# OPEN BOOKS, CLOSED SETS

A novel
by Dave Hughes

Prickly Pair Publishing
Chandler, Arizona, USA

This book is a work of fiction. All names, characters, places, and incidents are either the product of the author's imagination or are used fictitiously. Any resemblance to actual persons, living or dead, business establishments, events, or locales is purely coincidental.

Other novels in the "Gay Tales for the New Millennium" series:
     Maybe Next Year
     Instant Adult
     If I Seem Quiet…

Watch for two more novels in this series in 2024.

Visit AuthorDaveHughes.com to learn more about Dave and his books. You can subscribe to his newsletter to gain background information and insights into Dave's books and the writing process, and receive advance notice of upcoming book releases (and subscriber early-bird discounts). You will receive Dave's short story, *Cruise Virgins*, free when you subscribe to his bi-weekly newsletter.
If you would like to contact the author, please send an email to dave@authordavehughes.com.

Cover photos:
     Student: G Stock Studio (licensed from iStock)
     Bedroom set: CoCo Studios, Atlanta, Georgia. Used with permission. All rights reserved.
Cover design: Dave Hughes



Library of Congress Control Number: 2023903783

ISBN: 978-0-9970017-9-2

# FRESHMAN YEAR

# On the First Day

Monday, September 22, 2008

At 7:00 a.m., Ryan Robertson sprang out of bed, eager to begin his first day as a freshman at UCLA. He was already familiar with the campus. For the past year, he lived in a house a few blocks away in Westwood, where he and three other gay men named Ted, Darnell, and Ricky rented rooms from attorney and UCLA alumnus Hal Morris.

Until today, he had been a visitor, a future student, a Bruin wannabe. But today, he was a full-fledged UCLA student. Today, he *belonged* here.

After lunch, he headed over to Schoenberg Hall where his 1:00 class, Music Appreciation 101, would take place. Ryan had played trumpet in various school bands since fifth grade. He enjoyed many genres of music, especially jazz, so he figured this course would be an easy A.

He entered the combination auditorium/lecture hall and scanned the room for a good seat near the front. As he walked down the aisle, faces gradually replaced the backs of heads. His enthusiasm tanked when he spotted a face he hoped he would never see again: that of Jordan Harrington.

Jordan had been Ryan's nemesis during his senior year at Westwood High School. Jordan's jealousy and disdain toward Ryan culminated in an ugly incident at the holiday concert when Jordan smeared Vaseline throughout the valves on Ryan's trumpet, rendering the instrument unplayable. While Ryan spent 20 minutes in the restroom trying to clean the Vaseline off his valves, Jordan played the first trumpet parts and solos in his place.

At their graduation ceremony, Jordan apologized. And while

Ryan felt his apology was genuine and he accepted it, he didn't relish the thought of seeing Jordan around campus for the next four years.

Ryan spun around and headed for a seat several rows behind Jordan, hoping Jordan hadn't seen him.

After class, Ryan bolted for the door. But considering his 6'6" height and wavy dark blond hair, he knew Jordan would see him. He knew he would be unable to avoid contact with him for an entire semester.

***

Sure enough, Jordan caught up with Ryan after class on Wednesday. "Hey, Ryan! What's up, man?"

"Oh, hi. Just getting settled into college. How 'bout you?"

"Same. I didn't know you were going to go to UCLA!"

*Well, it's not like we had anything to do with each other last year,* Ryan thought. "Yeah. It's one of the reasons I came to LA when I left home. I'm glad I actually got in."

Jordan said, "Oh, come on, Mr. Valedictorian. Seriously? With your grades, of course, you were going to get in."

"Yeah, I guess. I didn't know you were coming here, either."

"Yeah. My dad's the head of the English department, so I just kind of assumed I'd go here. So how was your summer?"

"Pretty good. I worked a lot. How 'bout you?"

"It was okay." Jordan's demeanor, which had been strangely upbeat given everything that happened last year, turned more somber. "Actually, it was kind of rough. My mom and dad are getting a divorce, so things aren't great at home."

"Oh, wow… I'm sorry to hear that."

"Thanks. My mom moved in with a friend of hers from work, so at least she's away from him. He's kind of an asshole."

*Like father, like son,* Ryan thought.

Jordan said, "I'm still living with him because it's a lot closer to campus. But enough of that. I'm surprised I didn't see you in the marching band!"

Ryan said, "I couldn't because of work. It takes up too much time and there would be too many conflicts, especially on Saturdays."

"Ah. I'm sorry. Are you going to be in any of the jazz ensembles?"

"I wasn't planning on it. I probably won't have time for my trumpet while I'm in college."

Jordan said, "That sucks, man. You're good. The band I'm in is mostly non-music majors. The first rehearsal was yesterday. They're pretty good. You should audition for it! I think there's still one open trumpet spot."

The prospect of playing in a jazz ensemble excited Ryan, but he didn't want to be in a band with Jordan again after what happened last year. Still, he asked, "When does it rehearse?"

"Tuesdays and Thursdays at 3:00. Here in this building."

Ryan said, "I'll think about it."

Jordan said, "The director's office is upstairs. Let's go and see if he's there, and you can set up a time to audition. If I made it, you can make it." Jordan paused. "And for the record, it's totally cool if you get seated higher than me. You probably will."

Ryan looked at Jordan suspiciously.

Jordan said, "Really. I'm serious. C'mon, let's go see if he's there."

Ryan smiled. "Okay, sure. Why not? I can at least talk to him."

****

After Music Appreciation class on Thursday, Ryan auditioned for the jazz ensemble. The director was impressed with Ryan's talent and offered him a spot in the band playing $2^{nd}$ Trumpet. An hour later, he attended his first rehearsal.

That evening, he returned to campus for the introductory

meeting of the LGBTQ+ Student Network. Ryan belonged to his high school's Gay-Straight Alliance during his senior year, and that proved to be a lifeline. After moving from Prairie Village, Kansas, to Los Angeles the previous summer, Ryan knew no one at his new school. He was a shy kid to begin with, and being gay made his assimilation to his new school all the more challenging. The handful of friends he made in the GSA made all the difference. He hoped UCLA's gay group would enable him to form friendships and enjoy a social life during college.

Ryan was among the first to arrive, but by the time the meeting began, 22 students had gathered in the meeting room. There was a nice diversity of attendees. Judging by their appearance and demeanor, Ryan guessed most of them were upperclassmen. Most of them seemed to know each other from last year.

After the meeting, people hung around and chatted in small groups. Most of them were catching up with their friends from last year. Ryan approached a group of several guys and stood near the periphery of their cluster. A couple of them stepped aside to allow him into their circle. Ryan introduced himself and the others did likewise, followed by a series of handshakes. The other guys chatted for a bit longer, until the person in charge of the meeting called out, "Our time is up for this week. We need to vacate the room for the next group."

# A Big Favor

Tuesday, October 7, 2008

On Tuesday, when Ryan sat down next to Jordan in Music Appreciation class, he said, "Hey, I have a big favor to ask. I'm going to have to miss class tomorrow. May I borrow your notes afterward?"

"Yeah, sure."

Ryan hoped Jordan wouldn't ask why he was going to miss class. If he asked, Ryan would just say he had to work. Hopefully, Jordan wouldn't pry for details. He assumed Jordan heard the rumors about his occupation that circulated around their high school last spring. Jordan probably helped spread them.

Jordan didn't ask why Ryan would be missing class. He was pretty sure he knew the answer. The less said about that, the better.

It was for a porn shoot. Ryan knew that as demand grew for his talents, he wouldn't have the luxury of accepting only shoots that took place on Saturdays. He'd have to strike a balance between working and attending classes. Hopefully, in future quarters he would be able to schedule all his classes on certain days, leaving other days open for gigs. He realized he needed to cultivate friendships with people in each of his classes for sharing notes.

***

On Wednesday, after Ryan returned from his shoot and ate dinner, he logged onto his computer and checked his email. To his surprise, there was an email from Jordan with a PDF document and an MP3 file attached. He opened the PDF first. It contained five pages of meticulous notes Jordan had taken and scanned, as well as photos he took using his phone of things the professor had written on the whiteboard. The MP3 file was a recording of the entire lecture. This was especially helpful since the professor often played musical excerpts of musical pieces during the class. That was impossible to capture with written notes.

Ryan was amazed that Jordan would go to so much trouble since he had been so nasty to him last year.

He put on headphones and listened to the lecture while he followed Jordan's notes and photos. It was the next best thing to being there.

# Proposition 8

Thursday, October 9, 2008


On Thursday, Ryan wore his new 'No on 8 – No H8' T-shirt he picked up at an Anti-Proposition 8 rally the previous weekend. After their Music Appreciation class, Ryan said to Jordan, "I really appreciate everything you sent me last night. I was only expecting to copy your notes. I can't believe you recorded the whole thing. How did you do that?" Ryan assumed Jordan's phone didn't have enough memory to record a 48-minute lecture.

Jordan said, "My mom has one of those old Sony Walkman cassette players they used back in the 80s. She still has a few blank cassettes. Then I ran a cable from the headphone jack to the line in jack on my dad's computer and used his audio editor to transfer the cassette to an MP3 file."

"I can't believe you went to all that effort for me. Wanna go hang out in the Student Center until Jazz Ensemble? Let me buy you a soda or something."

"Yeah, sure."

Ryan bought them each a soda and a brownie. They sat down at one of the tables in the common area. Jordan commented on Ryan's shirt. "It figures you would be against Prop 8."

"Well, duh… And you're not?"

"I'm for it. I believe marriage is between a man and a woman."

"Really? Then fuck you." Ryan stood up, grabbed his soda, his backpack, and his trumpet case, and started walking away.

Jordan got up and followed him. "Now wait a minute. That wasn't very nice, especially after what I did for you. Besides, I have a right to my opinion."

Ryan turned to face Jordan. "You're correct on both counts. And I have a right to choose who I hang out with. Now if you'll excuse me…"

"No! That's not excusable. Come back to the table. We need to talk about this."

"No we don't, but all right." Ryan followed Jordan back to their table and they sat down. "Okay, talk."

Jordan said, "You liberals think you're so progressive and open-minded, but as soon as somebody comes along with a different opinion than yours, you shut them out. I think we should be able to be friends and have different opinions."

"I agree. Some of the other guys in my house have different opinions about things, but we all get along great. But this goes beyond opinions. This is about values. And we choose our friends based on their values."

"There's nothing wrong with my values. And in this case, I value the sanctity of marriage. If you don't value that, maybe we do have a problem."

"Of course I value marriage. That's why I believe I should have the right to get married when I meet the right guy."

"Okay, so I believe marriage is only between a man and a woman, and you think two dudes should be able to get married. Why isn't this just a difference of opinion?"

"Because… A difference of opinion might be whether or not we should be fighting in Afghanistan, whether taxes on the rich should be lower or higher, or whether Obama or McCain would be a better president. But when it comes to marriage equality, the question is whether I should have the same rights as you, or you get to have some rights that I can't have."

"I still don't see how that's about values rather than opinions."

"It's about whether you believe all people should have equal rights or not."

"You have equal rights."

"I DO NOT!!! How can you even say that? If I had equal rights, we wouldn't be having this conversation right now. If everyone had equal marriage rights, there wouldn't be a Prop 8."

"You have the right to get married – to a woman."

Ryan let out a derisive chuckle. "Yeah, but I don't want to get married to a woman."

"Well, that's your choice."

"Being gay is not a choice."

"I think it is, but that aside… A marriage is between a man and a woman. It's always been that way. It says so in the Bible. So if you want to get married to a woman, you have the right to do that. But two guys together isn't a marriage. It's… well, I don't know what it is. It's something else."

"Two men or two women together is two people who love each other and want to spend the rest of their lives together. Sounds like marriage to me."

"No, marriage is a man and a woman who love each other and want to spend the rest of their lives together. What you're trying to do is redefine marriage. You're trying to change the definition of marriage from one man and one woman to just any two people. Or three people. Or a guy and his dog. Who knows what you'll want next?"

"Ah, the slippery slope argument. That's not a valid debate tactic, it's a diversion. This isn't about three-person marriages or human-animal marriages. It's about two people who love each other and want the same rights as everyone else."

Jordan said, "Look, it doesn't bother me if you want to live your life with another guy and do whatever it is gay guys do together. Go ahead and spend the rest of your lives together. Don't let me stop you. I hope you live happily ever after. Just don't call it a marriage."

"Why not?"

"Because a marriage is between a man and a woman."

Ryan let out a dramatic sigh. "So here we go again, around and around."

"Why is it so important to you? Why are you trying to force this onto everyone else? Just live together, for Christ's sake. Why do you even need to get married?"

"Because marriage brings with it hundreds of rights, both at the federal and the state level. Like when one person dies. If you're married, all of your assets still belong to the other. If you're not married, all of the dead person's possessions and money have to go through probate, and a lot of times the family of the one who died thinks their stuff should go to them."

"So have wills."

"Yeah, that helps, but wills can be contested, and it still has to go through probate. Here's another example. When one person is in the hospital, their legal spouse can always get in to see them. If you're not married, they can treat you like a stranger. You have no rights. And there's filing taxes jointly, and social security benefits for the surviving spouse. All sorts of things."

"So for you, it's all about the money."

"That's part of it, for sure. But it's about so much more than just money."

"See, for me and most people, it's not about money. It's about living your life according to God's plan. And that's for a man and a woman."

Ryan laughed. "Oh, so now you're all Godly. Did God tell you to put Vaseline in my valves? Did God tell you to destroy our bulletin board display of famous LGBT people? Was that part of God's plan? Because let me remind you, my dad was a minister. I grew up in the church. And I'm not aware of anywhere in the Bible where it tells you it's okay to do those things."

"That was wrong and I apologized for all that. The Bible also teaches forgiveness, if you'll recall. But we're getting off track. Back to what the Bible says about marriage…"

"Yes, let's look at that. Earlier you said the next thing we would want is three-person marriages. Well, what about Jacob, Leah, and

Rebecca? Not to mention his 'handmaidens' – which is a funny way to describe them since they were obviously using more than their hands. According to the Bible, a man can have as many wives as he can afford. So you should be all for polygamy."

Jordan said, "Well, things were different back then."

"Yeah, right. But you know what? That's not even relevant. We're not voting on whether or not the Bible is right for what it says about marriage. We're voting on whether or not same-sex couples should be able to get *legally* married, like everyone else."

"But then you're forcing churches to marry gay people. What about the separation of church and state?"

Ryan exclaimed, "Yes! Separation of church and state! That's exactly what this is about! The government can't force churches to marry people. Nobody's pushing for that. Some churches will, and some won't. Fine. If a gay couple wants to get married in a church, there are plenty of churches that will do that. Or they can just go before a judge and get married, or have a secular ceremony with a wedding officiant. Whether or not you have a church wedding is irrelevant. It's being able to get a marriage license that matters. So no, there's no need to force churches to marry same-sex couples."

"Yeah, but you know that will be next."

"There's the slippery slope argument again. No, we don't know that. Frankly, a lot of gay people don't care about what churches think. They don't want the church to have anything to do with their marriage."

Jordan said, "Yeah, well maybe if they went to church and repented…"

"Listen, I don't have anything to repent for. I could talk for an hour about how my church treated me, but that's a conversation for another day. But let's get back to the separation of church and state. The state doesn't have any right to tell churches they have to marry same-sex couples, and conversely, churches don't have any right to tell the government what laws they should pass about who can get legally married."

"I suppose, but it's not the churches that are voting. It's people. And if the majority thinks same-sex couples should be able to get married, then I guess everyone else will have to go along with it. But most people think marriage is between a man and a woman, so Prop 8 is going to pass."

"So what you're saying is that people's rights should be decided by popular vote."

"In this case, yes."

Ryan raised his voice again. "No! Not in any case. Think about this. Women didn't use to have the right to vote. Only men could vote. So if it was up to men voting to give women the right to vote, do you think that would ever have happened? Same with segregated schools. In the 50s, do you think the white majority would have voted to let black kids attend their schools? Of course not. So if a minority having equal rights always depends on the majority to vote on it – well, history has shown that most of the time it doesn't happen."

Jordan said, "Yeah, but that was about gender and race. People can't help what gender or what race they are, they're born that way. Being gay is different."

"Well, yes. Sexual orientation is different from race, which is different from gender, which is different from physical abilities or disabilities, and so on. What's your point?"

"Your race, your gender, or your disabilities are not your choices. Being gay is. I don't think we should change our laws and the definition of marriage just to accommodate a small minority's choice, especially when the majority finds that choice objectionable."

"Being gay isn't a choice. Look, my father forced me to go into therapy with some ex-gay quack, and then he was about to send me off to some secret camp where they were going to try to use some kind of so-called gay conversion therapy on me. I had to run away from home. I was made fun of at school all last year. LGBT people get rejected by their families, discriminated against and fired from their jobs, and sometimes even beaten up or killed. Why would I choose that?"

"I have no idea. Is the sex really that great?"

Ryan smirked. "Actually, it is. But it's not about sex, it's about love. It's about equality. Trust me on this. People don't choose to be gay." Ryan glanced at his watch. "We need to leave to go to rehearsal in a couple of minutes. But let me ask you something. A moment ago you said the majority finds being gay objectionable. Do you find me objectionable?"

"No. I like you. I wouldn't hang out with you if I didn't. As I said, I hope you find someone nice to share the rest of your life with, if that's what you want. I don't have any problem with you being gay. Just don't try anything with me."

Ryan scowled at Jordan. "Believe me, you have nothing to worry about. But if you want to be friends… well, what kind of person doesn't want his friend to have all the same rights and privileges he has? Why would I choose to have a friend who would vote against my rights? What kind of friend is that?"

Jordan didn't have an answer.

Then Ryan thought of something else. "Think about this. My position takes nothing away from you. You'll still be able to get married to a woman and have all the rights and privileges you have now, regardless of whether gay people get equal rights or not. But your position takes a lot away from me."

Jordan didn't have an answer for that either.

Ryan looked at his watch and stood up. "C'mon, let's go."

# The Calendar

Saturday, October 11, 2008

At the University of Maryland in College Park, Chris Robertson's college career had gotten off to a wonderful start. He joined the Terrapin Marching Band, and was elated to be participating in college football games on Saturdays. College football, played in huge stadiums and often to TV audiences, was a far greater experience than Friday night high school football.

He was making dozens of new friends, most notably fellow saxophonist Seth Barnhart, a sophomore from Glendale, Arizona. During the first couple weeks of band practices and parties, they exchanged numerous glances, brief conversations, and dropped hints. Soon it became clear to both of them, and some of their more observant bandmates, that they were becoming an item.

Chris was grateful to be living near Washington, DC. Fall, 2008 was an exciting time to be near the nation's capital. In all likelihood, the next president would be not only a Democrat but also the first African-American to hold that office. The "hope and change" Barack Obama promised during his campaign included the hope of more rights for LGBT people, the end of Don't Ask, Don't Tell, and – maybe, just maybe – nationwide marriage equality. The nationwide LGBT community also had its hopes pinned on the defeat of California's Prop 8, which would be a giant step forward on the path toward marriage equality.

All these factors gave Chris just what he needed – new opportunities and a complete change of scenery.

His senior year had been difficult. His boyfriend, Bryan, had mysteriously disappeared in late July – just as they had made the transition from best friends to boyfriends. They had talked about going to college together – maybe at UCLA, where Chris's older brother Tyler went, or maybe someplace else. The place didn't matter as long as they were together and far from Kansas. He spent three years cultivating their friendship, coming to terms with his sexuality, and then trying to pull Bryan from his closet. But shortly after Bryan's homophobic parents found out he was gay, they did something that prompted him to disappear.

Chris did his best to carry on. He applied to UCLA, even though he didn't know where Bryan was or whether attending UCLA was still on his radar. He was accepted, but he received a better scholarship offer from Maryland.

On Saturday, October 11, the Maryland football team had a week off, which meant the marching band had a free weekend as well.

Chris' roommate went home for the weekend, so Chris and Seth spent the previous night together. In the morning, they ate breakfast in the dorm's dining hall.

Chris said, "It seems weird not having a game. It's like there's a whole day with nothing to do."

Seth replied, "I know, right? And it's a beautiful day. I want to get out and do something, not just stay in my room and study."

They both ate a few bites while they thought of possibilities. Then Chris said, "Let's go into DC. We could wander around Dupont Circle and see what's there."

"Sounds good! I went there several times last year, so I can show you around."

Shortly after 11:00, they emerged from the Dupont Circle station onto Connecticut Avenue. They strolled north on the west side of the street, then crossed over and headed back on the east side. They came to the Lambda Rising book store, which had a special National Coming Out Day display in their front window, with a selection of books about the coming out experience.

Chris said, "Is there really a National Coming Out Day?"

Seth replied, "Yep, there sure is. I think they started it the year after the 1987 March on Washington, where they displayed the AIDS quilt on the national mall."

Chris realized this had taken place two years before he was born. What must it have been like to be gay back then?

They stepped into the store and spent the next twenty minutes browsing. Chris found several books he wanted to buy. He was amazed there could be an entire store devoted to LGBT-related books. It was a far cry from the small section at the back of Book Galaxy at the Great Mall in Olathe, Kansas – or the Mediocre Mall, as he and Bryan called it.

The mere thought of Bryan prompted a cascade of memories and feelings.

Chris thought about Bryan less frequently since arriving at college. It was just as well – he needed to put all that behind him and move on with his life. Still, he wondered how Bryan would react to being in a store filled with gay books and gay-themed merchandise. That time he and Bryan were in Book Galaxy and he showed him a copy of *Gay Sex 101*, Bryan freaked out. Maybe this would be different, since Bryan would be a thousand miles away from his parents and the other patrons were also gay. Or maybe this would be too much gay for him.

"Hey!" Seth called out to Chris. "You still there?"

Chris had been staring into space, lost in thought about Bryan. Seth motioned for Chris to come to the back of the store. "Check this out!"

Chris walked back to an area where they had adult-themed greeting cards with photos of naked men. They also had a display of 2009 wall calendars featuring either scantily clad or completely naked men.

Seth was glancing through the unsealed display copies of the calendars. When he finished looking through a calendar called Student Bodies which featured naked college-age men, he handed it to Chris.

"Looks like 2009 is going to be a very good year!"

Chris thumbed through the first few months. "I dunno... we could be falling on hard times."

Seth snickered. "Yeah, I bet you'd like to fall on some of those."

"As if you wouldn't."

Chris reached the page for October and froze. Gazing at him from the page of the calendar, smiling seductively in all his magnificent, fully-erect glory, was Bryan.

Chris stared at the page. All sorts of thoughts raced through his mind.

Seth leaned over to see what Chris was staring at. "Yeah, that one's pretty amazing, isn't it?"

*You have no idea*, Chris thought. "*He*, not it."

Seth gave Chris a curious look. "Whatever."

Chris returned the display copy to the rack, picked up a sealed copy, and added it to the stack of books he was carrying.

Seth said, "Are you really going to put that up in your room? I'll bet your roommate will love that."

"Who knows, maybe he will. Besides, it's National Coming Out Day. What better way to let him know he has a gay roommate?"

"Like he doesn't already know?"

Chris said, "I don't know whether he's figured it out yet or not. But I can put it up in my bedroom when I'm home this summer. And if we share a room next fall, we can put it up then."

Chris wasn't sure how he would react to seeing this picture of Bryan every day next October. But he was glad to know Bryan was still alive.

***

Chris and Seth slept together again that night. They parted company after dinner on Sunday so they could have time to study.

After Seth left, Chris pulled out the calendar and gazed at

Bryan's picture. He wondered where Bryan was, and how it came about that he had been photographed for a nude calendar. Bryan had been self-conscious about people seeing him naked. Chris couldn't fathom how he could be comfortable posing naked and hard for thousands of men to see.

Chris found the name and website of the publisher in the fine print on the bottom of the back cover. After searching online, he found an email address to contact them.

Dear Sir/Madam:

I just purchased your 2009 Student Bodies calendar. I'm looking forward to admiring the handsome men in the calendar all next year.

I'm writing to ask if you can put me in touch with the model on the October page. He was my best friend in high school, but we've lost touch. I would love to re-establish contact with him.

Would you please forward my name, email address, and phone number to him? I would be most grateful.

Thank you very much for your help.

Sincerely,

Chris Robertson

chris-rob@hotmail.com

(913) 765-4321

He pressed Send. He tried not to get his hopes up too much.

***

On Tuesday, Chris received a response.

Dear Mr. Robertson:

Thank you for purchasing our 2009 calendar.

We regret that we do not have contact information for any of the models featured in our publications. We work with photographers, who submit photographs from their portfolios for our consideration.

I have forwarded your request to the photographer who submitted the October photo. He may or may not forward your request to the model, and the model may or may not choose to respond. Sometimes they receive a large volume of fan mail. I just want to manage your expectations.

Best regards,

Stefan

Oh well. Chris would just have to cross his fingers and wait.

# Not a Choice

Monday, October 20, 2008

After Music Appreciation class, Jordan wanted to talk. "Last time we talked, you said that when your father found out you're gay, he made you go to therapy, and then he was going to send you someplace that would make you straight. And then you said gay people face job discrimination and even being beaten up and killed."

"That's right."

"Well, if being gay is so difficult, why didn't you go along with the therapy so you could be straight?"

Ryan said, "Because it doesn't work that way. I've felt attracted to guys for as long as I can remember. I denied it and repressed it for years. My dad preached against homosexuality in his church all the time. But back at my old high school, I had this guy named Chris who was my best friend. We met at band camp my freshman year and started becoming friends right away. Finally, at the end of our junior year, we both figured out that we were in love with each other. I tried to resist, but finally, I couldn't deny it anymore. I knew I loved him. We went all the way only once before my parents found out and I had to run away. But it was the most beautiful, passionate, intense experience I've ever had. It was almost spiritual – like our souls joined together. It wasn't just sex, it was love. I knew, at that moment, that I would always be attracted to men and it's beautiful and there's nothing wrong with it. It's a natural part of who I am, like being attracted to women is a natural part of who you are." *I assume…*

Jordan had been listening intently. "So, you found a guy you connected with. But don't you think that maybe there are women out there you could have that kind of connection with?"

"In other words, maybe I just haven't met the right woman. And if I did, I could be straight."

"Yeah. Have you tried dating girls?"

"No. Have you?" Ryan couldn't recall ever seeing Jordan with a girl during their senior year of high school.

Jordan looked hurt. "That was pretty harsh."

"Yeah, I guess it was. Sorry." Ryan paused to let the tension ease a bit. "Here's another way to look at it. Let's say you and I are walking across campus and there are people all over the place. Do you notice the attractive women or the attractive men? I notice the attractive men. I mean, I can look at a woman and appreciate that she's beautiful, and you could look at a guy and say 'yeah, he's handsome,' but it's about who you naturally feel drawn to."

"It's about who you wish you could fuck."

"I guess you could say that. But it's not just about sex. Who do you feel more emotionally drawn to – men or women?"

Jordan thought for a moment. "Okay, so can I ask you a couple of personal questions?"

"Yeah, I guess."

"You don't have to answer. This might be off-limits."

"Okay."

Jordan lowered his voice. "So, when two guys are together, how do you decide which one is the woman?"

"Neither of us is the woman. We're both guys. That's the whole point."

"No, I mean how do you decide who's … on the receiving end?"

"We flip a coin."

"Really?"

"No, not really. I don't know. Some guys prefer being the bottom, others prefer being the top. A lot of guys are open to doing it both ways."

Jordan paused for a moment, then asked, "Have you ever… you know…"

"Been on the receiving end? No, not yet. The only time Chris and I went all the way, I was the top and he was the bottom. I wanted to do it the other way next time, but unfortunately, there was no next time."

"Do guys actually enjoy that? I mean, I get how putting your dick in a guy's ass would feel a lot like putting it in a woman. But I don't understand how getting someone's dick crammed in your ass would feel good."

"Well, guys tell me it does. Chris sure liked it. But the point isn't who's doing what to whom. It's about two people connecting. It's about intimacy. And, of course, it's fun and it feels good."

"Yeah. Well, I can't wait to see what it feels like."

Ryan looked at Jordan curiously. *Did he just say what I think he said?*

Jordan added, "With a woman."

*Well, you've got to start dating them first. But I shouldn't say that out loud.*

Jordan asked, "Where is Chris now?"

"I don't know. We talked about going to UCLA together. His older brother went here and liked it. We just wanted to get somewhere far away from home, where we could be more open."

"Why don't you contact him?"

"I guess I should. When I first ran away, I couldn't let anybody know where I was. I was still 17, so if they found me, they could force me to go back home. Then my dad probably would have tried to send me to the gay conversion place again. Now, I still don't want my parents to know where I am, but I guess I could tell Chris. He wouldn't tell them."

"You should totally get in touch with him. You might be able to get back together again. Who knows?"

"Yeah, you're probably right. I'll think about it. There are other factors, too." *Like the fact that I'm doing porn.*

Jordan paused for a moment and pondered whether he should ask the other question on his mind, or whether he had asked enough questions already. "Okay, so uh… Can I ask you one more thing?"

"You just did."

That flustered Jordan even more.

Ryan said, "Sorry. Yeah, sure. Ask away." *We just talked about guys fucking. I should be able to handle whatever else he throws at me.*

Jordan hesitated for a moment. *I don't know… maybe it would be better if I didn't say this. But I just said I had another question. Oh well… No turning back now.* "Do you find me attractive?"

"Oh God, no!" *Did he really just ask me that? I totally did not see that one coming.*

They stood and looked at each other. Neither knew what to say next. Ryan thought, *Why did he even ask that? What was he hoping I'd say? He looks hurt – or at least disappointed. Does he want me to be attracted to him?*

Finally, Jordan said, "Well… okay."

"I take it that wasn't the response you were hoping for."

"Well… I don't know… I guess I thought I was at least kind of decent-looking. But you just made it sound like I'm really gross or something."

"No, no… you're not gross at all. Actually, you're a pretty good-looking guy. I thought you were asking if I felt attracted to you. You know, like if I was interested in you romantically … or sexually. And no, I'm not."

Jordan breathed a sigh of relief. "Yeah, I can see how you could interpret it that way. I guess I wasn't very clear. But I figured if you, a gay guy, thought I was attractive, then maybe women would too."

"Well, I can't speak for straight women. There are all kinds of factors that combine to make up attractiveness. And everyone's looking for something different. Beauty is in the eye of the beholder, as they say."

Jordan remained silent. He looked like that wasn't the answer he was hoping for either.

Ryan said, "I'm sorry, I guess when I blurted out, 'Oh God, no!'

it sounded kind of harsh. I didn't mean it that way. It's just… that's kind of a difficult question. It puts me in a rough spot. It's like if I say I don't find you attractive, it sounds like I'm saying you're ugly. And you're not. But if I say I do think you're attractive, it sounds like I'm interested in you in *that* way. And I'm not."

"That's okay. I get it."

"And just to be clear… Yeah, I like guys. But I'm not interested in trying to get straight guys. I don't think most other gay guys are, either. I might look at a guy and think he's hot, but I'm not going to try to put a move on him – at least not unless I find out he's gay. And single. And maybe not even then. It all depends."

"So how can you tell whether a guy's gay or straight?"

Ryan sighed. "I wish I knew."

# Election Night

Tuesday, November 4, 2008

Hal hosted a party at the house to watch the election results and, hopefully, to celebrate the election of Barack Obama and the defeat of Prop 8. Both sides had poured millions of dollars into the Prop 8 campaign. The nationwide LGBT+ community knew that the future of marriage equality in the United States might be determined by the outcome of this election.

Hal and Ricky invited several of their friends, including a few people they knew from the porn industry. Ricky introduced Ryan to Michael Rodick, the Director of Casting and Talent Acquisition at Eagle Studios, one of the world's leading purveyors of adult gay male entertainment.

Michael said, "Pleased to meet you in person, Ryan. I've seen a few of your videos and I'm impressed by your work."

Ryan replied, "Thank you, sir. We have quite a few of Eagle's videos in our collection. I learned a lot from watching them when I was first getting started in the industry. Truly state-of-the-art productions!"

"How kind of you. So… may we step out onto the patio to chat for a few moments?"

"Sure."

Ryan led Michael out to the patio and slid the door closed behind them.

Michael said, "It is fortuitous that we met this evening. I always have my eyes open for new talent, and we have an opportunity for a man with your... um… *qualifications* in an upcoming project."

"I'd be honored to work for Eagle. Ricky has spoken very highly of your company. Please tell me more."

"We're planning a major release for our 20th anniversary, which is next year. We're going all out. This video will have everything – and I mean everything! Three-ways, four-ways, DPs, toys, fisting, watersports, you name it. And there's going to be a massive orgy at the end, starring the entire cast! We keep adding ideas and it keeps getting bigger. That's a good problem to have, right?" Michael paused to allow his attempt at humor to register. "It's gotten so big, we'll probably have enough for two videos. Anyway, we were originally planning to do it with twelve guys, but then we found out Stallion Studios did a 15-man orgy a few years back, so we're going to hire four more guys to make it sixteen. What do you think so far?"

"Hmmm… interesting. So would I just be in the orgy at the end?"

"No, no… we'll work you and the other three guys into some of the other scenes as well. We'll probably add in a couple more scenes for you guys. I could see you being in four scenes, maybe five."

"Okay, but just so you know, I'm not into fisting or watersports or anything like that. Toys, maybe, but not on the receiving end. I guess I'm kinda vanilla."

"That's fine. Only a few guys will be doing that stuff. Don't worry, you'll be bringing plenty to the party."

Ryan understood what Michael Rodick was implying.

"Okay, I'm interested. When will you be shooting?"

"After the first of the year. The scenario is a gay ski weekend in Breckenridge, Colorado. We'll be flying everyone out there on Thursday, January 8th. We'll shoot all day Friday, Saturday, and Sunday. Then we'll fly back on Monday, January 12th. We've rented a 5-bedroom chalet. It's unbelievable! Wait 'til you see it. It only sleeps ten, so some of the guys will be staying at rooms in the lodge – including you since you're a late addition. We'll do a few scenes in our studio in Chatsworth afterward, but most of it will be shot there."

Ryan said, "I'll have to check my calendar. I'm going to UCLA, and I'm not sure whether classes start on January 5$^{th}$ or 12$^{th}$."

Michael leaned in and lowered his voice. "I am prepared to offer you $12,000, plus travel to a very nice, very high-class resort. This will be the greatest porn video of all time. You may never get an opportunity like this again. Think about it." Michael handed Ryan his business card.

"Okay, I'll let you know by Friday."

Michael and Ryan returned to the party. Six people were seated around the television in the family room, while others were grazing in the kitchen and mingling in the living room. Ryan walked into the family room and asked, "What's the latest?"

Ted said, "It's looking good for Obama."

Ryan glanced at the electoral vote count at the bottom of the screen. The network pundits had just called Texas for McCain. "I don't know, it still looks pretty close."

Darnell said, "Relax. You know Obama's going to win California. That's 55 votes right there. Plus Washington, Oregon, and probably Colorado. Obama's got it."

One of the guests said, "Obama won Indiana and North Carolina! McCain hasn't got a chance."

Ryan asked, "How about Prop 8?"

Ted said, "So far, the Yeses are winning. But most of the smaller conservative counties are in. The big cities like LA and San Francisco are still counting."

"Thanks." Ryan wandered into the kitchen to get some more food and another Jack and Coke.

Hal was in the kitchen, and he pulled Ryan into the hallway leading to his bedroom. "I saw you talking to Mike Rodick out on the patio. What did he want?"

Ryan cracked up laughing. A little bit of his drink splashed onto the floor. "Sorry, I'll clean that up."

"What's so funny?"

Ryan lowered his voice and said, "I thought you said 'microdick.'"

Hal snorted. "Oh my God… I've never thought of that before."

"What an unfortunate name for someone in the porn industry."

"I'll say. God, I'll never be able to look at him with a straight face again."

"I know, right? I guess that's why he introduced himself to me as Michael."

Hal asked, "So anyway, what did he want?"

"He offered me $12,000 to be in this big 20th-anniversary video they're going to make."

"$12,000??? Are you shittin' me?"

"Nope. It's for four or five scenes. And they're taping it at some fancy ski resort in Colorado."

"I didn't know you skied."

Ryan said, "I don't. He didn't ask about that."

"I was joking. I know the video's not about skiing. Isn't that the one Ricky is doing?"

"Yeah. He's the one who introduced me to Microdick."

"You've gotta stop saying that."

"Yeah, I know," Ryan said. "Anyway, if I do it, that means I'd be gone from January 8th through the 12th. I'd have to miss, like, three days of classes."

"But for $12,000? Do it! It's the start of the quarter. You won't miss much. Besides, everyone in the industry is talking about this. It's gonna be really big, from what I've heard."

"I guess. That doesn't matter so much to me. I told him I'd think about it and let him know by Friday."

# Election Fallout

Wednesday, November 5, 2008

As they were leaving Schoenberg Hall after Music Appreciation, Ryan noticed Jordan seemed a bit down. Ryan was still mourning the passage of Prop 8, but he was trying to stay upbeat because at least Obama won.

As they walked toward the Student Center, Ryan said, "Well, it looks like we each won one and lost one."

Jordan said, "What do you mean?'

"I'm happy that Obama won but sad that Prop 8 passed. I'll bet you're sad that McCain lost but happy that Prop 8 passed."

"Nope. I'm also sad that Prop 8 passed."

"Huh? I don't get it."

"I voted no on Prop 8. I thought about what you said after we had that talk a couple of weeks ago. Even if I believe marriage should be between a man and a woman, that's a religious belief. I shouldn't force my religious beliefs on you when I vote. And like you said, this was about legal rights, not religious beliefs. You should have the same rights as everyone else. So yeah… I voted no on Prop 8 because of you. If you want to get married to a guy someday, well, I want you to be happy."

Ryan stopped. "Really? Thanks, man! Seriously. That means a lot to me."

"And I voted for Obama, although I wasn't thrilled about it. I thought McCain would be the better president. But if something happened to him – and let's face it, he's getting up there – I just couldn't see Palin becoming president. And besides, I think your rights have a better chance of advancing with Obama. Maybe you'll get nationwide marriage equality someday. Maybe he'll end Don't Ask, Don't Tell or maybe he won't, but you weren't going to get that from McCain."

"Wow," Ryan said. "Mind blown. You changed how you voted because of me?"

"Yeah, I guess so. Now that I'm getting to know you better, I think differently about a lot of things."

"Man, I… I don't know what to say."

"Could you say we're friends now?"

Ryan compared the Jordan from last fall, who put Vaseline in his trumpet valves, defaced the Gay-Straight Alliance's bulletin board display, and treated him coldly all year long, with the Jordan who was standing in front of him today. They seemed like two different people. "Yeah. Definitely. We're friends now. And I'm glad."

Jordan smiled and Ryan smiled back.

Ryan said, "May I hug you?"

Jordan said nothing but took a step closer to Ryan. Ryan gave him a loose bro-hug since they were out in the open with dozens of students passing by. But Jordan wrapped his arms around Ryan and gently squeezed. He held him for several seconds.

After they released each other, Jordan said, "C'mon, let's go get something to drink."

Once they were seated at the Student Center with their drinks, Ryan said, "I can't believe how much you've changed since high school."

"Good. I'm trying." Jordan took another sip of Coke. "You remember the night of the prom?" Ryan nodded. "You probably didn't see this, 'cause you were dancing with Mike, and LaTanya and Angelica were dancing, and everyone else was focused on that. Well, I was being a real asshole about it, like I thought it was wrong for two guys or two girls to dance together. And I was saying a bunch of nasty shit. So then Raul grabbed me and pulled me out on the dance floor and tried to get me to dance with him. And of course, I was furious, and Julio and

Connor were laughing at me and taking pictures. But Raul was gripping my wrists so hard I thought they were going to break off, and he looked me right in the eye and said, 'Listen, asswipe. You've done some shitty things to Ryan. Why don't you try being nice to him for a change?' That hit me hard. But I knew he was right. I was being an asswipe, as he put it. I did some shitty things to you. And for the next few weeks, I took a good look at myself. I didn't like what I saw. I decided I needed to work on being a better person. And I decided I'd try being nice to you. And uh… that's worked out a lot better."

Ryan was speechless. *I should get in touch with Raul and thank him.*

Jordan continued. "I realized I got a lot of my beliefs from my Dad. Or maybe because of him. Whatever. He's pretty racist and sexist. Homophobic, too. And I guess growing up around that, I absorbed a lot of that from him. I realized that even though I didn't like him for a lot of reasons, I was becoming just like him. And most of my friends were the same way. Starting college was a good chance to close that chapter and open a new one. When I saw you in class the first day, well, I was glad to see you. It was nice to see a familiar face, but I also realized this was my opportunity to fix things. Not just to make up for all the shitty things I did, but to practice being nice to you instead."

Ryan said, "You have been nice to me. And… well, I'm kind of ashamed to admit it, but for a while I was suspicious. I didn't know what to make of it. It's like, why are you treating me so nice now, after the way you treated me last year? Is this for real? But yeah, I guess it is. Anyway, as I said, I'm glad we're friends. And yeah… you're a totally different person now."

Jordan said, "And with my Dad, I always had to be the best. I had to be perfect. When I didn't get first chair, he came down on me hard. Can you believe he went to Mr. Scales and told him to put me in first chair?"

"Yeah, I heard that."

"He stopped giving money to the band boosters because of that.

And of course, when I got kicked out of the band, that made me a total failure. A disgrace to the family name. I was grounded for a month. He didn't let me forget that for the rest of the year. And when you were the Valedictorian? That was a big disappointment, too. I mean, I got a 3.92. That's not good enough? Well, it wasn't good enough for him because somebody else did better."

"Wow… that must have been rough."

"It was. And, oh yeah, when he saw you hugging those other guys after graduation he said, 'Is he queer?' I said, 'He's gay.' Then he told me I should stay away from you because you'll try to recruit me. So yeah… that's what I've had to deal with. Anyway, on graduation night, I finally said fuck it. Not to his face, just to myself. A 3.92 is good enough, dammit. And I shouldn't be first chair if someone else is better. And I've been hanging around you for six weeks now, and you haven't tried to recruit me."

Ryan said, "Too soon. We don't start on that until after three months."

Jordan looked startled.

Ryan said, "Just kidding."

"Not funny."

"Sorry. I guess this isn't the right moment for lame attempts at humor."

"Definitely not. But anyway, I decided he was full of shit and I wasn't going to be like him – not in any way. Besides, he sure as hell isn't perfect, so why does he have a right to expect me to be?"

"He doesn't. You know, my dad was kind of the same way. I mean, I got good grades and did well at everything, but there was always this assumption that I had to turn out exactly the way he wanted me to – like I was supposed to be a preacher like him, or at least be all religious and stuff. And he had a lot of bigoted, wrong opinions on things, too."

Jordan said, "So I guess you and I have that in common."

"Yeah. You know, it really changes your life when you realize your parents aren't perfect and they're not always right. Sometimes they're seriously imperfect and wrong about a lot of stuff. It's kind of liberating when you realize your parents are just messed-up humans like everyone else."

"I know, right?"

Ryan glanced at his watch. He didn't have any more classes today, but he was ready to head home. Maybe he'd study, or maybe he'd sit out on the back patio and chill for a while. "Well, I'm going to head out now. See ya tomorrow."

"Later." Jordan got up from his chair. "Thanks, man. I'm glad I have you to talk to."

They hugged again.

# A Walk in the Garden

Tuesday, November 18, 2008

Jordan missed his classes on Monday. He asked Ryan to take notes for him in Music Appreciation and loaned him his mom's Walkman to record the lecture.

On Tuesday, Jordan was visibly despondent when he arrived and sat down next to Ryan. He couldn't even force a smile to acknowledge him.

Ryan asked, "What's wrong?"

"Eh… just really bummed. Can we talk after class?"

"Sure."

Jordan sat through class, but he wasn't mentally there. Ryan took good notes so he could share them with Jordan later.

After class, Ryan asked, "Student Center or walk around campus?"

Jordan replied, "Is there somewhere else we can go? Someplace quieter?"

"How about the botanical garden? It's not too far."

"I've never been there."

"It's nice. I think you'll like it."

Ryan led Jordan a couple of blocks south to the garden. Jordan said little during their journey. Ryan tried to make small talk about what the professor covered in class, but Jordan had other things on his mind.

Once inside the garden, they walked a short while, then sat down on a bench. Jordan said, "This is nice. I had no idea this was here."

"Yeah, I discovered it one day when I was out running."

Jordan took a moment to compose his thoughts. Then he said,

"My parents had their day in court yesterday. Their divorce is now final."

"I'm sorry. Even if it's for the best, it's still painful to go through."

"Yeah, tell me about it."

"How did it turn out?"

Jordan said, "Mom got everything. She had a good lawyer. Dad hired one of those $200 divorce attorneys you see on billboards. Mom got the house, half of his investments, and a nice big alimony payment. Dad has until the end of November to move out, then Mom's going to move back in."

"Did they fight over custody of you?"

"Since I'm over 18, that doesn't apply. Nor does Mom get child support. But she made sure Dad would have to pay for my college. Since he's a professor here, he gets a discount on the tuition."

"Well, at least there's that."

"Anyway, Thanksgiving and Christmas will suck this year. They'll probably suck every year from now on. Things will never be the same again."

Ryan asked, "What do you think you'll do this year?"

"Mom has some relatives in Anaheim, so we're going there for Thanksgiving. That won't be so bad. I don't know about Christmas yet."

"I know how you feel – kind of. Last year I spent Thanksgiving and Christmas away from my family for the first time. Thanksgiving wasn't so bad. All the guys in my house had a nice dinner together. They're like my family now, so that was nice. But last Christmas it was every man for himself. A couple of the guys traveled to spend Christmas with their families. Hal is Jewish, so he doesn't observe Christmas. That left Ted and me. We went for a walk on the beach, hiked, and ate out a couple of times, so it was okay. But Ted told me something that makes a lot of sense, at least to me. He thinks of Christmas more as a season than as a day. There are concerts and parties and decorations everywhere, and everyone's happier and nicer. So the season's nice, but the day itself is anticlimactic. To him, Christmas day is a 'me day.' He does whatever he wants, like hiking or driving somewhere. It helped me to look at it that way."

"Yeah, I see what you mean. Still, it's going to be a big adjustment – and a reminder that things are different now."

"I get it. But in a few years, you'd be out on your own anyway. You may move to another city, and if you get married, you'll spend Christmas with your wife and family. So it was bound to change sooner or later anyway."

"Yeah, I guess."

Ryan asked, "How are your mom and dad holding up?"

"Well, Mom's happy. She's the one who wanted out of the marriage, and she got a great settlement. Dad has pretty much resigned himself to what happened. He's been in a sour mood ever since Mom told him she wanted a divorce."

"I suppose whenever a couple breaks up, one person suffers before the break-up and the other person suffers afterward."

Jordan said, "Yeah. Looking back, I can see that Mom's been suffering for years. I get the impression they just held it together until I got out of high school."

"Well, at least they were thinking of you."

"Yeah, but how do you think that makes me feel? My parents stayed in an unhappy marriage because of me. They probably resent me for it. And what I thought was a family was really just three people going through the motions, at least for the past few years."

Ryan put his arm around Jordan's shoulder. He could see Jordan's eyes were moist. "I'm sorry. I wish I knew what to say."

"You don't need to say anything. I just need someone who will listen."

Ryan thought about that. He didn't have any answers. Perhaps there were none. He wasn't a professional counselor, and there was nothing he could say that would change anything. "Well, I'm always willing to listen. We can talk anytime you want."

"Thanks. Mom said if I want to, I can see a counselor to help me work through things. I think I'll take her up on it."

"That will probably do you good. It can't hurt, anyway."

Jordan sat quietly for a moment, then stood up. "Well, thanks for listening. And thanks for caring about me."

Ryan stood up, and they hugged. He could tell that Jordan was crying, so he held him for a few moments. Then Jordan stepped back and wiped his eyes. Ryan glanced at his watch. "Crap. We need to get moving. Jazz Ensemble starts in five minutes."

"You go on. I'd like to spend some time alone."

"Okay. See you tomorrow. And call me if you need to."

Jordan nodded and turned away.

# Home for the Holidays

Monday, December 22, 2008

It was a cold, dreary Monday afternoon in Prairie Village, Kansas, but Chris was glad to be home for the holidays after a busy but satisfying fall semester. He completed his finals the past Saturday morning and flew home later that day.

Chris's mom, Kathleen, asked, "Honey, would you mind going to the grocery store to pick up some things for Christmas dinner?"

"Sure, no problem."

"Thanks. Here's the list. If you want to pick up some soda or snacks for yourself, go ahead. If you have any questions, I'll have my phone handy."

Chris drove to Price Cutter, which was one of the closest stores and it usually had the best prices. As he wandered the aisles, he noticed some of the shelves seemed disorganized and disheveled. He thought about Bryan, who worked there during the summer before he disappeared. The shelves would have been in perfect order on Bryan's watch.

As Chris pushed the cart with his bagged groceries out the front door, he glanced at the small area near the door with the restaurant booths. That was where Bryan told him his parents found out he was gay. They had grounded him, sent him to a shrink, and forbade him from seeing Chris again. That was also where Chris broke up with Bryan. That was the last time Chris ever saw him.

Chris loaded the groceries in the car and began his trip home. Suddenly, an idea occurred to him. He glanced in each of the car's mirrors, then made a U-turn and sped back to Price Cutter.

Chris practically ran to the Customer Service desk. Fortunately, there was only one customer ahead of him. He scanned the wall behind the desk and spotted a framed picture of a smiling 40-something man wearing a white shirt and a dark tie labeled,

Russ Simonton, Store Manager

When the customer in front of him turned and left, Chris stepped up to the desk and asked, "Is Mr. Simonton in today?"

"Yes, he is."

"If he's not too busy, I'd like to see him for a couple of minutes. Just to say hi."

Angela, the Customer Service Supervisor, picked up the phone, punched a button, and said, "Mr. Simonton to the Customer Service Desk, please." Her voice interrupted the piped-in Christmas music and echoed throughout the store.

Chris said, "Thank you," and stepped aside.

In a moment, Mr. Simonton arrived.

Chris said, "Hi, Mr. Simonton. I'm Chris Robertson. You probably don't remember me, but I was Bryan Bauer's best friend back when we were in high school a couple of years ago."

Mr. Simonton stood expressionless for a moment. He knew he needed to be careful about what he said, given the circumstances surrounding Bryan's departure and his desire for privacy.

"Uh… Yes, of course. How are you, Chris?"

"I'm fine. I'm going to college at the University of Maryland now. I just got home for the holidays on Saturday."

"Welcome home! So, how may I help you?"

"Well… I was wondering if you've heard from Bryan, or if you have any idea where he is."

Mr. Simonton considered what he should say. "I exchanged a couple of emails with him shortly after he left, mostly about how to handle his final paycheck. Have you had any contact with his parents? I wonder how they're doing."

"No. I have no desire to talk to them, considering what they did to him."

Mr. Simonton smiled and let his guard down a bit. "I don't blame you. So, like I said, he and I have exchanged a few emails. But it's been a while, so I'm not a hundred percent sure where he is now or if the email address I have for him is still good."

"Okay. But could I ask a big favor? Would you please send an email to the last address you have, and tell him I asked about him? And would you pass along my email address and phone number? Tell him I really miss him and I'd love to hear from him."

Mr. Simonton stepped behind the counter and retrieved a pen and a piece of paper. "Sure. Here, write it down. But I can't guarantee anything."

"I understand. But it's worth a try." Chris wrote down his name, email address, and phone number, and handed the paper and pen back to Mr. Simonton. "And tell him I said Merry Christmas."

"I will."

"And Merry Christmas to you, too!"

"Thanks. Merry Christmas!"

Mr. Simonton smiled. Chris seemed very nice. He was cute, too. He and Bryan – now Ryan – would have made a nice couple. As Mr. Simonton walked back to his office, he recalled the last conversation he had with Bryan as he drove him to the bus station on his last day in town. He remembered Bryan saying how he hoped he and Chris would one day be a happy couple like Russ and his husband Frank, living in a comfortable home in a suburb with a couple of dogs. He recalled how upset Bryan was that he wasn't able to say goodbye to Chris.

Mr. Simonton walked into his office, closed the door, and sent the email to Ryan.

# Christmas in Westwood

Tuesday, December 23, 2008

Ryan slept until 9:00 on Tuesday morning. It was a relief not to get up early for classes. He had no shoots scheduled until after Christmas. He had nothing to do today but relax and maybe wrap a few presents he had purchased for his housemates.

After breakfast, he checked his email. He didn't expect to find anything significant, but it had been a few days since he last checked.

He found the email from Russ Simonton. He was probably just checking in and wishing Ryan a Merry Christmas. It had been a while since Ryan updated Russ on his life, so he decided he would reply and bring him up to date.

Ryan opened the email and read it.

Dear Ryan,

I hope you're doing well.

I wanted to let you know that Chris stopped by the store and asked if I had heard from you. I didn't tell him anything except I thought I still had your email address. He asked if I would forward his email address and phone number to you, so here they are: chris-rob@hotmail.com and (913) 765-4321.

He would love to get back in touch. I'll leave that up to you.

He's going to the University of Maryland now. He just got home for Christmas. I asked if he had spoken with your parents. He said no, and he has no desire to do

> so. So, there's that for your consideration.
>
> Frank and I are doing fine. His father is starting to go downhill, so I guess it's good that we're here. I hate Kansas winters, though.
>
> Everything is the same at the store.
>
> Please write back and let me know what you've been up to. How's college?
>
> I hope you have a Merry Christmas and a Happy New Year!
>
> Best,
>
> Russ

Ryan stared at the computer screen. Finally, he decided to go for a walk around the neighborhood to sort things out.

Ryan walked up and down the curvy, hilly streets of his neighborhood. He hardly noticed the lovely homes and the Christmas displays in their front yards. All he could think about was Chris.

He thought about all the fun times they had in band and on the track team. He remembered the times they practiced their instruments together in his bedroom, and how they'd put on a jazz play-a-long CD and jam while his younger brother Brandon listened, smiling with admiration. He thought about the times they hung out at the mall or Slush Fun, their favorite fast-food hangout, and how they laughed and talked about all sorts of things. He remembered the time at the bookstore in the mall, when Chris took books with provocative titles and displayed them on the front table, and how that seemed so edgy and mischievous at the time. In hindsight, that was pretty innocent compared to what Ryan was doing for a living now.

He recalled the time they spent the night together in the cheap motel when they went to the state championship track meet in Wichita, and the subsequent times they got to know each other intimately in Chris's bedroom. He recalled the time that nasty policeman caught them kissing in the car and outed Ryan to his father, and how that started the whole downward spiral of events.

He realized he never fully appreciated those times while they were happening. He never imagined they'd be taken away. He couldn't have guessed that the last time they sat at Slush Fun and laughed so hysterically while they made up silly names for people and their professions, it would be the last time they would ever go there together. He thought they would be able to spend their senior year together, and then they'd go to college together. In other words, he took it all for granted.

He didn't fully appreciate Chris. Who knows, he may never meet someone like Chris again. No one he met at high school last year or at UCLA so far this year even came close. His housemates were nice guys and he felt close to all of them to some degree, but not like it was with Chris. He had feelings for Ted, but Ted made it clear that he didn't want any kind of relationship. Besides, Ted is eight years older and has plenty of his own issues to work through.

Bryan walked into Westwood and ate lunch at My Gyro, his favorite restaurant.

Up to this point, Ryan had been able to keep Chris relegated to his past life. But now what should he do? Should he reconnect with him? Would a friendship that existed solely on emails, texts, and phone calls be rewarding or frustrating? Would occasional contact with Chris from a distance be more depressing than rewarding?

How much should he tell Chris? Should he tell him where he lives now? What if that information made it back to his parents? Chris wouldn't tell them directly, but if he told his parents or his brother or any of their friends, it could get back to his parents.

And what would Chris think if he found out Ryan was doing porn? And what if that information started getting around?

Maybe it was best just to leave it all in the past.

After he finished lunch, he walked around campus. It was practically deserted since classes weren't in session. He walked up and down the grassy common areas of Wilson Plaza and Dickson Court and passed some of the buildings where he had classes. Even though he was now on campus five days a week, he was usually focused on navigating the crowds and getting to class on time, or whatever else was on his mind at the time. But without any of that distraction, he was able to admire the stately buildings and the attractive campus.

This, along with the beautiful home and the nice housemates he shared it with, was his life now. Maybe it was best to leave Chris and everything else in the past. Life has moved on.

Ryan walked back to his house and got on with his day. He wrapped the presents for his housemates, played some video games, joined his housemates in ordering pizza for dinner, then watched TV with them. All this kept him distracted from Chris most of the time, but the fond memories and the conundrum he faced about whether to contact him were never far from his mind.

He decided this would be a lovely evening to get in the hot tub, so he turned it on at 9:00 to heat the water and got in at 10:00. He gazed up at the night sky while the water jets massaged his shoulders, back, and legs.

A half-hour later, Ted came out. "Hey, do you mind if I join you?"

"Of course not," Ryan said. "That would be nice." Ted walked back into the house and returned with a bottle of Chardonnay in an ice bucket and two plastic wine glasses. He poured glasses for both of them and settled into the tub.

After a few minutes of small talk, Ted asked, "So, what's on your mind?"

"Chris, my boyfriend from back home. He's home from college, and yesterday he was in the grocery store where I used to work. He asked the manager if he knew where I was. So, the manager sent me an email with Chris's contact info."

"You mean you haven't had any contact with him since you left Kansas?"

"No. I didn't even get a chance to say goodbye to him before I left, because it came up so fast. Technically, we weren't boyfriends anymore because he broke up with me a week before that – not because he was mad at me, but… well, it's kind of a long story. But the main reason I haven't been in contact with him is that I didn't want anyone to find out where I am. You know, because my parents and the police were looking for me. I figured that if I told him, he might tell someone else, and then sooner or later it would get back to my parents. So, it was safer to not tell anybody."

"So now you're wondering whether you should get back in touch with him?"

"Yep."

"Why wouldn't you?"

"Mostly because I still don't want to let people know where I am. I've started a new life out here, and I want to leave the past in the past. Plus, he's going to the University of Maryland now, so it's not like we could hang out together like we used to or resume our relationship. We would be communicating by email or text or phone calls, which seems like it would be a pretty disappointing alternative. It just wouldn't be the same as it used to be. And then on top of that, I don't know how he'll react when he finds out I'm doing porn."

"That's all fair. But it's still gnawing at you, so part of you must want to."

"Yeah. I still love him. I've never met anyone else like him. I keep holding out this hope that maybe someday we can be together again. That won't happen if I never talk to him again. And besides, I feel I owe him an explanation for what happened."

"It sounds like your head is saying no and your heart is saying yes."

"Yeah, that's a good way to put it."

"Well, then follow your heart. Maybe someday it will work out, or maybe it won't. Maybe he'll freak out when he finds out you're doing porn, or maybe he won't. If it doesn't work out, at least you tried. You'll never know if you don't, and then you'll spend the rest of your life wondering, 'what if…?'"

"Yeah, I suppose you're right. But I'm still worried about people finding out where I am."

"Why? You're over 18 now. Your parents can't come and force you to go back home."

"Yeah, but I don't even want to hear from them again. I don't want them trying to get me to go back – even for a visit – or trying to convince me that I should convert to being straight, or whatever else they might do. The fact is, I don't even think of them as my parents anymore. It's like I've divorced myself from them."

"I get it. I feel the same way about my dad. I don't ever want to see or hear from him again, either. At least in my case, I think the feeling is mutual."

Ted lifted the wine bottle out of the ice bucket and refilled their glasses. Then he continued, "Still, you're letting your disdain for your parents prevent you from being in touch with the man you love. Do you want to let them have that power over you?"

"I guess not."

"Besides, if you continue to live your life with the fear that they could find out, that's like a dark cloud that's going to follow you around wherever you go. Do you want to live like that?"

"No."

"And here's another thing. You're holding out hope that you and Chris might be together again someday, and he's from your past. And what about your little brother? So, you can't say 'the past is the past.' You can never truly leave the past behind. Your past is part of who you are."

"Yeah, I suppose. But I still don't know whether I should get back in touch with Chris."

"Well, you don't have to tell him everything up front. Just send him an email and say you're interested in being back in contact, and explain to him why you had to leave. You don't have to tell him where you are just yet. Explain to him why you want to keep that private. If he promises not to tell anyone else, then maybe you can tell him. Same thing with the porn. Save that for later."

"Okay. But I still wonder if I can be satisfied with just having occasional contact by email or text or phone. Or will it be a constant reminder that we can't be together?"

"Well, you're going to have to decide which is worse – no contact or occasional contact from a distance. Only you can decide that. But I think you need to reset your expectations. This isn't going to be a relationship now or in the foreseeable future. It's going to be more of a pen-pal friendship. It may continue or it may fade away after a while. Just let it run its course, whatever that might be. And keep in mind if you give him your phone number, he'll figure out that you're somewhere in LA by the area code."

"Damn… you're right." It also occurred to Ryan that if he used his current email address, Chris will find out he changed his name. But he'll need to tell him that at some point anyway.

Ryan reached over and placed his hand on Ted's thigh for a few seconds. "Thanks a lot, man. You've helped me see things more clearly. Thanks for listening. And caring."

Ted smiled, "You're welcome. Glad I could help. And I do care."

Ryan asked, "So, how are you doing?"

"Okay. Overall, things are good. The lull between semesters is always kind of depressing for me. It's like I appreciate the break from studying, but then I have a bunch of time on my hands without much to do. Most of the other students have families they go back to, but I don't."

Ryan said, "Yeah, I know what you mean. I spent all day today just walking around."

After a silent moment, Ryan said, "Hey, you want to do something together tomorrow?"

"Like what?"

"Anything. Disneyland, Universal, the Getty Museum, drive along the beach, drive up to the mountains, whatever. It doesn't matter, just something to get us out of the house."

"Yeah, maybe. Let's see what we feel like doing tomorrow morning."

Ryan let a moment pass. "You're kind of bummed, aren't you?"

"Yeah, Christmas is kinda rough. It's supposed to be such a joyful holiday, but not having a family to go home to makes me sad."

"Yeah. Last year was my first Christmas away, and it was really hard. This year it wasn't so bad until this Chris thing came up."

Ted said, "On the other hand, I'm 25, so maybe I'm a little old for that, but still…"

"Maybe you could visit your mom and her partner next year."

"I did that a couple of years ago. It was the first year I was out of the Marines and going to school here. It was okay, but it was kind of awkward. For them, Christmas is all about their kids, which is as it should be. I felt like I was imposing on them or crashing their party a little bit. I mean, we love each other and we're cordial, and her wife and I get along fine, but their lives have moved on in one direction and mine has moved on in another."

Ryan said, "I think of you guys as my family. Hal is kind of like a father to me. Well, maybe not a father, but more than a big brother. Maybe a cross between a guardian and a mentor. But definitely, someone who cares about me and who I can turn to for advice. And you guys are like my brothers – especially you."

"Awww…"

"You are! Especially times like right now." Ryan put his hand on Ted's thigh again.

Ryan wanted to hug Ted. Not a quick hello or goodbye hug, and not as a sexual prelude, but just holding him in his arms for a while and cuddling.

They looked at each other. Ted must have seen Ryan's desire to be hugged in his eyes. Maybe he wanted to be hugged too. He smiled and whispered, "C'mere."

Ryan scooted over and snuggled up next to Ted, resting his head on his broad, muscular shoulder. They wrapped their arms around each other and held each other in silence for the next ten minutes until the jets shut off at the end of their cycle.

# What Ted Really Thinks

Wednesday, December 24, 2008

After lunch, Ryan and Ted decided to visit Venice Beach. It was Ryan's first time there, and he was surprised to learn LA had a neighborhood next to the ocean with a little canal system. They explored the narrow walkways along the canals through what was mostly a residential area.

Ryan said, "I wonder what it would be like to live here. These are cute little houses, and you'd be so close to the beach."

"Yeah, well these cute little houses probably cost a fortune. I mean, houses are expensive everywhere in LA, but places by the ocean are outrageous. You'd have to be rich."

"Yeah. And I think if I was that rich, I'd rather spend my money on other stuff than sinking so much into a small house."

Ted said, "I guess it's all relative. If you had five million dollars, then spending one million on one of these houses wouldn't seem like so much – if this is where you really want to live. I'd get tired of the tourists all the time. Besides, would you really go to the beach every day?"

"Probably not. But speaking of the beach..."

They left the canals and headed to the ocean. They walked south on Beachfront Walk, stopping in a few shops along the way. Since it was the day before Christmas, they weren't crowded. When they had gone far enough, they turned around and walked back along the edge of the ocean.

Ryan asked, "If you could live wherever you want after you graduate, where would you live?"

Ted gazed at some distant point along the coast while he

considered how much he wanted to share. "Somewhere like Canada or Australia or New Zealand. Or maybe somewhere in Europe. That's why I'm getting my Master's Degree in International Business. I want to get a job with one of the big accounting firms or some large international corporation and work overseas. Maybe spend a year or two in one place then move on to someplace else – unless I find a place I really like and decide to settle down."

That surprised Ryan. A wave of disappointment washed over him since he was hoping they could still see each other after they were out of college.

"Why do you want to leave the US?"

"A lot of reasons. This country's pretty fucked up, as far as I'm concerned. My views changed a lot when I got sent to Afghanistan and I saw what war was like first-hand. It made me think about what we're doing there. We think we have to be the world's policeman and the world's sugar daddy. Like we're this big world super-power and we can tell other countries what they should do. We're not really doing any of that to protect the United States, we're doing it to carry out Bush, Cheney, and Rumsfeld's foreign policy agenda. They don't give a shit if people in other countries get killed and their homes get destroyed. And if we lose some of our soldiers, well that's just the price you pay."

"Wow. I hadn't thought of it that way."

"Yeah, well, when you experience the killing and devastation first-hand, it opens your eyes."

"Don't those other countries you mentioned have militaries, too?"

"Yeah, and they may contribute a few troops. But it's all being driven by the US. So many people in this country glamorize the military like it's a great thing to send our poor young people off to other countries to kill and get killed. They buy into all this bullshit that we have to control the world and be the most powerful country on earth. They think it's all about freedom and democracy, but it's not. It's about cheap, plentiful oil. That's it. Period."

Ted was getting more and more worked up. "And along with all this military rah-rah, you have all these gun nuts who think everyone needs to be armed to the teeth. And people wonder why we have mass shootings all over the place. See, they don't have these problems in those other countries I mentioned. Nobody thinks they need to own a whole arsenal of weapons and carry guns around all the time. It's a totally different mindset, and it's a lot more kind and humane. And then there's the right-wing religious bigotry. Just look at all the constitutional amendments they've passed in states to stop same-sex marriage. We couldn't even stop it in California, of all places! But you can get married in Canada and some countries in Europe. And I bet you'll be able to get married in a bunch of other countries before too long. But not here, and we're heading in the wrong direction."

Ryan said, "I didn't think you were that interested in marriage. You always talk about being a loner and not wanting to be in a relationship."

"Whether or not I ever get married is irrelevant. I believe we should have equal marriage rights regardless. And who knows, someday I might meet Mr. Right and want to settle down. But even if I don't, I want to live in a place where I have equal rights."

"Do you think it will get better under Obama?"

Ted said, "Maybe. I hope so. But the number one thing I want to see him accomplish is healthcare reform. And that's another thing with all those other countries. Their healthcare systems are so much better. We have the most expensive healthcare in the world, and yet too many of our people are uninsured.

Ryan asked, "How come it's so much cheaper everywhere else?"

"There are a lot of reasons, and I don't understand them all. But in every other country, people view healthcare as a right, like we view public education. The government runs the system and pays for a lot of it. Here, we view healthcare as a benefit of employment, which is great if you work for a company that offers it. But where does that leave you if you're self-employed, a college student, or you work for a small mom-

and-pop business? That's why we need universal healthcare. Everywhere else, they spend much less on their military and more on healthcare and education. Says a lot about our values, doesn't it?"

Ryan sighed. "Yeah, it sure does."

"Anyway, I don't expect things to get better in the US anytime soon, so my best option is to live someplace that's more in line with my values. I don't think we'll ever be able to do anything about the gun culture or the religious fanatics. They've been around for a long, long time. And you can't change them with laws. You have to change people's hearts and minds. And I don't know how Obama – or anybody else – is going to do that."

That was a lot more information than Ryan was expecting when he asked Ted where he wanted to live. He was just asking for the sake of small talk. But it offered a bigger insight into Ted's psyche than Ryan had been able to discern up to that point.

After a few moments of silence, Ted said, "Sorry, I didn't mean to go off on politics and everything that's wrong with the world – especially when we came here to have a fun day and enjoy the beach."

"That's okay. It gives me a lot to think about. We never really talked about that stuff back in Kansas. It's like everyone there is a Republican."

"Yeah, I'm sure your parents have a much different worldview, based on everything you've told me."

Ryan said, "You got that right. I guess when you're gay you have to be a lot more politically aware, 'cause you have so much more stuff on the line."

"I wish a lot more gays were political. That might change some elections."

They returned to Ted's car. It was getting close to dinner time, so Ryan asked, "Hey, you wanna grab dinner someplace?"

"Yeah, sure. Do you have anything in mind?"

Ryan thought for a second. "Can we go to Burger Betty's in WeHo?"

That wasn't the sort of place Ted wanted to go, since the greasy, fattening food was well outside of his dietary boundaries. But it was Christmas Eve and he knew it would make Ryan happy, so he agreed.

They found a place to park and walked in. The décor was campy and a bit tacky, which made it fun. Since it was Christmas eve, it wasn't busy. Ryan tried to imagine what it must be like on a Friday or Saturday night.

After they were seated and ordered, Ryan said, "Thanks for agreeing to come here. Once I saw the menu I realized you probably don't want to eat most of what they have here."

"That's okay. The house salad with the roasted chicken is fine."

"I can't believe it's taken me a year and a half to get here. I've wanted to come here since I arrived in LA. It's too far to come here on a bike. Even though I have a car now, I'm always busy with other stuff. And it's the kind of place you go with other people, not by yourself."

Ted asked, "Why is this place such a big deal?"

"Well, it takes me back to the day I found out that my parents were going to send me off to the gay conversion therapy place and I had to leave home right away. Russ, my boss at the grocery store where I worked, took me to the Burger Betty's in Kansas City before I had to go to the bus station."

"They have Burger Betty's in Kansas City?"

"Yeah, believe it or not. Anyway, Russ and his husband Frank were the first gay couple I ever met. It's like they were the first role models I ever had. They gave me hope that maybe one day Chris and I could be like them, spending our lives growing older together. And I was amazed that there were places like this where gay people could go out and eat right along with everyone else, and it was okay. I know, that sounds stupid now, but that's how unaware I was at the time. There was nothing gay whatsoever in Kansas. I didn't even know there was a gay community right across the state line in Kansas City. It's like a whole new world opened up for me that evening. That day was tragic in many ways because I had to leave home and everything, but it was memorable in other ways. It was the first time I had ever been out in the gay community and been around other gay people – well, except for when Chris took me to the pride festival. And it's where I first learned about drag shows and stuff."

"So how does this compare?"

"Well, it's kinda the same and kinda different. It's still festive and everything, even though it's kind of dull here tonight. And the other thing is, my mom was always into healthier eating, so we would never go to a place that serves food like this. Chris and I used to go to this drive-up place called Slush Fun. We'd get these big slushies and all this food my mom didn't want me to eat, and it was fun. We'd sit in the car cracking each other up or sometimes talking about more serious stuff. And yeah, I know the food's not that good for you, but we were teenagers, you know? Teenagers are supposed to eat junk food. We were running fifty miles a week on the track team, so it's not like we were gaining weight or anything."

Ted said, "Well, you'd better be careful about what you eat now, especially in the business you're in. You've got to stay in great shape or they won't hire you anymore."

"Yeah, I'm pretty careful most of the time, and I still go running when I can. But anyway, I figured it's Christmas Eve so this is sort of like a Christmas present to myself."

"I get it. That's why I agreed to come along."

Ryan asked, "So, what's your favorite place to eat? Or maybe several of your favorites."

"I don't know. Eating out isn't a big deal for me. I'm pretty much of a loner, as you know, and it's not much fun to go out and eat by yourself."

"We can go out together more often."

"Yeah, thanks, but the other thing is, restaurant food isn't very healthy. You never know how much fat you're getting. Like steamed vegetables, for example. That sounds healthy until you realize they've been sauteed in butter."

They finished their meal, and Ryan grabbed the check before Ted could. "I insist. I'm making good money now. And you came here as a favor to me. Besides, you always bring the wine when we get in the hot tub."

Ted decided not to protest.

As they were driving back to the house, Ted asked, "Have you decided whether you're going to reply to Chris's email?"

"I'm leaning in that direction."

"Well, tonight at dinner you talked about him a lot. It was 'Chris and I' this and 'Chris and I' that. It's obvious that he still means a lot to you."

"Yeah… he does."

Ted said, "Well, let me give you something to think about. You're lucky. You have the option of emailing or calling your old boyfriend. I don't. You have no idea how much I wish I could talk to Alex right now. You have no idea how much I wish I could hold him right now and tell him how much I love him. You have no idea how badly I wish I could fuck his brains out right now. But I can't. Because he's dead. He's fucking dead. He was just 20. I saw him get blown to bits right in front of my eyes in Afghanistan. I'll never be able to unsee that. I'll have nightmares about that for the rest of my life. And now you're sitting there waffling back and forth about whether to get in touch with Chris? Well, at least you can. So call him! Maybe you'll get back together and maybe you won't, or maybe you'll at least be friends again. But it won't happen if you don't call him. And you'll never know. You'll live your whole life wondering, what if you had made that call? So get off your ass, stop being a fucking wimp, and call him, Goddammit!"

By the end of his rant, Ted was red-faced, yelling, and pounding the steering wheel. Ryan knew he couldn't say, 'But I'm still not sure I want him to know where I am,' because Ted would explode. That would just prove Ted's point that he was being a fucking wimp.

They drove the rest of the way home in silence. Ryan was afraid to say anything. He had never seen Ted so riled up before.

They walked into the house and headed toward their rooms. Ted stopped outside his door and said, "I'm sorry. I shouldn't have yelled at you like that."

"That's okay. You were right." Ryan stepped forward and hugged Ted. "I had a great time with you today. Thanks!"

"Sorry I had to go and ruin it."

"You didn't. See you tomorrow."

# Breaking the Silence

Wednesday, December 24, 2008

Ryan knew Ted was right. He should contact Chris. He paced around his room, thinking about what he wanted to say and how he was going to say it.

He sat down at his desk and opened his laptop. He decided not to disclose his new name to Chris yet, so he couldn't use his current email address, ry-rob@gmail.com, since that would reveal that he had changed his name. He wasn't ready to have Chris learn he had changed his last name to Robertson. He tried to use his old Hotmail account, but he discovered it had been deleted due to inactivity. So, he created a new one.

He began composing his email to Chris. He spent two hours typing, deleting, rewording, and fine-tuning his message. Finally, he settled on this:

Dear Chris,

I've been meaning to get in touch with you for a long time. I'm sorry I've stayed silent for so long. Once I explain why I hope you'll understand.

First, let me tell you what happened.

The day after the last time we saw each other at the store, I had a big confrontation with my parents. They were making me see this so-called counselor that Dad knew from college, who claimed he could help gay people turn straight. Yeah, you read that right. Of course, it wasn't going to work and this guy was pervy and creepy. I told my parents I wasn't going to see him anymore, and I refused to be subjected to anything else to try to make me straight. I demanded they accept me for who I am.

Long story short, the next Saturday, a whole bunch of weird stuff happened, and I discovered they were going to force me to go to this "camp" in Alabama where they practice some kind of "gay conversion therapy" to turn kids straight. And they were going to take me there the next day! No way was I going to do that.

So, I threw a bunch of my stuff into a couple of suitcases and my backpack and got on a bus. I didn't have any other choice. And of course, I took my trumpet.

Needless to say, I couldn't let anyone find out where I went. I'm sure the police and the FBI were looking for me everywhere, at least until I turned 18.

I really wanted to say goodbye and let you know what happened, but I couldn't. I'm really sorry. I figured I couldn't say anything to anyone about where I went without risking getting caught.

Even now, I'm flying under the radar. I thought a lot about whether I should even send you this email. But I want us to be in touch. Who knows what the future holds or if a relationship will ever happen, but I still want you in my life in one way or another, even if it's just an occasional email. So, I guess I'm starting the process now. Besides, you deserve an explanation.

It really hurts that I won't be able to see Brandon again until he grows up. Once he's out of the house and on his own, I will track him down and get in touch. I left him a letter telling him that. I gave him my first trumpet, too.

I changed my name when I turned 18, but you can still call me Bryan. I'm not quite ready to tell you where I am, but let's just say it's far from Kansas. I'm now going to a well-known university. It's been difficult sometimes, especially around the holidays. I have to work to support myself, so that means I can't do anything outside of school like marching band. I don't have much of a social life – no time for that. I am renting a room in a house with several other gay guys who have become my family. It's a beautiful place, almost too good to be true. You would be amazed. I'm very fortunate.

So overall, I'm doing okay. It sucks that I had to leave so suddenly, but I had no choice. It sucks that I can't have you and Brandon in my life and that I couldn't finish high school at Prairie Village and go to college with you. But in some ways, it's nice to be out on my own. I can make my own choices and live the way I want – including being openly gay. You would be proud of me for that. I don't have to put up with any more religious shit. My future is in my own hands, and it's going to be awesome.

Mr. Simonton told me you're going to Maryland. How do you like it? Have you decided what you're going to major in? How are your parents? What's Tyler doing now?

Please write back and let me know what's going on.

But please, PLEASE, don't tell anyone you've heard from me, except maybe your family – but only if they promise not to tell anybody. Don't give anyone else my email address. I don't want my former parents to find out anything, so I don't want any info about me to start getting around. I'm taking a chance with this email, but

> I decided I need to trust you.
>
> I'm looking forward to being back in touch.
>
> I love you. I'm sorry I never actually told you that in person. I should have. You're the best guy I've ever met and I'll always cherish the time we spent together. You changed my life in so many good ways.
>
> Merry Christmas!
>
> Love,
>
> Bryan

Ryan decided to save it and read it again tomorrow, then send it. It will make a nice Christmas present.

# The Best Christmas Present Ever

Thursday, December 25, 2008

Chris woke up at 7:15 on Christmas morning with the inexplicable feeling that something special was going to happen today – like maybe he would receive an especially thoughtful gift or his boyfriend Seth would have some good news to share when they talked on the phone later. Seth was spending Christmas with his family in Glendale, Arizona.

Chris had only a week to spend with his family this year. He arrived last Saturday, but this Saturday he would fly to Boise, Idaho. The University of Maryland Terrapins were playing in the Humanitarian Bowl on December 30, and the marching band was flying in on December 27. Chris was going to fly directly from Kansas City to Boise and then fly to Maryland with the band after the game.

Chris donned a long-sleeve T-shirt, comfy sweatpants, and pair of slippers lined with thick, comfortable faux fur. It was hardly gay apparel, but it was what he had available in the selection of clothes he hadn't taken to college.

He walked downstairs. His parents and his older brother Tyler were already in the kitchen. He smelled coffee and the tantalizing aroma of freshly-baked cinnamon rolls. Chris was 19 and Tyler was 23, so they had outgrown the child-like desire to head straight for the Christmas tree to discover what Santa had brought. Now, as an all-adult family, they enjoyed a leisurely breakfast in the kitchen before making their way to the tree.

They finished opening their presents at around ten. Chris went back upstairs to take a shower and put on the clothes he would wear for the rest of the day. Chris's father ventured onto the snowy roads to pick up his parents from their retirement community and bring them home to enjoy Christmas dinner and the rest of the day with the family.

During the downtime before his grandparents' arrival, Chris opened his laptop to check Facebook and his email. He had accumulated about a hundred friends on Facebook, and his news feed was filled with Holiday greeting memes and selfies. Chris wondered whether Bryan was on Facebook. He searched, but nothing came up. Chris wondered where Bryan was and what kind of Christmas he was having. He wondered whether the email Mr. Simonton sent to Bryan reached him.

When Chris was finished with Facebook, he opened his email and discovered the email from Bryan. He nearly jumped out of his chair with excitement.

He opened the email and read it. Many parts of it saddened him, but at the same time, he was ecstatic that he was hearing from Bryan.

He clicked on Reply and began writing an email to Bryan.

---

Dear Bryan,

You have no idea how happy I am right now! It's so wonderful to hear from you. Getting your email was the best Christmas present I could possibly have received.

Thanks for telling me what happened. Wow. Just wow. That totally sucks. But I'm glad you found out what they were going to do and got away in time. Now that I know the story, I understand why you did what you did. I'm glad you seem to be doing well. Heck, I'm just glad you're alive. When you first disappeared, I was afraid you might have killed yourself. I didn't think you would do that, but you never know, right? Anyway, like I said, it's so great to hear from you and know you are alive and well.

I'm doing well. I like going to the University of

Maryland. I'm in the marching band, and in fact, we're going to play in the Humanitarian Bowl in Boise on December 30. I will fly up there on the 27th. I thought bowl games were supposed to be in sunny, warm places, but whatever. It's still great that we get to go somewhere.

I'm majoring in Political Science. After I graduate, I hope I can get into law school at Georgetown or George Washington. I want to work for one of the legal advocacy firms that are working to get us equal rights or for some senator or representative. Now that Obama is president, I am optimistic we'll make progress, and I want to be part of making that happen. So, it's great to be so close to the action in Washington, DC.

I have a boyfriend. His name is Seth. I met him in marching band. We've been seeing each other for about three months now. It's starting to get serious. We'll probably get a dorm room together next fall if things keep progressing.

What about you? Are you seeing anybody?

You asked about Mom and Dad and Tyler. They're all fine. Tyler had to drop out of UCLA, though. For some reason, he lost his scholarship, so he couldn't afford to go there and pay out-of-state tuition. I think maybe he couldn't keep his grades up. He went to Kansas for his senior year. Now he has a job in downtown KC. He's still living with Mom and Dad, but he's talking about getting an apartment closer to his office. He has a girlfriend he's been seeing for about a year. He met her at school. She's still going there. After she graduates, they'll probably move in together.

But back to us. I am so sorry I broke up with you. Looking back, that was totally stupid and inconsiderate of me. I'm sorry the last time you saw me was when I did that. I'm sorry I never got to say goodbye. I wish it could have been different.

Dad just got back from picking up my grandparents, so I should go down and spend time with them. Can we talk on the phone sometime soon? Maybe tomorrow? If not tomorrow, then maybe after I get back to campus after the bowl trip – anytime starting January 1. I would love to hear your voice again and just talk for a while.

I love you. I always have and I always will.
Merry Christmas!
Chris

Chris decided not to mention the calendar. He didn't want his first contact with Bryan to contain anything that might be awkward. That could wait until later. Maybe it would be best not to bring it up at all.

Chris clicked Send, then shut his laptop down and went downstairs. He hugged his grandparents, then everybody sat down in the living room and opened the presents to and from the grandparents. Chris was so happy and excited he could barely contain himself. Tyler said, "Dude… what are you on? Whatever it is, I want some."

"Nothing! I'm just happy to be home. Happy to be with my family again. Happy it's Christmas. Happy I get to go to a bowl game."

"Oh. I thought maybe you were happy with the Christian Andrews underwear I got you."

"Yeah! That too!" The underwear was cool, but receiving sexy underwear from his brother in front of Mom and Dad felt awkward. But he knew Tyler meant well.

Later, as the family was sitting around the table enjoying a delicious Christmas dinner, Chris was still giddy with excitement. He was usually positive and upbeat, but never like this. Everybody could tell there was something he wasn't sharing.

During a lull in the conversation, Kathleen spoke up. "Honey, it's nice to see you so happy. But I've never seen you quite like this before. What's going on?"

The wine they were enjoying with dinner left Chris feeling even more festive and less inhibited. He weighed whether he should keep the news to himself or tell his family. He thought back to Bryan's email. He said not to tell anyone except maybe his family – but this was his family. So why not? Chris could no longer stand having this wonderful secret and not being able to tell anybody.

"Okay, so… something really great just happened. But you've got to promise me you won't tell anyone else. Okay?"

Everyone looked perplexed.

"Okay?" Chris repeated.

Tom and Kathleen mumbled, "Okay…"

"Seriously. This cannot leave this house. So… I just got an email from Bryan!"

Tom, Kathleen, and Tyler lit up. Kathleen said, "Oh, honey, that's wonderful! How is he?"

Tom added, "And where is he?"

"He's fine. He's going to college somewhere – he didn't say where, though."

Chris's grandparents looked puzzled. Why would receiving an email from someone be such a big deal? And why wouldn't this guy say where he is?

Grandma said, "Who is this guy?"

Chris said, "My best friend! He used to go to school here. I haven't heard from him in like a year and a half!"

While Chris's parents and Tyler were fully accepting of Chris being gay, this fact had not yet been mentioned to the grandparents. Tom wasn't sure how they would receive the news.

Grandpa said, "If he's your best friend, why haven't you heard from him in a year and a half?"

"Well, it's kind of complicated, but he had to move away on

short notice." He knew that wasn't a very satisfying answer, but he felt he shouldn't say any more.

The grandparents were still perplexed. Then Grandma said, "Wait... Bryan... Isn't that the name of that preacher's kid who disappeared a year or two ago?"

Uh-oh. Chris knew he shouldn't lie to his grandparents. "Yes, actually, it is."

Grandma said, "Do his parents know where he is now?"

"I don't know for sure."

"Well, don't you think they should know? For heaven's sake, if one of my kids went missing and someone else knew something about them, I'd be really upset if they didn't tell me. His parents have a right to know."

Chris said, "No, they don't. If you knew what they did that led him to run away, you'd understand. He doesn't want to have any further contact with them. He's an adult now, and that's his right."

Grandpa said, "I agree with your grandmother. You need to call them and let them know you've heard from their son."

Tom stepped in. "Kathleen and I have met them. They're not nice people, especially his father. I know how they were treating their son, and I understand why he left and why he wants to have no contact with them."

Grandpa said, "He's a pastor, and apparently a very successful one. His congregation is huge. He's a man of God. I can't believe he would harm his son."

Kathleen said, "Just because he's a pastor doesn't mean he doesn't mistreat his kids. As Tom said, we've met them. He's a pompous ass, and he thinks he's right about everything."

Tom said, "In any case, Bryan is an adult, and if he doesn't want to have contact with his parents, that's his choice. Don't even think about taking matters into your own hands and calling them."

Grandpa said, "Now listen here. You may be a grown man now, but I'm still your father. You can't tell me what to do or what not to do."

Tom glared at his parents. "Just. Don't."

There was an awkward moment of silence at the table. Chris's mood was now totally deflated. He was kicking himself for saying anything.

Kathleen finally spoke. "So what else can we talk about?"

After dinner, Chris went back up to his room. He powered up his computer and checked to see if Bryan had replied to his email yet. He hadn't, so Chris read the first email from Bryan again. His mood started to improve.

****

Bryan and Ted decided to spend Christmas Day hiking in Topanga Canyon, followed by dinner at a Chinese buffet. When they returned home, Bryan checked his email. He lit up when he saw the reply from Chris. He opened it and read the email three times. A wave of mixed emotions swept over him.

*Damn. I should have contacted him last Christmas. Maybe he could have applied to UCLA and we could have gone to college together.*

*Still, it's great to hear from him. I'm so glad he's not mad at me and he was happy to hear from me. As I read his words, I can see his face and hear his voice. He still touches me in ways nobody else can.*

*But he has a boyfriend now. Double-damn. It's only been three months. Maybe it won't work out.*

*What am I thinking? It's not like we could get together – not with him in Maryland and me out here. I should be happy he's found someone. I should be happy he's happy.*

*He wants to talk on the phone. It would be so good to talk to him. But he'll start asking questions I don't want to answer – not yet, anyway. And if I give him my number, he'll know where I am based on my area code.*

*Should I stop being so paranoid about this? I've already missed out because I didn't communicate with him. What if I'm letting another opportunity slip away?*

*Like Ted said yesterday, at least he's still alive. I can talk to him. Maybe I shouldn't squander my opportunity.*

*Besides, how can I tell him I don't want to talk to him on the phone after reaching out to him by email? We're both excited about being back in touch. That would just ruin it.*

Ryan paced around his room, debating what he should do. Then he walked out onto the back patio and gazed up at the evening sky as if he might receive some sort of cosmic message from the universe telling him what he should do.

After 15 minutes, he walked back inside. Maybe Ted or Hal could give him some advice. He knew what Ted would say – call him. He knocked on Hal's door.

"Come in."

"Hi, Hal. How were your movie and dinner?"

"Fine. We had a great time. We saw *Milk*. And the Chinese food was, well, Chinese food."

"What did you think of *Milk*? Mr. Perez, the advisor of our Gay-Straight group at school last year, told us about him."

"It was good. It was well done. Of course, I knew a lot of the stuff in the movie because I lived through those times, and I knew how it was going to end. But there were some things about his earlier life I didn't know. It was more of a history lesson than entertainment. But our other options were *Extreme Movie* and *Frost/Nixon*, so this was probably the best choice."

"And how are your friends?"

"Oh, they're the same. Just a year older. But anyway, how was your Christmas? What did you do today?"

"Ted and I went hiking in the Santa Monica Mountains. It was great! I'm glad there's still some nature left so close to this big city."

"Yeah – thank God people had the wisdom to preserve some of the land and create parks. Otherwise, all that would have been bulldozed for houses.”

“Then we ate at a Chinese buffet.”

Hal chuckled. “I’ll bet it was crowded.”

“It wasn’t too bad. They were prepared. They kept bringing out more food constantly.”

“Well, anyway, is there something on your mind? I saw you out there stargazing a few minutes ago.”

“Yeah. I wanted to ask your advice on something. A few days ago, I got an email from my old boss back at the grocery store in Kansas, and he said my former boyfriend Chris had been in the store asking about me. My manager passed along his email address and phone number. So this morning I sent him an email. I didn’t tell him where I am now, and I didn’t tell him my new name, but like I wanted to get back in touch with him, you know? Just to let him know I’m okay and tell him what happened and why I suddenly disappeared. So I just got a reply back, and he was happy to hear from me and everything, but then he asked if we could talk on the phone. And it would be great to hear his voice again and talk in real-time, but… well, I know this is going to sound paranoid, but if I give him my phone number, he’ll know where I am based on the area code.”

“You’re right, I think you’re being paranoid. Why not just give him your phone number and tell him where you are? You don’t think he would tell your parents, do you?”

“No, probably not. That’s one of the things I’ve been afraid of. But there’s something else. Remember Tyler, the guy that was supposed to live here, but now I’m in his room?”

“Yeah…”

“He’s Chris’s older brother.”

Hal nearly spat out the water he had just sipped. “What?”

“Yeah. And I don’t think Chris knows he’s gay. Or maybe he’s mostly straight and he just likes to fool around with guys. But whatever.”

“Sound like maybe he was sowing his wild oats while he was in college, then he was going to go back to Kansas and be straight again."

"Who knows? Anyway, the reason I changed my last name to Robertson was I was hoping someday Chris and I would be together again. Then when we got married, I'd already have his last name."

"Awww… that's sweet."

"But he has a boyfriend now, so who knows if that will ever happen. And now it's going to seem weird to tell him I changed my name to his, even though I totally disappeared and didn't talk to him for a year and a half. Like now he's with someone else, but he finds out his ex changed his name to be the same as his."

"That is kind of unusual, but I don't see why he would be offended. Anyway, I don't understand why you don't want to call him. That sounds like a no-brainer to me."

"Well, I do, but I just don't know what I should and shouldn't tell him."

"I'd say don't tell him about his brother. But aside from that, I don't see any need to hide anything from him. You trust him, don't you?"

"Yes, of course."

"All right, then. But here's an option. Are you familiar with Skype?"

"I've heard of it. I've never used it."

"If both of you have a webcam or a built-in camera on your computer, you can see each other as well as talk. And you can give him your username instead of your phone number."

"That sounds great! How much does it cost?"

"It's free. Just download it from Skype.com."

"Cool. Thanks, Hal! You've been a big help!"

Ryan ran back to his room, downloaded Skype, and set up his account. He asked Hal if he could call him to try it out. Then he sent Chris an email suggesting they hook up via Skype tomorrow at 2:00 Central time, which would be noon for Ryan.

# Nice to See You!

Friday, December 26, 2008

Ryan woke up at 6:30 a.m. He didn't have anything on his schedule today besides the Skype call with Chris at noon, but that was all he could think about.

He even had a dream about Chris. He dreamt they were getting married in the Santa Monica Mountains at a spot he and Ted passed on their hike yesterday. It was near the edge of the mountains, with a spectacular view of the beach and the ocean below. It was sunny and windy and their hair was blowing all over the place, but nobody cared. Brandon was his best man and Tyler was Chris's. The weirdest thing was that his dad showed up unexpectedly right before the ceremony started and insisted that he officiate the wedding. Somehow, that made sense in the dream and it was fine with everyone.

All morning, Ryan ran over what he wanted to say and how he envisioned the conversation would go. He couldn't wait to see Chris's face. He fantasized about Chris coming to visit and staying with him in the house. They would go sightseeing all over town. He fantasized that Chris would transfer to UCLA and they would live together in his room until they graduated. He knew that was unlikely, but he could dream!

At 11:50, Ryan launched Skype. He pulled a can of Dr Pepper from his fridge and waited eagerly for Chris to join. At 11:58, he did. As soon as Chris came into view, Ryan's heart skipped a beat. He could see part of Chris's bedroom behind him. He thought of the many times they had hung out, listening to music and practicing together. And there was his bed, where they had their first sexual experiences in the summer of 2007.

Chris said, "Oh my God – I can't believe this! It's so great to see you again!"

Ryan replied, "I know, right? You look great. I wish I could reach through the screen and hug you and kiss you right now."

"Yeah, me too. Anyway, how was your Christmas? What did you do yesterday?"

"I had brunch with my housemates and then we opened our presents to each other. One of the guys went home to visit his family, but the other three are here. In the afternoon, I went hiking with one of the other guys named Ted, then we went to this Chinese buffet for dinner."

"You went hiking on Christmas day? Man, it's freezing here. We have six inches of snow."

"Nah, it was around 70 degrees." Ryan realized he had just given Chris a clue about where he was living. "What did you do?"

"We had a nice time. My grandma and grandpa Robertson were here. Dad brought them over from the independent living place in Lee's Summit where they live. Seth and I talked on the phone at one point. He's visiting his parents in Glendale, Arizona now."

"Cool. So, tell me about Seth." *Tell me about my replacement. What makes him so great? I know, that's not right, but I can't help it.*

"Well… he's really nice. He's a sophomore, so he's a year older than me. He plays tenor sax. I met him pretty soon after marching band started, so we've been hanging out all semester."

"What's he majoring in?" *Have you slept with him yet?*

"Right now, he's thinking Economics. But he might change to Computer Science or something else. He's not sure. So for now he's getting all his general requirements done."

"And you're majoring in Political Science, right?"

"Yeah. I'm getting my general courses out of the way first, but I'm pretty excited about it. They have a good Poly Sci program here."

"Not surprising, I guess, being so close to Washington. How do you like living there?"

"Oh, I love it! The campus is beautiful. And I love that it's so close to Washington. This fall was taken up with marching band, but one weekend in October when we didn't have a game, Seth and I went into town. We went to Dupont Circle, which is like their gayborhood. They have a bunch of gay bars and restaurants and shops near there, and a lot of gay people live in the area. So that was cool." *And there's a gay bookstore where I bought this calendar.* "But enough about me. Tell me about where you live. You said you live in a house with a bunch of other gay guys?"

"Yeah. It's pretty unbelievable. It's in a kinda rich neighborhood, but it's only a few blocks from campus. I can walk there in ten minutes. Anyway, the guy who owns it, Hal, is in his early 40s. He's an attorney. He has this nice master suite with a home office. There are four other bedrooms, and he rents them out to gay college guys. I lived here my senior year, too. And there's a big kitchen with all these fabulous appliances, and you should see the backyard! Oh my God… There's a swimming pool and a hot tub and a tiki bar and… Here, why don't I show you?"

Ryan unplugged his laptop and picked it up. He turned it around so the camera and the screen were facing forward. "Can you still hear me?"

"Yeah."

Ryan walked out into the kitchen. "So this is the kitchen. Check out the stove! And the huge fridge!" Ryan pivoted slowly so Chris could see the entire room.

"Wow, that's pretty swank."

Ryan turned the computer so it was facing him again. "Yeah. And Hal's a great cook. Everyone is responsible for buying their own food and fixing their own meals. But on Sunday night, Hal cooks dinner for everyone. Then we watch a movie or play a game or something. It's like a family night. It's nice 'cause most of the time everyone is off doing their own thing, but once a week we all spend time together."

"So do you all get along okay?"

"Oh, yeah. They're great. They gave me so much support during the first few months after I got here. It's like I'm everyone's little brother and they all kinda help me along. As I said, we're a family. Everyone's different, but that's what makes it interesting. You should hear how they joke around and tease each other. It's really hilarious."

"Sounds sort of like a small gay frat house." *Have you slept with any of them? Or all of them?*

"I never thought about it that way, but yeah. Kinda. Anyway, let me take you out back." Ryan turned the computer so it was facing forward again, and walked out through the sliding glass door.

At the same time, Tyler knocked on Chris's door. He muted his microphone and said, "Come in." Tyler entered and Chris said, "I'm on a Skype call with Bryan. He's showing me where he lives. Look at this place!"

With the computer facing away from him, Ryan couldn't see Tyler. He was slowly rotating so Chris could see everything. "There's the pool. That raised part at the far end is a waterfall. And there's the hot tub." Tyler's eyes popped open wide when he recognized the familiar surroundings. Ryan continued, "As you can see, the whole backyard is completely private, so it's clothing optional. One of the guys, Ted, the guy I went hiking with yesterday, is like totally *haaawwwttt*! He's been working out for years and he is a *stud*! And he's really nice. Anyway, sometimes at night he and I come out here when it's peaceful and quiet, and he brings a bottle of wine, and we sit out here – in the hot tub during the winter and in the pool during the summer – and just drink wine and talk. We can be honest with each other and talk about whatever's on our minds. Or sometimes we don't say anything and just chill out together. But it's beautiful."

Chris thought, *Two naked guys in a hot tub? And he's obviously turned on by this Ted guy. What could possibly happen?*

"Anyway, let's go back inside. Oh, hey, I see Hal in the kitchen. Let me introduce you to him."

Tyler bolted from the room, which seemed odd to Chris. Ryan

stepped back into the house and closed the sliding glass door behind him.

"Hey, Hal. I'm on a Skype call with my best friend Chris from Kansas. Chris, meet Hal. Hal, meet Chris."

Hal said, "Hi Chris! Nice to meet you – on screen, anyway. Ryan's told us a lot about you."

Chris unmuted his mic and said, "Nice to meet you too. That's a pretty fabulous place you have there." *Did he just call him Ryan? Maybe the sound cut out for a second. Or maybe I didn't hear it right. Wait a minute… he said in his email he changed his name.*

"Oh, this meager hovel? Yeah, we like it. It's comfortable. You need to come out and visit sometime!"

"I'd love to." *But first Bryan needs to tell me where the heck it is.*

"Well, I'll let you get back to catching up with each other. Nice to meet you!"

"You too."

Ryan carried the computer back into his room and set it down on his desk facing him again. "So what did you think?"

"You were right. That place looks amazing!"

"Yeah, I totally lucked out."

"How can you afford that?"

"It's only $500 a month. Plus I have to buy my own food."

"Sweet." *Must be nice. I'm paying more than that to live in a tiny dorm room with a roommate.*

Ryan asked, "So how was your senior year?"

"It was pretty good – except you weren't there."

"Awww…"

"No, seriously. Especially the first few weeks. It just seemed so wrong not to have you there. I missed you. Every day, I wondered if you were all right, and where you were, and what happened to you. I mean, I still had all our other friends, and that was great, but it wasn't the same."

"Did you run on the track team in the spring?"

"Nah. I just did it because you were doing it too. And besides, every day would have been another reminder that you weren't there."

Ryan said, "God… I feel really bad about that. Believe me, I would have preferred to be there with you. On the bright side, at least you didn't have to put up with Rocket Crockett and his bullshit."

"Yeah, but you know what? Right after I found out you were gone, I sent a text to all our friends in the band and all the guys on the track team. And he replied in, like, two minutes. He said he was really sorry and he would spread the word. He asked me to keep him updated. Every couple of weeks when I'd see him in the hallways at school, he would ask if I heard anything about you. I think he was genuinely concerned. And despite all his teasing and acting like a dick, I think he actually liked you."

"He had a funny way of showing it."

Chris said, "Yeah, who knows why he acted the way he did? But you know, even though he was obnoxious at times, deep down I think he's an okay guy."

"I suppose. I wonder what he's doing now."

"He's going to TCU. He got a scholarship to play football there."

Ryan said, "Well, good for him. Seriously. He's a great football player. But anyway, who else do you know about?"

"A lot of our friends went to either Kansas or Kansas State. I'm on Facebook now, so I'm friends with some of them. Nobody I know is going to Maryland. Hey, are you on Facebook?"

"Nah… I'm staying away from that."

"How come?"

Ryan said, "Mostly because I don't want my folks or anybody from their church finding me. I value my privacy. Besides, a couple of the other guys here are on Facebook, and sometimes they spend hours at a time on it. Seems like a huge waste of time to me."

"Yeah, I guess. I try not to spend more than 20 or 30 minutes on it each day. But it's nice to keep up with people. Anyway, tell me about your senior year. What was your high school like?"

"It was different. Real different. And not in a good way. I mean, it was okay, but it was definitely a step down from Prairie Village."

"In what ways?"

"Well, first, the bands weren't nearly as good. I guess in the 90s the school system had to cut funding for schools. So a lot of schools had to drop their band programs. It's better now, but they're still trying to rebuild."

Chris said, "Wow. No band in school? That would suck."

"Yeah. Music is just as important as any other subject. The band director was pretty good, though, and really nice. Oh, and get this! His name is … wait for it … Mr. Scales."

"Nooo…!"

"Yes! And then I thought of that time we were sitting at Slush Fun thinking up names that would match people's occupations. I couldn't think of a good first name for Mr. Scales, but then I thought, what if he had been in the military and reached a high rank? He could have been Major Scales!"

Chris laughed. "That's funny! Wait… I know! His first name could be Dorian. Dorian Scales."

"Good one! I didn't think of that."

"So tell me more about your school."

Ryan said, "Well, the classes were easier. A lot of the kids came from lower-income homes, and maybe the elementary schools weren't quite as good, but anyway it wasn't as challenging. Oh, and I made Valedictorian!"

"Congratulations! But I'm not surprised."

"Yeah, but I might not have been at the top of the class at Prairie Village. And another thing, this school was much more diverse. I mean, I never thought about it while I was there, but Prairie Village is like totally White. Here, the school was maybe 10 or 15 percent White. It was over half Latino, and there were more Blacks and Asians too. I mean, none of that's bad, it's just different. When I first got there, I wasn't sure how well I was going to fit in, you know?"

Chris asked, "So how well did you fit in?"

"It was kinda rough at first. 'Cause you know me, I'm kinda shy. And it's like everyone already had their friends from last year, and now who's this new, tall, geeky White guy? But it worked out okay. I made some good friends. A lot of them were the kids in the GSA."

"The what?"

"The Gay-Straight Alliance. Yes, they actually had a club for LGBT kids and straight kids who wanted to be supportive."

"Man, they'll never have anything like that in Prairie Village."

"I know, right? But out here, it's a lot more liberal. Like for the election, there were a lot more yard signs for Obama than for McCain. And since the school is so racially diverse, they're better about acknowledging differences in religion and sexual orientation and things like that."

"And you joined it?"

"Yeah. I decided since I didn't have to hide being gay from my parents anymore, I was going to be more out. I mean, why not? I figured, if they don't like me, they don't like me. After what I went through with my parents, I'm through with trying to hide who I am."

"Wow. I can hardly believe it."

"Well, you were a big influence on that. So was this girl I met in the GSA. She's a Black lesbian named LaTanya. She and I became really good friends. She said she just puts herself out there and people either like her or they don't. That's their choice. She said she would rather have a few close friends who are real than try to change who she is to get more people to like her. So I decided I wanted to be the same way. One of my other friends was this Vietnamese guy named Mike, and another guy named Raul, who was straight and Latino."

"That's cool. Yeah, it's more diverse at Maryland, and certainly in the DC area. And I know what you mean about politics. DC and Maryland and Northern Virginia are much more Democratic."

"And my own house is diverse. One of my housemates is Latino, and another guy is a Black drag queen."

"Are you serious?"

"Yeah. He's totally fabulous. And you should hear him sing! Oh my God… he's amazing. When he's in drag, he sings with his real voice, and he sounds just like Whitney Houston. But he's real strong, like LaTanya, and I've learned from him a lot about standing up for myself and being proud of who I am."

Chris said, "Sounds like it. So… are you seeing anyone?"

"Nah… I kinda dated this guy for a few months, from February until the beginning of May. I met him in the GSA. Anyway, that crashed and burned big time. And we were about to go to the senior prom, but I got Mike to go with me instead."

"*What*??? You took a male date to the senior prom?"

Ryan said, "Yeah. The GSA talked about having our own little dance. But LaTanya said, 'I don't want separate but equal, I want full inclusion.' So yeah, I went with Mike and LaTanya went with her girlfriend. A few of our straight friends from the GSA were there too."

"Did you actually dance?"

"Not at first. But then, while they were playing a fast song, a couple of our straight friends pulled the four of us out onto the floor and we all danced in kind of a group, you know? But then this slow dance came on, and LaTanya and Angelica decided they were going to slow dance like everyone else. So I took hold of Mike and we slow-danced too. And at first, it was really scary, like everyone stopped and stared at us. But then two of the straight girls in the GSA started dancing together, and then their boyfriends did too. And then all the other couples went back to dancing like it was no big deal. And that was that. So we danced for the rest of the evening."

Chris said, "Wow… that's amazing! I can't imagine that happening at Prairie Village."

"Yeah, but you know? All it takes is someone to do it first."

"Would you have danced with me if we went?"

"I would have wanted to. But I don't know. I guess it would have depended on whether it felt safe or if it seemed like people might freak out. I mean, I never went to any dances, because I never had a girlfriend."

"Still… I think it's great that your school was so cool with gay people."

Ryan said, "Well, we had a couple of really bad things happen earlier in the year. But they ended up raising awareness, so I guess it wasn't all bad. But anyway, what's it like being gay at Maryland?"

"It's not a big deal. Most of the kids in the marching band know we're a couple and no one cares. I suppose some kids don't like it, but they keep it to themselves. And it's not like we hold hands when we're walking across campus. But we get treated the same as everyone else."

"That's good."

Chris asked, "What about where you are?"

"It seems like it would probably be okay. There's an LGBT student group here, and I've met some nice people in that. But I'm not in the marching band and I live off-campus, so I don't have much of a social life beyond that. I'm pretty busy." *Please don't ask about my job.*

"So you're not in any bands or anything?"

"I couldn't make the time commitment for marching band. But I'm in a jazz ensemble they have that's mostly non-music majors."

"Good. 'Cause you shouldn't quit playing your trumpet. You're too good, and I know how much you love it."

There was a brief pause. Then Ryan said, "Well, I should probably let you go, but it's been great to see you again."

"Yeah. You don't know how much this has meant to me."

"Me too. I mean, I've gotten on with my life and everything, but this has reminded me of how much I've missed you."

Chris asked, "Can we do this again? I really want to stay in touch, and hopefully see you in person again someday. The last year and a half have been hard."

"Of course. I'm sorry I kept out of sight for so long. Whatever the future holds for us, let's never be out of touch with each other again.

I mean, I'm glad you have Seth and everything, but you know…"

"Definitely. How about if we do this again after I get back from the Independence Bowl? I'm flying back to Maryland with the band on December 31st. So maybe on New Year's Day?"

Ryan said, "Sure. How about 2:00 your time?"

"That should work. I'll email you if anything changes."

Another pause.

Chris said, "This has been great."

"Yeah. Have a wonderful time at the Independence Bowl! I want to hear all about it."

"Thanks. I will."

Another pause. Ryan thought, *Should I say it? I mean, I already said it in the letter. But he has a boyfriend, and I don't want it to seem like I'm trying to cut in on him. What if he doesn't say it back to me? Oh, geez. Just tell him. You already regret that you never told him before.*

Chris said, "Uh, Bryan?"

Ryan blurted out, "I love you."

Chris laughed. "That's what I was getting ready to say to you. I love you too."

"It feels weird to say that to you on a screen. I wish I had told you in person."

"I know, but I'm glad we said it."

"Me too. I so want to hug you right now." *And so much more.*

"Same here. But it's the thought that counts."

Ryan said, "Okay, well… talk to you on New Year's Day."

"Yeah. I can't wait."

"Bye."

"Bye."

Reluctantly, Ryan clicked the button to end the call. He sat at his desk, staring at the screen. His emotions were pulling him in every direction. Seeing and talking to Chris had been wonderful. But it also reminded him of everything he had lost, and what he could no longer have.

Ryan threw on a light jacket and started walking toward Westwood. He ate lunch at My Gyro. He imagined taking Chris to this place and explaining everything on the menu, then sitting across the table from him enjoying the food and talking about whatever.

After he finished lunch, he decided to spend some time in the botanical garden on the southeastern edge of the campus. Perhaps that would provide the right atmosphere for reflection and sorting out his feelings.

# Meanwhile, Back in Kansas...

Friday, December 26, 2008

The day after Christmas was just another workday for Rev. Brad Bauer, head pastor of the Eternal Savior Christian Church. While the Christmas Eve and Christmas morning services could be re-used each year with minimal modification, they still took time. Now it was Friday, and he had barely started on his sermon for Sunday. He instructed his secretary to take messages whenever possible so he could work uninterrupted.

Shortly after 2:00, the phone rang. The secretary announced there was a caller on line 2 who said his call was urgent and insisted on speaking directly to Rev. Bauer. He sighed and pressed the button for line 2. "Greetings in the name of our Lord and Savior, Jesus Christ. Rev. Brad Bauer speaking. How may I help you?"

"Good afternoon, Rev. Bauer. I have some information about your missing son. My name is Walter Robertson. Yesterday, my wife and I were celebrating Christmas with my son and his family. While we were eating dinner, my grandson mentioned that he received an email from your son, Bryan. He was quite excited about it. Apparently, this was the first time he'd heard from him in a year and a half. I asked him if this was the Bryan that went missing last year, and he said it was. I asked him where Bryan is now, but he said he didn't know. He said your son had not disclosed that information. Now, I find that a little hard to believe, but for some reason, he wasn't going to tell me."

Brad said, "So your grandson heard from Bryan, but he doesn't know where he is."

"That's correct. At least that's what he says."

"That's not particularly helpful."

"Well, I figured you could at least talk to my grandson. If nothing else, he has Bryan's email address."

"That's true. So, what is your grandson's name?"

"Chris Robertson."

"Chris Robertson… oh, yeah. He's the kid who recruited my son into the homosexual lifestyle. If it wasn't for him, none of this would have happened, and my son would be here today."

"Now, wait a minute, sir! You're accusing my grandson of being a homosexual and recruiting your son? And you're blaming him for his disappearance?"

Brad said, "That's correct. And I'm not accusing, I'm stating a fact. We met with his parents shortly after Chris and Bryan were caught kissing in a car. For some inexplicable reason, they're proud of him for being a homosexual. They said they support him and they weren't the least bit interested in helping him recover. Apparently, they haven't shared that information with you."

"Well, I *never–*"

"You have now. Now, if you'll excuse me, I'm very busy today. May the blessings of the Lord be upon you. Goodbye." Brad hung up the phone and shook his head.

*That was the last thing I needed today. God, I hope he doesn't call the house. Brenda will insist on following up on it. She already wants to waste more money on a private investigator in El Paso, because Brandon got a Christmas card from Bryan postmarked from there. This, after we spent $6,000 last year on a Private Investigator in Macon after he got a Christmas card from there. What a waste of money that was – a total wild goose chase. And what's the point? Even if we find him, he's 19 now, so we can't force him to come home. And I can't have that hit the news when I go on my book signing tour next month. Besides, I don't ever want to talk to those vile Robertson people again.*

*Now, where was I? Oh, yeah... living the word of the Lord by loving thy neighbor.*

***

Chris wasn't saying much at dinner. He seemed distracted.

"How was your Skype call with Bryan?" Kathleen asked.

"It was good. It was great to see him again and hear his voice."

"How's he doing?"

"Really well, it seems. He carried the computer around the house and the backyard so I could see where he lives. He rents a room in this house that looks pretty fabulous. There's a pool and a hot tub in the backyard. It's really beautiful. And he says his housemates are nice."

Kathleen said, "Well, good. I'm glad things worked out well for him. Are you going to talk again?"

"Yes. We're going to do another Skype call on New Year's Day."

Tom said, "Well, make sure to tell him we said hi."

Kathleen studied the expression on Chris' face. "I'm surprised you aren't in a happier mood. You seem kind of down. Well, maybe not down, but contemplative."

"Yeah, contemplative is about right. I guess I'm wondering what it might have been like if he hadn't run away and we were still boyfriends. And what it would be like if we were going to college together."

Tom said, "Well, there's no point in pining for what might have been."

"I know, but I can't help it. And he sounded so happy and he lives in this great place and everything seems to be so good for him. It's like he's gone on without me and everything's just great."

Tyler said, "You mean you don't want him to be happy? Would you feel better if he was suffering?"

"Well, no, but…"

"'Cause that's kind of messed up."

Chris said, "I know, it doesn't sound right, and of course I want him to be happy, but… I don't know, I'm just feeling weird about it. I'm trying to sort it all out."

Tom said, "It sounds like you're glad he's doing well on his own and you want him to be happy. But you'd prefer that he was doing well and being happy *with you*."

"Yeah, that's pretty much it." Chris paused. "And there's another thing. The whole time we were talking, I felt so excited and so happy… almost tingly. It was just… magical. It's like everything was right with the world. And it occurred to me that the last time I felt that good was with him, the summer before last. So, like, where does that leave me and Seth? I mean, he's nice and everything, and we get along great, and I definitely have feelings for him. But he doesn't quite make me feel the way I felt with Bryan."

Everyone sat silently, wondering what would be the right thing to say.

Finally, Kathleen said, "I understand, honey. But Bryan isn't available to you right now, and we don't know if he ever will be. But you shouldn't resign yourself to a life of being alone because you can't have him. You've only been seeing Seth for a few months so far, right?" Chris nodded. "I'm sure your feelings for him will continue to grow."

Tom added, "Or maybe they won't, but the only way you'll find out is to continue dating him and see where it goes. You may date several people before you find the one you want to marry."

Chris said, "I guess."

Kathleen said, "You shouldn't compare Seth to Bryan. That's not fair to Seth. He'll never be Bryan. But he has his qualities, and you should decide based on what he has to offer."

Tyler said, "It's like that Stephen Stills song, 'Love the One You're With.'"

***

After dinner, Tyler stopped by Chris's room. "Hey, you wanna talk some more?"

"Yeah, sure. Come in."

"So what else is on your mind?"

"A couple of things. For one, he seemed different. He seemed… I don't know… a lot gayer. Back when he was here, he was still closeted. I remember when I took him to the gay pride festival. It seemed like a good idea at the time, but it totally bombed. He kept saying stuff like, 'Why do I have to label myself?' 'Why do I have to even say I'm gay?' 'Why do I have to identify as part of some community?' 'I can't relate to these drag queens and swishy guys, and I don't want to wear T-shirts with rainbows.' Now, he's like totally out and he's drooling over one of his roommates. And at one point he said that last year in high school, he and this other guy danced together at the prom! That seems so unlike the Bryan I knew."

Tyler said, "But isn't that good? Weren't you frustrated because you couldn't get him to be more out?"

"Yeah, I guess. I know, it doesn't make any sense. But he's different. He's changed. And who knows how else he's changed?"

"And you wonder whether you would still like the new Bryan as much as the old Bryan?"

"Yeah, kinda."

"But didn't you say he still made you feel all excited and tingly?"

"Yeah."

"Well, then…"

Chris said, "I guess I won't know until I talk with him some more. I like Skype, but I hope I get to see him in person again sometime."

"Well, maybe you can get together next summer, or maybe your spring breaks will line up."

"Yeah, but here's another thing. He won't even tell me where he is. And he said he changed his name, but he hasn't told me what that is. And it's like, how can we go much farther without him telling me those things? We need to be able to trust each other."

Tyler said, "Well… I can solve part of that mystery for you."

"Really? How?"

"When he was showing you that house he lives in? I've been there. I know exactly where it is. It's a few blocks away from UCLA."

"Yeah, with the swimming pool and the palm trees, I figured it must be southern California, or maybe Arizona or southern Florida."

"I know the other guys who live in that house. They were friends of mine. The one named Ted that he was saying was so hot? Well, he is. His physique is damn near perfect. Anyway, Ted and I had some business and accounting classes together. Sometimes we studied together and we'd meet at his house. Then I met the other guys. They're all really nice. One of them is a Black drag queen, and the other is a porn star."

Chris's eyes popped open wide. "What? You're kidding me. What was he like?"

"Pretty wild and crazy. He's quite the party boy. Sometimes they'd have parties and Ted would invite me. And let me tell you, those were some wild parties! So yeah, I know those guys and that house."

"Interesting. Small world, isn't it?"

"Yep. So, since Bryan lives with those guys, no wonder he seems gayer. Some of it was bound to rub off."

"Yeah, I guess. So how come you ran off so quickly when Bryan was going to introduce me to his landlord?"

"I don't know. I guess if Hal saw me and recognized me, he'd want to talk, and that would divert the call away from you and Bryan." Tyler knew that sounded lame, but it was the best he could come up with.

Now Chris had more information to process. "Okay, well, thanks for the talk."

"Any time. Don't worry, you'll work it out. I'm glad you and Bryan are back in touch again."

"Yeah, me too."

# The More You Know...

Thursday, January 1, 2009

On New Year's Day, Ryan dragged himself out of bed at 9:30. He had been up until 2:00 a.m. celebrating New Year's Eve with his housemates and about twenty other partiers. The booze flowed freely, and at one point there were eight naked guys in the hot tub. Ryan received a lot of attention.

He threw on a T-shirt and sweatpants and shuffled into the kitchen to make breakfast. Hal and Ted were watching the Gator Bowl on the large TV in the family room. Ryan carried his bowl of cereal and glass of orange juice into the family room and joined them. None of them had any affinity for either of the teams, but Ryan got swept up in the game and lost track of time. When halftime came a few minutes before 11:00, Ryan realized what time it was.

"Shit! I'm supposed to be on a Skype call with Chris in five minutes! And I haven't showered yet. I look like crap."

Ted said, "Looking like crap is not possible for you. Just comb your hair and you'll be fine."

Ryan rushed into the bathroom to wash his face and comb his hair. He ran back to his room and put on a nicer T-shirt, then opened his laptop and launched Skype. He joined the call a minute late. "Hey there, sorry I'm late."

Chris replied, "Hi! No problem. Happy New Year!"

"Happy New Year to you too! So how was the Humanitarian Bowl?"

"It was fun. Fortunately, Maryland won, 42-35. It was a wild game. Lots of back-and-forth."

"Cool. And how did the band do?"

"Really well. It was cold, though! I mean, it gets cold in Kansas, too, but we're usually done with football games by Thanksgiving. And it doesn't get nearly as cold in Maryland."

"What's Boise like?"

"It's kinda nice. The mountains surrounding the town are beautiful. Definitely different than Prairie Village."

Ryan asked, "So what did you do last night?"

"We went to a party one of the band members threw in Silver Spring. A lot of the kids who go to Maryland live in the DC suburbs. It was okay. What about you?"

"We had a party here last night. It was pretty wild. Hal throws these big parties two or three times a year and uh… let's just say they're a lot of fun."

"You look like you partied pretty hard last night."

*I partied hard, all right.* "It shows that much, huh? Yeah, I was a bit hungover. But I've been up a couple of hours and I have some food in me, so I'm feeling better."

"That's so unlike the Bryan I used to know. I remember when we were at that Memorial Day cook-out the summer before last, you were surprised my parents let me drink beer."

"Yeah. Obviously, drinking was out of the question with my parents. Anyway, now that I'm out on my own and living with older guys – yeah, I drink now and then. Just once a month or so. One of my housemates, Ted, is a wine drinker and we usually share a bottle of wine when we get in the hot tub together. So I'm learning about the different kinds of wine. I'm not a big beer fan, though."

"He's the one you said was so hot, right?"

"Right. A few days after I moved in, he and I went running together. And at one point, he took his shirt off and… OH. MY. GOD! His body is, like, perfect! He's a former Marine, and he's been working out for years, and… let's just say his effort has paid off."

"But what's he like?"

"He's really nice. He's probably my favorite housemate. He's kind of quiet and reserved. He had a difficult childhood and then he joined the Marines and got sent to Afghanistan, and I think maybe he has a little PTSD. He keeps saying he has issues he needs to deal with, although I don't think he is. But he's focused on his studies and he's working on a Master's in International Business. And now that we're comfortable with each other he lets his guard down a bit, so we have some pretty deep talks. And he's always there when I need someone to talk to. So yeah, we're really good friends."

Chris asked, "So, are you two, like, dating?"

"No. At first, I wanted to, but he didn't. See, he's eight years older than me. He spent four years in the Marines, then he was a senior in college when I was a senior in high school. And he has this thing he calls the 'half your age plus seven' rule that says you shouldn't date someone who's younger than half your age plus seven. Anyway, I'm kind of over that now. We probably wouldn't make good partners, but we're good friends."

"Well, good. So, when do classes start at UCLA?"

"Monday. We're on quarters, so fall quarter ended on December 12th. When do your classes start?"

"We're on semesters, but we have these short little terms between semesters. Winter term is January 5th through 23rd. Spring semester starts on January 26th. I figured I might as well take a class during winter term, rather than spend a few more weeks in Kansas doing nothing besides freezing."

"Hey, wait a minute. How did you know I'm going to UCLA?"

Chris grinned. "Busted!"

"Seriously, how did you know?"

"Well, on our last call, you know when you were showing me around your house? You couldn't see it because you had your computer facing away from you, but Tyler came into my room. And when he saw the backyard with the pool and the hot tub, he recognized it. He said he knows the guys who live there, and he's been there for some of those wild parties you were talking about."

Ryan was speechless.

"And you were talking about Ted? He and Tyler had some classes together, so they would get together in Ted's room to study. Then he met the others."

Ryan thought, *I wonder if they ever studied biology... each other's. Oh, wait... at that family night dinner last year ago when Ted, Ricky, and Darnell were talking about Tyler, they all said they fucked him.* "Did he tell you he was going to live here his senior year?"

"What...? No! Really?"

"Yeah. Remember at that cook-out, he said he lived in the dorms his first three years, but next year he was going to live off-campus with a few friends? This house is what he was referring to."

"Oh, wow. What a coincidence!"

"Yeah. He found out he lost his scholarship a few days before I arrived in LA. I'm sorry that happened to him, but who knows what would have happened to me if that room wasn't available."

"So how did you end up there?"

"You remember Hal, from our last call? The guy who owns this place? He's an attorney and he volunteers for the Los Angeles LGBT Youth Project. I went there when I first got to town. I asked them if I could see an attorney about getting emancipated from my parents and changing my name. They hooked me up with Hal. While I was talking with him about my situation, he said he had a room available because someone else had to back out. And later I learned that was Tyler."

"But didn't you say your house is all gay guys?"

"Yep."

"But Tyler's not gay."

Ryan asked, "How do you know?"

"Well, when I came out to the family and they responded so well, you'd think he would have come out then, too."

"Not necessarily."

"I mean, he did say he had some gay friends he hung around

with…"

Ryan said, "That was probably these guys. And maybe others. I know Ricky, one of my other housemates, has taken him out to the bars on several occasions."

"Still, none of that means he's gay. He's just cool with being around gay people. He's been really nice to me since I came out. We've gotten a lot closer."

"That's great. I'm sure being around these guys helped."

Chris said, "Besides, he has a girlfriend now. He's been dating her for about a year. She's probably going to move in with him after she graduates this spring. So no, I don't think he's gay."

*Should I tell him Tyler had sex with three of my housemates? No. I really shouldn't. Let's just wrap this up and move on.* "Maybe he is, maybe he isn't. Maybe he's bi. Only Tyler knows for sure. Or maybe he's still figuring it out for himself, which is why he didn't come out to the family when you did. But in any case, I'm living in the room he was going to be living in."

Chris said, "Tyler told me that one of the other guys there is a porn star."

"Yeah. That's Ricky, the guy he went out to the bars with."

"Really? I mean, what kind of person would do that?"

Ryan thought of several ways he might respond to that. None of them would have moved the discussion forward in a positive way. It was a rhetorical question anyway. So he changed the subject.

"Well, moving on… now that you know where I live, please don't tell anyone else, okay? I don't want it getting back to my family."

"Oh, I won't. Promise. And I know my parents and Tyler won't. So let me ask you something else. You mentioned that you changed your name. What did you change it to?"

"Ryan."

"Okay. On the last call, when you introduced me to Hal, I thought I heard him call you Ryan. But it sounds so much like Bryan, I couldn't be sure. And did you change your last name?"

*It will be interesting to see how he responds to this.* "Yes. I changed it to Robertson."

Chris looked startled. "Really? Why?"

"Because I hoped someday we'd be together again. Then when we got married, I'd already have your last name. Even if that never happened, I wanted to honor you. So now I'm Ryan Brandon Robertson. I chose Brandon for my middle name to honor him."

"Oh my God… That's so touching! I mean, seriously… That means so much to me!"

Ryan could see Chris's eyes tearing up. "That's how much you mean to me."

Chris's emotions were pulling him in so many directions. His internal debate about whether to stay at Maryland with Seth or transfer to UCLA to be with Ryan seemed more urgent than ever. He had no idea what to do. "Wow… That's just… I don't know… I really wasn't expecting that."

"I hope you're not offended."

"Offended? No way! I mean, that's like the greatest compliment I've ever received. It's just that… well, I have a lot to think about."

Ryan wasn't sure what he meant by that. But he could sense Chris was emotionally overwhelmed, so it was probably best to let it go. "Well, we've covered a lot of ground today, haven't we?"

"Yeah, I'll say. When do you want to talk again? Maybe next weekend? January 10th or 11th?"

"I can't. I have to work that weekend. Maybe the following weekend?"

"Where are you working?"

"It's kind of complicated. I'll tell you more next time we talk, okay?"

*Why can't he explain his job in a few words? But he wants to talk about it next time, not now.* "Okay. So is Saturday or Sunday better for you?"

"Probably Sunday." Ryan was much more likely to have a shoot on a Saturday than on a Sunday. "How about 2:00 your time?"

"Yeah, that's good. Sunday, January 18th, at 2:00 Eastern Standard Time."

"Okay, well take care. And good luck with your winter term."

There was a brief pause while they both waited to see what the other one would say next.

Ryan said, "I love you."

Chris said, "I love you too." Then he remembered the calendar. They talked about so much else, he forgot to ask about that during the call. But the call was ending, so that topic would have to wait until next time. He didn't know how he was going to bring it up, anyway. There was so much new information to digest. Bryan had changed so much, but he knew he still loved him.

# Where's Jordan?

Tuesday, January 6, 2009

On Tuesday afternoon, Ryan entered the music building for the jazz ensemble's first rehearsal of the winter quarter. To his surprise, Jordan wasn't there. There was a new trumpet player in his chair.

After rehearsal, Ryan asked the director if Jordan had enrolled for this quarter. The director replied that he had not.

After he returned home, Ryan texted Jordan.

Jordan didn't reply until 9:30.

Fifteen minutes passed.

Tue, Jan 6 2009, 9:51 PM

Full schedule. Not much free time.

Ryan could tell Jordan was blowing him off, but why? Especially after Jordan had gone out of his way to be so nice to him last quarter. Ryan realized Jordan's holidays were probably difficult since his parents were now divorced. But why take it out on him?

# The Boys of Breckenridge

Thursday, January 8, 2009

Ryan's winter quarter got off to a great start. His classes seemed like they would be interesting and his first impressions of his instructors were favorable. He chatted with each of them after class on Wednesday to let them know he would be absent Thursday afternoon and all day Friday and Monday. Fortunately, there would be no quizzes or tests, and no assignments would be due so early in the quarter. He'd have plenty of time to catch up.

Ryan had accepted Michael Rodick's offer to travel to Breckenridge, Colorado for three days of shooting porn scenes. He was hesitant to accept the gig because it meant he would miss two and a half days of classes. But Ricky, who recommended him for the gig, insisted that he accept it. He said, "Man, this is Eagle Studios! They're the biggest studio in the business. They hire only the best talent. They sell tons more videos, so they pay better. Dude, you need to be part of this! I guarantee you it will be the best thing that's ever happened to your career."

Ryan figured if he could get his foot in the door with Eagle Studios and these videos ended up being as big as Ricky said they were going to be, it would indeed be very good for his career. So he accepted.

On Thursday, Hal drove Ricky and Ryan to the airport. Ricky spotted several guys he knew from his past work who were also traveling to Breckenridge for this project. He introduced Ryan to the other guys. Several of their names were familiar, but Ryan had not worked with any of them yet. Most of them seemed to know each other already. They chatted and laughed easily and speculated about what would be in store for them this weekend. They seemed like nice guys.

The guys all looked to be several years older than Ryan, and they were no strangers to the gym. Ricky was right – Eagle Studios hired very high-caliber guys. He wondered which ones he would be working with and whether he would look scrawny by comparison. He recalled some of the activities Michael Rodick said would be taking place and wondered which of these guys would be doing what to whom. *This is going to be a very interesting weekend*, he thought.

# Yield Not to Temptation

Thursday, January 15, 2009


After Ryan's last morning class let out a few minutes before 11:00, he started walking toward Westwood Village to beat the lunch rush. As he crossed Bruin Plaza, he spotted Jordan. He waved. Jordan saw him and quickly decided he couldn't pretend he had not. He thought, *Might as well get this over with.*

Ryan walked up to Jordan. "Hey, how's it going?"

"Okay, I guess. My classes this quarter are pretty tough."

"How were your holidays?"

"They sucked, like I thought they would."

"I'm really sorry. Any updates on your situation?"

"Yeah. Dad moved out and Mom moved back in. But I think she's going to sell it and move somewhere else. Then I'll have to find someplace else if I want to live near campus."

For an awkward moment, neither of them said anything. Ryan didn't want to prolong the conversation about Jordan's home situation. But he noticed Jordan wasn't engaging with him, like asking how his holidays were or how his quarter was shaping up. Jordan didn't seem to want to talk to him. Finally, Ryan said, "Are we okay? Did I say or do anything to upset you?"

Jordan took a deep breath. "No, you haven't done anything wrong. But, uh… We can't hang out together anymore. I'm sorry."

"Why not?"

"Well… Okay, so a couple of months ago when my parents were going through their divorce, Mom asked if I wanted to see a counselor to work through my feelings and help me deal with everything. So I did.

I'm still seeing him. At one point I told him I was starting to have feelings for you I didn't think I should be having. At first, I thought it was just because I knew you and it was nice to see a familiar face on campus when I was starting college. Then, when I needed to talk about my parents, you were there. And I appreciate your support. You were there for me when I needed someone. But then it kinda started going in other directions. Like remember that day we went to the botanical garden, and you hugged me for like ten or fifteen seconds? It felt comforting, and I think that's all you meant, but I felt something else. And, uh… it bothered me that I was having those feelings."

"Now wait a minute. I was just trying to comfort you. I wasn't trying to come onto you. I would never try to take advantage of you like that. I don't think I've ever said or done anything inappropriate to you."

"You haven't. Except maybe that one time when you said you don't start recruiting guys for at least three months."

"Good lord, I was only kidding. Believe me, I have no interest in you."

Jordan said, "Well, anyway… my therapist said the best thing for me to do would be to cut off further contact with you. Just to avoid the temptation, I guess."

Ryan was dumbfounded. He felt angry, offended, hurt, sad for Jordan, and sad for himself. He thought of several things he wanted to say but realized that none of them would improve the situation. So he simply said, "Well, alrighty then." He stepped around Jordan and resumed his journey toward Westwood.

After six steps, he looked over his shoulder at Jordan. He hadn't moved. Ryan called out, "Have a nice life."

***

That night at the LGBT+ Student Network meeting, something felt different. Ryan sensed several guys seemed to be looking at him more than usual. It was only a handful of the guys – most of the other group members were engaged in planning the quarter's activities and forming committees to work on things.

When the meeting ended, everyone filed out the door. Ryan exited along with the group of guys he had gotten to know last quarter. Once they were outside, Jason said, "So I hope you don't mind, but I have to ask you something. My boyfriend gave me the 2009 Student Bodies calendar for Christmas, and – is that you in it?"

"I don't know." The other guys seemed surprised Ryan wouldn't be aware that a naked picture of him had been published in a calendar. Ryan thought quickly. *There was that photo shoot back in June with the guy Hal introduced me to at the LGBT Youth Project gala. Maybe one of those pictures ended up in a calendar. Shit. Now someone in this group has seen me naked. I wonder if he's shown it to the other guys.* "I guess it could be."

Another guy named Nathan said, "I think I saw you in a video I was watching online. Was that you in *Men on a Mission*?"

Ryan's heart sank. But there was no point in trying to deny it. "Yeah, that was me."

Nathan turned to his friends and smiled as if to say, 'I told you it was him.' He said, "Dude, you're really packin'. Seriously!" Nathan smiled at Ryan with a look that suggested he'd like to examine that package in person.

For the next few minutes, Ryan was peppered with questions.

"What made you decide to do porn?"

"I need the money to pay for college."

"What's it like? Is it fun?"

"It's just a job. It's not as fun as you might think."

"How much do you get paid?"

"It pays really well. How much is kind of personal."

"Do your parents know?"

"No."

"What if they find out?"

"I don't care. I'm not in touch with my parents."

"Why not?"

"I had to leave home when they found out I'm gay."

The questioning continued for several more minutes. Finally, Ryan said, "Hey look, guys, I kinda don't want to talk about this anymore. I'd appreciate it if you wouldn't spread it all around campus, okay? I just want to be an average student here like everyone else."

A couple of them mumbled, "I get it." "Yeah, that's cool."

But Ryan knew he had been defined and that was unlikely to change. "Well, I need to get some homework done. See you next time."

They all waved, and Ryan started heading toward home. He wasn't sure if there would be a next time.

# The Big Reveal

Sunday, January 18, 2009

Chris had trouble concentrating on the Philosophy class he was taking during the winter term. Winter term only lasted three weeks, so the entire course was condensed into that time. Chris was in class for four hours every morning, then he had an accelerated amount of homework and studying each afternoon and evening.

Since the last Skype call, all he could think about was Ryan. That, and the revelation about his brother. Back in high school, he and Ryan talked about going to UCLA together. But after Ryan left home and they lost touch, Chris had no idea where Ryan was, let alone where he was going to college. But now… maybe?

Chris's roommate wasn't there for the winter term, so he had the room to himself. He and Seth ate all their meals together and spent the night together most of the time. Often, they'd spend the evening studying in silence and chatting with each other when they wanted a break.

Last Thursday, Chris asked Seth for an evening apart. He told him he needed to devote extra focus to studying for an exam the next day. That was true, but he also wanted to be alone when he called his parents to talk.

"Mom… Dad… I had another Skype call with Bryan. He's going to UCLA! And he's living in the same house Tyler was going to live in during his senior year until he lost his scholarship."

Kathleen exclaimed, "Really! What a small world!"

"Yeah, I know. What a coincidence, right?" He didn't tell them the part about the house being all gay guys. "Anyway, it's been great to see him and talk to him again. He's changed a lot."

Kathleen said, "Well, we all change as we get older, especially as you go through your teenage years and you start college. Tyler changed, and you're changing. In a good way."

"Yeah. I'm sure part of it was growing up and going to college, and part of it was because he was thrust out into the world on his own. For one thing, he's a lot more out than he was before he left. And that's a good thing. Anyway, I've been thinking. He and I always talked about going to UCLA, and… well, what would you say if I applied to UCLA and got a scholarship? Would you be okay with me transferring there if I could do it affordably?"

Tom said, "Well, let's look at this objectively. Up to this point, you've been happy with Maryland. It's close to Washington, DC, where you want to work after you graduate. And you want to apply to law school at Georgetown or George Washington. Do you think you will be as well prepared for the career you want if you go to UCLA?"

"They have a good law school there."

Kathleen said, "But let's be honest. We know what's really driving this. You want to be with Bryan again. You're following your heart."

"Yeah, you're right. But what's wrong with that? You've always told me to enjoy each day as I go through life."

Tom said, "UCLA is a fine school and I know you'll get a good education there. But what about Seth?"

"He's nice and everything. We get along great, and I enjoy spending time with him. But I don't click with him quite the way I clicked with Bryan. The spark isn't quite the same."

Kathleen said, "We saw how you were floating on air after you got that email from him on Christmas day and you talked the next day."

"Yeah. Even after a year and a half apart, and after all the ways he's changed, he still does it for me."

Tom said, "Well, take some time to think about it. Don't make a hasty decision. I suppose you can go ahead and apply. Even if you get accepted, you can change your mind between now and then. And if you don't get accepted, well, that kind of settles it."

Kathleen added, "Besides, you have the rest of your lives after college. Maybe Bryan would be willing to take a job in the DC area after he graduates. What's he majoring in?"

"Computer Science."

Tom said, "Then he should be able to get a job anywhere."

"Yeah, you're right. Oh, and one other thing. After he left home, he changed his name so it would be harder for his parents to find him. Do you know what he changed it to? Ryan Brandon Robertson. That's right. He chose our last name. He said if he and I got together again and got married, he'd already have my name. And even if not, he did it to honor me."

Tom and Kathleen were speechless. Finally, Kathleen said, "That's really sweet. So you see, he's also thinking of being with you in the longer term."

"Yeah. Well, thanks for listening and for your advice. I'm going to talk to him about it on our next call. I'll think about it some more and I promise I won't make a hasty decision."

Tom said, "Okay. Well, whatever you do, we love you and we'll support you."

"Thanks. I love you too."

***

At lunch on Sunday, Seth asked Chris, "Wanna go see *Extreme Movie*? It's a nice day and we need to take a break from studying."

Any other time, seeing a movie together would be a great idea. And a frivolous comedy would make an excellent diversion. But Chris had a Skype call with Bryan at 2:00. "No, I need some time alone this afternoon. Maybe you can get one of our friends to go."

Seth looked puzzled. "Come on, it'll be fun."

"Yeah, but... I promised one of my high school friends I'd call him this afternoon."

"Can't you call him tonight?"

"No, we agreed on 2:00. Anyway, I'll call you when we're done. Maybe we can go to a later show."

Seth realized it wasn't open for negotiation, so he went back to his room after lunch.

Chris couldn't wait to talk to Ryan. In his mind, he repeatedly rehearsed how he was going to bring up the various topics he wanted to discuss. He tried to anticipate what Ryan might say, and how he'd respond. He opened his laptop and logged into Skype at 1:45. A few minutes before 2:00, Ryan joined.

Chris said, "Hey! How're you doing?"

"Great. How's your winter term going?"

"Pretty good. I'm taking Philosophy, just to get a Humanities requirement out of the way as quickly as possible. It's like they take a class that would otherwise run a whole semester and cram it all into three weeks. It's really intense. We had a test on Friday. I think I did okay."

"I'm sure you did fine. Anyway, it will be over in a week."

"Yeah. So how do you like UCLA?"

"It's good. I mean, it's a lot different from high school. I'm sure you know that. It's a lot harder. And it's up to you to be disciplined enough to pay attention and study and manage your time. It's a lot less social than high school, too. It's like there are these other kids in my classes, but everyone's just there for the class. Everyone goes their separate ways afterward."

Chris said, "Really? It's not like that here. I mean, yes, the classes are harder and I have to study a lot more. But between the marching band and the guys in my dorm, I've got a lot of friends here."

"Yeah, it would probably be different for me if I lived in a dorm. Living off-campus is definitely not as social."

"How do you like living in LA?"

"Overall, it's great. I love the warm weather. I am so through with snow! And it rarely rains. I love having the pool and the hot tub to use whenever I want. Once I get out of college, I want to get a job someplace where it's warm enough to have a pool. I could definitely get used to this lifestyle. But on the other hand, it's pretty expensive out here. And crowded. The city is huge – it goes on for miles and miles. And sometimes the traffic is horrible. So it's not perfect. But I like it. How do you like Maryland?"

"It's pretty good. It still gets cold and snows here, but not nearly as much as in Kansas. And I know what you mean about a bigger city. College Park, where the campus is, is okay. Just a bunch of restaurants and bars and shops. But the campus is really beautiful, with lots of trees and green space. I've only been to DC a few times, but I love it! All the monuments and museums and government buildings and stuff. It's all so stately. Dignified. Important-looking. There's so much I want to explore. I think I'd love living here."

"I'd love to come and see it sometime."

"Yeah, that would be great. Our spring break is from March 14th to 22nd. When's yours?"

"Let me see… Shit. That's finals week for us. Our spring break is the next week."

Chris asked, "When are you done for the year?"

"June 12th. How about you?"

"May 20th. Darn."

"I guess quarters and semesters don't line up very well. But you could come out and visit sometime during the summer! I'm here all year. There's all kinds of stuff I can show you. And we could go to Disneyland!"

"That sounds great. We'll see. I'll probably be working at the pool again, but I'll see if I can find a few days to come out." *Seth wouldn't have to know*. "But that reminds me. You were going to tell me about your job."

Ryan took a deep breath. *Here goes*. "Well, when I first got here, I got a job at this grocery store called Pure Foods. It's really expensive and fancy. It's where the rich people shop. Anyway, it was okay but it took up all my time. During my senior year, I was in marching band and jazz ensemble, and they both rehearsed after school. So that cut into the number of hours I could work. Still, I got in 25 or 30 hours a week. But I was just making enough to get by and I had *no* extra time. And I knew I'd need more money to be able to pay for college, and I wasn't going to get it at this job. So anyway, I talked to Hal, and he suggested something else."

Chris thought, *Well, what is it? Quit beating around the bush and tell me.*

Ryan said, "Anyway, well, how do I say this? So you remember the time at the end of our junior year when we went to that party with the track team guys at Trevor Zimmerman's house?"

"Yeah…"

"And remember how Rocket Crockett got Trevor to put on one of his dad's pornos?"

"Yeah…"

"And remember when Rocket said, 'Hey PK, you should have that schlong of yours in porn. You'd make a fortune!'"

"Yeah…"

"Well, I took his advice."

"I don't get it. What are you talking about?"

"I'm doing porn. And he was right. I'm making a fortune."

"You can't be serious. Please tell me this is some kind of joke."

"Nope. It's no joke. I star in gay porn videos. I couldn't call you last weekend because I was in Breckenridge, Colorado shooting a bunch of scenes at a ski resort."

Chris was stunned, and it showed on his face.

Ryan said, "Yeah, I know. But I didn't see any other good options for making enough to pay for college, on top of rent and food."

"Yeah, but it's dirty money."

"What do you mean? It's not like I'm selling drugs or doing anything illegal."

"That's actually legal?"

"Sure it is."

Chris took a deep breath. "Okay. Well. So… How long have you been doing this?"

"A little over a year. I started not long after I turned 18."

"You've got to be shittin' me. I can't... I can't believe you'd stoop to that level to make money. Doesn't it make you feel dirty? And cheap?"

"No, it doesn't. But believe me, I struggled with it at first. I went back and forth on whether I should do it. I had a lot of baggage from Dad's church to unload. But I needed the money and I didn't see any other good options. I guess I could have kept working at Pure Foods and tried to go to a community college part-time. But I wouldn't get as good an education, it would take longer, and I'd still be scraping by. Anyway, it's the path I chose and I'm okay with it."

"But it seems so sleazy. And so unlike something you would do."

"I guess it depends on how you look at it. There's making love and there's having sex. And this is just having sex. We're actors, playing a role for other people's fantasies. We're giving people something they can get off to. I don't think it's dirty or sleazy at all."

Chris said, "Like it's just a business transaction."

"Yeah. It's just a job. A very well-paying job."

"So I guess that explains the calendar."

"What calendar?"

"The Student Bodies calendar for 2009. You mean you haven't seen it?"

Ryan shook his head. Chris reached over and pulled the calendar out from one of his drawers. He opened it to October and held it in front of the camera for Ryan to see.

"Ah, yes, I remember now. I did a photo shoot for a professional photographer I met last spring. He was going to add it to his portfolio and submit it, along with others, to various magazines and calendars and stuff. He never told me where it ended up. All I know is, I got paid $1,000 for the photo shoot. Where did you get that?"

"One Saturday back in October when there was no football game, Seth and I went down to Dupont Circle in DC. That's the gay part of town. And there's this gay bookstore there. I had no idea there were so many gay books! Anyway, they had this area in the back of the store where they have magazines and calendars and stuff. We were looking through the 2009 calendars, and there you were."

"Surprise!"

"Yeah, it sure was."

"Are you going to put that up in your room?"

"Not this year. My roommate's straight. He's okay with me being gay, but I figure he might not want to see naked guys with hard cocks on his wall all the time. But Seth and I plan to share a room next year, so maybe I'll put it up then."

"Does Seth know that's me?"

"No. I haven't told him about you." *And I don't know whether I should.* "Well, anyway, I'd better get going. Seth wants to see a movie this afternoon and I told him I'd go."

"Okay." *I kind of expected we'd talk longer.*

Chris said, "So, uh, take care. And good luck with your classes."

"Yeah, you too." *Is he going to ask when we'll talk next?*

A few awkward seconds passed.

Chris said, "Bye."

*No 'I love you,' just 'Bye.'* "Bye."

Chris disappeared from his screen.

Ryan sighed. *Oh well. Chris wasn't in my life a month ago, so I guess I'll continue with life as it is. Besides, he's still got his parents helping him pay for college. I don't. So he has no right to judge me for my choices.*

***

Chris texted Seth.

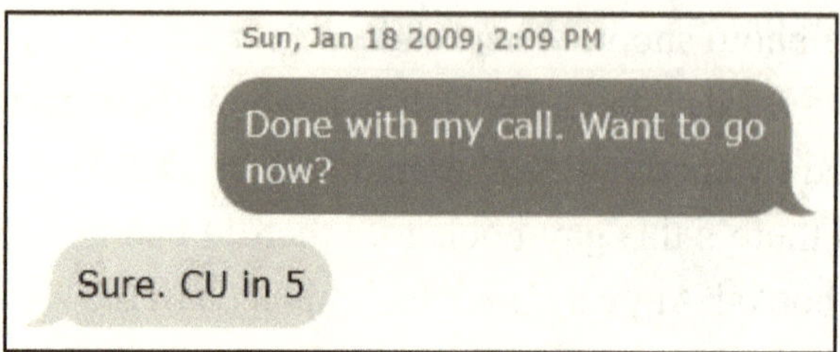


Chris was stunned by everything he had just learned. He couldn't wrap his head around the idea that pure, wholesome, naïve Bryan, whom he loved so much in high school, was now doing porn. But on the other hand, he was relieved. He had one less dilemma to contemplate. *So much for transferring to UCLA. Maryland will be fine. And Seth will be fine.*

# Consequences and Acceptance

Sunday, January 18, 2009

Ryan was depressed all afternoon. He was in no mood for the weekly family night dinner, but he knew he should go. Maybe being surrounded by his housemates would cheer him up. He tried to act like nothing was wrong, but he wasn't doing a very good job.

As soon as everyone sat down and began eating, Ricky started regaling everyone with tales of what had taken place in Breckenridge the previous weekend.

"Guys, it was unbelievable! First of all, the scenery. I've never been in the mountains in the middle of winter. There was, like, two feet of snow on the ground. And they rented this super-nice chalet where we did most of the scenes. Some of us stayed there and some of us stayed in rooms at the lodge, but man, it was all nice! I mean, is this how rich people live?"

Ryan said, "I remember when I was riding the bus to come out here from Kansas a couple of years ago. When the bus drove through the mountains on I-70, I remember thinking how beautiful it was. That was July, and there was still some snow on the mountaintops. So it was nice to go back and see more of it."

Ricky continued. "Anyway, they did a bunch of scenes with three or four guys in them, including one out in the hot tub on the back deck. I mean, it was like 20 degrees and there was snow everywhere, but we were out there naked in a hot tub! We'd shoot for a minute, then duck under the water for two minutes to warm up again. But we got it done! And then on Sunday… Oh! My! GOD!!! They had all sixteen of us in the living room of this place for this huge orgy! You heard right –

sixteen guys!"

Ted said, "Okay, I'm not sure I want to know, but how many of them did you take?"

"You mean during the orgy or the whole weekend?"

"Either."

"Well, let's see. Four of us were total bottoms. The rest of the guys were either tops or versatile. So I'd say probably twelve, over the course of the weekend."

Hal said, "Sounds like you'll be a shoo-in for the 'Bottom of the Year' award at next year's Adult Video Academy Awards."

Ricky said, "Shoe in? I'm surprised they didn't think of that. They thought of everything else."

Ryan said, "Wait a minute. They have academy awards for porn?"

Hal replied, "Yep, they sure do. The ceremony takes place in Las Vegas every year as part of the industry's annual convention."

Darnell said, "You mean you've never watched it live on network TV?"

Ryan said, "What do they call them – the Rammies?"

Everyone laughed.

Ricky said, "I'd accept 'Bottom of the Year,' but I'm aiming for a 'Lifetime Achievement' award! Greatest bottom ever. After all, not many people can take three at once."

Everyone around the table was speechless. Not surprised, just speechless.

Finally, Ted asked, "How is that even possible?"

"I promise you, it is. Just ask Ryan."

Darnell said, "Wait a minute. You mean you two…"

Ricky replied, "It was strictly for business."

Ryan said, "Really, Ricky? Did you have to mention that?"

"Dude, they're going to see it when the video comes out."

"I know, but… Can we please talk about something else?"

Ricky let it drop, but the atmosphere at the table became

subdued. Between moments of awkward silence, others mentioned what was going on in their lives. But nothing took hold as a new conversation topic.

After about 15 minutes, Darnell turned to Ryan and said, "Honey, what's wrong? You look like you just came from a funeral."

Ryan made a feeble effort to smile. "Oh, I don't know. A few things have happened recently that wouldn't have happened if… well… if I wasn't doing porn."

Darnell said, "Uh-oh. What happened?"

"Okay, well first… before we get into that… So there's this guy named Jordan I went to high school with who also goes to UCLA now. Last quarter we were in Music Appreciation class together, and he's the one who encouraged me to audition for the jazz ensemble."

Ted said, "Wait a minute. Jordan. Please tell me this isn't the same guy who put Vaseline in your valves right before the holiday concert back in high school."

"Actually, it is. But he apologized for that, and I think he really meant it. And like I said, he encouraged me to play in the jazz ensemble with him. Anyway, last quarter we hung out a lot and we were getting to be pretty good friends. Like, one day we had this conversation about Prop 8, and he said he was for it. But then after we talked about it, he changed his mind and voted against it, because of me."

Hal said, "Or at least he said he voted against it. You'll never know."

"Yeah, I guess not. But anyway, he was going through a rough time because his parents were getting divorced, and we talked a lot about that. And by the end of the quarter, we had gotten pretty tight. But so far this quarter I've barely seen or heard from him. I reached out to him a couple of times but it seemed like he was ignoring me. So then I ran into him on campus last Thursday, and I asked him what was wrong. And get this – he told me he started having feelings for me. And he's seeing a therapist who told him not to associate with me anymore."

Ricky said, "Dude, that guy's a tool. You don't need people like that in your life. I'd say, 'Good riddance.'"

"Yeah, I guess. But still, it hurts to have someone say they don't want to be around you anymore because you're gay. And then on Thursday night, I went to the LGBT Student Network meeting. Last quarter I made a bunch of new friends there. But then after the meeting, some of the guys were standing around and one of them said, 'Hey, is that you in the new Student Bodies calendar?' So now, they've seen a picture of me and my boner. Then one of the others asked if that was me in *Men on a Mission*. So then they started bombarding me with questions about what it's like to be a porn star. And by now they've probably all seen me in videos having sex. So now I'm like, how can I ever face those guys again? Like, I just want to be a regular guy and have friends, but from now on I'll be Ryan the Porn Star to them."

Ted said, "Not necessarily. They'll look beyond that if they're really your friends."

Darnell said, "Yeah. This will be one way you can tell who's a real friend and who's not."

Hal said, "I know what you mean. I experienced that myself. It cost me my job at the law firm. I guess you could call it an occupational hazard."

Ricky said, "That's part of the price of being a celebrity. They're probably jealous of you. I'll bet most guys secretly wish they could be in porn."

Ryan said, "I wouldn't say I'm a celebrity."

Ricky replied, "Oh, you are! And after *The Boys of Breckenridge* comes out you are going to be legendary! You were there. You know it's destined to become a classic!"

"Great. Just great. I'll never have a normal life again."

Darnell said, "Oh, honey, you don't want to be normal. Normal is highly overrated. Normal is boring."

"Yes, I *do* want to be normal. I want to have a normal life doing normal things with normal friends."

Darnell said, "Honey, that ship has sailed. Your life stopped being normal when you had to run away from home. You are special and your life is an adventure. Embrace it!"

"I guess. But then this happened. Earlier today, I talked with Chris on Skype. When we talked on Christmas and New Year's Day, it was like we were best buds again. It was just like we were back then, except on a screen. But then when we were talking today, he asked what my job is, and I told him. He said he thought doing porn was dirty and sleazy, and I could tell he totally lost respect for me. And as it turns out, he's seen the Student Bodies calendar too. So whatever hope I had that he and I might get back together someday is now gone. I'll be surprised if he ever talks to me again."

Darnell reached over and placed his hand on top of Ryan's. "Oh, honey, I am so sorry."

Ted said, "Yeah, that sucks. I can see how that hurts."

Hal said, "So, are you going to stop doing porn?"

Ryan said, "See, that's the thing. I still need money to buy food and pay rent and pay for college. I'm only doing this for the money, anyway. And even if I stopped now, the damage has already been done. And if *The Boys of Breckenridge* ends up being as big as Ricky says, it'll only get worse. And I can't stop them from releasing it."

Darnell said, "Honey, it sounds like there's nothing you can do about it. And since that's the case, the best choice you have is to accept it and move on."

Hal said, "You haven't done anything wrong."

"Apparently some people think so."

Hal said, "So what? You're doing what you have to do to earn a living and pay for your education. You can't stop other people from judging you, but you can decide you're not going to be a prisoner to their judgment. Unless they're offering to pay for your education or they have a better solution, they need to mind their own business and keep their judgment to themselves."

Darnell said, "Haters be hatin'. You've gotta ignore 'em and keep on keepin' on."

Ted said, "We love you for who you are. There will be other people who love you for who you are, too. Those are your people. Those are the ones who matter."

Ryan sighed. "Yeah, I guess so. Thanks, guys. I love you too."

# SOPHOMORE YEAR

# Empowered

Friday, May 28, 2010

At 3:30 p.m., Hal turned his BMW into the parking lot of the Topanga Retreat Center and parked. He pulled a small carry-on suitcase from his trunk and headed toward the main lodge. Given his flexible work schedule and the fact that the retreat center was less than 15 miles from his home, he was among the first to arrive. He noticed a couple of RVs in the parking lot and assumed those people preferred to stay in their RVs rather than the retreat center's group accommodations.

When he entered the lodge, he approached two men seated behind a rectangular folding table draped with large rainbow flags. One of the men was a 60-ish hippie who looked like he was still living in that era. His long, stringy gray hair was gathered into a ponytail behind his neck. His wrinkled face was accented by a gray mustache and goatee, and he wore an oversized tie-dye shirt and beads. The other man was a chubby cherubic fellow in his 30s who wore a stretched-out T-shirt and cargo shorts. He was fretting over the placement of each item on the registration table. His fussy, frenetic energy was a jarring counterpoint to the relaxed, almost disinterested calm of the aging hippie.

Hal wore a fashionable patterned short-sleeved shirt, well-fitting off-white shorts, casual loafers, and aviator sunglasses perched on top of his head. He realized his sartorial choices were better suited for a resort on Maui than a retreat in a woodsy mountain lodge, but he had no idea what to expect.

The younger one looked up at Hal as he approached the table and said, "Welcome to the 44th gathering of the California Men's EmpowerMen(t) Retreat!" He separated 'empower' and 'men' into two separate words and appended the nearly-inaudible 't' as an afterthought to drive home the play on words intended by the name.

The older man nodded slightly with a warm look that seemed to say, 'Peace, brother.'

"Hi. I'm Hal Morris."

The younger man said, "Hi! I'm Trevor, and this is Norbert." Hal extended his hand, which Trevor shook enthusiastically and Norbert merely held for a few seconds. Trevor started thumbing through a five-page printout of registered attendees. Norbert slowly reached over to a plastic storage tub on the left side of the table and retrieved a large manila envelope.

"Let's see..." Trevor said as he scanned the second and third pages. "Ah, here you are. Morris, Hal. It says here you're paid in full, and you have requested a lodge room." Norbert handed Hal the large envelope without saying a word.

Hal said, "Yes, that's correct. So, this is my first time at one of these retreats. What's it like?"

Trevor said, "Our goal is to create a relaxed, nurturing space of unconditional acceptance that's free from judgment and pre-conceived expectations of what it means to be a gay man in today's world. We offer a selection of workshops and guided activities to help you release the internalized pain and suffering that's buried deep within your psyche, and guide you on your journey toward discovering your true purpose."

That was almost too much psychobabble for Hal to comprehend. He recalled seeing a similar statement on the organization's website. "Okay, that's great, but what actually happens?"

Trevor replied, "There's a schedule in the packet Norbert gave you. There will be some activities in which everyone participates, such as meals here at the lodge and a talent show on Saturday night. During the mornings and afternoons, there will be workshops of all sorts. They're all described in the packet. There's no sign-up, you choose whichever one calls to you. There's also free time for meditation, journaling, socialization… whatever you feel drawn to. There's a map in the packet that shows you where everything is."

"Uh… okay."

"The weekend is whatever you want to make of it. The old saying that 'you get out of something what you put into it' definitely applies here. But the part that doesn't show up on the schedule is the relationships you create. Open yourself up to people. Talk. Listen. Connect. Hundreds of lifelong friendships have been formed at these retreats. Many people return for each one. Norbert, here, is one of the founders. He's been to every one. This is my fourteenth."

It looked and sounded a lot more new-agey than Hal anticipated.

Norbert stood up. "Be. Just be." He walked around the table and hugged Hal. He held Hal for at least ten seconds. It seemed almost creepy, but at the same time, it felt disarming and comforting. After Norbert released him, Hal felt like he had just enjoyed a 90-minute massage on a warm, sunny tropical beach. Norbert said softly, "Just let go."

Hal wasn't sure what he needed to let go of, but maybe he would discover that this weekend.

Trevor said, "The lodge rooms are down that hall. Feel free to pick any available bed."

Hal walked down the hall and peeked into several rooms. The rooms were simple. Each contained between four and eight beds, some of which were bunked. They were just a step above the metal military-style beds reminiscent of summer camp. Hal surmised that this facility was designed for youth camps and church groups.

He found a four-person room with beds that weren't bunked and placed his suitcase on one of the beds. He sat down and pulled the contents out of the envelope. There was a single sheet with the retreat schedule, another with a map of the grounds, and a stapled bundle of eight sheets printed front and back with brief descriptions of each workshop. The first two pages listed which workshops would be offered during which sessions. Most were offered more than once. They dealt with every topic imaginable, and some Hal never could have imagined, such as:

> Meditate Your Way to Regularity
> How to Design and Knit a Macrame Sling
> Feng Shui for Your Love Nest
> Haiku for Hard-ons: How to Write Erotic Poetry
> 69 Other Uses for Water-based Lube

Hal had no idea what he should pick. Maybe he would just go with what he felt called to at the time, as Trevor suggested.

Hal inserted everything but the map back into the envelope. He took a walk around the property to discover where everything was. The retreat center was located next to Topanga State Park, so there was easy access to hiking trails.

He was surprised to note the facility had a large hot tub about a hundred feet from the lodge on the edge of a wooded area. A temporary sign posted near the hot tub announced that it would be clothing-optional after 9:00 p.m.

Hal took a brief hike into the state park, then returned to his room about ten minutes before dinner. A suitcase sat on one of the other beds, but its owner was elsewhere. Participants would be arriving from all over the state and beyond throughout the evening. He ventured into the dining room. The food was served cafeteria-style and the dining room contained long tables and benches – just like summer camp. Hal spotted a group of three other men who were about his age and asked if he could join them.

***

Saturday morning after breakfast, everyone remained in the dining hall for Retreat Orientation. One by one, Retreat Leadership Committee members introduced themselves and went over the myriad rules and guidelines for the weekend. Hal guessed many of them had been implemented in response to situations that had occurred at previous retreats.

- Accept each person as he is.
- Don't post pictures of people on the internet without their permission.
- Avoid discussing politics or religion, except in workshops devoted to those topics.
- While people are encouraged to wear whatever attire they choose, full nudity is permitted only in bedrooms, communal showers, the hot tub after 9:00 p.m., and workshops specifically designated for nudity, such as Naked Yoga and Sensual Erotic Massage.
- Smoking is permitted only in the parking lot. Please do not leave cigarette butts on the ground.
- Alcohol and illegal substances are prohibited.

Hal smiled. He had a bottle of vodka in his trunk, just in case.

- Be open to giving and receiving hugs. That said, no means no.
- No complaining. If you have an issue that needs to be addressed, please bring it to the attention of a member of the Issue Resolution Committee.
- The use of electronic communication devices is strongly discouraged. Participants are encouraged to disconnect from the rest of the world for the weekend.
- While friendships formed during previous Retreat weekends are to be celebrated, strive to introduce yourself to someone new at each meal and each workshop you attend.

Each of these policies sounded reasonable to Hal. But when taken as a whole, it seemed this weekend would require balancing openness and spontaneity against conformity and structure.

After the orientation session, Hal consulted the schedule to see which workshops were being offered during the first session. None appealed to him, but one that caught his attention was Naked Yoga. He had never tried yoga, let alone naked yoga, but his friends and acquaintances who practiced yoga raved about its physical and mental benefits. He was in good shape for a man of 42 and had no hang-ups about his body image or being naked, but he wasn't particularly interested in seeing many of the retreat participants naked. He suspected this workshop might resemble a nude beach, where most of the naked people were the ones he'd rather not see naked, and the ones he'd like to see naked remained clothed. Then he realized he was being judgmental, and one of the guiding principles of this weekend was to accept people as they are. Plus, naked yoga was unlikely to be a sexual activity. So he decided to try it.

The workshop would take place outdoors in a grassy area near the hot tub. It was far enough that the other retreat participants could see a group of naked men but wouldn't be able to see specific information. He wondered whether the workshop would attract spectators. That would probably violate retreat protocol, but men will be men.

Hal walked toward the workshop space. An energetic, slender young man in his early 20s was arranging yoga mats into two concentric circles, about three feet apart. Hal was the first person to arrive. He asked the workshop leader, "I've never done yoga before. Will that be a problem?"

The leader replied, "Not at all! This workshop is designed for beginners. It's not difficult to learn. I'll demonstrate each step as we go along. Just do what I do."

"Okay, and uh… just curious. Why is this naked? And outdoors?"

"So we can let down our barriers, release our feelings of embarrassment, shame, and self-consciousness, and become one with nature."

Then Hal thought of one more thing. "What if someone … you know … gets an erection?"

"It happens from time to time. It's nothing to be embarrassed about. It's a natural part of male physiology."

Hal decided to give this a try. Perhaps he had barriers he needed to let down.

Over the next few minutes, more participants arrived. Hal nonchalantly checked out each man as he arrived. He knew he was supposed to simply accept each man for who he was, but – well, old habits die hard. Most of the others were of no interest to Hal. But he noticed one man who was in his mid to late 30s, just over six feet tall, and looked like a business professional. Hal realized that was a rare look at the retreat.

The workshop leader glanced at his watch. It was 10:32. Fourteen participants had arrived and selected a mat. Nobody else was heading toward the circle of yoga mats, so he stepped up to his mat in the center of the circle.

"Welcome, friends, to Naked Yoga. I'm your leader, Mykel. That's spelled M-Y-K-E-L. Thank you for joining this session. No matter whether you are an experienced yoga practitioner or this is your first time, you are welcome here. Yoga is easy to learn. I'm often asked why we should practice yoga naked, and I say, why not? Nakedness is our natural state. We are beautiful just as we are. When we shed our clothing, we shed our feelings of embarrassment, shame, and self-consciousness. We allow ourselves to be vulnerable. We give ourselves permission to be in touch with ourselves, each other, and nature. Shall we begin?"

Mykel began removing his clothing as if it was the most natural, comfortable, and carefree act in the world. As he dropped each article of clothing into a pile, he looked as if he was releasing a burden he had been bearing or a shackle that had been holding him back. The calmness and ease with which Mykel stripped provided a reassuring example for the other participants. Hal glanced around, not wanting to appear as if he was checking anyone out. Everyone else seemed comfortable removing their clothes, so he dismissed his remaining hesitation and followed suit.

Mykel began giving instructions, which he demonstrated as he spoke. Everyone joined the flow. Hal became so focused on the movements Mykel was leading them through he forgot everyone was naked.

When the session ended and the men were putting their clothes back on, Hal realized that throughout the session, he never got an erection. He hadn't even thought about it. He wasn't aware that anyone else had either, although he hadn't paid much attention. He glanced over to the handsome professional-looking guy. He had finished dressing and was kneeling to tie his shoes. As the men began heading back toward the lodge, Hal caught up with the handsome guy and introduced himself.

"Hi! I'm Hal Morris." Hal extended his hand, which the other man shook.

"Brent Seiter. How did you like it?"

Hal didn't know how to answer. He had been so absorbed in the yoga session he hadn't even thought about whether he liked it. He seemed rejuvenated, so that was good. "I wasn't sure what to expect, especially with the naked part. But I guess I liked it."

"First time?"

"Yep."

"First time doing yoga or first time doing it naked?"

"Both. And you?"

Brent said, "I've been practicing yoga for about six years. I try to do it several times a week. The only other time I've done it naked in a group was here. I practice naked at home all the time."

"So it must benefit you."

"Oh, absolutely. It keeps me in good shape physically, and it keeps me centered. Yoga is as much mental as it is physical."

"I have friends who do it and they say it helps them."

Brent nodded.

Hal wanted to keep the conversation going. "How many of these retreats have you attended?"

"This is my third. I've come to the one here in LA for the past two years. And you?"

"First time."

"How do you like it so far?"

Hal said, "I don't know. The jury's still out. I wasn't sure what to expect, but I'm trying to take things as they come and be open to whatever may happen. Like naked yoga, for example. If you had told me a week ago I'd be doing that, I wouldn't have believed you."

"How come?"

"I don't know. I guess I never thought to put the two together."

Brent asked, "So why did you come here this weekend?"

"I don't know. Curiosity, I suppose. I know that sounds funny, but I don't have a better answer. I saw an article about this group and their retreats in the gay paper, so I checked out their website. I guess I wanted to try something new and different."

"Well, it *is* different."

"Why did you come?"

"To push my boundaries and maybe learn new things about myself. It gets me out of my usual world. When I meet all these people from other walks of life, with different experiences, challenges, and world views, it expands my horizons. It puts a lot of things in my life into perspective."

Hal wasn't sure what to make of all that. It sounded centered or enlightened or something, but what did it mean in concrete terms? But to keep the conversation going, he said, "Yeah, I hear what you're saying. There are a lot of very different people here." Hal hoped that sounded sufficiently neutral and non-judgmental, but Brent glanced at him with a look that said otherwise.

Brent said, "I believe we can learn something from each person who passes through our life if we can be open to it."

Hal realized he could probably learn some things from Brent. He hoped he would have the opportunity.

***

After lunch, Hal reviewed the choices for workshops. He noticed Mykel was leading a psychic medium group reading. The workshop description stated, 'Mykel, a psychic medium, will attempt to bring forth and communicate with the spirits surrounding those who are in the room. Mykel cannot guarantee that a spirit you wish to communicate with will be present, nor can he guarantee a reading for each person. Limit 12 participants.'

Hal was skeptical about the concept of talking to the dead and of people who claimed they could do so. But he formed a good impression of Mykel during Naked Yoga. He seemed genuine, positive, and … enlightened, for lack of a better word. Hal decided to give it a try just to expose himself to something new. It would assuage his curiosity if nothing else.

Hal arrived at the room where the group reading would be held. He saw twelve chairs arranged in a circle, filling up most of the room. Mykel was making minor adjustments to the spacing of the chairs to make the circle as perfect as possible. He looked up at Hal and smiled.

Hal said, "Good afternoon, Mykel. I enjoyed the naked yoga session this morning. That was a new experience for me."

Mykel smiled. "Good. I'm glad you enjoyed it. Have you ever had a reading from a medium before?"

"No, this will be a new experience for me too. But when I saw you were leading it, I felt I could trust you."

"Thanks. That's very kind of you."

"So how does this work?"

"I'll explain everything when the session starts. There's nothing for you to do but sit and be open to the experience."

Hal took a seat near the door, so he could quietly excuse himself if he wanted to leave.

Before three minutes had passed, eleven more people arrived. Mykel taped a sign to the outside of the door that read, 'Sorry, full.' He walked to the middle of the circle, took a deep breath to center himself, and said, "Welcome, and thank you for choosing to take part in this group reading. Who has never participated in a reading with a medium before, either individually or in a group?"

Hal raised his hand, as did two other men.

"Good. Let me explain what I do and what you can expect from today's session. A medium is a person who has the ability to communicate with the spirits of those who have passed from our lives. When you die, your physical body remains, but your spirit leaves your body and returns to the universe. The spirits of your deceased loved ones visit you more often than you probably realize. You may not be aware they are present, but they are. Sometimes they visit to watch you and be with you for a while, and other times they have a message they would like to communicate to you. I can help facilitate that communication. Now, to manage expectations, I cannot guarantee that a spirit will come through for you. Even by limiting the group to twelve, I may not be able to deliver a message to each of you. Nor can I summon a particular spirit. They are not constantly available at our beck and call. You may be hoping to hear from your grandmother, but your uncle may come through instead. That's one of the fun things about group readings. We never know who is going to show up and what they're going to say. So before we begin, do you have any questions?"

A man raised his hand. "What if the message a spirit wishes to give is too personal or embarrassing to share in front of others?"

Mykel replied, "That's usually not the case. Often, the spirit wants to apologize or seek forgiveness, or perhaps they want to let you know they've forgiven you for something. Sometimes they just want to let you know they're okay. Sometimes they offer advice. But I won't say anything in front of the group that could be embarrassing or incriminating."

Hal raised his hand. "Is the spirit going to be someone you're related to?"

"Not necessarily. It could be a friend or a former lover. It could be a spirit who's connected with someone you know, who wants to give you a message they hope you'll relay to someone else. I try to discourage that, though."

A few seconds passed and nobody else had a question, so Mykel said, "Then let us begin. There are many spirits here already, so I'll try to get through as much as I can." He turned to Jeremy, the man who had asked the first question, and said, "Your grandmother is here."

"Which one?"

"She says you used to call her Nana when you were little. She says she's doing well, and she loves you." Mykel stood still. He was gazing into the distance as if he was trying to make sense of what he was hearing. He shook his head a couple of times as if to say, 'I don't understand you.' Finally, he looked at Jeremy again and said, "She says there are a lot of things you have started but you haven't finished, and you need to get back to work on them. One is your degree. Another is something you started writing, but gave up on several years ago."

Jeremy looked like he knew exactly what she was talking about. Mykel stood still, like he was receiving more. "She says you're wasting your time on people and activities that aren't helping you move forward. They're keeping you in a rut. You need to stay focused on your goals and let go of people who are sucking up too much of your time and energy. Especially Caden."

"Oh my God... Caden's my boyfriend."

"Yes, she says he's holding you back. He's draining you – and your bank account."

Jeremy looked alarmed.

"And she has one more thing." Mykel listened some more. "Check in on your mother. She has less time left than anyone realizes."

Jeremy looked overwhelmed. "Wow... that's amazing."

Mykel asked, "Does that make sense to you?"

"Oh yeah, totally. I was majoring in theater, but I dropped out for a while because I needed to work and save up some more money. But then I met Caden, and we moved in together. Now it seems like all my money is going to pay for our apartment and our bills. And I was working on a play, but he keeps saying I need to be realistic and I'll never be able to sell it, so I should forget about it and move on. And he always wants to hang out with our friends and stuff, and we're spending beyond our means, and… yeah, he's totally draining me, both spiritually and financially."

Mykel turned to someone else, whose brother had died in a car accident.

The hour passed quickly. Hal was fascinated by what he heard. Some of it was vague enough that the message could be applied to many circumstances, but most of the time Mykel hit the nail on the head. He referred to people's loved ones by name, even though he couldn't have known that information ahead of time. Hal was becoming a believer, but as the end of the workshop approached, it looked like he would be one of the few who didn't receive a message. He had been cast out of his family for being gay over twenty years ago, so he didn't expect any of his dead relatives to have any interest in him.

The workshop ended. People got up from their chairs and filed out the door. Most were filled with a sense of wonder and exhilaration from the messages they had received.

"Hal?" Mykel said. "Are you able to stay behind for a few minutes?"

"Um… sure." Hal quickly reviewed his interactions with Mykel during this session and the naked yoga session from that morning. He couldn't recall that he had ever told Mykel his name.

After the room had cleared, Mykel said, "I wanted to give you this message privately, since some of the information is rather personal. Vincent is here."

"Vincent?"

"Your partner, who passed away 20 years ago."

Hal was visibly taken aback. He decided to sit for this. Mykel moved the chair next to Hal so he could face him, and sat down.

"How is he?" asked Hal. He wasn't sure whether it made sense to ask a spirit how he is, but he didn't know what else to say.

"He says he's fine. Since spirits don't have physical bodies, they don't experience any of the illnesses or aches and pains we do. He says he was sorry to leave you, but he was suffering so badly he wanted it to be over."

"Yes, he had AIDS. Sadly, AZT was the only drug that was available at the time, but he didn't tolerate it well. His case was too advanced for it to help him."

Mykel looked as if Vincent had already explained that, and he simply nodded.

Hal continued, "I feel so guilty. I'm probably the one who gave it to him. I was doing porn back then because I had to support myself and pay for college. That was before they started using condoms. I figured I got it there, then gave it to him before I realized I had it. I've never been able to forgive myself for that."

Mykel paused while he listened to Vincent. Then he said, "Vincent says it probably wasn't you. He says it was probably a guy he had a few dates with before you met."

Hal said, "What??? How come he never told me that?"

"He didn't know it at the time. It's something he learned after he crossed over."

"So he might have given it to me."

"Possibly. But does it matter now?"

"No, I guess not. But I still feel guilty because I survived and he didn't."

Mykel listened to Vincent some more. "He says you need to let that go. He's not bitter about it. And he says even if you're the one who infected him, he forgave you back when he was still alive. He says he loves you, and he watches over you all the time."

"Oh, I love him too. It's like there's a hole in my heart that will never be filled."

"He says you'll have other lives where you can be together. So your separation is temporary."

"What do you mean?"

"We live many, many lives," Mykel explained. "Our spirits live forever, and periodically we choose to incarnate into human form. Then we die, and we return to the other side."

"So each of our lives is just a chapter in our overall journey?"

"Yeah, that's a good way to look at it. And using that analogy, your chapter and his just started and ended on different dates. In the grand scheme of things, it's a short time."

"So if I took my life now, I could be with him again."

"Yes, but don't. Please don't. Your work here is not finished. You survived, and you remain on this earth for a reason." Mykel listened to Vincent for a few seconds, then he turned his attention back to Hal. "You have helped many, many LGBT youths with your time and money. There are many more who will benefit from your help in the future. You're helping the guys who live with you now. Think how many people would be less fortunate if you weren't here."

"Yeah, I suppose so." Hal was amazed that Mykel had received all that information from Vincent.

"Don't worry, you'll be reunited with Vincent. He will be there to greet you when your time comes. You might decide to find each other in your next incarnation."

The door opened, and people started entering the room for the next workshop. Mykel said, "Let's take a walk outside. I think Vincent has more for you."

They left the building and started walking across the large grassy open area. Hal said, "So you said he watches over me all the time."

"Yes, spirits frequently visit our world to check in on their loved ones. Often, they try to communicate with us, but not everyone can hear them as I can."

"You know, sometimes I get the feeling he's with me. I just assumed that was wishful thinking."

"No, he's probably there. Anyway, he has one more message for you. He says you need to start moving forward again. He says you've been in the same routine for a long time, and new opportunities are waiting for you. You should allow yourself the freedom to pursue them. Remember, your work here isn't finished yet."

"Is he talking about business opportunities? A career change?"

"Yes. But also…" Mykel stopped walking and gazed upward while he received more information. "Personal opportunities. You need to start dating again. He says there's a good chance you are going to meet someone special."

"But… I've always felt Vincent was the one I was destined to be with. I don't think there's anyone who will ever take his place in my heart. And besides, I have HIV."

Mykel shook his head. "There will never be another Vincent, but there are other men who are special in their own way. And don't let HIV stop you. Other guys have it, and others will love you for who you are, regardless."

"But… I know this sounds crazy, but it feels like I would be cheating on him."

"He says you have his blessing to go out and find somebody else. He wants you to be happy for the rest of the time you have in this life." Mykel paused. "Now, this is me talking. What if it was you who died and Vincent lived on? Would you want him to spend the rest of his life mourning you and feeling lonely, or would you want him to find someone else to be happy with?"

"I'd want him to find someone else and be happy."

"Well, he wants you to be happy, too. And he wants you to get on with your life."

Hal stood silently for a moment to let this new information sink in. Then he said, "Wow, Mykel. That's incredible. You have no idea how much this means to me."

"I'm glad I could help. Being a medium can be challenging sometimes, but at times like this it's incredibly rewarding."

"I enjoyed the yoga too. Do you offer yoga classes in town somewhere?"

"Yeah, at a couple of community centers. Those aren't naked, of course. But my goal is to open my own studio where I can offer a variety of services, such as yoga, Pilates, guided meditation, vibrational energy healing, and so on."

Hal glanced at his watch. "I need to run. I'm going to be late for my next workshop. I'd like to stay in touch and maybe take some more yoga classes from you. May I have your contact info?"

Mykel gave Hal a business card and they said goodbye. Hal then hurried to his next workshop, Living Positively. It was described as a facilitated discussion group for HIV+ men, in which they could discuss healthy living, dating, and other concerns related to living with HIV.

Hal's viral load was undetectable and having lived with HIV for twenty years, he felt he had adapted pretty well. Still, it seemed like the most relevant workshop offered during this period.

Hal arrived at the room where the workshop was taking place. He opened the door quietly and tried to slip in without causing a disruption. He spotted an open chair and sat down. He glanced at the man sitting to his left. It was Brent Seiter.

Hal spent most of the workshop listening to others. Most of the participants were younger, and many of their comments led Hal to assume they had acquired HIV within the past year or two and were still coming to terms with their situation. Some of the participants seemed to have a victim mentality, but Hal couldn't think of anything to say that would be received as constructive rather than judgmental, so he remained silent. He noticed Brent wasn't saying much either.

Near the end of the discussion, an anguished guy in his mid-20s said, "The thing I keep asking myself is, why did this happen to me? Is it punishment for being gay? What did I do to deserve this?"

Hal raised his hand, and when the facilitator acknowledged him, he said, "I've been positive for over twenty years. I know why it happened to me. I was having unsafe sex." He opted not to reveal the context, namely performing in porn videos in the 80s. "But soon I realized it was pointless to wonder why it happened to me. It did, and I had to come to terms with it. I had to accept it and move on. This was my new reality, and I decided to make the best of it. Here's an analogy. If you were in a car accident and you become paralyzed, how would you respond? Would you spend the rest of your life sitting at home in a wheelchair being bitter about what happened to you? Or would you decide to live your life as fully as you could, despite your limitations? Here's another thing. Life isn't supposed to be easy. If it's too easy, you stagnate and you don't grow. Life throws challenges at all of us. Each challenge is an opportunity for us to become stronger and grow. Living with HIV is a challenge. How can you grow from it? How can you still live a full, happy life? And if I could say one last thing while I still have the floor... My partner back in the 80s wasn't so lucky. He died from it. I miss him every day, but I'm grateful that I have been given the chance to live on. I realize that at any time, the meds could stop working and I could die. So having HIV has led me to appreciate my life more."

The room was silent for a moment while everyone absorbed Hal's message. He glanced at Brent, who smiled and nodded in return.

The facilitator decided to wrap up the discussion a few minutes early. As people got up to leave, Brent said to Hal, "I admire your attitude. And I'm sorry about your partner."

"Thanks. Hey, would you like to sit together at dinner? I'd like to get to know you some more."

"Sure. We can try to sit by ourselves, but if other people want to join us, we should be sociable."

"I understand. If that happens, let's find some other time to talk. We'll see how it goes."

Brent glanced at his watch. "Dinner starts in half an hour. I'd like some time alone to meditate and get cleaned up for dinner. See you there?"

"You bet."

***

Hal and Brent met for dinner. They were able to find a spot at the end of the last long table in the far corner of the dining room. Nobody else came along wanting to join them.

Hal asked, "So, what do you do? I know, that's a lame way to start a conversation."

"It works as well as anything. I'm a director at one of the studios. I was an editor for years, then worked my way up through production assistant, and now director."

"That's fascinating. TV or movies?"

"Some of both. I worked on the editing for the last two seasons of the Golden Girls, for example. I'm doing mostly mini-series and made-for-TV movies now. And how about you?"

"I'm an attorney. I work in another segment of the movie industry – adult films."

Hal watched Brent's face closely to gauge his reaction to that statement. Over the years, he learned his occupation was often a make-or-break factor in his relationships. So he usually presented that information up front to see how it would be received. Fortunately, Brent showed no indication of disapproval.

"Well, I'll bet that's interesting. How did you end up there?"

"It's not as interesting as you might think. It's not like I'm present on the set. I do all my work behind the scenes. I work from home a lot, which I appreciate. Anyway, I began my career working for one of the big law firms downtown, but my career kind of ground to a halt when they found out I'm gay."

Brent said, "Really? They discriminated against you because you're gay?"

"Yep. I sued them and won a nice settlement. I bought my house with that money. But that effectively blackballed me in the mainstream law profession."

"That's a shame."

"I suppose, but things have turned out okay. I like my work and it pays pretty well."

"Where do you live?"

"In Westwood, a few blocks from UCLA. That's where I went for my undergrad and law school. I rent several bedrooms in my house to gay guys who are going to UCLA. They're like my family. How about you? Where do you live?"

"Sherman Oaks. Not too far from you."

With those preliminary topics exhausted, there was a lull in the conversation. Both men ate a few bites of their food.

Brent said, "What are some of your interests outside of work?"

Hal said, "I volunteer my services for the Los Angeles LGBT Youth Project. I serve the organization itself and kids who need legal help. I served on the board for a few years and I donate to the organization as well."

"That's very generous of you. My work takes up a lot of my time and my schedule is unpredictable, so it's hard for me to belong to organizations. I sang in the LA gay men's chorus for a while, but I missed as many rehearsals as I attended, so I let that go. Aside from that, I'm into photography. I have an RV, so any time I can take several days off, I head out to someplace beautiful and relaxing – usually a state or national park in California or Arizona."

"Oh, cool. That sounds like fun. Is your RV one of those in the parking lot?"

"Yeah, I decided I would rather do that than take my chances with random roommates."

Hal said, "Good idea. I have to admit, I rarely take vacations. I know I should. I can afford it, and I'm not getting any younger. But being single, I don't always enjoy traveling by myself."

"You mentioned that your partner passed away twenty years ago. Have you had any relationships since then?"

"Nothing serious. I've had some dates here and there, but that's about it. I have a lot of friends, so there are plenty of people in my life. I belong to a gay Jewish social group. And the guys who live in my house are kind of like sons to me. I cook dinner for them every Sunday night, then we play games or watch a movie together or something. Sort of like a family night. So, while I've been single a long time, I have plenty of love and companionship in my life."

"That's really sweet."

"How about you?"

Brent sighed. He wasn't fond of recounting the story of his breakup, but it was part of getting to know someone. It would inevitably come up sooner or later. "I've been single for about three years now. I was with my ex for eight years. I thought he would be the one I spent the rest of my life with. I mean, it wasn't perfect – no relationship is – but it was fine. But then I discovered he was cheating on me – a lot. That's how I got HIV. He and I didn't use condoms because I thought we were monogamous, you know? So, I'll always have that little reminder of him and our breakup. But life goes on."

"Wow, that sucks. I'm really sorry."

"Thanks. But as you said so eloquently, it happened. I have to accept it, make the best of it, and move on. And I'm grateful the meds make it possible for me to remain healthy and go on with my life. But it does put a crimp on dating."

Hal said, "That's for sure. Another reason I haven't dated much over the years is I'd rather not have to go through the whole disclosure thing every time. It gets old fast."

"You got that right. At least we have that in common."

"Yeah. The other disclosure I always have to go through is my occupation. A lot of people get turned off because I work in the adult entertainment industry. That, and I performed in gay porn films back in the 80s. I had to do that to earn a living and put myself through school after my parents disowned me. That's probably where I picked up HIV." Hal decided to wait until another time to tell Brent about the message he had just received from Vincent.

Brent said, "So you were disowned by your parents, you got HIV, you lost your partner, and your employer discriminated against you. You've had it pretty rough."

"Yeah, I guess. But you know, when I got kicked out onto the street, I decided I was a fighter; a survivor. I was bound and determined to make it on my own. As I said earlier, life throws challenges at us all the time. Each challenge is an opportunity to become stronger and grow."

"I can tell you're a very strong person."

"Thanks. As they say, living well is the best revenge. And I live pretty well. I have a lovely house, four great guys to share it with, and lots of wonderful friends. I make plenty of money. So yeah… life is pretty good." *Although it would be nice to have somebody special to share it with. Somebody like you.*

"For the record, I don't have any problem with what you do for work or the fact that you were a porn star in the 80s. I mean, let's be honest. I watch porn. So do most other guys. It gets me through those lonely nights. So if I watch it, I can't really be critical of those who make it, can I? That would be hypocritical."

By this time, they had finished their dinner. Brent asked, "Are you going to the talent show tonight?"

"I guess… That's the only thing going on, isn't it? What's it like?"

"It's a lot of fun. Nobody takes themselves seriously. Some of the performers are quite talented, and others… not so much. But it's all for fun."

"Okay. Wanna sit together?"

"Sure. See you there."

They got up from the table and took their trays to the conveyor belt. They exited the dining hall and turned to go their separate ways until the talent show started at 8:00. They both stopped, glanced at each other, and smiled. Simultaneously, they decided to take a few steps toward each other and hug.

***

Brent was right. The talent show, while not always featuring talent, was filled with good-natured, frivolous fun. They laughed a lot. Hal enjoyed it, and he enjoyed sitting next to Brent. He wondered how he could prolong the evening.

After the show ended, Hal, Brent, and all the other attendees filed out of the dining hall and into the night. Hal guessed many would head to the hot tub. He wondered if there would be any water left in the tub by the time it was all over. He turned to Brent. "It's a lovely evening. Would you like to go for a little hike? I brought a flashlight."

"That would be nice. But you don't need a flashlight." Hal looked puzzled. Brent said, "You'd be surprised how well you can see by the light of the moon and the stars. C'mon, I'll show you."

They headed across the clearing toward a path into the woods. Brent was right. Once they were 50 feet into the woods and the lights of the retreat center buildings were no longer visible, Hal could see the path beneath his feet and the trees and shrubs that surrounded them. If he brought his flashlight, he would be able to see only what it illuminated.

Hal said, "It's so peaceful and beautiful."

"It sure is."

A few minutes later, they reached a small clearing. In the dim light from the moon in the night sky, they could see each other's faces. Hal liked what he saw, and it seemed Brent did too.

Hal whispered, "I had no idea what to expect when I came here this weekend. But I'm so glad I did."

"See what happens when you get out and try something new?"

They smiled at each other. Hal had taken several chances this weekend – the naked yoga, the medium reading, and coming to the retreat in the first place. He decided to take another chance. He stepped forward until he was inches from Brent's face. He placed his arms around Brent's waist and leaned in for a kiss. Their lips met, and they kissed under the moonlight for at least ten minutes.

They stopped for a moment and Brent said, "I have a nice bottle of Cabernet and some Manchego cheese in my RV. It would be wonderful to have someone to share them with."

Hal nodded and smiled, and they walked hand-in-hand down the path back to the retreat center. When they reached the clearing, Hal decided to take another chance. "Would it be okay if I swung by my room and picked up my stuff?"

"Absolutely!"

# Ted Graduates

Friday, June 11, 2010

On Friday, June 11, Ted graduated from UCLA's Anderson School of Business, with an MBA in International Business.

All of his housemates attended the ceremony. It was a picture-perfect, 70-degree, sunny day. Afterward, the gang headed to The Brewin' Bruin in Westwood for beer flights and bar food to celebrate.

Ryan said, "You know, I'm not a beer guy, but these are pretty good!"

Ted said, "Yeah. There's a huge difference between the mass-market stuff that comes in cans and craft beers brewed on the premises."

Hal asked, "How does it feel to finally be done with school?"

Ted replied, "Fantastic! After four years in the Marines, four years in undergrad, and two years in grad school, I finally get to start my career. I'm really looking forward to it. But at the same time, it will be a big change. In some ways, I'll miss it."

Darnell said, "I'll bet you won't miss the studying and the exams."

"Yeah, but I'll miss you guys. I'll miss the campus and the college environment."

Ricky said, "What you mean is, you'll miss being around all those college boys." Ted didn't argue.

Hal said, "You're right – it will be a big change. The corporate world will be entirely different. I remember when I graduated from law school and started working at that big law firm. It was quite an adjustment."

Darnell said, "I know what you mean about school going on

forever. I've been going for five years, and I'm still a year away from becoming a Nurse Practitioner."

Ryan said, "Tell us about the company you're going to be working for."

Ted said, "Powers Whitehurst & Collins is an international firm providing accounting, auditing, and a wide range of other professional services. They have offices all over the world, which is one of the main reasons I'm so happy I'll be working there."

Hal said, "What will you be doing?"

"Well, at first, I'll be going through a lot of training."

Ricky said, "So basically, more school."

"Yeah, I guess it never ends. Anyway, I'll be in the division that supports multinational companies and domestic companies that want to start expanding into other countries. Accounting laws and tax laws are different in every country, so we help them remain in compliance with all the various laws in the countries in which they do business."

Ryan said, "Sounds impressive!"

"Oh, it will be fascinating! At least I hope so."

Ricky asked, "So, are you going to keep living with us?"

Ted replied, "No, it's time to move on. I'll be making a nice salary, which will be another big change. I'll be able to afford my own place, and I need to move out so Hal can rent my room to a college student who needs it. My company is located in El Segundo, just south of the airport. I'm looking at apartments in Manhattan Beach and Redondo Beach so I'll be close to work."

Hal said, "Come to think of it, the four of you have lived in my house for three years now. Ryan was the last one to move in, and that was in July of 2007. I used to get a couple of new guys every year."

Ryan asked, "How do you go about finding a new tenant? Do you just go down to the LGBT Youth Project and see who comes in on the next bus?"

Everyone chuckled.

Hal said, "No. Remember, I made an exception for you. I usually

148

rent only to college guys."

Ryan asked, "Do you have anyone in mind?"

"Actually, yes. There's a guy I met at the EmpowerMen(t) Retreat named Mykel. He's going back to school to study kinesiology and nutrition."

Ricky said, "What the hell is kinesiology?"

Ted replied, "It's the study of human physiology and movement. People study kinesiology when they want to become personal trainers or physical therapists."

Hal said, "He's big into yoga, physical fitness, healthy living, and that sort of thing. His goal is to open a studio where he can offer classes and coaching. I think you'll like him."

Darnell said, "Sounds like you're replacing Ted with another gym bunny. Is he built like Ted?"

Hal said, "No, he's slender and well-toned. He's more into yoga and Pilates and stuff like that than weightlifting. And he's vegan."

Everyone wondered how that would impact Hal's family night meals.

***

On Sunday, Hal grilled steaks in honor of Ted's graduation. It was a special occasion for another reason: Hal wanted to introduce the guys to Brent, whom he met at the EmpowerMen(t) Retreat. During the two weeks following the retreat, Hal and Brent had gotten together several times for lunch and dinner. They emailed and texted each other throughout the day. Brent was all Hal could think about, and every indication was Brent felt the same way about Hal.

At around 5:30, Ryan emerged from his room and entered the kitchen. Hal was scurrying about the kitchen, tending to every detail so the dinner would be perfect.

Ryan asked, "Hey, Hal. What can I do to help?"

Hal stopped assembling tossed salads long enough to say, "If you would set the table, that would be great. There's a new tablecloth and a new set of cloth napkins and placemats there at the end of the counter. Then please get out my stainless steel silverware and the nice plates. We'll need salad forks and dinner forks, and please put dessert forks and spoons at the top of each place setting. And a wine glass and water glass at each place too, please."

"Wow… You're going all out for this, aren't you?"

"It's a special occasion. I want everything to be nice."

Hal took pride in his cooking skills and his weekly family dinners, but Ryan had never seen him so excited or obsessed about a meal before. He removed the new tablecloth, napkins, and placemats from their plastic pouch and arranged them on the table. Hal stepped out onto the patio to fire up the grill. The doorbell rang, so Ryan hurried to the front door to answer it.

He opened the door to find a handsome man carrying a colorful spring flower arrangement in a vase. His hair was meticulously trimmed and groomed, and he wore an expensive-looking pale blue polo shirt, neat dress jeans, and a perfectly polished pair of loafers.

Ryan said, "You must be Brent."

"Live and in living color."

"I'm Ryan. Please come in."

Brent stepped into the living room and shifted the vase to his left hand so he could shake Ryan's hand. "Pleased to meet you."

"Come with me. Hal's out on the patio."

Ryan led Brent into the kitchen just as Hal was returning from the patio.

Brent said, "Hi! I hope I'm not too early."

"Not at all!"

"I brought this for the table. Or I guess you could put it on the island. Whatever works."

"It's lovely! Thank you! Ryan, would you…"

Ryan stepped forward and took the vase from Brent. Hal and Brent greeted each other with an affectionate kiss and a warm hug. Ryan carried the floral arrangement to the table and placed it in the center. When he turned around, Hal and Brent were still hugging.

Both men were glowing. They radiated excited, nervous energy – Brent, because he wanted to make a good impression on Hal's housemates, and Hal, because he wanted Brent's first impression of his home and his cooking to be perfect. Ryan had never seen Hal so animated and giddy.

Hal asked Brent, "How do you like your steak?"

"Medium to medium-well is fine."

Hal reached into the refrigerator and pulled out the large rectangular plastic container in which he had been marinating the steaks for the past two days. He carried it out onto the patio.

Brent turned to Ryan and said, "He's really going all out for this. Does he do this for you guys every week?"

"No, this is a special occasion. One of the other guys who lives here just graduated from grad school. He grilled steaks when I turned 18 a couple of years ago. Most of the time, it's something simpler like pizza or chili or hamburgers. But it's always good. He's a great cook."

"I think it's wonderful that he does this for you guys."

"Yeah. We usually play games or watch a movie afterward. It helps create a family environment here. Most of us don't have much contact with our biological families. Hal and I have no contact with ours at all. So this really helps. He's not just renting rooms, he's providing a home."

"Hal has told me about you guys. I can see how much he cares about you. He talks about you guys like a straight guy would talk about his kids. Ted's the one who's graduating, right? And he used to be a Marine."

"Yeah, that's right."

"And you're the one from Kansas. Your father's the big-shot minister."

"Yep, that's me." Ryan wondered if Hal had told Brent about his livelihood.

Brent continued. "You're majoring in Computer Science and you play the trumpet."

Hal came back in from the patio. He walked over to the stove to check on the mashed potatoes and the mixed vegetables. "The steaks should be ready in about ten minutes. Ryan, would you please round up the other guys?"

"Sure." Ryan headed to the bedrooms and started knocking on doors.

Brent walked up to Hal. "This is amazing. And you're amazing!" He touched Hal's arm and gave him a quick kiss on the cheek. "What can I do to help?"

Hal said, "There are two bottles of Malbec on the top row of the wine fridge. Would you please open one? When we're ready to sit down, you can ask the guys if they want some and pour the glasses."

"Sure. I can do that."

"Asking is a formality. They'll all say yes."

Brent chuckled.

The other guys arrived, and Hal said, "I'm going to go check on the steaks. Ted and Ricky, would you please come out with me? Darnell and Ryan, please carry the mashed potatoes, vegetables, and dinner rolls over to the table. And get out the salad dressings. Look around and see if there's anything else missing."

Everyone pitched in. In less than a minute, everything was on the table and everyone was seated. Brent asked, "Would anyone like wine? Or maybe I should ask, is there anyone who doesn't?"

Everyone chuckled. Brent poured wine for everyone, then sat down.

For the first few minutes, everyone passed the food and the salad dressing. Once everyone had what they wanted, they started eating. Other than the occasional 'Mmmm... this is delicious!' nobody said much of anything.

Everyone was mindful not to say or do anything that might be embarrassing in front of their guest. They were curious to learn more about this guy who had rocked Hal's world for the last two weeks, but they didn't want to bombard him with questions. Brent was nervous about the first impression he was making in front of these guys who were obviously an important part of Hal's life. They would effectively become his sons-in-law if this relationship progressed, as he hoped it would. He realized they were part of the package. Hal was still nervous about everything being perfect. Despite everyone's desire to be on their best behavior and create the best impression, the dinner was sinking under its own weight.

Brent said, "Ted, congratulations! Tell me about your new job."

Ted said, "I'll be working for Powers Whitehurst & Collins, one of the world's largest accounting and professional services firms. I'll be in the division that serves multinational corporations."

"That sounds interesting."

"I hope I can get assignments in other cities around the world, so I can learn what it's like to live in other places."

Everyone took a few more bites in silence.

Brent turned to Darnell and said, "I understand you've got quite a talent for singing and performing in drag."

"Why yes, thank you! Next week, I'll be heading out to Provincetown for an eight-week run. This will be my fourth summer there."

Hal said, "Tell him about the gay cruise you'll be doing later in the summer."

"Whitney Austin will be performing on Pacifica's Mediterranean cruise in late August."

Ryan recalled the hilarious, dishy banter that had taken place at the table when Darnell returned home from performing on his first cruise in 2007. Nobody launched into that here. Another conversation topic had fallen flat.

Brent turned to Ryan and said, "I understand you're going to Prague for a few weeks."

Ryan thought about how to answer. The fact that Hal told Brent that he was going to Prague probably meant he told him what he was going there to do, but he wasn't entirely sure. Was his porn career an appropriate topic for conversation now?

Ricky settled that question. "That's right! He'll be fucking his way across the continent with a bunch of uncut European twinks!" Darnell and Ted laughed out loud. Ryan blushed. Hal almost shat his pants.

Darnell turned to Brent and said, "I do apologize for that unseemly outburst. Miss Thang here has no sense of decorum."

Ricky said, "Oh, please. Everyone knows Ryan and I are porn stars. Why beat around the bush? He's going over there to shoot a bunch of scenes for Kinky Twinkies. Hell, I wish I was doing it too, but they only want skinny young White guys with huge uncut dicks. There, I said it. Now, everyone please get over yourselves."

Ted said, "Really? 'Cause I'm pretty sure Ryan's cut."

Ricky shot back, "And how would you know? Oh, wait…"

Darnell said, "It's a shame they're not interested in a Latino guy with, shall we say, 'extensive experience.' Not to mention an ass you could smuggle a kilo of cocaine in."

Ricky said, "No problem. There's plenty of demand for that here."

Ted said, "The ass or the cocaine?"

"The ass, bitch."

Ryan sniffed and said, "Speaking of ass… Do we have a gas leak?"

Ted, who was sitting next to Ricky, jumped up from his chair and backed away from the table. "OH. MY. GOD!!! Jesus Christ, dude!"

Ricky feigned embarrassment and said, "Sorry… Anal makes me gassy."

Darnell jumped up and covered his nose and mouth with his napkin. "Damn, gurrl! Did you shove a dead animal up yo' ass?" He ran out of the dining room toward his bedroom.

Ryan said, "I think she just shat 'n 'er panties."

Ted said, "He probably got invaded by Klingons."

Hal was mortified – and furious. He spent a lot of money on the steaks and wine, and he wanted this dinner – the first meal he cooked for his new boyfriend – to be perfect. He was on the verge of exploding when Darnell ran back into the room with two fans. He snapped them open with a theatrical flourish and waved them frantically in front of Ricky.

Hal looked across the table. Brent was laughing his ass off. Hal said nothing and tried to calm down.

The commotion died down and the foul stench dissipated. Everyone sat back down and resumed eating their meal.

Brent said, "I've been to Vienna and Berlin, but not Prague. I hear it's amazing! I look forward to hearing all about it. Take lots of pictures."

Ricky added, "And lots of videos."

Ryan said, "Dude…"

After dinner, all the guys pitched in and helped clear the table and transfer the leftovers into storage containers. When they had finished, Hal asked, "What do you guys want to do this evening? Movie or a game?"

Brent held back to see what the other guys would say.

Ted, Darnell, and Ricky all said, "Game."

Ryan said, "How about The Big Black Deck?"

Hal jumped in. "Um… no. I just bought 7 Wonders. It's popular now. Let's check that out."

Everyone sensed that, after the shenanigans at dinner, they should go along with whatever Hal wanted. Brent said, "That sounds interesting. Let's try it."

***

They played 7 Wonders for about an hour, then switched to the card game Hand and Foot. Now that there were six people instead of their usual five, they were able to divide into two teams of three. By the end of the game, everyone had let their guard down and Brent seemed like one of the bunch.

After the group dispersed, Ryan went back to his room to catch up on his email.  It was approaching 10:00, and he realized that in a few days, he would be heading off to Europe. When he returned, Ted would no longer be living there. Ryan walked over to Ted's room and knocked softly.

"Yeah?"

Ryan let himself in. "Hey. I was thinking this would be a nice night for the hot tub. What do you think?"

"Yeah, sure. That would be great."

Ryan went back to his room, took off his clothes, and wrapped a towel around his waist. He walked into the hallway at the same time Ted, also clad in only a towel, emerged from his room carrying a bottle of Pinot Grigio. They walked into the kitchen to get a couple of plastic wine glasses.

"Wait," Ted said. "It would appear the hot tub is already in use."

Ryan joined Ted at the window. Hal and Brent were sitting in the hot tub, wrapped in each other's arms.

Ryan said, "Want to check back in a half-hour or so?"

Ted said, "Nah… let's try again tomorrow night."

They looked out the window again.

Ryan said, "That's sweet, isn't it?"

"Yeah. I'm really happy for Hal." Ted paused. "But if you'd like to join me for a glass in my room, that would be nice."

"Come as you are?"

Ted paused. "Sure. Why not?"

# JUNIOR YEAR

# Mykel

Sunday, August 15, 2010

Hal drove to LAX and picked up Ryan, who was returning home after spending six weeks in Prague filming scenes for Kinky Twinkies Studios. Hal easily spotted Ryan along the pick-up curb at the Tom Bradley International Terminal. Ryan quickly loaded his suitcases in the trunk, hugged Hal, and got in the car.

Hal said, "Welcome home! How was your trip?"

"Totally awesome in every way! Where do I even start?"

"Well, just give me the highlights now. I know the guys will want to hear all about it at dinner tonight."

"Okay, well… First of all, Prague is amazing. It's so beautiful! So much European charm, yet it's modern too. I could totally live there. Now I understand why Ted wants to go live in other countries."

"I've never been to Prague, but I've heard nothing but good things about it. But I know what you mean about European cities. I've been to Barcelona, Paris, and Amsterdam, and they're lovely."

"And the guys! The guys I got to work with were, like, damn near perfect! Every one of them was drop-dead gorgeous, and they're hung like racehorses! And they take porn to a whole new level. I mean, it's classy and beautiful … and hot! Sizzling hot! And they had all these beautiful places for us to do it in. I mean, Kinky Twinkies is a high-class operation. There wasn't anything even remotely sleazy about it. They have truly raised porn to an art form."

"Yeah, I've seen some of their releases. I can't imagine what their budgets are."

"But aside from all that, the guys were really nice. They invited me to hang out with them and they showed me places. It's like they have this camaraderie off the set, and it shows on the set."

"Sounds wonderful. So I take it they were happy with your work?"

"Oh yeah. The producer talked to me about going to South Africa next year for some shoots."

"That's amazing. I never would have dreamed about that when I was in the business back in the 80s."

"I never would have dreamed I'd be doing any of this three years ago – let alone all over the world. But anyway, how are you? What's been happening at the house?"

"Well… as you know, Ted moved out. He found an apartment in Redondo Beach, not far from where he works. And the guy I met at the retreat, Mykel, has moved in."

"Isn't he the guy who led your Naked Yoga workshop?"

"Yep. Also, he's a medium. You know, someone who can communicate with the spirits of the deceased. While I was at the retreat, he received a message from Vincent, who was my partner back in the 80s. Unfortunately, he died from AIDS. It was nice to communicate with him, and he said some things I needed to hear. It really helped me. Anyway, between that and getting to know Brent, I have a whole new lease on life. I realized that I've been kind of stuck for years, and now I'm unstuck if that makes sense."

Ryan loved seeing Hal so optimistic and happy. "Yeah, I get it. I can tell. Anyway, I look forward to meeting him."

"He's quite a character. I mean that in the nicest possible way. He's kind of new-agey, but in a good way. He's into yoga and meditation and positive living, that sort of stuff. It has definitely changed the dynamics around the house."

"Interesting. So what does he think of Ricky?"

"Well, they're as different as night and day. But Mykel's good at accepting people as they are. He's all about 'live and let live' and so is Ricky. They seem to get along fine."

"So when does Darnell get home?"

"In another couple of weeks. He's had another successful summer in P-town, and he's on his Pacifica gay Mediterranean cruise now. It will be nice to have the house back to full strength."

"I'll bet it's been quiet around the house with just you, Mykel, and Ricky."

"Not as quiet as you might think."

Ryan wasn't sure what Hal was alluding to, but he didn't say anything.

They pulled up to the house shortly after 3:00. Ryan noticed there were more cars than usual parked along the street near their house. He assumed someone in the neighborhood was throwing a party.

Hal helped Ryan carry his suitcases to his room, then disappeared into his master suite.

Before Ryan started unpacking, he walked into the kitchen to get a glass of water. When he looked out the sliding glass door, he saw about a dozen naked men sitting on padded mats and practicing yoga. One of them looked like Brent. A slender young man sporting a man-bun was leading the group. Ryan guessed that must be Mykel.

The outside door to the master suite opened, and a naked Hal walked out and joined the group. Ryan shook his head, then returned his attention to filling his glass at the cold water dispenser in the refrigerator door. He recalled the time shortly after he moved in when he came home to find an orgy scene being shot in the backyard. After that and everything else he had seen over the past three years, seeing a group of naked men practicing yoga was far below the threshold of what it would take to shock him.

Ryan went to the store to pick up some food and sodas for the coming week. When he returned home at 4:15, the yoga session had ended and most of the naked men were cooling off in the pool.

The guests were gone when Ryan emerged from his room at 6:00 for their traditional Sunday family night dinner. Hal, Brent, and Mykel were clothed and Hal was pulling a couple of pizzas out of the oven.

Ryan walked up to Mykel and introduced himself. "Hi, I'm Ryan. You must be Mykel." He extended his hand.

Mykel stepped past Ryan's outstretched hand and hugged him. "I'm a hugger."

"Good, so am I." Ryan was still picturing Mykel naked on the back patio. "So, how long have you been teaching yoga?"

"About five years. Now that you're home, you should join us. We meet Monday, Wednesday, and Friday at 5:00, and Sunday at 3:00."

Brent said, "It does wonders for your mind as well as your body."

Mykel said, "Hal has told me a lot about you."

Ryan said, "Well… I don't know what he's told you, but whatever it is, I swear it's not true!"

Ricky entered. "Oh, yes it is."

Mykel said, "Hal has told me nothing but excellent things about you."

Ryan replied, "Like I said… it's not true!"

They all chuckled. Ricky said, "Welcome home!" and gave Ryan a big hug. "So you're back from fucking your way across Europe?"

*Great,* thought Ryan. *I'm meeting Mykel for the first time, and this is the initial impression he gets.* "Gurrrl, please. I was only in Prague, not all across Europe."

Ricky turned to the others and said, "And when he says he was in Prague, he was literally *in* Prague."

"Oh, stop!" Ryan tried to say it humorously, but he seriously wanted Ricky to stop.

Hal finished slicing the pizzas and carried them over to the kitchen island. "Dig in! The one on the right is vegan and gluten-free." Everyone grabbed a couple of slices and sat down. Ryan noticed that everyone was going for the pizza on the left except Mykel. He took one slice of each.

After the meal was underway, Ryan asked Mykel, "So I totally get yoga. But why do it naked?"

Mykel said, "So we can let down our barriers, release our feelings of embarrassment, shame, and self-consciousness, and become one with nature."

Ricky said, "Oh, please. Everybody just wants to see some dick."

Hal gave Ricky some side-eye and said, "It's a completely non-sexual experience. I can attest to its benefits. It helps me feel free and uninhibited."

Ricky feigned a derisive snort. "Like you were ever inhibited."

Hal said, "Regardless, I find it liberating."

Mykel said, "Sessions are free for you guys since it's your home. I scheduled the sessions at times when they wouldn't be too much of an imposition. You're always welcome to join us."

Ryan said, "Thanks, but I'm kind of shy about having strangers see me naked."

Ricky spat up his drink. "Dude! You've been in, what, fifty movies? Including *The Boys of Breckenridge* and its sequel *Slippery Slopes*, which are now the biggest-selling gay porn videos of all time. And now you're in a bunch of Kinky Twinkies videos. The whole world has seen your cock."

"Yeah, but not in person. I don't want to create a distraction and disrupt the flow. Now can we please move on to something else?"

Brent said, "I'd love to hear about your visit to Prague. What did you get to see and do?"

"Oh, man, Prague was amazing! So much beautiful architecture. I got to see Prague Castle, the Charles Bridge, the Astronomical Clock, and so much more. And the people are so friendly. The guys I worked with were really nice to me. They took me around to show me places and let me come along to their parties. They were so friendly – not to mention gorgeous and sexy!"

"And hung!" Ricky added.

Ryan said, "Yes, they were. But there's more to life than big dicks."

"There is?"

Hal asked, "Did you get to go anywhere else?"

"Yeah. I got to see Vienna, Bratislava, Munich, and Nuremberg. It's so easy to get around on their trains. It's too bad we don't have a better train system in the US. Their public transportation is so good. It would be easy to live there without owning a car."

Hal asked, "Did you take a lot of pictures?"

"Yeah, but I haven't had a chance to go through them and pick out the best ones yet. Can we do that next week?"

"Sure."

Brent said, "It sounds like you had quite an experience."

Thankfully, the conversation moved away from sex and dicks. Ryan wondered what Mykel thought of him after this introduction. Oh well, nothing he could do about it. It was a worse reflection on Ricky than on him.

# A Big Announcement

Sunday, September 12, 2010

This week's Sunday family night dinner was particularly festive. Darnell had just returned from a summer of performances as his drag alter-ego, Whitney Austin – first in Provincetown, then on a ten-day gay Mediterranean cruise. Ryan, Hal, and Ricky had heard about these trips in years past, but each year there were new ports, new pictures, and new stories.

Brent and Mykel were hearing about Darnell's summer exploits for the first time, so they were all ears and full of questions. Darnell was thrilled to have a new audience to entertain.

After Darnell finished telling everyone about his travels, Hal said, "Everyone, I have an exciting announcement to make."

Everyone stopped eating and focused on what Hal was going to say next. Brent looked like he knew what was about to come.

"As most of you know, Mykel is a medium. At the EmpowerMen(t) Retreat back in May, he held a group reading, and one of the spirits that came through was my late partner, Vincent. Part of his message was that I was stuck in a rut. I was living my life on auto-pilot. I needed to expand my horizons and be open to new opportunities and possibilities. Part of being open to new possibilities has resulted in my relationship with Brent. For a long time, I have been subconsciously holding myself back from dating again, for many reasons. But thanks to Brent, and as a result of my message from Vincent, I am able to love again. I'm willing to try a relationship again. And it's been going well. This man has brought so much happiness into my life!"

Everyone glanced at Brent and smiled. He was gazing at Hal in admiration. The feeling was obviously mutual.

Hal continued. "But there's more. With Brent's support and encouragement, I have decided to embark upon a new business venture. I am going to start my own production company!"

The guys clapped and offered their congratulations.

Ryan said, "Just so I'm clear, is your new production company going to produce porn or something else?"

Hal replied, "Porn. It's what I know best. See, I think the industry has become stagnant. If anything, I see the quality of the products being produced nowadays going downhill. It's cheaper. Lower production values. Skankier performers. A lot of these companies that have started up in the past few years are cranking out low-budget crap. No one is advancing the art form except Kinky Twinkies. In fact, Ryan's experience with them this past summer has confirmed the direction I want to go with this. I want to create the US-based equivalent of what they're doing at Kinky Twinkies. Handsome performers, beautiful surroundings, playful and passionate sex. Good lighting and camera work. In short, I want to produce a higher-quality, more artful product. I want to show sex that's beautiful and sensual. Sometimes romantic, sometimes just playful and fun. Tasteful, not trashy. So no fetishes, gangbangs, or guys trying to prove they can squat on a fire hydrant."

Darnell turned to Ricky and said, "Well, darling, that pretty much cuts you out."

Ricky replied, "Bitch! I can be fucking romantic!"

No one said anything for a few seconds. Then everyone burst out laughing.

Ricky rolled his eyes and shook his head dismissively. "*I can't even* with you people."

Ryan said, "That sounds wonderful, but where are you going to get the money to launch a business like this?"

"I'm well aware that to produce a higher quality product, it's going to take a higher level of investment. But I have a lot of connections I've built up over the years and I'm going to be approaching them. And Brent has a lot of contacts in Hollywood who might be willing to work on these projects – editors, set designers, lighting people, and so forth. Both Brent and I have some financial resources we are willing to invest in this, and I'm working on getting some other investors on board now."

Ryan said, "That sounds exciting! So, uh… let me know if you need me to be part of this."

Ricky said, "Me, too."

Hal said, "That reminds me of another thing I'm going to do differently. For my performers with exclusive contracts, I'm going to offer residuals."

Ricky asked, "What does that mean?"

Hal said, "That means you might not get as much pay upfront, but you will get a percentage of all sales going forward. So the more videos we sell, the more money you'll make."

Ricky turned to Ryan and said, "If you and I were getting residuals for *The Boys of Breckenridge*, we could retire in Hawaii!"

Ryan said, "So it's like the performers have a stake in the quality of the product."

Hal said, "Exactly. And I want to build a website that lets viewers get to know the performers a little better. I'm envisioning having a page for each performer with some professional-quality photos, a short bio, and maybe an interview. Nothing too personal, of course. I want to give people the opportunity to bond with their favorite performers. That will build a loyal fan base, which of course means repeat customers."

Mykel said, "Sounds like some pretty lofty goals. I hope you can pull it off."

# 21

Friday, October 15, 2010

Back in August, shortly after Ryan returned from his six weeks in Prague, Ted asked Ryan if he could take him out for dinner on his birthday. Ted wanted to show Ryan his new apartment and take him to a nice restaurant nearby.

Ryan navigated his trusty Toyota Corolla twenty miles through LA rush hour traffic. He allowed himself an hour for the journey, and still arrived 15 minutes late. It didn't help that he had to circle the surrounding blocks several times looking for a parking space. After about ten minutes, he lucked out and claimed a spot right after someone pulled out.

Ryan located the correct unit and rang the doorbell. Ted opened the door with a huge smile on his face. As Ryan entered the apartment, he heard jazz piano trio music playing softly in the background. Ted had selected the Classic Jazz channel on his TV. Ryan said, "Sorry I'm late. Traffic was hell, then I couldn't find a place to park."

Ted didn't seem to mind at all. He planted a kiss on Ryan's lips and then gave him a prolonged hug. "No problem – it's LA. Traffic jams are a way of life. The reservation's for 7:00, so we still have 45 minutes."

"How close is it?"

"About two blocks. We can easily walk." Ted hugged Ryan again. "Aw, man… It's so great to see you! It's nice to be out on my own and have my own place and everything, but it's quiet here. I miss the guys." He clasped his hand on Ryan's shoulder. "And I really miss you."

Ryan smiled. He missed Ted too. But Ted was, by his own admission, a loner. When he lived in the house, he stayed in his room most of the time when he wasn't going to classes or visiting his escort clients. It seemed strange to hear Ted talk about missing everyone.

Ted said, "So, how about starting the evening off with a celebratory cocktail?"

"Sure!"

"What would you like?" Ted led Ryan to a small cart that contained about a dozen liquor bottles of various types.

"I don't know. Suggest something."

"How about a lemon drop martini?"

"Sounds great. Nice music, by the way. Are you into jazz now?"

"It's okay. But I figured you'd like it."

Ted poured some ice, some expensive-looking vodka, and a couple of other ingredients into a shaker and shook it vigorously for a few seconds. Then he removed the cap and strained the chilled contents into two martini glasses. He expertly carved two spirals of lemon rind, dropped one in each glass, and handed a glass to Ryan. "Cheers! To legal drinking!"

They clinked glasses and Ryan took a sip. It was just the right combination of tart and sweet. "It's delicious!"

Ryan's housemates, especially Ted, offered Ryan alcoholic beverages even though he was underage. He usually accepted whatever he was offered, and was still discovering which drinks he liked better than others. It hadn't occurred to him until this moment that as of yesterday, he could legally purchase alcohol for himself and order drinks in a bar or restaurant.

Ryan marveled at the expertise Ted displayed while preparing their drinks. He was a bit taken aback by how much booze Ted owned. Ryan wondered, *Is he having people over? He just mentioned that it was quiet here and he missed being around people. Had he owned that much in the house? Is that why he stayed in his room so much?* He said, "That's quite an assortment of liquor you have there."

"Thank you. Yeah, I want to be prepared in case I have people over. Like tonight."

"You sure seem to know what you're doing. Were you a bartender at some point?"

"No, but I took a mixology course during my freshman year."

"They offer that at UCLA?"

"No, it was off-campus. It was one of those adult ed classes. And a couple of my regular clients had nice home bars, so I learned a lot from watching them make drinks."

Ryan looked around. Ted had done a nice job selecting furniture and accessorizing. "Wow. This place is a pretty swank."

"Yeah, I really like it. It's kind of small, just one bedroom, but that's all I need. And the beach is only a couple of blocks away. I go running on the beach a lot."

"How far is it from where you work?"

"Just over a mile. That's one of the reasons I picked this place, so I would be close to work. For the first few weeks after I started my job, I commuted every day from the house, and you saw what that was like. I have no interest in spending two hours a day on the freeway. That's no way to live. On the other hand, this little place costs an arm, a leg, and my left nut."

"Yeah, that would be a big adjustment after paying $500 a month at the house."

Ted said, "True, but my job pays quite well. It's weird to have all this money show up in my bank account twice a month after being a Marine for four years and a college student for six."

"Well, it's not like you were without income while you were in college."

Ted showed no reaction.

Ryan asked, "Are you still doing that?"

"No. I gave up escorting when I started my job. I kinda miss my clients, though. You know, at the time I felt like I was providing companionship for them. Now I realize it kinda worked both ways."

"Couldn't you still do it?"

"I could, but I don't want to. I don't need the money anymore. I've closed that chapter. Now I finally get to start on my career."

"How do you like your job?"

"It's pretty good. It's definitely an adjustment. Working eight to five Monday through Friday takes a lot more of your time than attending classes. I've only been there four months, so I'm still taking a lot of training and learning stuff. But I can tell the work is going to be challenging."

"How do you like the people?"

"Most of them are nice. They're definitely smart. There's some office politics, but you'll find that anywhere."

Ryan finished his lemon drop. "That was really good. Thanks!"

"You want another one?"

"No, thanks. How soon do we need to leave?"

Ted glanced at his watch. "We can probably go now. It won't hurt to be a little early."

They left the apartment and walked down the street toward the ocean. When they reached the oceanfront drive they turned right. A block later, they reached Sailor Sam's, a fancy-looking restaurant that faced the ocean. Ted led Ryan up the steps and into the lobby. "Wait here." He stepped forward and spoke quietly to the maître d'. "I have a reservation for two for 7:00. Ted Purcell. I requested a table facing the ocean. We're celebrating my friend's birthday."

The maître d' checked her reservation book, nodded, grabbed two menus, and said, "Right this way, gentlemen." She led them through the dining area, past the longest salad bar Ryan had ever seen, to a table next to the window at the far end of the room. It was covered with an elegant white tablecloth, folded cloth napkins, an array of knives, forks, spoons, water and wine glasses, a lit candle, and a small vase with a few fresh flowers. Ryan and Ted sat facing each other, and the maître d' handed each of them an opened menu. "Sebastian will be your server this evening. He'll inform you of today's specials. Have a wonderful evening."

Ryan had never eaten in a place so upscale and fancy. He glanced out the window. The golden sun, against a brilliant red and orange sky, was about to dip below the surface of the Pacific.

Then he looked down at the menu and almost fainted. The appetizers ranged from $15 to $25, and the entrees started at $24 and went up from there. A few items simply said, 'market price.' He shuddered to think what that might be.

"Um... Ted..."

Ted sensed Ryan's obvious discomfort. "Don't worry, it's on me. I can afford it, and you're worth it. You only turn 21 once. Order whatever you want. Don't pay any attention to the right column."

That did little to assuage Ryan's self-consciousness. The macadamia-crusted chicken breast, at $24, would be fine.

Ted said, "The bacon-wrapped filet mignon is to die for. It's the best piece of meat you will ever put in your mouth." He paused. "And I know, that's saying something."

Ryan smiled at Ted's attempt at humor, but he still felt embarrassed about Ted spending this much money on him.

Ted continued, "I recommend the surf-n-turf, which is the filet mignon paired with a lobster tail."

"What are you going to have?"

"The surf-n-turf. And the salad bar is amazing! Try the Caesar salad and the clam chowder. And they even have caviar!"

Ryan had never eaten at a place even remotely like this before. *Is this how rich people live? Does Ted really make that much?* He knew he shouldn't ask.

Sebastian appeared at the table with a basket of cloth-wrapped, freshly-baked sourdough bread, along with two ramekins of whipped garlic butter. "Good evening, gentlemen. Would you like to see a wine list?"

Ted replied, "Yes please." Sebastian handed it to him. Ted scanned it and asked, "What would you recommend to accompany the surf-n-turf?"

Sebastian replied, "The Pinot Noir from the Marlborough region of New Zealand would be an excellent choice."

Ted glanced at Ryan with his eyebrows raised optimistically, as if to say, 'sound good?'

Ryan shrugged his shoulders and nodded slightly.

"Thank you. We'll try a bottle."

"Very well, sir." Sebastian turned to Ryan. "Sir, I apologize for the inconvenience, but I am obligated to verify your age if you will be consuming wine."

Ryan reached for his wallet and produced his driver's license. Sebastian glanced at it and handed it back. "Happy belated birthday, sir. Now, would you like to start with an appetizer?"

Ted glanced at Ryan with a look that said, 'go ahead, order something if you like.'

Ryan was already wondering how he would be able to eat so much food. "Nothing for me, thanks. That salad bar looks intense."

Ted looked back at Sebastian. "Nothing for me either."

"Are you ready to order or would you like a few more minutes?"

Ted looked at Ryan. Ryan nodded.

Ted said, "I would like the surf-n-turf. Medium."

Sebastian turned to Ryan. Ryan decided bacon-wrapped filet mignon and lobster sounded better than macadamia-crusted chicken breast and ditched his original plan. "I'll have the same. Also medium."

"Very well." Sebastian collected their menus and returned moments later with a bottle of Pinot Noir. He expertly uncorked it and poured a small amount into Ted's glass.

Ted swirled it, inhaled the bouquet, and took a tiny sip. "MMMmmm… oh, yes! That will do nicely."

Sebastian smiled and poured five ounces into each of their glasses. He set the wine bottle on a small white saucer that had been placed on the table for just that purpose. "Enjoy! And please help yourself to the salad bar when you're ready." Sebastian turned and left.

Ryan was about to take a sip of his wine. He remembered the night soon after he moved into the house, when he and Ted spent a couple of hours in the pool talking. Ted showed him how to swirl the wine and inhale the bouquet before drinking it. While he was performing the obligatory swirl, Ted raised his glass and said, "A toast! To friendship and fine living!" They clinked their glasses and took a sip.

That night in the pool was the first time Ryan had ever tried wine. That was a white wine, a Pinot Grigio if he remembered correctly. And this was a Pinot Noir. Ryan wondered what Pinot meant – and Noir and Grigio, for that matter.

That night, they had a heart-to-heart talk about loneliness and fitting in at school. They talked about Ted being an escort, and how that compared to being a prostitute or a porn star. They talked about Ryan's attraction to Ted. Ryan thought about the times they went running, how much he admired Ted's physique, and how much he lusted after him. That night in the pool was the first time they were naked together. Nothing happened, both because Ted wouldn't allow it and because Ryan had lost interest after discovering Ted was an escort. Still, that night was special. In hindsight, it was when they bonded and their friendship began.

Ryan recalled one particular statement Ted made that night. "A lot of times you never really appreciate something until it's gone." *Maybe that's how Ted is feeling now that he's out on his own. Maybe that's why he's being so extravagant tonight.*

"Hey, you still there?" Ted asked.

Ryan snapped back to the present. "Yeah. Sorry, I was recalling a few memories from the past."

"Pleasant ones, I hope."

"Yeah. Very pleasant." Ryan smiled.

"Well, let's go check out the salad bar."

Ryan had been to restaurants with salad bars before, but they were nothing like this. This one had shrimp, oysters, and smoked salmon. There were all kinds of cheese – some in cubes, some in slices, and some you sliced right off the wedge. There were all kinds of fruits and vegetables, and a station dedicated to Caesar salad. Since Ted raved about it, he took some. Ryan's plate was already loaded with enough exotic treats to make a full meal when he arrived at the last display on the line. Ted was waiting there for him. "This is the caviar I was telling you about. You have to at least try it."

Ryan looked at the small bowl filled with tiny black balls. It didn't look appetizing at all. "What is it?"

"Fish eggs. Put some crackers on your plate, then spoon some on each cracker."

Ryan glanced over to Ted's plate. He had five crackers loaded with caviar. Ryan decided to start with two.

They returned to the table and dug into their food. Ryan took a bite of the caviar. It tasted salty and fishy. There was another taste, and it took Ryan a moment to pinpoint it. He took another bite. It wasn't bad, but it wasn't his new favorite thing. Then it hit him – it tasted like ocean water.

Ted asked, "What do you think of caviar?"

"Honestly? It's okay. I guess I don't understand why people make such a big deal about it." The fact that the caviar was staining the crackers black added nothing to the appeal.

"Probably because it's expensive. They say people attach value to things based on what they have to pay for them, so I guess this is one example."

Ryan realized Ted was attaching a lot of value to this night out.

They finished their salad course. Like clockwork, a young nameless man who looked to be about Ryan's age unceremoniously appeared and removed their salad plates and the silverware related to that course.

Ted took another sip of his wine and smiled with satisfaction. Then he said, "So, tell me all about your summer in Europe!"

"Oh, man, it was amazing. Everything about it was fantastic. Europe is so… I don't know, quaint? Classy? Tasteful? It's like it's both historical and modern at the same time. The ambiance is so relaxed. I mean, around here, people are always in a hurry and everyone drives everywhere. And so many people are pretentious. There, everyone walks or takes public transportation. People are friendlier and not in such a big hurry. Like, people hang out in sidewalk cafés for hours on a nice evening, or they go sit in the park and read or just hang out."

Ted was nodding and taking in every word.

"So, I was based in Prague, and it's incredibly beautiful. There were all these magnificent old buildings, but it's still alive, you know? And you can go anywhere else on a train. I went to Berlin and Nuremberg and Munich and Vienna, and they're all just as fascinating. I could live in any one of them, but especially Prague and Vienna. Most of my scenes were shot in Prague, but they also have a studio in Bratislava – that's the capital of Slovakia – so I was there for a week. And they put me up in these nice furnished apartments. I mean, they treated me royally. And the other guys? They were so nice! They took me around to places and invited me to their parties and stuff."

"So, they spoke English?"

"Yeah, some more than others, but we got along fine. That's another thing. In Europe, everyone speaks at least some English. Sometimes they speak several languages. I never had any trouble getting by."

Sebastian arrived and presented their surf-n-turf entrees. The presentation was perfect. In addition to the filet mignon, which was smaller, rounder, and thicker than any steak Ryan had seen, the lobster tail rested on a frilly green lettuce leaf. Five stalks of asparagus were wrapped with a sliver of bacon and topped with a dollop of yellow sauce. A pat of butter was melting over a perfectly-shaped mound of garlic mashed potatoes. A carved radish and a sprig of rosemary adorned the plate. Ryan wanted to whip out his phone and take a picture of it, but he wondered if that would be uncouth in a place like this.

"Wow, Ted, this is incredible. It's so perfect I almost don't want to cut into it."

"As they say, food is consumed by the eyes before it is consumed by the mouth."

Ryan lowered his voice slightly. "Can I take a picture of this, or would that be frowned upon?"

"I don't see why not. Here, let me take a picture of you!"

Ted pulled his phone out of his pocket. He refilled their wine glasses and set the bottle aside. He framed the picture so that both Ryan's face and his plate were in frame. "Smile!"

Ryan smiled and Ted touched the photo button on the screen.

"Now raise your glass. That's it. Smile!"

Ryan retrieved his phone and took a picture of Ted and his place setting, and one aimed down at his plate.

At about that time, Sebastian arrived with a camera. "Gentlemen, please allow me to take a photo of you." He took a few steps back. "Now, lean in a little. Okay, smile!"

Sebastian snapped a picture, looked at the image in the viewfinder, then said, "Excellent," and scurried away.

Ryan wondered if there would be a charge for the photo added to their bill.

Ted said, "Okay, the moment has been memorialized. Let's enjoy!"

Ryan cut a slice of the filet mignon and tasted it. Ted was right, it was by far the best piece of meat he had ever put in his mouth. The best anything, for that matter.

For the next ten minutes, there was not much conversation while they both savored their meals. The sun had sunk below the horizon, but there were still some streaks of orange remaining in the sky. The ocean water lapped up against the shore outside their window. Light piano jazz was playing unobtrusively in the background, setting a relaxed yet elegant mood. Everything was perfect. Ryan glanced across the table at Ted. As kind as Ted was, he always seemed to exude a hint of sadness or pain, as if he constantly carried some quiet burden. He was always pleasant to others, but still quiet and shy. His self-protective barriers were high. Over time, he had let down his guard for Ryan more than anyone else. But Ryan still assumed that a lot remained locked deep inside. But tonight, Ted looked happy. Not kid-at-Disneyland happy, but content – like he was finally enjoying himself. Maybe that was worth all the money Ted was spending this evening. Ryan decided to stop worrying about that.

Ted stopped eating long enough to split the remaining wine between their two glasses. As if on cue, Sebastian appeared, picked up the empty wine bottle, and asked, "Would you care for more?" Ted looked promisingly at Ryan.

Ryan said, "There's no way I can drink another half bottle of wine. I mean, it's delicious, but…"

Sebastian said, "I could bring you a carafe."

Ted replied, "Yes, that would be about right."

Sebastian turned and left.

"What's a carafe?"

"You'll see. It's basically a half-bottle. Enough for one more glass each, maybe a bit more."

A moment later, Sebastian arrived with the carafe. He topped off each of their glasses and set the carafe on the little saucer. As soon as he was out of earshot, Ted said, "So back to Prague. Tell me about the scenes you shot."

Ryan looked around. The restaurant was almost half full, but the tables immediately surrounding them were still empty. He didn't want to talk about making pornographic movies in an elegant environment such as this, but perhaps he could share some information without getting too graphic.

"First of all, the guys were amazing – in every way. They're drop-dead gorgeous. They have beautiful, smooth bodies and perfect hair and, well… they're highly qualified for the job."

"Just like you."

"I kept thinking, I'm getting paid for this? I should have to pay to be with these guys. I mean, have you ever seen a Kinky Twinkies video?"

Ted said, "I may have seen one or two. You definitely fit their profile."

"Thanks. I guess they thought so too. Anyway, the whole operation is so high-class. Like they totally raise this genre to an art form. I mean, just the way they had us kiss each other, and do foreplay and everything. It's hot, but it's also sensual and playful, and… well, it's almost innocent and pure. They treat sex like it's a beautiful thing. Whereas here, it usually comes across as impersonal or rough or sleazy or whatever. And they found these beautiful places, like country houses out in the woods. Everything was so classy. And the guys… not only are they hot, but they're nice. I'm going to stay in touch with some of them. And we didn't just show up and shoot a scene. They allowed us time to get to know each other and develop a rapport and an attraction for one another, and it shows in the finished product."

"Nice. I can't wait to see some of the videos you're in."

Ryan wasn't crazy about that possibility, but there was nothing he could do about it. It came with the territory.

They finished the remaining food on their plates. Ryan was stuffed and a little drunk.

Ted asked, "So, do you think you'll go back to Prague next summer?"

"They asked, but I said no. I need to get an internship so I can get some real job experience."

"Yeah, that makes sense."

"They are going to fly me down to Cape Town for a week in January, though. They're going to send like 20 or 30 guys down to some fancy house on the beach and do a whole bunch of scenes, including one with everyone in it."

"You're kidding me!"

"Nope. That's what they said."

"My God, are they trying to set some kind of Guinness world record?"

"I don't know, but if nothing else I'll get to see Cape Town."

The nameless busboy came and cleared everything away except their wine and water glasses and the half-empty carafe. He used a small flat tool to scrape the crumbs off the tablecloth. Then he placed a small fork and spoon sideways across the top of their place settings.

A moment later, Sebastian arrived carrying two dessert plates. Ryan's plate contained a small, round individual-sized chocolate cake and a scoop of vanilla ice cream. 'Happy Birthday, Ryan!' was written across the plate in drizzled chocolate syrup. There was a single lit candle in the center of the cake. "Happy birthday, sir, compliments of Sailor Sam's." He handed Ryan a nice cardboard folder that had the photo he had taken earlier inserted into the opening.

Ted's dessert was also chocolate cake and vanilla ice cream, but minus the candle and the birthday greeting. A few dollops of some sort of raspberry sauce adorned his plate.

Ted reached for the carafe and split the rest between their two glasses. "Cheers! To 21!" They clinked their glasses and took a sip.

Ryan picked up his fork and sliced it into his cake. A thick, hot chocolate filling began oozing out. "It's chocolate lava cake!" Ted explained.

Ryan somehow managed to stuff every sinfully delicious bite of the chocolate lava cake into his mouth. He dutifully finished his wine. He figured since Ted was spending all this money, he didn't dare leave anything uneaten.

Ted paid the check and they departed into the cool, breezy October evening. The sound of the ocean washing up onto the beach and the smell of the ocean breeze created an environment of peaceful serenity. After that incredible but gluttonous meal, it felt good to walk and breathe in the fresh air.

Ryan said, "It's a beautiful night out. Can we go for a walk on the beach?"

"Sure."

The sun had set an hour ago and the moon had appeared. There were dots of light from the pier in the distance and the buildings across the street, but the beach was dark and romantic.

For a minute, they walked side-by-side and enjoyed the calm beauty in silence. Then Ryan said, "Ted, I can't thank you enough for that dinner. I've never experienced anything like that in my life."

"My pleasure. I'm glad I could be the first one to give you that experience."

"Do you eat there often?"

"Only a couple of times. I ate there at the end of my first week on the job, and I also went there on my birthday. You were still in Prague."

It seemed sad to Ryan that Ted had to celebrate his birthday by himself. Or maybe he wasn't by himself, but Ryan didn't think he should ask.

Ryan said, "You really seem happy tonight. I don't think I've ever seen you this happy before."

"Well, life's getting better. I've achieved my goals of going to college and getting my MBA. Now I'm starting my career with a great company that has offices all over the world. And while I liked the house and everything, I really like my new apartment."

"Yeah, it's pretty sweet. You did a nice job decorating it."

"Thanks. You know, I've worked hard for this. I've had to overcome a lot of shit. I came from a poor, broken home in Pennsylvania with a drunk, abusive asshole for a father and a lesbian mother who got separated from me when I was ten. I got sent off to Afghanistan, where I saw all the horrors of war. Then I had to have sex for money to make my way through school. But now, I've made it. I've got a great job and I make decent money. I've put up with enough shit to last my entire lifetime. Now, I'm going to treat myself well. I'm going to eat nice meals and drink fine liquor and wine. I'm going to live in safe, comfortable, beautiful surroundings. I'm going to travel and live in different parts of the world until I find the place that's just right. This is what I've dreamed of and worked for, for over ten years. So yeah, I'm happier now than I've ever been. And it's only going to get better."

Ryan took a moment to let all that sink in. He already knew those things about Ted's past, but now they all came together in a way that shed light on Ted's psyche and his emotional burdens. This was one of those few times when Ted was opening up. "Yeah, I can see why you feel that way. And yes, you deserve this success. You deserve to live well."

Ted said, "I learned a lot from Hal. Think about his story. He was disowned and kicked out by his parents. There were nights he had to sleep at the Youth Project, or on someone's couch, or even on the street. He had to support himself and work his way through school by doing sex work, and he ended up getting HIV. He got a job with a big, prestigious law firm, only to be told they wouldn't promote him because he's gay. But now, he has a fabulous house, wears nice clothes, drives a nice car, and donates his time and money to the Youth Project. Not to mention giving us a nice place to live for next to nothing. He's slogged through a lot of shit to get to the nice life he lives today."

"I didn't know Hal had HIV."

"Oh. Well, maybe I shouldn't have told you. He's open about it if it comes up, but it's not like he needs to volunteer that information."

"At least not unless he's going to have sex with you."

"Right. Which he never does with guys in the house."

They had walked at least a mile. Sailor Sam's was just a few twinkling lights in the distance. Ted asked, "So, are you ready to turn around and head back?"

"Sure," Ryan said. "You know, until Brent came along, I wondered why Hal was still single. I mean, he's nice, he's good-looking, he's successful… although I suppose not everyone would approve of the industry he works in. And until Brent, I never saw him date anyone or even hook up, at least not that I noticed. Maybe it's because he has HIV."

"Yeah, that might be a factor. It's like, every time he meets someone, he has to disclose his status at some point. I'm sure that's awkward and it probably scared a lot of guys off."

"I wonder if Brent also has HIV."

"It's possible. In any case, they've figured out how to deal with it. I'm really happy for Hal."

They walked in silence for a moment. Then Ryan asked, "So, are you seeing anyone? None of my business – just curious."

"No. You know, I've never really dated anyone. I don't even know how you go about it. When I was in high school, I knew I could never ask a guy out. I couldn't risk having anyone find out. And of course, in the Marines, they had 'Don't Ask, Don't Tell,' so I'd get kicked out if they found out. Alex and I just kind of figured each other out. After our unit was deployed to Afghanistan, we had very little privacy and no place to go on a date even if we could. And at UCLA, I wanted to stay focused on my studies. Plus, there probably weren't many guys who would want to be boyfriends with someone who was an escort."

"Yeah, I know what that's like. Whenever I meet someone nice, as soon as they find out I do porn, it's game over. Either that, or it's a big turn-on for them to be fucking a porn star. So, they aren't really interested in me, the person, they're interested in me, the porn star."

"Yep. Anyway, now they have all these websites and apps for finding men. I tried that, but for me, it was frustrating and depressing. Most of the guys on there are either lying about themselves or looking for a hookup. And I've never liked going to bars and trying to pick people up."

Ryan said, "There has to be a better way. Maybe you could join some gay organizations or volunteer someplace. That way you could meet people in places where the focus isn't on dating or sex."

"Yeah, but you know, I'm still not interested in a relationship. I want to focus on my career. I want to try living overseas. So, even if I met someone, I'd be leaving in a year or two anyway."

"Wouldn't you stay in one place for the right guy?"

"I don't know. Why are you asking me all this stuff? Can we just drop it?"

*Uh-oh,* Ryan thought. *I've hit a sore spot. Now he's going to explode.* "Sorry."

Ted rapidly became agitated. "Everyone thinks you have to be in a relationship. Everyone thinks your goal in life should be to find that special someone to spend the rest of your life with. It's like you're not a complete person or you're not a success unless you're in a couple. Well, that's bullshit. My happiness doesn't depend on having a boyfriend or a partner or a husband or whatever."

"I said I'm sorry."

After an awkward pause, Ted said, "Sorry I went off."

Ryan wanted to ask, 'But are you really happy?' but he knew he shouldn't.

They passed the restaurant, then turned up the street to Ted's apartment. They walked the rest of the way in silence. Once they were inside, Ted hugged Ryan. "Hey, I'm sorry I snapped at you. I'm not mad at you or anything. Are we okay?"

"Yeah."

"I wanted this to be a nice night for you."

Ryan smiled and did his best to appear upbeat. "And it was! Really! This has been a wonderful night. That meal was incredible. I've never tasted food that good. I'm still full. And the walk on the beach was beautiful!" *And rather romantic, at least until the end.* "Most of all, I feel I got to know you a little better. And I like hanging out with you."

"Do you really?"

"Yes, really."

"Thanks. I enjoy hanging out with you too. Like I said, I've missed you."

Ryan said, "Well, we should get together now and then. Maybe do things together. There's lots of stuff around LA I haven't seen yet."

"Yeah, that would be nice."

Ryan wondered if the evening was about to conclude, and this was the moment he should say thanks and goodbye, kiss him, and leave.

He wanted to stay, but he didn't know how to broach that topic. He was having trouble reading what Ted wanted. In the past, Ted made it clear that sex was off the table. But somehow, tonight seemed different. He couldn't quite put his finger on it.

Ted said, "Why don't you have a seat on the couch? I have a little something to top off the evening."

As Ryan walked over to the couch and sat down, he wondered, *What? Has he bought me a present, too? After spending all that money on dinner? I hope not – that would be a bit much.*

Ted walked into the kitchen and returned with two small wine glasses and a dark bottle he had just uncorked. "This is a dessert wine. It's called Porto Coco. It's port wine, which is a dark red, infused with chocolate. Lemme tell you, this stuff is sex in a glass!" He poured a few ounces into each glass.

"Uh, Ted? I'm already kind of drunk. I've never had this much alcohol in one night. I shouldn't be driving with what I've had already."

"So, why don't you spend the night?"

Ryan tried to hide his delight at this sudden turn of events. Even so, he wasn't sure if this meant he'd be sleeping on the couch or…? Better not leap to conclusions. It would be awkward if he made the wrong assumption.

"Well… okay."

"Good. It's settled. Now, to good friends and fine living!"

They clinked their glasses and took a sip.

Ryan said, "Oh. My. God! This is, seriously, the most delicious thing ever!"

"See? Like I said, it's sex in a glass. Would you like some cheese and crackers?"

"That would be delicious, but no. I'm stuffed. And I can't have any more wine, either."

They didn't say much as they took tiny sips from their glasses and savored each drop. Ryan wondered how much Ted drank each day, but he knew it would ruin the moment if he asked.

They finished, and Ted took their glasses and the remaining wine back into the kitchen. Ryan wondered what would happen next and how the evening would play out from here. Ted returned, and Ryan stood up and said, "Well… I know it's still kind of early, but I'm starting to fade."

"Yeah, we did consume a lot of food and alcohol."

"So, uh… Should I sleep on the couch?"

Ted chuckled. "Well, I guess you could if you would be more comfortable with that. But you're more than welcome to sleep with me."

"But you've always said–"

"Yeah, well, that was then. This is now. We're no longer living together in the house. And you're 21 now."

Ryan looked confused. "What's that got to do with it?"

"I'm 28." Ted looked at him like it should be obvious. "Do the math."

It took Ryan a moment, then he remembered. "Ah, yes… Half of 28 is 14, plus 7 is 21."

"Ding-ding-ding-ding-ding!"

Ryan laughed. "I dunno, that still seems kind of arbitrary."

Ted replied, "Well, I guess you have to draw the line somewhere. Besides, you've grown a lot over the past three years."

"Have I?"

"Yes. You're not an innocent, naïve, almost virginal teenager anymore. You're a lot wiser to the world now, and you're growing into the person you're meant to be. I just graduated, and you'll be graduating in less than two years. We're much more on the same plane now."

Ryan hadn't thought about how he had changed since coming to LA, but he guessed he had. But whatever. He could contemplate that another time.

Ted turned toward his bedroom and held out his hand. Ryan took it and allowed Ted to lead the way.

# The Morning After

Saturday, October 16, 2010

The next morning, Ryan gently woke up and opened his eyes. It took him a few seconds to process the strange surroundings and remember where he was. He glanced at the alarm clock – 7:15. He was lying on his left side, and he had a surging erection and a desperate need to pee. Ted was snuggled up behind him with his right arm draped over Ryan's midsection.

Ryan gently lifted Ted's arm and slid out of the bed. As he walked toward the bathroom with his flagpole pointing the way, Ted stirred.

When Ryan exited the bathroom, Ted was waiting to take his turn. Ted said, "Good morning!" and kissed Ryan sweetly. "You want to hang out in bed a little longer?"

"Sure." Ryan climbed back in bed and laid on his back. He recalled the time near the end of his junior year in high school, when the track team traveled to Wichita for the state championship track meet and he and Chris spent the night in a cheap motel. He recalled how he couldn't sleep in the strange bed and the anticipation and uncertainty about what might happen. He realized what he wanted to happen on that night over three years ago was exactly what had happened last night. Oh, well. As Ted said last night, back then he was an innocent, naïve, virginal teenager. Those days were long gone.

About five minutes later, Ted returned and snuggled up under Ryan's arm and rested his head on his shoulder. He draped his right arm across Ryan's chest and his right leg over Ryan's right leg, just below his crotch.

He kissed the side of Ryan's face and whispered, "Did you sleep okay?"

"Yeah." Between the drowsiness caused by all the wine he had consumed and the post-coital energy drain, Ryan had slept soundly.

Ryan whispered back, "How did you sleep?"

"Like a baby."

Ryan smiled. "Well, if you woke up every two hours and cried, I sure didn't hear it."

"Silly."

"It's what I do."

"Well, I sure enjoyed what you did last night." Ted planted a gentle kiss on Ryan's cheek while his right hand drifted across Ryan's chest and fondled a nipple. "Now that you're fully rested, wanna go another round?"

Rather than answer verbally, Ryan turned toward Ted and draped his left arm over his body. They locked lips. Their tongues danced while their free hands explored each other's smooth bodies.

***

After a half-hour of intense, passionate sex, they snuggled in each other's arms for another twenty minutes, basking in the afterglow and drifting in and out of light slumber.

Ryan realized he was experiencing 'the morning after' for the first time. Those two nights when he and Chris had sex in Chris's bedroom they enjoyed the afterglow, but Ryan always had to return home. Spending the night was out of the question. Since then, it was all porn scenes – always physical, never emotional.

Ryan kissed Ted's cheek. "This is so wonderful."

"Yes, it is. You know… maybe I was crazy for pushing you away these past three years."

"Well, whatever. We're here now. Maybe this is the way it was meant to be."

They kissed a few more times. Then Ryan said, "There's another reason this was so special. You remember last night, when I said I had never experienced a dinner like that before? And you said you were glad you could be the first one to give me that experience?"

"Yeah…"

"Well, you were the first one to give me another experience, too."

"Huh? What do you mean?"

"I've never bottomed before, until last night."

"What? You're kidding me! But…"

"Yeah, I know… all the porn. But they always want me to be the top. You know, the whole big dick thing."

"Speaking of the big dick thing, that is by far the largest thing I have ever had in there. But I'm always up for pushing my physical limits."

"Well, you did a great job. Anyway, Chris and I never got to do that. We only went all the way once, and I topped him. I was going to have him top me the next time, but there was never a next time. I got outed and my parents grounded me, so I couldn't see him anymore. Then I had to escape and come here."

"That's too bad about you and Chris. Do you think you'll ever get back together with him?"

"I don't know. Probably not – at least not anytime soon. He's on the other side of the country and he's still with his boyfriend. They've been together for two years now. So yeah, who knows if I'll ever have that chance? Anyway, I didn't want my first time as a bottom to be with some stranger in a porn scene. When I was in Prague last summer, the producer asked if I would bottom, but I said no. I explained why, and he understood. So… I decided you would be the right one."

"Wow… I'm honored! I mean, seriously… I hope it was okay for you."

Ryan kissed him. "It was wonderful. Even better than I thought it would be." *I can see why Ted had so many repeat clients.*

They lay entwined for a few more minutes in silence. Then Ted said, "Well, we should get up. How 'bout if we take a shower, then I'll whip up a little something to eat?"

Ryan glanced at the alarm clock. It was 8:10. "Oh, and just so you know, I have to be up in Chatsworth for a shoot at 10:30. So I need to be out of here by 9:15 at the latest."

"Well then, you go ahead and shower and I'll cook. I can take my shower later."

"Sounds good."

"Oh, and… I hope I didn't wear you out too much." Ted smiled.

Ryan smiled back. "I should be okay, although it probably won't be my biggest cum shot."

"Oh, to be young again. Anyway, I'll get busy."

Ryan wasted no time in the shower. He emerged from the bedroom 20 minutes later, wearing the same nice clothes he wore to the restaurant yesterday. As he headed toward the kitchen, he smelled the tantalizing aroma of sizzling bacon. When he entered the kitchen, he spotted six thick slices of peppered bacon drying on a bed of paper towels. Ted was pouring a whipped egg mixture into the skillet.

"That smells amazing."

"Thanks. What would you like in your omelet?"

"Whatever you're having. There's nothing I don't like."

"Okay, then… diced ham, black olives, mushrooms, roasted red peppers… and cheese, of course."

"Sounds wonderful."

Ryan looked around. He saw two plates on the counter with a small assortment of fruit – strawberries, blueberries, and cubed cantaloupe. *This was 'whipping up a little something?'*

As the eggs congealed in the skillet, Ted frantically chopped up the olives, mushrooms, and peppers. Then he added half of the mixture and a generous handful of cheese onto the omelet and let it cook while he whipped up another three eggs. He rolled the omelet up and transferred it to one of the plates. Then he poured the second egg mixture into the skillet. While it congealed, he transferred three slices of bacon to each plate. Then the toaster popped up with two slices of whole-grain toast, which he sliced diagonally and added to the plates. He added the ingredients to the second omelet, then took three quick steps over to the fridge. He reached into the freezer and pulled out two champagne flutes. He retrieved champagne and orange juice from the refrigerator and poured mimosas, then set them on the table. Then he rolled up the second omelet, added it to a plate, and carried the two plates to the table.

Ryan was impressed with the expertise and efficiency Ted had just displayed. All of this had taken place in less than five minutes. He was a bit taken aback that Ted would go to all this trouble for him.

Ted proudly announced, "brunch is served!"

They sat down. Ted raised his glass in what had become a routine. Ryan raised his and said, "It's my turn. To amazing meals, an amazing 21$^{st}$ birthday celebration, and an amazing friend!" He resisted the temptation to add, 'and an amazing stud machine.'

"Cheers! You're too kind. But I'm glad I could do something nice for you on this momentous occasion."

They remained focused on eating, given their time constraint. At one point, Ryan said, "All this food is delicious. Where did you learn to cook like that?"

"I'm mostly self-taught. I've watched some cooking shows and some videos online. And a lot of trial and error."

"Do you cook for yourself a lot?"

"Yeah, I try not to eat out too much, or eat a lot of pre-processed frozen meals. I cooked for myself at the house, too, but I tried to time it so I wouldn't be in the other guys' way. Most of the time I'd cook up a bunch of food to last several days, then portion it out into containers I could reheat later. Now, it's easier. I have the whole kitchen to myself and I can cook more in real-time."

"Well, you're really good at it."

"Thanks. It's nice to have someone to cook for. It's a nice

change from always cooking for one."

Ryan hoped this meant he'd be invited back occasionally. He said, "Someday, when the time is right and you're ready for it, you'll be a really good husband for some lucky guy."

"Yeah, maybe someday. I still have a lot of shit to work through."

Neither of them said anything, not wanting the topic of conversation to turn dark on an otherwise wonderful morning.

Finally, Ted spoke. "My company has very good benefits, including mental health counseling. I'm thinking about checking that out."

"Yeah, maybe it will help. Couldn't hurt."

"We'll see how it goes."

As they neared the end of their meal, Ted said, "I'd offer you another mimosa, but I know you have to drive across town."

"Yeah, definitely not. I probably shouldn't have drunk this. It was delicious, though."

Ryan knew this wasn't the right time to bring up how much drinking Ted seemed to be doing. Maybe it will work itself out after he gets counseling.

Ted sensed that Ryan had something on his mind but wasn't saying anything. "In case you're wondering, I don't drink this much every day. Usually just a glass of wine with dinner. But I figured this was a celebratory occasion."

"Yeah, I was wondering about that. Just don't let it get out of hand."

"Don't worry."

They finished their food and got up from the table. Ryan helped carry the dirty dishes to the sink. "Well, I hate to eat and run, but I need to get going."

"I know."

They walked to the door.

Ryan said, "This has been fantastic. Everything! The dinner last night, the walk on the beach, the brunch this morning… and… I'm glad we finally got to do what we did."

"Me too."

They hugged.

Then Ted took both of Ryan's hands into his hands. "You know…" He took a deep breath. "You're my best friend in the whole world. Nobody else gives a shit about me."

This left Ryan speechless. Even though it had been over three years since he left Kansas, he wasn't quite ready to shift the title of Best Friend away from Chris. That seemed kind of stupid since they were only in touch occasionally and were no longer a part of each other's day-to-day lives. And Chris had a boyfriend. What could he graciously say at this moment?

"Yeah. We do have a very special friendship. And I care about you a lot."

Ted smiled. They hugged again.

"Well, I've got to head off."

"Yeah, I know."

They kissed.

Ted asked, "Can we get together again soon?"

Ryan smiled. "Sure. I'd like that."

The moment was sweet but it was quickly becoming awkward. Better just go now, Ryan decided.

***

Thankfully, traffic was light for a Saturday morning. Ryan figured he had enough time to make a quick stop at the house to change clothes since it was near the freeway.

At 9:30, Ryan parked in the driveway and hurried into the house.

As he passed the kitchen, Ricky called out, "Well… look what the cat dragged in."

Hal, Darnell, and Ricky emerged from the kitchen. Ryan

wondered what was up.

Darnell said, "Oh, don't mind us. We're just here to observe the 'walk of shame.'"

"What are you talking about? I'm not ashamed of anything. In fact, I'm feeling really good this morning."

Darnell replied, "OOOooo…!!! You must have had quite a night, darling. I can't wait to hear alllll about it."

"In your fantasies. I don't discuss my personal business with others."

Hal said, "Seriously, we were getting a little worried about you. We thought we might have to send out a missing person alert."

"Well, thanks for your concern, but everything is fine. Now, if you'll excuse me, I'm kinda in a hurry."

Ryan hurried into his bedroom, closed the door, and changed into more casual clothes. He emerged from his room three minutes later and headed toward the front door.

Darnell said, "You look like a man on a mission. Where are you off to?"

"I've got a shoot today."

Ricky said, "Well… aren't we in demand?"

Hal said, "Wait a minute… Didn't you have dinner with Ted last night?"

Darnell and Ricky let out exaggerated gasps.

"Yes. He treated me to a very nice dinner at Sailor Sam's. It was amazing!"

Ricky said, "And apparently he treated you to dessert afterward."

Darnell added, "Oh, honey. I'm glad you finally got what you've been wanting all these years."

*Really? Was it that obvious to the others?*

Ricky asked, "So… is he a ginger down there, too?"

Ryan said, "Seriously? You guys are a bunch of skanks."

Darnell stepped forward and waved his finger back and forth like a miniature windshield wiper. "Oh, no, no, no! Let's examine what we know, shall we? *You're* the one who stayed out all night with another man, and now *you're* heading off to shoot pornography. Now, who's the skank?"

"Yeah, right. Let he who is without sin cast the first stone. We had quite a bit of wine, so I didn't want to drive home and get a DUI. You don't know what we did or didn't do last night."

Darnell said, "Yes, so we can only assume…"

Ricky said, "So, what *did* you do?"

Ryan couldn't believe he was being subjected to this. Then he had an idea. He leaned forward and said in a hushed voice, "Okay. So, you really wanna know?" He flashed an I'm-going-to-tell-you-a-secret grin and paused for dramatic effect. Darnell, Ricky, and Hal eagerly awaited what he would say next.

"We went to this huuuuuge all-night orgy. There were at least 50 guys there. It was incredible!"

They stood speechless. Ryan spun on his heels and hurried out the door. "Later, bitches!"

Ryan got in his car, drove back to the freeway, then headed north to Chatsworth, the epicenter of the San Fernando Valley's porn industry. As he drove, he replayed everything that had happened last night and this morning. It was all wonderful, but it raised questions.

*Why did Ted spend so much money on me? Is he really that flush with cash? Or was it just to get me in bed?*

*Was he interested in me all this time, but he didn't think he should let it happen?*

*He said he wants to get together again. Is it just to hang out together? Is it for sex? Or is it dating?*

*He keeps saying he doesn't want a relationship with anybody. Is that true, or is that a nice way of saying he doesn't want a relationship with me?*

*Or does he want a relationship with me? Why would he treat me to such an extravagant, romantic evening if he wasn't interested in me?*

*Is that something you do for someone who's just a friend?*

*Maybe it's a 'friends with benefits' thing. Do I want that?*

*Do I want a relationship with him? I've always been attracted to him, but maybe that was more physical. He has some emotional issues he keeps pushing down. And now it looks like he might have a drinking problem.*

*Am I overthinking this?*

Ryan pulled into the parking lot of the studio. He decided it was probably best just to see how things played out in the weeks ahead. They could talk if and when they needed to.

For now, he needed to stay focused on the job at hand.

# The Bar Scene

Saturday, October 16, 2010

Ryan arrived home after shooting his scene and eating dinner. On his bedroom door, there was a sticky note that read:

> Come see me
> – Ricky

Ryan expected to be either teased or questioned more about last night. If Ricky believed they had gone to an orgy, he probably wanted to know why he wasn't invited. Ryan didn't think anyone actually believed his fib, but who knows?

Ryan knocked on Ricky's door, and Ricky yelled, "Come in."

Ryan entered and said, "Hey, man, what's up?"

"Dude! Hey, you're 21 now. Let's go out tonight and let me show you the bars. Drinks are on me!"

"I'm really tired. Can we do it another time?" Ryan wasn't particularly excited about doing it at all.

"Aw, c'mon man! It's your birthday weekend. You can sleep in tomorrow."

Ryan wasn't convinced.

Ricky said, "You can take a disco nap for a couple of hours. I'll come by and get you at ten."

"What's a disco nap?" Ryan couldn't imagine how he could sleep if there was dance music playing.

"It means you take a nap earlier in the evening so you can stay out later. Stuff doesn't start happening until at least eleven."

"Oh, all right. But only for an hour or so. I don't want to stay out all night."

"Cool, man. I'll come to get you at ten." Ricky knew that once Ryan got out there, he'd want to party all night.

***

At 10:00 sharp, Ricky knocked on Ryan's door. Ryan was wearing the same red polo shirt, blue jeans, and running shoes he had worn to the studio. Ricky was wearing a tank top and shorts, which showed his muscular chest and round buns to good advantage. The tank top had 'BED ROMANCE' written in bold letters, a play on Lady Gaga's recent hit.

Ryan realized he had no idea what guys wore to gay bars in WeHo on a Saturday night. He asked, "Uh… do I look okay?"

Ricky's expression conveyed, 'Not really.' He said, "It's a little plain. Do you have, like, a T-shirt that fits kinda tight? Maybe a black one?"

Ryan mentally scanned his wardrobe. "I've got dark blue."

Ricky said, "That'll do."

Ryan went back into his room and put his dark blue T-shirt on. It wasn't as form-fitting as Ricky's tank top, but he didn't have the muscular definition that Ricky had. Oh, well, he wasn't going there to hook up. It would be a learning experience.

Ricky drove them to a stretch of Santa Monica Boulevard that seemed to be the nexus of gay nightlife. He somehow found a parking spot on a side street. He led Ryan to the Temple, which he said was one of the most famous gay bars anywhere. As they approached the club, there was a line to get in. Fortunately, they only had to wait about ten minutes. Ricky said if they had arrived at midnight, they would have waited for a half-hour or more.

Ricky gave Ryan a quick tour. "This place is amazing. The food is great if you ever come here to eat." There was a restaurant area with booths and tables, a dance floor, and an outdoor patio. The place was packed. On the throbbing dance floor, techno music blasted from the speakers and go-go boys danced on elevated perches. Ryan plugged his ears with his fingers. It looked dorky, but he didn't care. Ricky led Ryan out to the patio bar and said, "What can I get you?"

"I don't know. What's good here?"

"Everything! This is one of the best bars in town."

"That's not very helpful. What are you having?"

"Hmmm… It's getting close to Halloween. I'm going to try their special pumpkin spice martini."

"That sounds disgusting. What else is there?"

"Maybe try a mojito."

"What's that?"

"It's like lime and mint and rum, I think. It's refreshing."

"Sounds good."

"Okay. Stay here. I'll be right back." Ricky nudged his way through the crowd and elbowed up to the bar.

Standing alone, Ryan felt conspicuous. At 6' 6", he could easily scan the crowd, and the crowd could easily see him. Although he couldn't tell for sure, he felt like he was being pointed out.

About ten minutes later, Ricky returned with their drinks. Ryan took a sip of the mojito and liked it. "So, how's the pumpkin spice martini?"

"Pretty good. You want a sip?"

"No thanks."

Ricky spotted a couple of guys he knew and waved them over. He introduced Ryan to Jorge and Carlo. They seemed upbeat and friendly. Ryan got the impression that if he was a friend of Ricky's, he was now a friend of theirs. He wasn't sure if they were a couple or just buddies. After the obligatory 'hey, whatcha been up to?' small talk, Carlo asked Ryan, "So, how do you know Ricky?"

"We live in the same house."

"Oh, cool. I've been there a couple of times. Nice place. I

thought maybe you did a movie together or something."

Ryan shook his head, unsure of what to say. They did a couple of scenes together in *The Boys of Breckenridge*. But he was first and foremost Ricky's housemate, and he preferred to leave it at that.

Jorge spoke up. "But you do porn, don't you? I'm pretty sure I've seen you."

"Well, actually, yes I have." There was no use denying it. He had, and they knew it. They acted like it was no big deal. They were already friends with Ricky, after all. Are they, or were they, in the business too? He wasn't going to ask. He realized that even though he was wearing clothes now, they had seen him naked. And they could be thinking about that right now. That made him more uncomfortable.

He snapped back into the present. Jorge, Carlo, and Ricky were joking about something else. Ryan didn't have much to add to the conversation, so he just stood and sipped his drink.

A few minutes later, a guy who had consumed enough alcohol to lose all sense of decorum tapped Ryan on the shoulder and said, "Hey, you're Luke Loadstar, aren't you?" He turned to the other three and said, "Oh, hey, sorry to interrupt," although clearly, he was not.

This was the first time Ryan had been identified by his porn name in public, so he was caught off-guard. "Uh, yeah…"

"Oh, wow, man, you're like my favorite porn star! That cock of yours is unbelievable! That scene you did in *Covet Thy Neighbor's Ass* was so fucking hot! Hey, can I get a picture with you?" Without waiting for a response, he handed his phone to Ricky and said, "Take a picture of us." He pressed himself against Ryan's side and put his arm around his waist.

Ricky said, "Okay, smile!" Ryan tried his best to force an obligatory smile.

The guy took his phone back from Ricky and said, "Wait a minute. You're… wait, don't tell me… oh yeah, Juan Knight." He turned back to Ryan and pulled him a step away from the others. He leaned closer and said in a lowered voice, "Uh… I know this is kind of bold, but I'm going to ask anyway. Would you come home with me tonight?"

"No."

"I've never had a dick as big as yours, but I'd love to try."

"I said no."

"Oh, come on. It'll be fun. I'll even pay you."

"NO! Now if you'll excuse me, I want to get back to my friends." Ryan turned his back on the guy and moved closer to Ricky, Jorge, and Carlo.

"Pleeeease??? I'll let you bareback me if you promise to pull out."

Ricky, Jorge, and Carlo glared at him. Ricky said, "Go away."

The guy didn't move. He looked shocked that anyone would say that to him. For a few tense seconds, Ricky, Jorge, and Carlo stared down the drunk guy. Ryan feared a fight was going to break out.

Jorge commanded, "You heard him. Get the fuck outta here. NOW."

The drunk guy turned and disappeared into the crowd.

Carlo diffused the tension by turning to Ricky. "Gurrrl, you just got upstaged. Looks like there's a new star in town."

Ricky said, "Eh… the tops always get all the love."

Ryan needed a change of scenery. "Guys, where's the restroom?"

Ricky replied, "On the other side of the dance floor, to the right."

"Okay. Be right back."

Ryan went back inside and weaved his way through the crowd along the right side of the dance floor. Every five or ten seconds, someone would turn and look at him and then whisper something to someone else.

He entered the restroom and discovered there were no dividers between the urinals. The walls and ceilings were covered with mirrors. He walked to the farthest urinal, unzipped, pulled it out, and started to pee.

Another guy entered a few seconds later and strode up to the urinal next to him. Out of the corner of his eye, Ryan could see the guy had pulled his dick out, but he didn't hear any pee splashing into the urinal. He kept his gaze focused on the mirrored wall immediately in front of him and turned his body slightly away. He finished as quickly as he could.

He worked his way through the crowd, past more looks of recognition. He returned to the patio, but Ricky, Jorge, and Carlo had moved from the spot where he left them. He looked around and spotted them at the bar. After he navigated around the clusters of people and reached the bar, Ricky turned around. He had a pumpkin spice martini in one hand and a mojito in the other. Jorge and Carlo turned around with fresh drinks in their hands, too. Ricky handed him the mojito and said, "Cheers!"

Ryan said, "Thanks, man, but I didn't want another one."

"I thought you liked it."

"I did, but–"

"Don't worry, man, I can afford it. It's your birthday! Celebrate!"

They moved a few steps away from the bar. Jorge eyed each of their drinks, then asked Carlo, "Okay, so which one of those is the girliest drink?"

Carlo looked at them both and said, "Definitely the pumpkin spice martini. Dude, pumpkin spice is for suburban rich bitches at Starbucks."

Jorge said, "On the other hand, a mojito in a gay bar? They should call it a Homojito."

Everyone chuckled.

Someone Carlo knew approached him, so he excused himself and stepped away.

Ryan turned to Ricky and asked, "So does that kind of stuff happen to you?"

"You mean getting recognized? Yeah. Don't worry, you get

used to it after a while. Comes with the territory."

Jorge said, "The only thing worse than getting recognized is *not* getting recognized."

Ricky laughed and fist-bumped Jorge.

Ryan asked, "Doesn't it bother you?"

"Not really. Think of it this way. They are your adoring fans. They're the ones who buy the movies you make so you can get paid. To them, seeing a porn star in person is like a fantasy come to life."

"Yeah, but do they always try to get you to go home with them?"

"Not always, but sometimes."

Jorge said, "Yeah, but the difference is, she says yes."

"Bitch."

"Gurrrl, you know it's true." Jorge turned to Ryan. "We don't call her Juan Knight Stand for nothin'."

"Shut! Up! Don't be hatin'." Ricky turned back to Ryan. "They're not always drunk and obnoxious like that guy was. Usually, they're pretty nice. Anyway, I don't mind. You've got to be nice to your fans."

Carlo returned.

Ryan finished his drink and said to Ricky, "Listen, I'm really tired. Can we go home?"

"Go home? We're just getting started! Lemme get you a Red Bull. Wait, I know! Let's head over to the dance floor, A little dancing will pick you up!"

Ryan dreaded the thought of the loud, pounding music assaulting his eardrums and the knowing eyes staring at him and undressing him. "No, thanks. Seriously, I'm fading fast."

Carlo said, "You wanna tweak?"

Ryan looked puzzled. "What do you mean?"

Carlo gave him a look that said, 'Come on, you know what I mean.'

Ryan figured it out. "Oh, no. No. No thanks."

Ricky said, "I'll take some if you're offering."

They glanced around.

Ryan said, "I'm outta here. Thanks for the drinks." He glanced at Carlo and Jorge. "Nice to meet you." Then he turned and made his way through the bar to the front door as fast as he could.

Once he was out on the sidewalk, he turned and started walking west. He passed another bar and a couple of restaurants and coffee shops with sidewalk seating. They were all full of guys who were checking out everyone who walked by. WeHo was in full swing on Saturday night.

Ryan considered walking all the way home but decided to call an Uber instead.

***

Fifteen minutes later, an Uber car pulled up to Ryan and he got in. He glanced in the rear-view mirror as he gave his address to the driver. The eyes looked familiar.

Ryan started to give the driver directions, but he cut him off. "Ryan, if that's the same house you lived in three years ago, I know exactly where it is."

"Oh my God… Payton?"

"Yeah."

The ride suddenly turned awkward. Payton and Ryan dated for three months during their senior year of high school. That ended badly when Payton wanted their relationship to become physical, forcing Ryan to disclose that he starred in porn movies. Payton spread that news all over school. Thankfully, there was only a month to go before the school year ended. They hadn't seen each other since.

They rode in silence for a couple of minutes. Ryan thought, *This is stupid. We can be civil with each other. It's been three years, after all. Water under the bridge.* He asked, "So, how have you been?"

"Okay, I guess. I got an office job at an insurance company. I'm studying to become an agent. I'm doing this to pull in a little extra money."

"Oh, cool."

"And how about you?"

"I'm going to UCLA. I'm a junior now."

There was a pause for about 15 seconds. Then Payton asked, "Are you still doing porn?"

"Yep. It's how I'm paying for school."

More silence. Ryan wondered, *If I wasn't, would he suggest we try dating again? No thanks, not interested.*

Payton said, "Hey, look. I want to apologize for what I did. I mean, I wish you had told me about what you do before we got to that point, but I shouldn't have told everyone at school about it. That was just wrong."

"That's okay. Don't worry about it. You're right, I probably should have told you sooner. But it's like, how do you bring that up, you know? I was new to it back then, so I didn't know what to do."

"I guess I was just kind of shocked by it. But it wouldn't bother me now."

*Oh no, here it comes. Please, don't...*

Payton turned the corner onto Ryan's street. *It's now or never,* he thought. *Nothing ventured, nothing gained.* "So, uh... I was wondering... Do you think maybe I could come in and we could pick up where we left off? You know, finish what we started?"

"No. I'm exhausted."

Payton pulled up to the curb in front of Ryan's house. "Oh, come on. Please? You have the most amazing cock I've ever seen. At the time, I wasn't even sure I could handle it, but now, I'm pretty sure I can. Anyway, I'd love to find out!"

"NO." Ryan opened the door, got out, and slammed the door behind him.

Payton rolled down the front passenger side window. "I'll refund the charge for the ride!"

Ryan scampered up the steps to his house without looking back.

# So Much to Be Thankful For

Thursday, November 25, 2010

This was Ryan's fourth Thanksgiving dinner with his housemates. Darnell and Ricky were living in the house when Ryan arrived in late July 2007, and they were still here. Although Ted had moved out in June after he graduated, Hal invited him back for this occasion. Mykel was a new addition, having replaced Ted. And this year's dinner was augmented by Brent, who had been dating Hal for six months now.

Ryan looked at Ted and wondered what he was feeling. Did he miss living here? Was he happy in his new life as a working man with a fashionable apartment?

Ryan looked at Mykel. He seemed disengaged, like he was physically present but mentally absorbed in something else. Mykel looked at Ted a lot, but Ryan couldn't tell from his facial expressions what he was thinking. He was looking at Hal a lot, too.

There were some weird dynamics at the table, lurking just beneath the surface. Ryan couldn't figure it out. He could tell Darnell was sensing it too.

After dinner, people started clearing the table, loading the dishwasher, and putting away leftovers. With seven people, the kitchen was a bit crowded and people were getting in each other's way. Mykel pulled Ted aside and whispered, "May I speak to you outside for a few minutes?"

Mykel opened the sliding glass door, and he and Ted stepped onto the patio. Mykel led Ted to a couple of lounge chairs near the far side of the pool. They sat down on the sides of the chairs, facing each other.

Mykel said, "I don't know whether Hal or anyone else mentioned this to you, but I'm a medium."

Ted looked a Mykel quizzically.

"A medium is someone who can communicate with the spirits of those who have passed before us."

"Yeah, I've heard of that. I'm not sure whether I believe it, but whatever."

"Okay, well… There's someone here who has a message for you. You can take it or leave it, as you see fit. Would you like to hear it? If you'd rather not, it's okay. No harm, no foul."

"Yeah, sure. Why not? Who is it?"

Mykel took a deep breath. "It's Alex."

Ted wasn't sure what to feel. Delighted? Sad? Afraid? Suspicious? What would Alex have to say? Did he want to hear it? Yet, he was skeptical. Ted had never met Mykel before today, so how could Mykel know about Alex? Maybe Ryan or Hal or one of the other guys told him about Alex.

"Ask him what his middle name was."

Mykel looked beyond Ted's right shoulder to something only he could see. "Yiannis. It's the Greek equivalent of John."

He got that right. "And what's my sister's name?"

Mykel paused while he waited to hear from Alex. Then he smirked. "He says you don't have a sister."

"Okay, I'm a believer. So… how is he?"

"He's fine. He says he's very proud of you for graduating from college and getting your Masters." Ted smiled. Mykel paused as he listened some more. "And he says he loves your new apartment. Very tasteful."

"He can actually see that? How can he see if spirits don't have physical eyes?"

"I don't know, but they can. He's watching us and listening to us now."

"So… does he follow me around everywhere?"

"Not all the time. He comes and goes. He has other loved ones he checks in on, and he spends some of his time with other spirits in their world. But he visits you a lot."

Ted smiled. He thought of Alex every single day. It was comforting to know that Alex thought of him too. "Will you tell him I love him and I miss him?"

"He knows. But he says it's nice to hear. Anyway, one of the things he wants to tell you is, you need to move on. You shouldn't spend the rest of your life mourning him."

"I guess, but I've never met anyone who comes close to Alex."

"He says thanks and that's very kind, but you can't look for another Alex. You have to look for someone who's special in his own way."

"Yeah, but… I don't know how to say this, but with him, I felt like I had found my soul mate. I know, that sounds corny, but it's like I could tell we were meant to be with each other at a deep, spiritual level. I've met some nice guys, but I've never connected with any of them on that level. Well, I guess I connect with Ryan to some extent."

Mykel listened while Alex told him something, then chuckled. "He said that was quite a connection you had with Ryan when he turned 21."

"OH MY GOD… he saw that???"

"Yep. He said it was totally hot. He wished he could have been there … physically, that is. He was there, spiritually."

Ted thought, *Okay, this is getting weird. A three-way with Alex and Ryan? Maybe that would be hot, but we would never have done such a thing. And Alex can watch me have sex? Will I think of that every time I have sex again?* Ted tried to shake those thoughts out of his head. "I think that's part of what's holding me back. It's like, if I get emotionally involved with someone else, I feel like I'm cheating on him. Especially now that I know he can see it."

"But you're not. You're here on earth, and he's not. And there's no reason you shouldn't enjoy your time on earth. You've been given that gift – don't waste it."

Ted looked like he was still uncomfortable about all this.

Mykel said, "Besides, he's giving you permission. He wants you to. He doesn't want you to spend the rest of your life being a lonely widow."

Ted was still processing all this new information, wondering how to respond.

Mykel continued. "He says he'll be waiting to greet you when your time comes and you cross over. He says you are soul twins. You have lived lives together before, and you probably will again. And you will be together in the spirit world, in between your physical lives."

"Are you sure?"

"That's what he's telling me. And that's how I understand it works. See, on the other side, souls are part of 'soul clusters' of six or eight souls, give or take. It's kind of like the families we have on earth. A few of the people you meet here on earth are part of your cluster. They may be your parents, children, siblings, spouse, or anyone else who's significant. It's like you and some of the others in your cluster get together and decide to choose bodies whose lives might intersect with one another."

"So Alex is in my cluster?"

"He says yes."

"Who else?"

Mykel paused. "He's not saying. But you know other souls besides those who are in your cluster. You know how once in a while you meet someone for the first time, but you get the feeling you've met them before?" Ted nodded. "That's probably either someone from your cluster or someone you've known in a previous life."

Ted said, "But getting back to me and Alex. So you're saying our souls planned that we would meet each other in the Marines and fall in love?"

Mykel paused as he listened to Alex. "That was one possibility."

"But then, him getting killed – was that part of the plan too?"

"Not necessarily. Souls can't predict what's going to happen to them during their lives on earth. There are many possible outcomes and many variables. Human beings have free choice. Every decision you make alters your path. And decisions others make often impact your path. Souls can't accurately see the future, but they see multiple possible outcomes. It's like once you start walking down a road, every time you get to a fork in the road you can choose to go one way or the other. So the future is unwritten."

"So him getting killed was just one possible outcome."

"That's right. Even you two meeting at the place and time you did was just one possible outcome. But the most important thing to remember is that even though he got killed and you got separated in this lifetime, in the big picture, you'll be together again. Your souls have known each other for many millennia. And in a way, because he comes and spends time with you, you're together like you are right now."

Ted's mind was swimming. "Wow. This is a lot to take in."

"Yeah, I know. I can recommend a couple of good books on the topic of what happens to your soul between lives. Anyway, there are a couple more things Alex wants to tell you. Then we'd better get back to the party. First, he says Ryan is someone special. He has a role to play in your life. Stay in touch with him, even as you move around the world. And second, you need to cut back on your drinking."

"Oh. Okay."

"And that's it. Alex says goodbye for now."

"Tell him I love him."

Mykel smiled. "He loves you too." Mykel paused. "Shall we go back in?"

"You go. I need a few minutes to myself."

"Okay."

"And… thank you. Thank you so much. You have no idea how much this means."

They stood up and hugged. Then Mykel went back inside.

# Black is the New Black

Saturday, December 18, 2010

Hal received an invitation to a holiday party hosted by an old friend named Charlie Kresler. He asked Charlie if he could extend the invitation to Brent and a couple of the guys from his house, and Charlie was happy to oblige.

Charlie lived with his partner of 18 years, Stuart, in a fashionable home in the Silver Lake neighborhood. As Hal drove the 45-minute drive to Charlie and Stuart's house, Ryan asked, "So, how do you know this guy?"

Hal said, "We met back in the 80s. He was in the business too. He and I did a few scenes together. We've stayed in touch off and on over the years."

Ricky asked, "What was his porn name?"

Hal replied, "Woody Long. Yeah, I know – everybody groan in unison. It was accurate, though."

Ricky said, "Woody Long? Are you kidding me? Oh man, that dude was legendary! I've seen a couple of his videos."

"Yeah, he was quite a big star back in those days. And I do mean *big*."

"No shit!" Ricky thought for a second. "So, do you know if he and his partner are… open?"

Ryan said, "Jesus, dude. You are the biggest size queen."

"And?"

Hal said, "I don't know. But you might want to wait until you meet him. I mean, he's a great guy and everything, but… let's just say the years haven't been kind to him."

"As long as his dick hasn't shrunk."

Brent said, "Moving on… What is he doing now?"

"He's an interior designer. And it's *designer*, not decorator, just so you don't commit that faux pas. When he was phasing out of being a performer, he did set design for Eagle Studios for a while. Now, he designs interiors for wealthy people's homes. I understand he's developed quite a clientele."

Ryan asked, "What does Stuart do?"

"I believe he's an architect. He designs plans for custom homes."

Brent said, "That works out well. One designs the home itself, then the other designs the interior."

Hal said, "I haven't been to their home in about four years. The last time I was there, it was pretty fabulous. Charlie told me he completely redid their interior a couple of years ago, so I can't wait to see what it looks like now."

Ryan said, "You know, if he used to do set design for adult movies, maybe you could get him to design sets for some of your movies."

Hal said, "Bingo! Yes, I fully intend to mention that to him tonight. If he's interested, we'll set up a meeting soon."

Brent said, "If he's gotten to the point where he's being hired by the elite, he might be too expensive for you."

"Yeah, probably, but it never hurts to ask."

Ricky said, "Maybe I could help you negotiate lower rates."

Hal sighed and said, "Down, boy."

They entered the neighborhood where Charlie and Stuart lived. Narrow, curvy roads snaked around the hilly terrain. The houses were packed tightly and close to the street. There were very few options for on-street parking, but Hal found a spot he could squeeze into a couple of doors down from Charlie and Stuart's house.

As they approached the modern, stylish house, Hal turned to the others and said, "A word of warning: Don't drink from a punchbowl or eat anything that looks homemade until you've determined what may or may not be in it. And it's okay to ask. Just say, 'Is there anything in this?' They'll know what you mean."

Hal rang the doorbell. A few seconds later, Stuart answered and welcomed the four guys into his home. Stuart and Hal hugged. Stuart said, "It's so nice to see you again! You're looking great."

"Thanks! You too! And thank you for inviting us. Guys, this is Stuart. Stuart, this is my boyfriend Brent, and these are two of my housemates, Ricky and Ryan." Everyone shook hands.

A small white dog ran up to Stuart and barked at the strangers invading his home. He was a Pomeranian, with long, straight hair that was as pure white as the driven snow. He looked like a small white poof ball with eyes. Stuart scooped the dog up into his arms. "And this is Phuqueles. It's spelled P-H-U-Q-U-E-L-E-S, but it's pronounced 'Fuckles'." Hal, Brent, Ricky, and Ryan were speechless. Stuart rolled his eyes. "I know. Charlie insisted on naming him that. Don't worry, he'll calm down after 30 seconds."

Stuart led them down a short hall toward the main living area. Hal, Brent, Ryan, and Ricky couldn't wait to see how fabulous a home decorated by one of Beverly Hills' most celebrated interior designers would be.

When they arrived in the great room, they were aghast. Every inch of surface area was solid black. Black walls, black ceiling, black carpet, black curtains, and black furniture. Hal looked up to the top of the tall wall along the back of the house. On previous visits, there had been a row of small square windows near the ceiling to let in the natural light. They were blocked with precisely cut wood squares that were painted black.

In contrast to the completely black surroundings, a tall white artificial Christmas tree stood near one corner. It was adorned with strings of twinkling white LED lights, silvery ornaments, and white ribbon garlands. All the presents under the tree were wrapped with white paper, ribbons, and bows. Hanging above the tree was a small, slowly rotating disco ball illuminated by a spotlight mounted on the ceiling.

Around the walls, a few modern paintings featuring geometric designs and bold colors were mounted within garish, oversized gold-painted frames. Each piece was illuminated by a strategically placed spotlight on the ceiling.

Phuqueles was no longer concerned with the new humans in his home, so Stuart lowered him to the floor. He scampered toward the kitchen in search of accidentally dropped food items. Stuart said, "There are all sorts of goodies in the kitchen. Help yourself!" He excused himself and headed to the kitchen.

Ryan whispered, "I'm surprised they don't have a black dog. If Phuqueles sheds, there would be white dog hair all over the place."

Brent whispered back, "You'd never see him. They would constantly be tripping on him or sitting on him."

Eight guests had already arrived. Some were mingling in the kitchen near the food, and a few were standing in a cluster near the Christmas tree, talking. As Ryan, Ricky, Hal, and Brent scanned the group standing near the tree, they noticed a slender, almost anorexic man who appeared to be the center of the conversation. He wore a loose-fitting striped shirt that was unbuttoned down to his navel, revealing a dense forest of salt-and-pepper chest hair. He was holding a pink martini in one hand. His other hand, palm up, held a cigarette casually dangling from his fingers, which never strayed more than a few inches from his head. Between sentences, he alternated sips on his martini and drags on his cigarette. His longish hair was streaked with blond and light brown highlights in an attempt to cover the gray hairs that were slowly overtaking his head. His coif was held firmly in place with a generous layer of product.

Ricky whispered into Ryan's ear, "If that cigarette gets any closer to his hair, it will start a fire." Brent heard that and chuckled. Hal shot Ricky a stern glance.

One of the other guests shifted her position slightly, and this man's most striking feature came into view. His skin-tight jeans and apparent lack of underwear accentuated a massive mound that ran from his crotch down one pant leg, halfway to his knee. It was so prominently featured that no one who glanced in his general direction could avoid noticing it.

Ryan was taken aback. He always wore underwear and loose-fitting pants to avoid calling attention to his endowment. He glanced at Ricky. Ricky's eyes were wide-open and, for the first time Ryan could remember, he was speechless.

Hal led Brent, Ryan, and Ricky toward the small group. When Charlie saw Hal, he said to the others, "Will you excuse me for a moment?" Then he took a few steps forward to greet Hal. "Darling! So great to see you! You look *fabulous*!" Once they were within a few inches of each other, Charlie said, "Mwah! Mwah!" to each side of Hal's face.

Hal said, "Charlie, I'd like you to meet my boyfriend Brent…"

Charlie transferred his cigarette to the space between the third finger and pinky of his martini hand, then shook Brent's hand. "Delighted! And congratulations on getting this one to settle down!" He nodded toward Hal.

Brent said, "I am the lucky one."

Hal said, "And these are two of the guys who live in my house now – Ricky and Ryan."

Charlie shook both of their hands and gave them a look that indicated he recognized them from their videos.

Ryan said, "This is quite a place you have here. I've never seen anything quite like it."

Charlie took that as a compliment. "Thank you. I chose this theme to honor and celebrate our first Black president, Barack Obama."

Ryan and Brent caught each other's eye. It was all they could do to not crack up.

Charlie took a sip of his martini and said, "After everyone has arrived and things settle down a bit, I'll take you on a tour. In the meantime, help yourselves in the kitchen." He turned and went back to the group he had been chatting with.

The four guys headed toward the kitchen. Ryan said, just loud enough for the four of them to hear, "I wonder if we'll need flashlights for the tour."

Brent said, "I wonder if their bedroom is completely black."

Ricky said, "I certainly intend to find out."

Hal shook his head. "Behave yourselves. Geez, I can't take you anywhere."

In the kitchen, they discovered a lavish spread of everything from shrimp with cocktail sauce to festive Christmas cookies. The kitchen was, thankfully, a little less dark. The oven, microwave, refrigerator, and dishwasher were all black, but the cabinets and the kitchen table and chairs were dark brown wood, and the granite countertop was marbled with various shades of lighter and darker brown. The room was better illuminated than the rest of the house.

Ryan spotted a platter of delicious-looking brownies. He started to reach for one, and Hal said, "Uh-uh. Remember what I told you."

"You mean there are drugs in the brownies?"

"I wouldn't be surprised. Better ask Stuart."

Ryan walked over to Stuart and asked, "Those brownies look delicious. But I was wondering…"

"Yes, they're fortified."

"With…?"

"Pot. And if you don't wish to partake, you should also stay away from the punch bowl."

"Is there alcohol in it? I'm 21 now."

"No, Ecstacy. There's bourbon in those bourbon balls – lots. Everything else is safe for general consumption."

"Okay, thanks."

Ryan glanced back at the plate of brownies. *What a shame – they look delicious.* He saw Ricky take a couple of them. He walked over to Ricky and whispered, "Uh, there's pot in those."

"Oh, good. I was hoping so."

More guests arrived. Ryan, who was naturally shy around new

people, did his best to mingle. He didn't say much. It appeared to be a mixed crowd – men and women, gay and straight. Nobody seemed to care. He assumed some of the gay men recognized him, but nobody said anything.

Charlie and several other guests had been smoking in the house, so the air was imbued with the stench of cigarette smoke. Ryan decided to step out onto the back balcony for a breath of fresh air. About ten feet away, he spotted Charlie, Hal, and Ricky standing in a small cluster. Hal was engaging Charlie in what looked like a serious discussion. Ryan started walking toward them but stopped when he smelled something odd. It smelled like a cross between burning wood and skunk. As he watched a few seconds longer, he could see they were passing around a joint. He turned and went back into the house. He found Brent, who was chatting with a few people about his career in the film industry. At one point, someone asked Ryan what he did. Rather than reveal he performed in adult movies, he said, "I'm a student at UCLA." A couple of the others had gone there, so they conversed about that.

Ryan was ready to leave, but his departure was dependent upon when the others wanted to go. He looked around. He didn't see Ricky anywhere. Maybe he had gone to the bathroom. Hal was in the kitchen getting another drink and chatting with Stuart. Ryan didn't see Charlie either.

A few minutes later, Hal joined the group with Brent and Ryan, a fresh cocktail in hand. Hal seemed unusually smiley and happy – even a bit giddy. Brent sniffed and frowned. He pulled Hal off to the side and asked, "Are you going to be okay to drive home?"

"Of course! I haven't had that much."

"I think maybe I should drive."

Hal didn't want to start a scene with his boyfriend, so he said, "Okay, if that would make you feel better."

"It would."

Ryan wandered back into the kitchen. He already had plenty to eat, but grazing was the best diversion available. He had eaten several bourbon balls and drank a couple of Captain and Cokes, so he figured he shouldn't have any more alcohol. He reached into a cooler and found a can of Dr Pepper. The shrimp was all gone, sadly, so he munched on some veggies from the veggie tray. A few minutes later, he gave in to temptation. He ate one of the brownies.

After ten minutes had passed, Hal wandered in. "Are you about ready?"

Ryan didn't want to come across as too eager, so he paused and said, "Yeah, I guess so."

"Let me round up the others, then we should say our goodbyes and thank our hosts."

Ryan walked back into the great room. Ricky had returned from wherever he had been. Hal and Brent walked up to him and asked him if he was ready to leave.

They said thank you and goodbye to Stuart and Charlie. As Charlie shook Ryan's hand, he winked and said, "Keep up the good work."

Hal handed his car keys to Brent, who sat down in the driver's seat. Once they were on their way, Hal said, "I had a chance to talk to Charlie about our business venture. He seemed interested. I'm going to have lunch with him after the holidays to go over more of the details. But I think he's in."

Ricky said, "Oh, he was in, all right."

Ryan said, "Are you serious?"

"Absolutely. And I can confirm that, yes, their master bedroom is completely black."

Ryan sighed. "You are such a whore."

"Hey, I figured the greatest top of all time should have a chance to hook up with the greatest bottom of all time." He turned to Ryan. "Nothing personal."

"Oh, please. It isn't a contest."

"It isn't?"

Nobody said anything. Ryan, Hal, and Brent wanted to discuss anything else – anything at all – but nobody could think of a different topic. Hal and Ricky were a bit tipsy, and Ryan was starting to feel a strange new sensation as a result of eating the pot-infused brownie. Brent seemed annoyed.

Ricky said, "You know what, Hal? Maybe you could convince Charlie to come out of retirement and do a movie for you. You could call it, *The Return of Woody Long*. I'll bet you'd sell millions!"

Hal said, "I don't think so. His porn days are long gone, and I'm pretty sure he feels that way too. He moved on a long time ago."

"No, I'm serious. He could dye his hair blond again, and with some make-up… besides, nobody's going to be looking at his face anyway."

Ryan said, "Co-starring you, right?"

"I wouldn't turn down the opportunity. Besides, daddy porn is becoming more and more popular."

Brent said, "Moving on…"

# An Ethical Debate

Wednesday, February 9, 2011

Ryan was eating breakfast in the kitchen before heading off to class when Hal walked in. "Hey, Ry."

"Good morning, Hal."

"How's your quarter going?"

"Pretty good so far. I've got a systems architecture class that's kicking my butt, and a couple of programming and app development classes I'm really into. They're taking a lot of time, though."

"Cool. Hey, I want to ask you a favor. And it's okay to say no. Actually, it's a favor for a friend of mine – a guy I knew when I was in college. His name is Emmett Drake. He's a professor in the Philosophy Department and he teaches a class called Introduction to Ethics. It addresses a lot of topics like values, morality, virtue vs. vice, and that kind of thing. A lot of it is in-class discussion. Anyway, he likes to bring in guest speakers from various disciplines to provide perspectives on whatever the topic for that day is. One of the topics he has coming up next week is pornography. And since he knows I'm an attorney in that industry, he asked me if I could recommend someone. Is that something you would be interested in doing?"

Ryan took a bite of his cereal and thought about it for a moment.

"So, what would I talk about? How would it work?"

"Well, it's not like you have to give a speech or anything. Dr. Drake will probably have you say a few words to introduce yourself, like what you're majoring in and why you're doing porn. He'll ask a couple of opening questions to get the discussion started, and that usually results in a pretty lively debate. The students will probably ask a lot of questions. There's a lot of back and forth among the students. You may not say all that much."

"Well, I guess so. Do you know when it is?"

"Next Tuesday at 11:00."

"I'm free then. So yeah, I don't see why not. It'll be different."

"That's for sure. Okay, thanks. I'll let him know. I'll give him your email address and phone number, and he'll get in touch with you. If you think of any questions, don't hesitate to ask him."

***

Tuesday, February 15, 2011

On Tuesday, Ryan arrived at the classroom at 10:45. The previous class hadn't let out yet, so he hung around outside the door and pondered how a discussion among college students about the ethics of pornography might play out. He was confident he could handle whatever came up.

He noticed an attractive woman standing across the hall with a curvaceous figure, blonde blown-out hair, and a bit too much makeup. She was dressed more fashionably than most college kids, and she appeared to be a few years older. Ryan didn't think too much about it, since people of all types went to school there.

At 10:48, the bell rang, the door opened, and the students from the previous class emptied the room. After the traffic cleared, Ryan and the woman across the hall walked in the door. Both of them headed up to the front of the room rather than taking a seat.

The woman looked like she wasn't sure why Ryan was standing in the front of the room with her, but she introduced herself to break the ice. "Hi. I'm Stacy Campbell, better known as Brianna Summers." She extended her hand.

"I'm Ryan Robertson, better known as Luke Loadstar."

A smile of relief crossed her face. "Oh. Are you speaking too?"

"Yeah, that's why I'm here."

"Oh, cool. You look so young, I thought maybe you were a fan and wanted to get a picture with me or something."

"I do go to school here. But yeah, I'm also in the business."

"I don't think I've heard of you yet."

"I do gay porn."

"Okay, well that would explain it." She smiled.

Dr. Drake hustled into the room. He wore a plaid shirt, a festive bow tie that was a poor match for the shirt, and round-rimmed bifocals. He sported a thick, bushy mustache and frizzy, curly, graying hair that was a bit too long for a man his age. He seemed a little wacky, yet professorial. He would be completely out of place in a corporate office setting, but he was exactly what Ryan imagined a philosophy professor should look like.

He took the courier bag he had been toting off his shoulder and placed it on the desk, then turned to his two guests. "Stacy! Wonderful to see you again." They shook hands. "And you must be Ryan." He offered his hand, which Ryan shook.

"Yes, sir."

"Emmett Drake. Nice to meet you. Thank you so much for coming. Here, let me get a couple of chairs for you."

This was a smaller classroom that held about forty chairs with little half-desks for taking notes. He pulled a couple of chairs from the first row up to the front of the room and turned them around to face the class. He turned back to his guests. "Would you prefer that I introduce you using your real name or your nom du porn?"

Stacy answered right away. "Brianna Summers, please."

Ryan hadn't even thought about this. But if he knew any of the students in the class, or if he met them in the future, he would want them to know him as Ryan Robertson, not as Luke Loadstar. So, he answered, "I would prefer my real name, Ryan Robertson."

Stacy turned to him and asked, "Are you sure? Since you're here in your professional capacity, you might think twice about whether you want your real name to get out."

"Thanks, but I'm good with this. I doubt that anyone will remember, anyway."

The room was filling up. Ryan scanned the room to see if he knew anyone. There were a few people he had seen before on campus, but no one from any of his computer science classes.

The bell rang, and the students who had been buried in their screens put their phones down. Stacy and Ryan sat down in their seats, and Professor Drake turned toward the class and spoke.

"Good morning. Our topic for discussion today is pornography. We are fortunate to have two guests who work in the adult entertainment industry, Brianna Summers and Ryan Robertson. Please help me welcome them."

Dr. Drake led the students in a brief round of applause.

"Brianna and Ryan, thank you so much for making time in your busy schedules to be here today. Now, I would like to remind the class that this topic, like many others we discuss, might be controversial to some people. There will be many different opinions expressed. That's perfectly fine as long as they are expressed respectfully and we don't attack others who have different viewpoints. I encourage everyone to remain open to opposing viewpoints and seek to understand why someone else may feel differently than you do. In other words, don't assume you're always right, and don't just dig in your heels and defend your viewpoint automatically. None of us are right 100 percent of the time. Even if you don't change your mind about anything it's good to gain a broader understanding of why others feel differently. Now with that said, I would like to start by asking each of our guests to tell us a little bit about themselves, and in particular, why they chose to become involved in this line of work. Then we'll open the floor to questions and discussion. Brianna, would you please start?"

"Sure. I've been in the business for about six years. I'm under contract with Libertine Studios, one of the largest producers of adult videos in the world. I have three children – a 10-year-old daughter and twin 8-year-old sons. I work in the adult entertainment industry to support myself and my children, and so I can save money for their college. My husband passed away unexpectedly seven years ago, leaving me to provide for my kids on my own. This business enables me to do that better than just about anything else I could do."

Ryan said, "Hello. I'm Ryan. I'm a student here at UCLA. I've been doing gay porn for a little over three years now. I started soon after I turned 18. Like Brianna, I do it for the money. Really, that's what it boils down to. In my case, my parents found out I'm gay after my junior year of high school, and – well, it's a long story, but let's just say I had to leave home quickly. I've been out on my own since the beginning of my senior year in high school. I soon learned I could barely support myself working at a grocery store part-time while I went to school, so I needed to find something that paid a lot better, especially if I wanted to go to college. And this does."

Dr. Drake said, "Thank you both for sharing a bit of your story. So, who would like to get things started?"

There was a brief pause while everyone waited to see if someone else was going to raise their hand first. Then, a couple of people hesitantly raised their hands. Dr. Drake pointed to a woman in the middle of the room and said, "Yes, Jennifer?"

"This question is for Brianna. How do you balance being a single mother and being a porn star? And how do you explain what you do to your kids?"

"Well, it's easier now that they're all in school. Before that, I had to put them in daycare on the days I worked. One good thing about this business is, I only need to do three or four shoots a month. They're usually one day, or maybe two. So, I'm home most of the time.

"As to what I tell them, I just tell them I have a job at a movie studio. At their age, that's all they need to know. They're too young for detailed discussions about sex, let alone pornography. That's not even on their radar yet. When they get older and I think they're ready for it, I'll explain it to them. But my goal is to save enough money to get out of this business in the next couple of years and find something else that may not pay as much, but is a bit more mainstream."

Another woman asked Brianna, "So, you're single, right?" Brianna nodded. "Would you still do this if you got married?"

"I don't know. It would depend on how much my husband makes and how he feels about me doing this. Of course, I'm not even going to make it past the first date with anyone who has a problem with me doing porn. So, we wouldn't get anywhere near marriage if he wasn't cool with it."

"Does being in porn make it harder for you to date? I mean, if you're even into dating."

Brianna said, "Yes, it definitely presents a challenge. But dating isn't a priority for me right now. My priority is providing for my children. And doing this earns me real good money, and it allows me to be home except for several days a month."

Ryan added, "Dating has been very hard for me. I had a boyfriend for a few months in high school. When I started doing porn, I had to do all my shoots on the weekends 'cause I was in school during the week. So that made it hard for my boyfriend and me to do stuff together. But when he found out I was doing porn, he broke up with me and started telling the other kids in school. So that didn't help my social life, either. Since then, I haven't dated anyone. Either they get turned off when I tell them what I do, or they're just interested in having sex with me because I'm a porn star. And there's still the issue of having enough free time. So like Brianna said, dating isn't a priority for me right now, and it probably won't be until after I graduate."

Another student asked Ryan, "Do your parents know what you do?"

"I'm not in touch with my parents." Many of the students looked shocked. "They got real bent out of shape when they found out I was gay. They even tried sending me to therapy to try to make me straight. I didn't have any choice but to get out of there. I haven't had any contact with them for three and a half years. They don't even know where I am."

The classroom was a sea of stunned faces.

Following a brief, awkward silence, a woman in the front row asked, "Okay, so here's a two-part question. First, is what you're doing even legal?"

Brianna replied, "Yes, it is – as long the people involved are over 18."

Dr. Drake interjected, "That's true today in most places in the country. There might be local laws in conservative states or locales that prohibit it. But that's difficult to enforce. Selling pornographic materials may still be illegal in a few places. There's an interesting history of how the laws have changed since, say, the fifties and sixties regarding what you could make and sell, and what kinds of material you could send through the mail.

"During the Reagan administration in the early eighties, they formed a commission to examine ways to suppress or completely prohibit pornography. But that backfired spectacularly. That was about the time VCRs started becoming widespread, and pornographic movies could be distributed on videocassette and watched in the privacy of your home. Before that, people had to go to adult theatres if they wanted to watch pornography. That was obviously inconvenient and possibly unpleasant on many levels."

The woman in the front row said, "The second part of my question is, do you think it's ethical?"

Brianna said, "Yes, I do. Why not? I work and I get paid. The company sells a product and people buy it. It's the same way everything else works. There's nothing dishonest or dishonorable about it."

"I guess where I was going with the question is, do you think it's ethical to sell sex this way? Maybe ethical isn't the right word. Maybe right, or desirable, as a society? I mean, I think sex is an intimate act shared between two people. It should be beautiful, loving, and private. What you're doing is putting it out there as entertainment, or as ... I don't know ... titillation. It's like you're turning it from a loving, intimate act into some sort of marketable commodity that's bought and sold."

Brianna said, "Well, yes. Porn is selling sex as a commodity for entertainment and titillation. No question. What we're really selling is a fantasy. That's all porn is – fantasy. We're selling what guys want to fantasize about when they masturbate. I mean, sure… it's great when two people have sex for love and intimacy and all that. But not everybody can have that all the time, you know? What about single people? What about men who are away from home on business trips? What about guys who want to get off on a little more than what they're getting from their wives? If it was your husband, wouldn't you rather have him jerk off to some porn fantasy than cheat on you with another person?"

"I don't think that's appropriate behavior for anyone who's married. To me, a man should be focusing all his attention on his wife. If he's watching porn and masturbating, that's practically cheating because he's not doing it with his wife."

Brianna asked, "You're not married yet, are you?"

"No."

"Well, good luck with that."

Most of the guys in the room chuckled.

Ryan said, "So, if a married man has sex with another woman – or a man, for that matter – that's definitely cheating. But if he's masturbating to porn, he's not having sex with another person, so is that still cheating?"

"But he is. In his mind, he's having sex with whomever he's watching in the video."

Ryan asked, "What about if he simply masturbates but he's not watching porn?"

"Well, that's not as bad, but he's still having sex not involving me."

Brianna said, "So, it's like the porn video is his mistress."

"Yeah."

Another guy in the room said, "And you don't know what he

thinks about when he masturbates."

Brianna added, "Or even what – or who – he's thinking about while he's fucking his wife."

Dr. Drake said, "Let's back up to a statement Brianna made a few minutes ago and explore that further. She claimed that porn is selling a fantasy. And people's fantasies can be all over the place. Setting aside illegal things like sex with minors, rape, or physically injuring someone, do you think the government should get involved with legislating what sort of activities can and cannot be depicted in a pornographic movie?"

Nobody answered right away. The students were either pondering how they felt about that issue or waiting to see what someone else would say.

Then one of the guys said, "I don't know. That's kind of a slippery slope. I mean, where would you draw the line? Like, a sex scene with four people is okay, but five is not? Spanking someone is okay, but whipping them is not? And how can they anticipate every possible scenario that someone could dream up?"

Another guy added, "And who would get to evaluate that and provide the recommendations? Would there be some committee sitting in a screening room watching porn for days, trying to decide where to draw the line between what's acceptable and what's not?"

Another guy said, "I'd be on that committee. Where do I sign up?" Several people chuckled.

One of the women said, "Maybe they could come up with some sort of rating system like they have for video games, to let you know what kinds of activities are in that particular movie."

Dr. Drake asked, "Should the government get involved with that, or should the industry police itself, like the Motion Picture Association of America does for mainstream movies? By the way, the MPAA rating system came about as a result of parents demanding to know what was being shown in movies."

Again, the students took a moment to think. Then one woman

said, "I think the government needs to stay out of it. I mean, if they get into the business of deciding what can or can't be in porn, then next thing you know, they'll be trying to regulate song lyrics and what's in books. In other words, censorship. As much as I may not like what's in some porn movies, I like censorship even less."

Dr. Drake added, "In fact, the issue of censorship of song lyrics and comedy routines was something the government and our society wrestled with for decades, as recently as the '80s. Ultimately, it comes down to the fact that all forms of expression are protected by the First Amendment."

One of the guys asked, "So if making pornography is legal, why shouldn't prostitution be legal? In both cases, someone is paying you to have sex."

Brianna said, "That's a really good question. Personally, I don't think prostitution should be illegal."

Ryan said, "I know a few guys who are escorts. In some cases, they do porn so they can get more customers and charge more for escorting. They're not standing on a street corner in the red light district, but they're still having sex with someone for money. No one's being harmed, so I don't think it should be illegal."

Brianna added, "And there are women who dance in topless bars and strip clubs. They have laws about how much you can take off, and what kinds of touching are allowed or not, but otherwise, that's legal. Besides, if prostitution was legal, the government could tax it and regulate it."

Another woman said, "But is it really true that no one is being harmed? I mean, first of all, there are sexually transmitted diseases. And the risk of pregnancy. But aside from all that, it's dehumanizing. It's objectifying and oppressing women. It's psychologically harmful."

Dr. Drake interjected, "Just a process check. We're getting away from pornography and onto prostitution, which can be a different discussion for a different day."

The woman said, "Well, okay, but porn dehumanizes and

objectifies women. It's also psychologically harmful, and it sends the wrong message to society."

Ryan replied, "What about gay porn? That doesn't dehumanize or objectify women. We should put a disclaimer in the credits: No women were harmed during the making of this movie."

Several people laughed.

The woman replied, "I wasn't thinking about gay porn because, well, I'm not gay. But it seems like men in porn are objectified and dehumanized, too. Just maybe not oppressed."

Ryan turned to Brianna and asked, "Are you being oppressed? Do you feel dehumanized?"

"Nope. And you?"

"Nope. You know, I suppose doing porn makes me a sex object. As I said earlier, I've met guys who only see me as a porn star, not as a real person. And they're only interested in me because I'm a porn star. I've learned it comes with the territory. It's a trade-off I have to accept. Remember, I'm on my own. This provides the money I need to support myself and put myself through college. I make a lot of money for someone who only has a high school diploma and not much other job experience. So, it's not oppressing me, it's supporting me."

Brianna added, "You know, women are treated as sex objects in all kinds of ways. Everything from conservatives who still think women should be at home making babies and keeping house, to cheerleaders in skimpy outfits, to waitresses at Hooters, to the swimsuit edition of Sports Illustrated. All that doesn't make it right, but porn is hardly unique."

Ryan added, "And again, there's gay porn."

A guy off to the right side of the room raised his hand, and Dr. Drake acknowledged him.

"So how do you get started with doing porn? I'm not saying I'm interested, I'm just curious." A few other guys around him chuckled as if to say, "Yeah, right."

Ryan smiled and said, "You're asking for a friend."

Brianna replied, "In my case, I searched on the internet. I found some of the companies that produce porn, and I contacted them. They had me send in some pictures. They asked me a bunch of questions about what I would and wouldn't do. The first few gigs I got were with some little fly-by-night start-up company that didn't pay worth a shit, but it got me in the door. One of the guys I did a scene with recommended me to someone else he knew, then it grew from there. This business is all about networking. It's all about who you know."

"…and who you blow," Ryan added. "Sorry, I couldn't resist."

Brianna said, "It's true."

Ryan said, "In my case, I lucked into it by chance. I even lucked into where I live by chance. I rent a room in a house a few blocks from here. The guy who owns it has four bedrooms he rents to gay college students. Anyway, he's an attorney in the adult entertainment industry. I got into porn through my landlord's connections in the business. I've also posed for photos that have ended up in magazines, calendars, and greeting cards."

The same guy asked a follow-up question. "What sort of qualifications do they look for?"

Brianna replied, "For the women, big boobs, a pretty face, and being in decent shape. Oh, and nice hair. Being curvy is good. Being too heavy or too scrawny isn't, in most cases. The more things you're willing to do – like anal or having sex with another woman or doing more than one guy – the more you'll get hired and the more they'll pay you."

Ryan said, "I can't speak for straight porn, but in gay porn, they look for three things: a handsome or cute face, a great body, and a big dick. If you have two of the three, you'll do pretty well. If you have all three, you'll get all the work you can handle. In a few cases, if your face and your body aren't that great but you have a huge dick, that'll be enough. And like Brianna said, the more you're willing to do, the more you'll get work and the more you'll get paid."

Brianna said, "Yeah, that's one thing I'll say about gay porn –

not that I've seen all that much. You have much better-looking guys. In straight porn, the emphasis is on the women, especially their boobs. They've let some pretty skanky guys in the door."

Ryan added, "And believe it or not, some of the guys who do gay porn are actually straight. But they're willing to do it with a guy to get paid for it."

Brianna said, "Oh, so that's it. That's why there are so many … I'll be charitable and say *unremarkable* guys in straight porn. You took all the good-looking ones."

Ryan smiled and shrugged. Some of the guys in the room chuckled.

One of the women asked, "Is there such a thing as lesbian porn?"

Brianna and Ryan looked at each other. Ryan shrugged. Brianna said, "I doubt it. If there is, it's a tiny segment of the business. Here's the thing. Porn is created almost exclusively for a male audience. Men watch porn, women read romance novels. Almost all romance novels are written by women, for women. And almost all porn is produced by men, for men."

One of the guys said, "But there are lesbian scenes in most straight pornos." He paused, then added, "Or so I've been told."

Brianna said, "Yeah, well, I hate to break it to you, but none of the women in those scenes are lesbians. And I've had lesbians tell me that what the women in those scenes do isn't what real lesbians do at all. It's all about what men want to see."

Another one of the guys on the right side asked, "So what's it like to make porn? Is it fun?"

Brianna replied, "Let's clear up that misconception right now. It's not fun, it's work. It's hard work, and often it's not all that pleasant. If it was fun, everyone would be lining up to do it and they wouldn't have to pay people."

Ryan added, "Yeah. Very little of what happens on the set ends up in the finished product. Like sometimes it takes all day to shoot what ends up being a fifteen-minute scene. They're constantly adjusting the lighting and getting different camera angles. There's more waiting around than there is action. And you have to be able to perform with three of four cameras pointing at you, lights shining down on you, other people in the room, some director telling you what position he wants you in, and even when and how he wants you to cum. And for the guys, you have to be able to get it hard when they're ready to shoot the next thirty seconds of footage. And most of the time, you're paired up with some stranger you'd never fuck in real life, but you have to act like you're into him and be passionate. So yeah, it's a job. It's work. We don't do it 'cause it's fun or 'cause it's great sex. It's a job, and we do it for the money. It's the same reason everyone else does their job."

There was a pause, so Dr. Drake said, "We have about 15 more minutes. There are a couple aspects of pornography that haven't been discussed yet. So, how about this: Is pornography good or bad for society?"

The woman who earlier asked if porn was ethical said, "I know I'll get flamed for this, but I think it's bad. I think it cheapens sex. It takes something beautiful and makes it trashy."

Dr. Drake said, "Remember, we can have differences of opinion without flaming anyone."

Brianna said, "I get that. I really do. It's easy to have this idealized concept of sex as only something two people in love do. But humans are sexual beings. People crave sex regardless of whether they're in a happy marriage or single and lonely. People think about it all the time, and sometimes people have some pretty wild fantasies and turn-ons. And most of them aren't bad, they just are what they are – neither good nor bad. So, I think people should be able to indulge in their fantasies and desires, as long as it's not harmful to others. Porn is a way for them to experience that, especially when they need to keep it a secret or when finding someone else to engage in those fantasies with isn't practical."

Ryan said, "I wonder if all this talk about porn being bad or distasteful doesn't come from a belief that sex is bad or dirty. In other words, if we accept that sexuality is just one of the many aspects of being human, and it's healthy and there's nothing wrong with it, then I think we, as a society, wouldn't have so many hang-ups about porn. Think about this. We have violent movies, where people are killing each other and blowing things up all over the place, but nobody's talking about whether that's good or bad for society. A lot of people watch that kind of stuff for entertainment. So I ask, what's worse? Watching people kill each other or watching people have sex with each other? I think the answer should be clear. But most people don't think twice about violent movies, yet they get all hung up about porn."

Brianna added, "We can debate whether all kinds of things are good or bad for society. Cigarettes, alcohol, junk food, guns, lots of things. We can talk about it all day, but I don't think we want the government to decide what's good or bad for us. We want the freedom to decide that for ourselves. I'd rather leave it up to the free market – supply and demand. Some people may say porn is bad for society, but the industry is selling more of it than ever. And that goes for kinky stuff, too. They make it because people want it."

A woman in the back of the room raised her hand.

"You were saying earlier that doing porn is a job, and you're only having sex with another person the way someone directs you to, and there's no love or feelings between you and the other person. Has doing porn changed how you view sex? Or I guess another way to put it is this. If you fall in love with someone in the future, will sex go back to being a romantic, lovemaking thing, or will you still look at it as just a physical transaction?"

Brianna replied, "In other words, has doing porn ruined sex for me?" The woman nodded. "I don't know. That's a good question. I guess I won't know the answer until it happens. As I said, I'm not focused on dating right now, and I probably won't be until I stop doing this in a few years. But I would like to think when I fall in love with a man, I'll be having sex with him because I love him – and because it's fun. I've never shied away from the fact that sex can be fun – or at least it should be."

Ryan said, "You know, that's an interesting question. I had to deal with that when I first started doing porn. Before I left home and come out here, I had a boyfriend whom I loved very much. I still do, even three and a half years later. I truly believed he would be the guy I spent the rest of my life with. It took me a long time to come to terms with being gay, let alone having sex. Anyway, I only got to go all the way with my boyfriend once before I had to leave. And it was the most beautiful, intimate, mind-blowing experience – more than I could ever have imagined. We had this indescribable emotional connection. And I thought that's how sex would be every time. Now I know that's pretty naïve even in the best relationships. Anyway, I'll never forget the guy I did my first shoot with. He was a nice guy and cute, too. So, I tried to create something emotional with him, rather than just going through physical motions for the cameras. Like I wanted to kiss him a lot, but the director kept saying, 'forget all the kissy-kissy stuff, just fuck him.' Oh, and I found out afterward that he was straight. That was an eye-opener. So, I had to completely readjust my beliefs about what sex is. I'm just an actor doing things with my body parts to another guy's body parts. It's all an act. It's a role I'm playing. It's like an actor who has to play a murderer in a movie, even though he would never shoot someone in real life.

"So anyway, back to your question. I don't know. I hope when I fall in love again, sex will be the same beautiful, intimate, emotionally intense experience I had before, but I don't know. I guess I won't know until I get there."

A woman in the front of the room asked, "Are you still in touch with your first boyfriend? Do you think you'll ever get back together with him?"

"He's going to the University of Maryland, so we're on opposite ends of the country. And he's had a boyfriend for two and a half years now. But we're in touch. We send each other emails and we've talked on Skype a few times. I'm not counting on getting back together with him, but you never know."

The room was silent. Everyone's attention was focused on Ryan. As he scanned the room, everyone's face showed sadness and empathy.

Dr. Drake glanced at the clock on the wall. "Well, we're almost out of time. Once again, I'd like to thank Brianna and Ryan for sharing their perspectives as industry insiders, and for sharing their personal stories to help us put a human face on what's often viewed as a very impersonal industry. And I thank all of you for contributing to a very lively and well-rounded discussion." The bell rang. "See you tomorrow. Remember, there's a test on Friday."

The students filed out of the room. Dr. Drake reached into his courier bag, pulled out two small envelopes, and handed one to Brianna and one to Ryan. "This is just a little thank-you for contributing so much to our class today."

Ryan said, "Thanks for inviting me. I enjoyed it. Feel free to contact me again."

Brianna said, "Oh, he will." She smiled. "It was wonderful to see you again, Emmett."

Dr. Drake bid farewell and hurried on his way.

Brianna said, "It was a pleasure to meet you, Ryan. I have a question for you. Would you be open to the possibility of doing straight porn?"

"I don't know... I've never thought of it until now. Why?"

"There might be some opportunities for you at my studio if you're interested. You might fit into some of the types they're looking for. You're good-looking and if I had to guess..." She glanced downward. "...You're very well qualified. You seem well-grounded and I'll bet you'd be good to work with. A lot of the young guys they find just get into porn so they can get laid, and they have no idea what doing porn is really like. Some of them have substance abuse issues, too. Anyway, think about it. They have a gay division, too. Let me give you my phone number."

Ryan reached for his phone and created a contact for Brianna

Summers. She gave him her phone number. He texted a message to her so she would have his.

"Okay, thanks. I'll think about it and let you know in a day or two."

"Ta-ta for now!" Brianna waved, then turned and left.

Ryan noticed one of the guys who had been sitting in the back of the room was still there. He got up and started walking toward the front of the room. "Hi, Ryan. I'm Cody."

Ryan and Cody shook hands.

Cody continued, "I enjoyed hearing about your experiences. Well, not the part about your parents or your boyfriend, but you know…"

"Yeah. Thanks."

"It made me think about some things in new ways – which is the point, I guess. Anyway, you seem like a nice guy. Would you like to go grab lunch somewhere?"

It was noon and Ryan didn't have any plans for lunch. "Yeah, okay. Where would you like to go?"

"I don't care. You pick."

"Okay. Are you familiar with My Gyro in Westwood?"

"I've walked past it, but I've never eaten there. I'm willing to try it."

# Lunch with Cody

Tuesday, February 15, 2011

As Ryan and Cody walked from the campus into Westwood Village, Ryan said, "So, tell me a little bit about yourself. You know, the standard stuff. Where are you from? What's your major?"

Cody said, "At least you didn't ask, 'What's your sign?' I'm from American Fork, Utah. That's south of Salt Lake City, between there and Provo. I'm majoring in journalism."

Ryan said, "You're not interviewing me for a story, are you?"

Cody chuckled. "Not without your permission. But seriously, no. As I said, you seem interesting. I just wanted to learn a little more about you."

"Fair enough. So, just curious. I hope you don't mind me asking, but since you're from Utah, are you a Mormon?"

"Technically, yes. I mean, I'm in the books, as we say. But I'm not observant."

"I'm surprised you're not going to Brigham Young."

"That's why I'm going here. I wanted to get away from that environment where practically everyone is LDS. Same with Utah and Utah State. I'm what we call a Jack Mormon – a Mormon in name only. I don't go to church very often. And I drink." He paused and smiled at Ryan. "And I've been known to have sex."

"Interesting. I've never heard the term Jack Mormon before. Anyway, here we are." Ryan held the door open and let Cody enter first.

Cody asked, "What's good here?"

"Everything. I think I've had everything on the menu. But I know, that's not very helpful. The gyros are really good."

They ordered, and once they sat down at a table, Ryan asked

Cody, "So, did you go on a mission?"

"Yeah. I got to go to New Zealand."

"Really! What was that like?"

"It was awesome! It's like totally beautiful there. The people are so nice. They're laid-back and friendly. Society is different there. It just feels more comfortable. It's hard to put my finger on it, but for example, there's no gun culture. Nobody has guns, and nobody wants them. So you're not reading always about mass shootings and robberies and stuff like that. They don't have hard-core religious fanatics like we do here. I mean, people go to church, but there are no right-wing churches trying to shove their beliefs onto everyone else and get laws passed based on their religion."

Ryan wondered whether Cody comprehended the irony of what he just said in the context of being a missionary for the LDS church. He decided not to press him on it. "Sounds nice."

"Yeah. I would live there if I could."

"Well, why don't you? I mean, after you graduate."

"I guess I could, but I have my family here. And besides, you can't just say, 'I'm going to go live somewhere.' You have to be able to get a work visa. And they have plenty of journalists there, so they're not looking to bring in journalists from other countries."

There was a pause in the conversation while they both enjoyed their food.

Then Cody asked, "So where are you from?"

"Kansas."

"Where in Kansas?"

"I'd rather not get any more specific than that. I don't know whether my parents are making any effort to try to find me at this point, but I'd be happier if they didn't know where I am."

"I'm not going track them down to tell them where you are."

"I know, it sounds stupid. I probably don't need to worry about it anymore. Still, I'd rather not have them in my life. If they didn't like me being gay, they sure aren't going to like me doing porn."

Cody said, "Yeah, I see what you mean. What are you majoring in?"

"Computer Science."

"Ah, so you're a nerd." Cody smiled, letting Ryan know this wasn't intended as a put-down.

"Yeah, I guess so. I like it, though. I want to be an app developer or a website designer when I graduate. When I was still in Kansas, I was the webmaster for my father's church. I redesigned their website. Their old one was designed back in the 90s, and it looked like it."

"You were designing websites in high school? Impressive."

"Yeah. I guess that's what got me interested."

Cody said, "So besides computer science and porn, what do you like to do?"

"I didn't say I liked to do porn."

"You know what I mean."

"I love music, especially jazz. I play the trumpet. I'm in one of the jazz ensembles here."

"Cool. I don't know much about jazz, but maybe you could play some for me."

Ryan asked, "And how about you? What are you interested in besides journalism?"

"Sci-fi. I want to be an author. But I figure being a journalist will improve my writing and give me a reliable paycheck while I'm working on my novels."

"Sounds like a good strategy. If I could do anything I wanted, I'd be a jazz musician. But that doesn't pay very well unless you're really good. So I plan to play music for my enjoyment while I pursue a career in something a bit more secure."

"How long do you think you'll keep doing porn?"

Ryan wished they could talk about other topics than his current livelihood. But considering they had just come from a class where it was the focus of the discussion, it wasn't out of line.

"Just until I graduate, maybe a little before. I'm only doing it to pay my way through college and support myself. Once I get a job as a software engineer, I won't need the money anymore. I've saved up enough to pay for the rest of school, so now I'm saving for a down payment on a house. Despite all the minuses of what I do, it pays well."

"What are the minuses?"

"Well, we talked about some of them in class. It messes with my schedule. They do a lot of shoots during the week, so sometimes I have to miss classes. I would have liked to be in the marching band, but that would take too much time away from work. There's the fact that I have to have sex with someone whether I want to or not – and it's usually not. I worry about picking up HIV or some other STD. Sometimes I get recognized when I'm out somewhere. And I have no idea whether doing this is going to have a negative impact on my career or my life in the future. Like, I don't have any desire to run for public office, but if I did, this would surely come to light. But most of all, it has a huge impact on dating or even making friends. You wouldn't believe how many times people have rejected me, or at least distanced themselves from me, because of what I do. And then others are only interested in me *because* I'm a porn star, like it's some kind of fantasy for them. So yeah, there are a lot of negatives. The money is the only positive."

Cody thought about all that while he took another bite of his food and chewed it. Then he said, "Well, I know what you do for a living, and it doesn't bother me. I'd hang with you."

Up to this point, it hadn't occurred to Ryan that Cody might be gay. He still wasn't sure. He hadn't set off Ryan's gaydar, although that still needed a lot of fine-tuning. *Maybe he just wants to be friends. On the other hand, Mormon kids could be gay just like anyone else.*

Ryan said, "Oh. Well, thanks. That's nice of you to say."

"I mean it. You seem like a nice guy. You seem like you're well-grounded and you have your head on straight. And like I said, the fact that you do porn doesn't bother me. I hope the fact that I'm LDS doesn't bother you."

Ryan thought, *Really? You know, I'll bet people do reject him because he's LDS. There was the whole Prop 8 thing, after all. I'm not sure how I feel about that. But that aside, he seems nice. It wouldn't hurt to at least get to know him a little better.* "No, that's okay. So yeah, we could hang out sometime."

"Wanna have lunch again later this week?"

Ryan mentally reviewed his schedule. He had a shoot on Friday, but tomorrow or Thursday would work. Or sometime next week. "How about Thursday? And you pick the place."

"Thursday it is. And how about the burrito place a couple of doors down?"

"Yeah, that works."

# Hangin' with Cody

Thursday, March 31, 2011

Ryan decided to take it slow with Cody. Between his porn work, his studies, and practicing the trumpet, he had enough going on in his life. He was a year and two months away from graduating anyway.

But after a month and a half, Cody was still around. They got together for lunch once or twice a week and had dinner and a movie a couple of times. Today during lunch at Chito's Burritos, Cody asked, "So I've noticed that whenever we have lunch on a Thursday, you bring your trumpet along."

"Yeah, my jazz ensemble rehearses on Tuesdays and Thursdays at 3:00. I have classes at 1:00 and 2:00, so there's no time for me to go home between classes to get it."

"Does your band ever perform for the public? I'd like to hear you sometime."

"As a matter of fact, we have a concert tonight at 7:00. It's in the Schoenberg Music Building, in Lani Hall."

"Do I need to buy a ticket or anything?"

"No, it's free. Just show up. There will be plenty of seats."

"Cool. I'll try to make it. Maybe we can go out for a beer or something afterward."

"Yeah, okay. Hopefully, the music won't scare you away."

"Why would it scare me away? Is it that bad?"

"Oh, I love it, and the band is pretty good. But I realize jazz isn't for everybody."

"I'll try to keep an open mind."

***

That evening, Cody showed up for the concert. After the show, he met up with Ryan and they started walking toward The Brewin' Bruin.

Ryan said, "Thanks for coming! So what did you think? And you can be honest. If you didn't like it, that's okay."

"It was good. I mean, I could tell everyone was very talented and some of the music seemed pretty complicated. Is it hard to play?"

"Sometimes. But that's part of why I like it. If it's too easy, it's not as much fun. When it's harder, I have to work at it and I become a better player."

"So… and I know this is probably a dumb question, but… those times when somebody would stand up and play a solo, like that one you played in the last song, were you playing that from memory? It didn't look like you were reading your music."

"No, those solos were improvised."

"You mean you make it up as you go along?"

"Yeah. Jazz is all about improvisation. They give you chords, but you decide what you want to play at the time you play it."

"How do you know whether the notes you decide to play will sound good or not?"

"Practice. Trial and error. And sometimes it's just luck. Sometimes, you have a good day, and your ideas fit the chords and the flow of the music. Other times, you don't do as well. But that's part of the fun and part of the learning process."

"Okay. Well… I kinda liked the parts where everyone was playing together. During the solos, well… sometimes they lost me. I couldn't understand what they were playing. It didn't make sense."

"Yeah, I get it. And some of the guys are better soloists than others. But the more you listen to jazz, the more it makes sense."

"Obviously, you like it."

"I love it. It's my favorite kind of music by far."

They arrived at The Brewin' Bruin and ordered flights and a

large basket of wings.

Ryan asked, "So what kind of music do you like?"

"Oh, mostly popular stuff. You know, Britney Spears, Lady Gaga, Jennifer Lopez, Adele. That sort of thing."

"Sounds like you like female singers."

"Yeah. And that's another thing about jazz. I like songs that have words. I don't listen to much instrumental stuff. It just seems like something is missing. Like if there are no words, what is the song trying to say?"

"Yeah, I get it. But there are singers in jazz, too, just not as many."

"Really? Like who?"

"Well, there's Diane Schuur, Dianne Reeves, Diana Krall…"

"Never heard of 'em. And is there some rule that says all jazz singers have to be named some form of Dianne?"

"No. For example, there's Norah Jones."

"Yeah, I remember her. She sang 'Don't Know Why,' right?"

"Yeah."

"That was jazz?"

"Well, not really. But some of her stuff is more like jazz."

"Maybe you could play some of the Diannes' music for me sometime."

"Yeah, okay. Are you doing anything this weekend?"

"I've got to study for midterms. But I could get away for a few hours."

"Why don't you come over to my place on Saturday night? You don't want to study on Saturday night, do you?"

"Of course not. Sure, let's do it. I can finally see that house you live in."

"Cool. You wanna grab dinner somewhere, then go there afterward?"

"Yeah, okay."

They were about halfway through their beer flights at this point, but all the way through the basket of wings.

Cody said, "I'm still hungry. You want something else?"

"Yeah, maybe a couple of sliders."

Cody flagged down the server and they ordered. Then Cody asked, "So there's something else I've been meaning to ask you. So… I'm still trying to figure out this gay thing." He paused. "I'm not sure how to say this…"

"Just say it. It's okay."

"Okay, so… how do two guys decide if they're going to start… you know…"

"Having sex?"

"Yeah."

"I don't know. I think it's different with different guys, or even in different situations. It kinda depends on whether you're just hooking up for one night or if you're trying to develop a relationship. Even then, I guess some guys want to start having sex sooner than others."

Cody took a moment to process that information and choose what to say next. Then he said, "What do you do? How do you decide when you're ready to start having sex with someone?"

"I don't know. I've thought about that a lot. When I was in high school back in Kansas, I was still struggling with coming out. I was scared to admit to myself that I was gay, 'cause you know, my upbringing. Of course, the church taught that you don't have sex until you're married, and that's to a woman. So I didn't know what to do about having sex with my boyfriend. But I decided it was okay because I loved him. So we did it a couple of times, but then I have to leave and come out here. Then I met this guy, and he was cute and friendly and everything, but he wanted to start having sex right away. And I wasn't comfortable with that. But anyway, since I started doing porn, I haven't been too interested in having sex with guys outside of that. And I don't even know if I want to have a boyfriend while I'm in college. I'm busy enough as it is. So I guess it's something I'm not dealing with for the time being."

"Okay, well… I was just thinking about it, 'cause you know, we've been hanging out for several weeks now, and I thought maybe we could start doin' it at some point. I mean, if you don't want to, that's okay. But I kinda want to."

Ryan thought about it for a few minutes while they ate their sliders. "Let's talk more about it on Saturday night."

# The Bottom Line

Saturday, April 2, 2011

Ryan and Cody met for dinner at the Westwood Pizza Kitchen. They talked about all sorts of things – everything except what might happen later in the evening. Ryan had questions he wanted to ask, but not in such a public setting. Cody didn't want to talk about it, he wanted to do it.

After dinner, they walked to Ryan's house. Once they were settled in his room, Ryan selected *Diane Schuur and the Count Basie Orchestra* to introduce Cody to the ladies of jazz. It was one of Ryan's favorite CDs, but Cody wasn't getting into it. During the gap between the third and fourth song, Cody said, "Can you stop that for a second?"

Ryan pressed Pause. "You don't like it?"

"It's okay, but… I know when we said we'd get together tonight it was so you could play some female jazz singers for me, but I'd kinda rather do something else."

"Okay." Ryan ejected the CD and put it back in its case. "Can I ask you a couple of questions?"

Cody wanted to get right into it, but he said, "Sure."

"So, just curious. And there's no wrong answer. The other night you said you were still trying to figure this gay thing out. Have you ever done anything with a guy before?"

"I've gone down on guys a couple of times, but I haven't done anal yet."

"Well, if you just want to do oral, that's okay. I mean, I don't want to do anything you're not comfortable with. Were you thinking you would–"

"I want you to fuck me."

"So I'd be your first time?"

"Yeah."

"Well, okay, but… it's pretty big–"

"I don't care. I've always wondered what it would feel like to have a guy's cock inside me, and I want to find out."

"Okay, but I insist we wear condoms."

"That's fine."

Cody moved closer to Ryan and started feeling his crotch. Ryan was already getting hard.

Ryan put his arms around Cody and started to kiss him. Cody let him, but he didn't seem very interested in kissing. Ryan wondered if Cody's only previous exposure to men having sex together was from watching porn, where the guys don't usually kiss much, if at all. Maybe he hadn't even seen that.

Cody dropped to his knees, unbuckled Ryan's belt, and unzipped his pants. For someone who had only gone down on guys a couple of times, as Cody said a moment ago, he was pretty good at it. He certainly had enthusiasm.

After five minutes or so, Ryan said, "Okay, I'm starting to get close. Do you wanna finish like this, or–"

"You know what I want." Cody stood up and peeled off his remaining clothes. Then he climbed onto the bed, laid down on his back, and raised his legs into the air.

Ryan finished removing his clothes. He walked around the bed to his nightstand and retrieved a couple of condoms, a bottle of lube, and a hand towel. "Well, someone's eager."

"What gave it away?"

Ryan chuckled. "Well, since it's your first time, maybe it would be better if we started with me on my back. That way you can control the rate of entry."

"Yeah, okay, whatever."

Ryan unrolled the condom and slathered his cock with lube. He laid down and Cody eagerly straddled him. Ryan said, "Take a few deep breaths. Try to relax. Go slowly.”

Cody wasn’t interested in going slowly. Again, Ryan wondered whether this was really his first time.

Ryan asked, “Are you doin’ okay?”

“I’ve never been better.”

After three years in the porn industry, Ryan had developed complete self-control. He was prepared to stop anytime Cody wanted to or if he showed any signs of pain. But Cody went at it vigorously.

Twenty minutes and four positions later, Ryan was ready to finish. After he pulled out and wiped them both off with the hand towel, they collapsed onto their backs next to each other. Ryan worked his arm under Cody’s head.

Ryan asked, “So, was your first time okay?”

“Oh my God… it was amazing. You’re a total pro at this.”

“Well, yes, I think you knew that.”

“No, seriously. That was even better than I thought it would be.”

Ryan said, “I didn’t hurt you, did I?”

“It hurt a little at first, but I didn’t care.”

“Well, okay, good… I was concerned. Anyway, next time – assuming there’s a next time – I’ll let you do it to me.”

Cody said, “Nah, that’s okay. I only want to be the…” He searched for the right word. “Catcher? Is that what you call it?”

“Bottom.”

“Yeah, I guess. Except I liked it when you were on your back and I was on top of you, riding it.”

“When you’re on the receiving end, we say you’re the bottom even if you’re above me, sitting on it.”

“Yeah, okay, then… I want to be the bottom.”

Ryan wished he had more opportunities to bottom, especially after he had done it with Ted. At work, he was always cast as the top. But whatever. Maybe he could get Cody to try being versatile sometime down the road.

# SENIOR YEAR

# Summer in Scottsdale

Saturday, June 11, 2011

With his junior year completed, Ryan looked forward to his summer internship at Technovations with a mix of excitement and apprehension. What was the real work world actually like? He would find out soon enough.

On Saturday morning, he loaded two suitcases, his laptop, and his trumpet into his trusty Toyota Corolla. Most of his CD collection was packed into a large cardboard box which he placed in the trunk, but he selected a dozen to listen to along the way. He headed to the 405 freeway, then east on I-10. He drove through miles and miles of endless suburbia. Soon, he lost track of how many times he passed signs for the same fast-food chains and big-box stores. It seemed to go on forever.

Seven hours later, the western outskirts of the Phoenix metro area came into view. In contrast to Los Angeles, Phoenix was browner, sunnier, and more spread out. Like Los Angeles, every interchange seemed to feature the same fast-food restaurants and big-box stores.

The downtown skyline and the tall office buildings of the Central Avenue corridor looked appealing against their backdrop of mountain ranges. Phoenix seemed a bit newer and fresher than LA, and the freeways were wide and well-maintained. After he passed downtown, he exited onto Loop 202, which would take him to Scottsdale. He admired Tempe Town Lake and the shiny new office buildings and condos that lined the opposite shore. Then he turned north onto Loop 101 and marveled at the beautiful mountain ranges to the north and east.

Finally, he exited onto Shea Boulevard. He weaved his way through several residential neighborhoods to the house where he would live for the next three months. He was impressed with how upscale everything looked. It was like his neighborhood in Westwood, but with a decidedly more southwestern flair.

Technovations recommended a website that connected interns with people who offered rooms for rent in their homes. He signed up with a man named Eddie who also worked for Technovations. His listing stated, 'The homeowner is an openly gay man. Anyone is welcome as long as you're comfortable with that.' Obviously, Ryan would be comfortable with that, as long as this guy wasn't harboring any assumptions or expectations about what might happen.

He arrived at a quarter to six, double-checked the address, and rang the doorbell. A nice-looking man who appeared to be in his mid- to upper-30s answered the door. "You must be Ryan."

"Yes, sir. And you must be Eddie." They shook hands.

"May I help you carry stuff in?"

"Sure." Ryan unlocked his trunk and handed Eddie his smaller suitcase and trumpet. He slung his laptop case onto his shoulder and carried his larger suitcase and the box of CDs.

Eddie led him to one of the secondary bedrooms. There was a bed, a chair, and a dresser. It was nothing special, but it seemed comfortable and it would be fine for three months. Another bedroom served as Eddie's office. He had set up a computer desk from an office supply store on one side of the room for Ryan to use.

Eddie showed him around the rest of the house. It wasn't as large or as fabulously appointed as Hal's house, but it was nice. Eddie led Ryan into the backyard. It wasn't as lush and resort-like as his backyard in Los Angeles, but there was a pool and a hot tub, a trio of palm trees, some cacti, and a barbeque island. Ryan noted there were no two-story houses in view of the backyard. Eddie said, "Since I live here by myself, I usually get in the pool and hot tub naked. You're welcome to or not, as you choose. If that makes you uncomfortable, I can put something on."

"No, that's fine. The house where I live in LA has a private backyard with a pool and hot tub, and we go naked in it too."

Eddie showed Ryan the kitchen and the laundry room, then said, "It's six o'clock. Have you eaten?"

"No, and I'm starving. What do you have around here?"

"Just about everything you could imagine. And if we don't have it near Shea and the 101, we can drive three miles north on the 101 to Frank Lloyd Wright Boulevard. They have everything in the world around there. But anyway, for tonight – do you want Asian, Mexican, or hamburgers and beer? Or something else?"

"Burgers and beer sound good."

"Cool. Then after dinner, I'll drive you around a little and show you where the grocery stores are and stuff like that."

The restaurant was only a couple of miles away. Along the way, Eddie pointed out various drug stores, restaurants, and discount department stores as they passed.

Once they had ordered, Ryan asked, "So, how long have you worked at Technovations?"

"About six years."

"How do you like it?"

"Overall, it's great. I like being part of a company that develops cutting-edge new technologies, especially if they'll make life better for people. It's very fast-paced and competitive. We have to stay at the forefront of new technologies, so it can be high-pressure at times. As an intern, you probably won't be placed under as much pressure since they'll give you work that can be wrapped up in three months. But you'll get a good look at what it's like to work for the company. You'll know what you're getting into if they make you an offer. You might decide you don't want to work there."

Ryan said, "Sounds like it's kind of a two-way street. They're checking me out as a future employee and I'm checking them out as a future employer."

"That's right."

"Yeah. No pressure there."

They both laughed.

Ryan told Eddie a little bit about UCLA. Eddie talked about how much he enjoyed living in Scottsdale and the Phoenix area in general. "It'll be really hot most of the time you're here. But that's why we have pools. For the rest of the year, the weather's great. Living here isn't for everyone, but I like it. It sure beats blizzards and freezing temperatures. You don't have to shovel sunshine."

Eddie seemed like a nice guy. Ryan felt comfortable with him and confident that he made a good choice for a place to live.

After dinner, Eddie drove Ryan past a couple of grocery stores. Ryan wondered whether he would ever learn his way around the winding, crisscrossed streets to find these places again.

Soon after they returned home, Eddie said, "I have a party to go to tonight. I feel bad about leaving you alone on your first night here."

"No problem. I'm exhausted. I think I'll go to the store and buy a few things, unpack, and turn in early."

"Sounds good. I probably won't be home until 11 or 12."

"Okay. Well, enjoy your party! And thanks for dinner."

"You're welcome. And I will. See you tomorrow."

***

Sunday was a beautiful sunny day, so Ryan decided to explore his new surroundings. He spent a few minutes studying the map of Scottsdale online to familiarize himself with the major roads and local points of interest. He plotted an approximate route he would travel, leaving open the possibility that he might stop somewhere or take a different turn if something aroused his curiosity.

He headed west on Shea Boulevard and crossed the freeway. When he reached Scottsdale Road, he turned south. He was amazed by all the lavish homes that sat on decent-sized lots. The spread-out, wall-enclosed properties were a stark contrast to the wealthy areas of Los Angeles, such as Beverly Hills and Bel Air, where the lots were smaller and greener.

When he reached Scottsdale Fashion Center, he decided to check it out. The chic, upscale mall seemed to go on forever. He didn't buy anything, but walking the full distance of the mall on every floor and browsing the stores ate up an hour and a half.

From there he continued south into Old Town Scottsdale. The tourist shops had storefront facades that attempted to recreate an old cowboy town in the wild west. He parked and walked around. He checked out the tourist shops, then crossed Scottsdale Road. On the other side were trendy, elegant art galleries. He stepped in a few of them but quickly realized everything on display in these shops was well beyond his budget. He wondered who could afford that kind of money to buy art, but then he remembered the neighborhoods he had just driven through.

By this time, it was late in the afternoon. Ryan ate dinner at a pizza restaurant on Scottsdale Road, then drove a mile east to Hayden Road and turned north. He drove past numerous parks, golf courses, and greenbelts, and noticed there was a bike trail that appeared to connect them all. Maybe that would be a place he could go running.

That evening, he sat down at his desk in Eddie's office. After he checked his email, he looked up more information about things he had seen on his journey. Reflecting on his day, he realized that he liked most of what he saw. A sign he passed at one point said, 'Welcome to Scottsdale – America's most livable city.' He decided that was a reasonable claim. If things worked out at Technovations, he could easily see himself living here.

Shortly, Eddie entered the room and sat down at his desk. After he spent a few minutes checking his email, he said, "How's your day been? I haven't seen you around."

"Yeah. I decided to get out and drive around. You know, just to see what the area looks like."

"Where did you go?"

"I went down Scottsdale Road, then came back up on Hayden. I stopped for a while at Scottsdale Fashion Center and Old Town Scottsdale."

"Cool. Yeah, there's a lot to see and do here."

"I like what I've seen so far. Hey, I was wondering. On Hayden, it looks like there's a bike path in some of the parks. Is it only for bikes, or can people go running on it too?"

"All of the above. Lots of people walk on it too. It's a great path – it goes through lots of beautiful areas."

"Cool. How long is it?"

"It's around 12 miles each way. It starts not too far from here, at 92$^{nd}$ Street and Shea, and it goes all the way down to Tempe Town Lake. I've ridden the full distance on my bike before, but that would be a long way to run unless you're training for a marathon or something. There are places along the way where you can park your car and run a section of it."

"I'll have to check it out. I was on my high school's track team, and I still like to run to stay in shape."

"Yeah, it's great exercise. I ran a marathon once in my 20s, but I can't run too much anymore because of my knees. So I switched to biking. I go hiking a lot too. There are some great hiking trails around here."

"Cool. So, let me ask you another question if it's okay. In your listing, you said you're gay. What's it like to work at Technovations as a gay person?"

"It's pretty good. When I first joined, I was pretty closeted at work. They have a small LGBT employee group, so I joined that. They do things like monthly lunches, game nights, and that sort of thing. Some of those people are now my best friends. I'd be happy to bring you along and have you meet them."

Ryan thought about it for a moment. Chances were good that at least one person would recognize him from his videos. Better not take the chance. "I don't know. Let me think about it."

"They're very friendly."

"I'm sure they are. That's not the issue. Let me think about it and I'll get back to you."

"Okay. Anyway, as I was saying, I was pretty closeted at first. But then after a couple of years, the company held a Diversity Day and they needed people to staff the booth for the LGBT group. So I took a chance and volunteered."

Ryan said, "Oh, God. I remember in high school our Gay-Straight Alliance group set up a table outside the cafeteria to hand out little stickers that said 'I'm an LGBT Ally.' It was a disaster. None of our so-called straight allies showed up to staff the booth, and nobody stopped to pick up a sticker. How did yours go?"

"About the same. They had tables for other groups, like African-Americans, Latinos, Native Americans, women engineers, and so on. Lots of people came to the event, but most people visited every table except ours. They hurried past and tried not to make eye contact."

"That doesn't sound gay-friendly to me."

Eddie said, "It's not like they're homophobic, it's more like it was awkward and they'd rather not deal with it. Anyway, I was scared shitless the entire time. But after that, nobody treated me any differently. In fact, some people became more friendly. Since I didn't get any negative reactions, I decided not to be so closeted anymore. I put a picture of my partner and me on my desk – that was when we were still together – and I put a rainbow magnet on my cubicle wall. And I stopped being evasive about what I did over the weekend. I discovered most people didn't have any problem with it."

"Sounds like the opposite of what happened to me. After the day I stood at that table, I was shunned by a lot of kids. I found out some of them were making fun of me behind my back. And there were a couple of people who did some really nasty things to me. So yeah, it wasn't so easy for me."

"That's too bad. I guess in the workplace, people are a little more mature than they were in high school. Plus, the company has policies that prohibit discrimination and harassment on the basis of sexual orientation and gender identity, so they know they're not supposed to do it. I'm sure there are still some people who are homophobic, but they know enough to keep it to themselves. It's improved a lot over the time I've been there."

Ryan said, "So you're glad you came out at work?"

"Oh, absolutely! It's a cliché, but it's like a giant weight was lifted from my shoulders. My work improved. I could build better relationships with people. I didn't realize how much energy I was wasting trying to keep people from finding out. Now, I don't worry about that stuff and I can focus on my work."

"Cool. So, at one point you said you had a partner."

"Yeah. We broke up a year and a half ago. We were together for a little over ten years. I bought this house after we sold the house we owned together."

"Sorry to hear that. What happened, if you don't mind me asking?"

"Well, the short answer is, I found out he had been cheating on me. But there's a lot more to it than that. It's complicated, as they say. Maybe I'll tell you the full story in all its gory detail sometime if you really want to hear it. So, what about you? Do you have a boyfriend?"

"Kinda. There's this guy I've been seeing for about four months now. It's like we hang out a lot, and we started having sex about two months ago. But I don't know where it's heading. He seems to be okay with things the way they are."

"Well, there's nothing wrong with taking it slow and letting things happen when they're meant to. I think a lot of people – especially gay men – tend to rush into relationships. I remember when Wade and I met, we pretty much fell head over heels for each other – or at least heels over head. We moved in together after only three months. In hindsight, I wish we had gone slower."

"Do you think he wouldn't have cheated on you if you had gone slower?"

"I don't know. Maybe it would have turned out the same either way. But I think we were so ga-ga over each other that we couldn't see each other's faults. We thought we were perfect for each other. We were in that 'you're the man of my dreams' bubble for a long time. It was wonderful for a while. But then, as time went on, reality set in and we started having problems. They weren't any worse than the problems every couple has, but we didn't know how to deal with them. We kept ignoring the issues that were developing and acting as if everything was still perfect. In other words, we never learned how to have difficult conversations with each other and address problems."

Ryan said, "I had a boyfriend in high school. His name was Chris. We were best friends for three years before we finally figured out we were gay and came out to each other. But anyway, at the time, I thought he was the greatest guy in the world, and we'd go to college together and then spend our whole lives together. And I always assumed we were perfect for each other and everything would be wonderful all the time. You know, the whole 'happily ever after' thing. But yeah... who knows how it would have turned out?"

"What happened with him?"

Ryan told Eddie the story about how his parents found out he was gay. How they sent him to Dr. Babcock for conversion therapy. How he found out they were planning to send him to an conversion therapy place in Alabama to try to turn him straight. How he ran away to avoid it, and how that meant he had to leave Chris behind.

Eddie said, "Wow. That's really intense. I'm sorry all that stuff happened to you."

"Yeah, it was pretty rough. Chris has a boyfriend now. He met him at college. That's been going on for three years, so it seems pretty serious. Anyway, I've learned how to get by on my own."

He proceeded to tell Eddie about how he arrived in LA and the house where he lives. He told him about Hal, Ted, Darnell, and Ricky, and how they provide him with love, friendship, and support. "So, all things considered, I'm pretty fortunate."

"Yeah, I guess things could have turned out a lot worse."

There was a lull in the conversation. They had been talking for almost two hours. They covered a lot of ground for a conversation that began with 'How was your day?'

Eddie said, "Thanks for sharing all that with me."

Ryan replied, "Yeah. Thanks for telling me your stories about being gay at work and your relationship with Wade."

"Well, I need to fold some laundry." Eddie got up, but before he left the room, he said, "I enjoyed our talk."

"Me too."

Eddie seemed like a nice guy. They were bonding quickly. It looked like this summer was going to turn out fine.

Ryan thought of Russ Simonton, his boss from his grocery store job in Kansas, and his husband Frank. They had been together for twenty-five years at the time, and they seemed to get along well. Ryan wondered what kinds of challenges they had to overcome through the years. Ryan decided to send Russ an email to ask how they were doing and bring him up-to-date on his internship and everything else going on in his life.

# Technovations

Monday, June 13, 2011

Ryan's first day at work was both fascinating and, at times, boring. He spent the morning in a training room with 11 other summer interns. For the first hour, the interns introduced themselves and the orientation leader led them through a teambuilding activity. Then a parade of Human Resources representatives subjected the interns to lengthy PowerPoint slideshows about company policies, corporate culture, and diversity training. At one point, the Diversity Director showed a slide listing the company's employee resource groups and said, "These groups are open to all employees. For example, you don't have to be a woman to join the Women Engineers group. If you're interested in learning more about Latino, African-American, or Native American culture and issues, you're welcome to join those groups or attend any of their events." Ryan saw the LGBT group listed along with the others, but the speaker made no mention of that. He looked around the room and wondered if any of the other interns were LGBT.

At lunchtime, the orientation leader handed each intern a cafeteria voucher good for up to ten dollars. "Just to manage expectations, we won't be treating you to lunch every day." She led the group to the company cafeteria, showed them around the various food stations, and instructed them to get their food to go and bring it back to their classroom.

A vice president joined them for lunch. He was older, white, and pudgy. Ryan guessed he probably drove a Mercedes and lived in one of those neighborhoods he drove past along Scottsdale Road. It was clear he would much rather be enjoying a two-martini lunch at a fancy restaurant than sitting in a room with a bunch of college kids. After a stiff, perfunctory welcome speech, he offered to answer questions from the group. There weren't very many. He left after about 20 minutes.

After lunch, a more personable vice president talked about the various organizations within the company and the exciting innovations the company was working on. His enthusiastic, animated manner made it easier to stay awake. By the time he was done, Ryan's brain was overloaded. He wondered how much of the information from today he'd be expected to remember. Would there be a test at the end of his internship?

Next, the orientation leader led the group on a tour of the campus. She pointed out some of the testing labs, the auditorium where company-wide meetings and other special events were held, a small medical center, and a store that sold company logo merchandise, snacks, and other nick-nacks. They ended up at the tech support center, where they were each issued a laptop, a power cable, a wireless mouse, and a carrying case.

At 4:00, they returned to the cafeteria dining room. Most of the tables were occupied by employees in pairs or small groups having informal meetings. Each person sat with their laptop open and a coffee or soda at hand. The intern group stood in an open area near the middle of the dining room. Managers arrived to meet their interns and lead them to their offices. Ryan's manager, Kendra, was among the last to arrive. She hurried in, shook Ryan's hand, and led him into the next building and up to the third floor. She led him to a two-person cubicle, half of which would be his workplace for the summer. There was a monitor and external keyboard for him to hook his laptop up to. She introduced him to his cubemate, Wendy, a tech writer who had been hired as a contractor to write some training manuals. She took him around to the cubicles of his teammates, most of whom were not at their desks. "They're probably in a meeting" or "they're working from home today," Kendra said. "You'll meet them tomorrow morning at our weekly team meeting."

Kendra led Ryan to her cubicle and said, "This is where I work.

Feel free to stop by anytime, unless I'm on a call or my 'Do Not Disturb' sign is up. I've got some stuff I need to wrap up by the end of the day. Please stop by in the morning and I'll get you started. I'm sure you've had a full day, so why don't you go back to your cubicle and get settled in? You can leave whenever you're done."

"Okay, thanks. See you tomorrow!"

Kendra nodded, then turned toward her monitor and dove into answering emails.

Ryan returned to his cubicle. He hooked his laptop up to the docking station, where the monitor, mouse, keyboard, and power supply had already been plugged in. He logged on for the first time and opened his email. There were already 15 emails in his inbox, including invitations to meetings, email blasts to his team, and more introductory information from HR. Ryan read them all, then surfed the company's intranet. Even though Kendra said he could leave whenever he wanted to, he felt he should stay until 5:00 to make a good first impression.

When 5:00 came, he shut down his laptop and locked it in one of his drawers. As he walked through the cubicle farm toward the door, he saw very few other people at their desks. Nobody saw that he had dutifully stayed until 5:00, and nobody would have cared anyway.

***

That evening, Eddie asked, "So… how was your first day?"

"To be honest, it was pretty boring. There was all this orientation stuff. I mean, it was kind of interesting and I know they have to go through it, but there was so much. And *sooo* many PowerPoint slides."

Eddie laughed. "Well, get used to it. That never stops. I think the reason they call them 'bullet points' is that after twenty slides, you wish someone would shoot you."

"I know, right? Some of my professors just talked to PowerPoint slides too."

"Did you get to meet your boss?"

"Yeah, just for a moment though. She seemed really busy and kind of frazzled. I'm supposed to have a meeting with her tomorrow. Her name's Kendra Clifton. Do you know her?"

"I know who she is. I haven't worked with her. There are rumors she might be a lesbian, but I don't know for sure. If she is, I don't think she's out at work. So I wouldn't say anything."

"I won't. I don't think I want to be out at work – at least not at first. Maybe if I end up getting a permanent job here, I'll think about it once I get settled in."

"Well, you do what you think is best. As I said, I don't think you'll have any problems, especially if your boss is a lesbian."

"Yeah, but it's like I don't want that to be the first thing people know about me. I don't want to be like 'Hi, I'm Ryan and I'm gay,' you know?"

"Yeah, I get it. You don't want to be labeled right away."

They talked about a variety of other topics. The conversation flowed freely. Ryan realized he was starting to look up to Eddie as sort of a big brother/mentor figure, much like Hal and Russ Simonton.

As they were wrapping up their conversation, Eddie said, "So, the LGBT group is having their monthly lunch this Friday. They're going to a Mexican place near the 101. Do you want to go?"

"Thanks, but no. Like I was saying earlier, I don't think I want to be out at work yet."

"Suit yourself, but I'm sure no one in the group is going to out you to anyone."

"Yeah, I know, but there are other reasons I'd rather keep it on the down low."

Eddie didn't say anything, in case Ryan wanted to offer more information. Ryan wondered whether he should tell Eddie why. He felt comfortable with Eddie and felt he could trust him, so he decided to talk.

"So, there's a reason I want to be kind of discrete at work – at least while I'm still an intern. Hmmm… How should I say this? So, um… Do you ever watch porn?" Ryan immediately realized this might be an inappropriate question. "You don't have to answer that."

Eddie smiled. "Yes, I may occasionally entertain myself with viewing material of an adult nature. I might even own a small collection of said material."

Ryan chuckled nervously. "Well, then, it's theoretically possible that you might have seen me in one of those videos. If you haven't, you might in the future."

Eddie grinned. "Yes, in fact, I have a few videos you're in. Or at least I'm pretty sure it was you. But I wasn't going to say anything."

"I appreciate that."

"By chance, was that you in *The Boys of Breckenridge*?"

"Yep, that was me. My housemate Ricky was in that too. He's Juan Knight."

"I just saw that movie this past weekend. All I can say is, wow! Especially that 16-man orgy scene."

"Yeah. It took us, like, an entire day to shoot that."

"You're kidding! Anyway… well, you've been open with me, so I'll be open with you. You remember that party I went to last Saturday night?"

"Yeah…"

"Well, that was an orgy. And they were playing that movie."

"I bet that fueled the fire."

"I'll say. It was quite a memorable event."

"So, orgies are really a thing? I wasn't sure if that was just something they did in videos to be outrageous or if people actually did that in real life. What's it like?"

"It's pretty hot, at least they can be. Sometimes they can be duds. It all depends upon the people and what kind of mood they're in. I think it's safe to say they're usually not filled with young, hot guys with well-built bodies and big dicks."

"I've never been to one in real life. And I'm not sure I want to. Despite everything I've done in videos, I'm a one-on-one kind of guy."

"That's cool. When I'm in a relationship, I'm a one-on-one guy too. But I figure, I'm single now, so why not get a little wild? At least before I find another partner or get too much older. Whichever comes first."

"You're a nice guy! I'm sure you'll find someone else soon."

"Thanks. So, if you don't mind me asking, why did you decide to be in porn?"

"Well, remember how I told you I had to leave home when I found out my dad was going to send me to that conversion therapy place in Alabama?" Eddie nodded. "Well, once I got to LA, I realized I needed to earn a lot more money than I was making at my grocery store job to pay for college. And that seemed to be my best option. Anyway, the main reason I don't want to get involved with the gay group is that I don't want other people to recognize me and start spreading it around."

"I don't think they would do that."

"Maybe not, but I'd rather not be identified as 'Ryan the porn star' right off the bat, or have people accidentally call me Luke instead of Ryan."

"Sounds like an occupational hazard. I hope you don't plan to run for office."

"Nope. But yeah… It's definitely an occupational hazard. It's gotten in the way of a lot of other things already – like making friends and dating. So maybe I'm being too paranoid, but I don't want it to get in the way of me getting offered a job when I graduate."

"Got it."

Eddie wanted to press Ryan for details on what it was like to make porn videos, but he decided not to. Maybe later in the summer after they had bonded some more.

# Summer's End

Friday, September 2, 2011

The summer flew by quickly. Eddie and Ryan got along famously. Some evenings, they would spend two or three hours talking about everything from what happened at work that day to their life experiences. On the weekends, they went hiking or visited local museums or art galleries. They ate out together often. Ryan even convinced Eddie to go with him to a couple of jazz concerts.

The dynamic between Ryan and Eddie was curious. Mostly, they were good friends. To Ryan, Eddie was like Hal in that they had a landlord-tenant relationship, but also a big brother/mentor relationship. In other ways, Eddie was similar to Ted in that they could have deeply personal conversations based on trust. And as with Ted, there was a degree of underlying sexual tension between them – although in this case, the attraction flowed mostly in the other direction. Eddie never said or did anything inappropriate or unwelcome, but Ryan could sense he harbored some unrequited desire. Eddie was a nice-looking man, but Ryan simply didn't feel that kind of attraction to men his age. Besides, there was Ted's half-your-age-plus-seven rule. Yet Ryan realized that, on certain levels, he loved Eddie.

In the interest of not complicating their relationship, both Ryan and Eddie knew it was best not to go there. Ryan avoided swimming naked with Eddie and only got in the pool naked when he was home alone.

***

On Wednesday of his final week, Ryan presented the results of his summer project to Kendra and several managers from adjacent workgroups. Ryan felt uncharacteristically nervous throughout the presentation. He knew a permanent job offer was dependent, at least in part, on this presentation. If he wasn't offered a job, at least this internship would look good on his resumé. There would be plenty of other companies he could interview with. But over the course of the summer, he realized he liked Technovations, he liked Scottsdale, and he liked Eddie.

The next day, Kendra led Ryan into a small conference room. She said, "Everybody was impressed with your presentation yesterday."

"Thanks! I was pretty nervous about it. I mean, I thought I did a good job on the project, but I wasn't sure how well my presentation went over."

"It was fine. Yours was one of the best presentations we've received from an intern. We don't expect college students to be polished presenters yet. I also wanted to let you know I have been pleased with your work all summer. How has your experience working here been for you?"

"I enjoyed it. It was a bit overwhelming at first. But once I got into the swing of things and got used to working in this environment, I liked it. And I'm really impressed by the people I've worked with and the new technological advances this company is working on."

Kendra asked, "Would you be interested in working here full-time after you graduate?"

"Yes, I would! That would be fantastic!"

"I'm glad to hear that. So let me explain how the process works. I can let you know now that we intend to make you a job offer. Since you've already worked here for three months, you won't have to interview for it. We can't make you an official offer with a specific salary until after the first of the year. This fall, the company will finalize the budget for 2012, including headcount. It's possible they won't approve any headcount for new college graduates, but that's unlikely, given how well the company is doing and our growth projections. We'll also receive guidance from HR regarding the starting salaries we can offer. So, the bottom line is, I'll be able to make you an official offer in January or early February. How does that sound?"

"That sounds excellent!"

"Good."

Ryan thought for a moment. "So, I have a question. Technovations has an office in Lehi, Utah, right?"

"Yes. It's not as large as this site. I think they have around three hundred people."

"Do you know if there will be any job openings there that I would be a good fit for?"

"Probably, but I don't know for sure. I could ask and find out. But like here, they won't know how many people they'll be able to hire until after the first of the year. Why do you ask?"

"Well, I really like this organization and I could definitely see myself living in Scottsdale. But there are other reasons why I would prefer to live in Utah. It's kind of personal."

"Do you have family there?"

"Well… potentially."

Kendra smiled. "Sounds like you're following your heart."

"Yeah, I guess you could say that."

"Well, they do have some good opportunities there for someone with your skillset. Since it's a smaller site, there may not be as many opportunities for moving around within the company. But in any case, I can't give you a tentative job offer for a job at another site. You would have to go through the application and hiring process like all the other upcoming college graduates. But I would be happy to give you a recommendation. And the fact that you interned here this summer will look very good on your resumé."

Ryan said, "Okay, thanks. It's only a possibility at this point, but it's good to know my options."

"Sure. And you have half a year to think about it. When I contact you in January with an offer, you can let me know whether you wish to take it or you'd prefer to apply in Utah."

"Sounds good."

***

On Friday evening, Eddie treated Ryan to dinner at a Brazilian steak house. Ryan was heading back to Los Angeles the next morning, so Eddie wanted to end the summer on a celebratory note.

Ryan had never been to a Brazilian churrasco restaurant before. Eddie suggested they begin with a caipirinha in the bar, which was also a first for Ryan. Once inside the restaurant, Ryan and Eddie headed for the buffet, which was brimming with appealing appetizers and side dishes. "Don't load up too much here," Eddie suggested. "Leave plenty of room for the meat."

As the meal progressed, gauchos appeared at their table every few minutes, each carrying a giant skewer of meat. Ryan tried at least one of everything. "This is amazing!"

"Isn't it, though?"

"For real! Usually, at all-you-can-eat places, the quality isn't that good. But here? Oh my God… I've never had so much meat before in all my life!"

Eddie almost blurted out, 'That's what he said!' But he thought better of it.

Ryan and Eddie thoroughly enjoyed their dinner. They were both in good spirits from the delicious, plentiful food and the perfectly-paired Brazilian merlot. Ryan told Eddie about his meeting with Kendra and her interest in offering him a job after he graduates. He recounted their conversation about him applying for a job in Utah. Eddie found this possibility disappointing, but he tried to remain objective. "From what I understand, they're working on some good projects there. On the other hand, it's a smaller site, so you may have fewer opportunities in the years to come."

"Yeah, Kendra said the same thing."

"Another thing to keep in mind is, they're very conservative. A large percentage of the population is LDS. Believe it or not, there's a large gay community in Salt Lake City. But in the outlying areas… that's another story. Plus, it gets really cold there in the winter."

"Yeah, those are all things for me to think about."

"So, are you that serious about Cody?"

"Yeah, kinda. He's nice and we get along well." Ryan glanced around at the nearby tables. He leaned toward Eddie and whispered, "And the sex is amazing!"

"Well, that's nice, but a good relationship is based on a lot more than great sex."

"I know. And it's only been a few months. We'll see what happens this fall. Kendra can't give me an official offer until January or February anyway, so we'll see how it goes."

Eddie pondered whether he should say anything else. He decided to. "So, it's none of my business, but… Has he contacted you very often over the past three months?"

Ryan paused. "Not really." Ryan was always the one to initiate contact.

Eddie changed the topic to the fun things they had done together during the summer. He tried to keep the mood upbeat and celebratory, but just beneath the surface lurked the reality that at this time tomorrow, Ryan would be gone.

***

When they returned home, Ryan said, "Thanks for dinner! That was amazing."

"You're welcome. I enjoyed it too. I wanted to send you off in style."

"That was really above and beyond." Ryan thought back over the entire summer. Eddie had been generous and friendly and caring all summer long. Ryan realized he had received so much more than a rented room in someone's house. He was filled with gratitude for everything Eddie had done for him. "Hey, it's a beautiful evening. Would you like to get in the pool?"

Eddie was pleasantly surprised but tried not to let on. "Sure, why not? Ummm… are we going to wear swimsuits?"

"We don't have to, unless you'd prefer. I didn't bring one anyway."

"Okay. No suits it is."

Soon, they were in the water. They each clung to a floatie and drifted in the water as the jets slowly pushed them around the pool.

They made some small talk and spent some time enjoying the pool and the beautiful evening in silence. Then Ryan said, "When I first arrived, I had no idea what to expect, other than a room to sleep in. But I really enjoyed my stay here. We did a lot of fun stuff together. And you've been so nice to me."

"Thanks. To be honest, I had no idea what to expect either. I mean, I signed up to let a total stranger come live in my house for three months. That person could have been obnoxious or a total slob or whatever. I almost talked myself out of it several times. But you've been wonderful. I couldn't have asked for anyone better."

"Yeah. I feel like we became friends – good friends. I hope we stay in touch, even if I end up living in Utah."

"That would be nice. Are you on Facebook?"

"No. I don't want to get involved with social media. I don't want fans stalking me and I don't want my parents to find me. Most of the guys I live with are on Facebook, and it seems like it takes up a lot of their time."

"Okay, we can communicate by email or text or something. Maybe talk on the phone now and then."

"Yeah. Skype would be good for that. Anyway, I'll never forget this summer and all the fun stuff we did."

"I'll never forget it either. It's been a special time. It was just what I needed to get my mind off Wade and start enjoying my life again."

They looked into each other's eyes and smiled. This was a tender moment and both of them wanted to make it last.

Ryan pushed his floatie away and walked toward Eddie. When they got close, Eddie stood up and placed his hands on Ryan's sides. He kissed Ryan tentatively, but when Ryan opened his lips he knew their desire was mutual. Their tongues explored each other's mouths while their hands caressed each other's shoulders and backs. Ryan reached down and clasped Eddie's buns. Eddie hopped up and wrapped his legs around Ryan's waist, with his butt positioned just above Ryan's rapidly hardening cock. They hugged each other tighter as their kisses grew increasingly passionate and urgent.

Eddie said, "Hold on a second. Let me run inside and get some lube and a condom."

"You can bring two if you like."

Eddie grinned as if he had hit the jackpot. "I'll bring the whole box. Just in case."

# If You Really Love Me

Saturday, November 12, 2011

Brent came over to the house in the late morning to spend time with Hal. They enjoyed lunch at a table on the back patio in the 70° sunshine. Hal prepared a delicious lunch of Reuben sandwiches, Caesar salads, and a crisp, cool Vinho Verde.

Brent said, "This is delicious! You certainly went out of your way to create an exceptional meal for just an average Saturday lunch."

"Lunch is never average when I get to enjoy it with the man I love." Hal held up his glass. Brent picked up his and they clinked their glasses. "Seriously. I've been happier over the past year and a half than I've been since… I don't know, at least 20 years."

"The feeling's mutual. You came along at just the right time. You've given me a new lease on life. You've given me hope that I can live happily ever after again."

They continued eating. Despite the effort Hal put into lunch and the beautiful sentiments he expressed, Brent could tell something was worrying Hal. Maybe one of the guys in the house was having difficulties.

After they finished eating, Brent approached Hal and put his arm around his waist. "Thank you for a delicious lunch." He kissed Hal gently on the cheek. Hal tried to smile. Brent said, "I can tell there's something on your mind. Would you like to talk?"

Hal nodded and led Brent back to his desk in the master suite. Hal sat down at the desk and motioned for Brent to sit in the comfortable reading chair.

Hal said, "So, it's been a little over a year since we started Purebred Productions. And, uh… it's been fun and exciting to build a new business, and I'm proud of the videos we've produced so far."

Brent said, "It's kind of you to say 'we,' but the truth is, you're the one who's doing all the heavy lifting. I'm only an investor. And your number-one cheerleader, of course."

"Well, yeah. But you've done the editing, which has been top-notch."

"Still, I think of this as *your* business. It's your dream and your show. I'm just here to support you every step of the way."

"But you know, as we've grown together over the past year and a half, more and more I find myself thinking in terms of two. Not you and me, us. *Our* business. *Our* investment. *Our* dream."

Brent said, "Well, okay, so what's on your mind?"

"Our business. Sales aren't where I expected they would be at this point. We exhausted this year's marketing budget back in August. And I owe Charlie Kresler over $20,000 for his set designs. Christ, I can't believe he charges so much."

"He designs interiors for the richest socialites in Beverly Hills and Bel Air. Surely you didn't think he'd work for you for minimum wage."

"I'm not paying him minimum wage! I know his hourly rate, I just didn't think it would take so many hours."

"Well, whatever. I know other people who have started businesses. They always find that marketing costs two to three times what they budgeted for. Everything takes longer than they expect. Most of the time, it takes at least two years before a new business starts making a profit."

Hal said, "But are these other people in the adult entertainment industry, one of the most profitable industries there is?"

"Well, no…"

"So that doesn't necessarily apply here. It's apples and oranges."

"In any case, what are you going to do?"

"I've been talking with a guy from Titan Marketing and Analytics. They're pros at driving traffic to websites using targeted online advertising. They took Banged for a Buck from a startup to a ten million dollar a year company in only two years."

Brent said, "Banged for a Buck – isn't that the company that finds allegedly straight guys who are strapped for cash and offers them money on camera to have sex with other allegedly straight guys?"

"That's the one. And their sets are cheap, like just an old couch with a sheet thrown over it or something. The guys aren't even that good-looking. And look how far they've come, and how fast."

"Yeah, but that's different. They're playing to a fantasy – straight guys who can be talked into having gay sex. And they're profitable because they're keeping expenses down. So it's apples and oranges like you just said."

"But that's my point. If they can make a fortune with cheap sets and mediocre guys and the same plot each time, think how much more we should be able to make producing classy, artful videos."

Brent said, "Maybe people don't want classy art. Maybe they just want to see guys sucking and fucking and cumming. Maybe they just want to get off while they watch their fantasy played out."

"Maybe, maybe, maybe. I've been in this business for almost 30 years. I think I know what people want and how to deliver it to them. Besides, look at Kinky Twinkies. They produce top-quality porn and they're extremely profitable."

"And how many years have they been in business?"

"Around twenty."

"Bingo. And back in their early years, they shot guys fucking in barns and empty warehouses, not elaborate sets. They didn't start with big production budgets. So anyway, how much does Titan Marketing and Analytics charge?"

Hal said, "$30,000 a month, or $300,000 for an annual contract. And they claim with that package, clients should be able to make at least three million by the end of the first year."

"*Should.* Do they guarantee that? What will they do if you don't make that much – pay you the difference?"

"No, but even if we make two million the first year or even just one, we come out ahead."

"And where are you going to get $30,000 a month to pay these guys? Let alone $300,000. You don't have any more money for marketing this year and you can't pay Charlie his $20,000."

"It means we're going to have to invest another million dollars in the business. I figure I can take out a home equity loan on the house and get a half million. You can sell some of your investments to get the other half million. I'll pay you back and you can invest it again as soon as the increased revenue starts flowing in."

Brent said, "No. I've already invested a million dollars in your business–"

"*Our* business."

"No, *your* business. At this point, it's questionable when, or even *if*, I'm ever going to see that money again."

"So much for you supporting me every step of the way. And as for all that talk about me giving you a new lease on life and us living happily ever after, apparently there are monetary limits to that."

Brent said, "Now hold on a minute. Yes, I love you, and yes, you make me happier than I've been in years, and yes, I want to spend the rest of my life with you. But I shouldn't be expected to flush all my money down the toilet to make that happen."

"Oh, is that what it is? Investing in my dream is flushing your money down the toilet?"

"Your financial statements certainly seem to support that conclusion."

"Well, as you said earlier, maybe it's going to take up to two years before we start showing a profit."

"And as you said earlier, that doesn't apply in the pornography business."

Hal said, "So, Mr. Know-it-all, what do you propose we do?"

"Scale back. Cut back on your expenses. Maybe push out your timeline so you're issuing six releases a year instead of twelve. And maybe you should pivot from full-length DVD releases to scenes people can subscribe to and download. Manufacturing and distributing physical media is a lot more costly than distributing something on the internet."

"In other words, be just like everyone else. Don't create a higher-quality product that's better than anything else. Just be average."

"Maybe the reason everyone else is doing it is that it works. And maybe the reason everyone else is offering an average product is that's what most people want to buy. Hollywood can't sell art films. They make money by selling stuff that appeals to the widest possible audience. And this is porn. People don't want art, they want to see guys fucking and shooting loads."

Hal said, "So you're telling me I have to give up on my dreams and do it your way if you're going to invest any more money in *our* business."

"No, I'm saying I'm not going to invest any more money in *your* business."

"What I hear you saying is there are financial limits to how much you're willing to see me fulfill my dreams and be happy."

"And what I hear *you* saying is, 'If you loved me, you'd give me the money.'"

"I didn't say that."

Brent said, "Not in so many words. But it's what you're implying. Anyway, the bottom line is this. I love you with all my heart, I want to spend the rest of my life with you, and I'm not giving you another penny."

"Then you don't really love me."

"And there you have it. Well, fuck that. If your love has a price tag, and a damn high one at that, I'm out." Brent stood up and headed for the door. "Don't bother getting up. I can see myself out."

# The Last Thanksgiving

Thursday, November 24, 2011

When Thanksgiving came, everyone tried to be as upbeat as possible to offset the fact that Brent would not be attending. Hal allowed Ryan to invite Cody to participate in their annual tradition. Cody spent the night with Ryan at least once a week, so he was no stranger to the others.

Ted flew to Massachusetts to spend Thanksgiving with his mom, her wife, and their two younger children.

By 5:00, everything was ready and everyone sat down to dinner.

Ryan thought back to his first Thanksgiving in this house. It was his first Thanksgiving away from his biological family. While he had been welcomed and assimilated by his housemates, he remembered how his heart still ached for his loved ones back in Kansas. He recalled how truly thankful he felt by the end of the meal, because he was surrounded by people who loved him, looked out for him, and accepted him for who he was.

Today, four years later, he had much to be thankful for. He was filled with gratitude. Still, he knew this would be the last year he and his housemates would be together for this occasion. Darnell was close to graduating. Ricky was no longer pretending he might resume taking classes. Somehow Ryan knew Ricky would be moving on with his life before too long. And of course, he was half a year from graduating himself. If Technovations offered him a job, he planned to accept it. That meant he would be moving away next summer.

He decided not to think about the future and to focus on enjoying today. He didn't want to become depressed on an occasion that should be joyful. As the dinner progressed, he observed everything – the smiling faces, the playful banter, the delicious food – with heightened awareness. It was as if he was making a mental recording he could replay in the future.

After dinner, everyone pitched in to clean up. Then, they sat down at the table again to play Eclipse. Ryan realized one of the things he enjoyed most about living in this house was the opportunity to play challenging, strategic board games with other college-educated guys. Back in Kansas, he had been limited to easier games Brandon could do well with.

At around 10:00, people started heading back to their rooms. Ryan and Cody retreated to Ryan's room to cap off Thanksgiving with a different kind of stuffing.

***

The next morning, Ryan and Cody decided to eat brunch at Eggstravagance before going their separate ways for the rest of the day.

After they had ordered and their food was delivered, Ryan said, "I probably should have ordered something lighter. I'm still stuffed from last night."

Cody replied, "I know, right? That was so good, though."

"Yeah. Hal's an amazing cook."

"It was nice of him to let me be part of it."

"Well, you're my boyfriend."

Cody didn't say anything as they both took a few bites of their food.

Ryan asked, "So, what do you want to do for Christmas?"

Cody replied, "I'm going back to American Fork to spend Christmas with my family."

"When are you leaving?"

"On December 9th. My last final is on the 8th. The dorms close the next day."

"You could stay with me at the house for a while."

"I kinda want to get back and see my family. And I already bought my plane ticket."

Ryan contemplated what to say next. "I've got some work scheduled up through December 22nd. Maybe I could fly there on the 23rd and join you. I really want to spend Christmas together, and it would be nice to meet your family." *And have them meet me.*

Cody hesitated, then said, "Uh… That wouldn't really work. That's, like, family time. We have stuff we always do together. And you wouldn't be allowed into the temple."

"Oh, I wouldn't do that anyway. I'm through with organized religion. I thought you said you weren't into it, either. I thought you were a Jack Mormon, as you called it."

"Well, yeah, but I still go to services with my family during the holidays. It's pretty much expected."

Ryan debated how he should proceed. There were plenty of things he wanted to say, but he knew they would have consequences. Finally, he said, "You haven't told your family about me, have you?"

Cody shook his head.

Ryan asked, "At what point are you planning to tell them?"

"I don't know. I guess I haven't thought about it until now." Cody paused. He knew he had to come up with something better than that. "I'll try to do it while I'm home if I can find a good time."

Ryan said, "There's never going to be a good time. You just have to decide you're going to do it."

"Maybe it would be best if I did it right before I leave to come back. You know, so it doesn't mess up Christmas."

"Yeah, I guess that would work. Then they'll have some time to think about it and get used to the idea."

Cody nodded.

"Will you at least call me on Christmas?"

"Yeah, I'll try, if I can get away for a little bit."

# Crappy New Year

Sunday, January 1, 2012

New Year's Day 2012 was quiet. Since it was a Sunday, the Rose Parade, which Ryan watched every year, was pushed to Monday. After last night's party, he was in no mood to get up early anyway. Cody would not return from Utah until next weekend.

At 5:00, Hal, Ryan, Ricky, and Mykel sat down for their usual Sunday evening family night meal. Hal served pork, collard greens, black-eyed peas, and cornbread.

Ryan said, "Everything is delicious, Hal. Too bad Darnell isn't back from Georgia yet. He would have loved this!"

Hal replied, "Yeah, I know. But speaking of Darnell, he called me a little while ago. His dad's not doing well. He had a heart attack last Friday and he's been in the hospital ever since. He's scheduled for a triple bypass on Tuesday. So Darnell's going to extend his stay for at least a week. He'll probably miss the first few days of classes. A lot depends on how well his father does and what his recovery looks like. He may have to stay longer."

Mykel said, "Oh, wow. That's awful."

Ryan said, "We should send him a card we all sign, and maybe flowers."

Hal said, "I'm sure he would appreciate that."

They ate in silence for a few minutes. The year was getting off to a slow start and no one had much to say.

Ricky said, "Hey, Ryan, have you heard anything from Cody? Wasn't he supposed to come out to his family while he's home?"

"Not a word."

"Are you going to call him?"

"I think I'm going to leave that ball in his court. He said his family and relatives do a lot of stuff together over the holidays, so I don't want to call and catch him at a bad time."

Ricky said, "Wasn't he supposed to call you on Christmas?"

"Yeah, if he could get away from his family."

Mykel said, "You know, I don't get a good vibe from that guy. I never have. It's like I get this feeling he's not authentic. Like he's not being completely open with you."

Hal said, "Yeah. He always seems guarded about what he says and does."

Ryan said, "I know what you mean. He's still pretty closeted. I doubt that anyone in his dorm knows, and up until now, his family doesn't know. I used to be there myself, so I know what that's like. So I'm trying to give him a break. My old boyfriend Chris kept trying to get me to be more open, and that created some conflict. I've learned you can't force people. They'll do it when they're ready."

Ricky said, "Yeah, but where does that leave you?"

"Well, we still have half a year to work stuff out."

***

Darnell's father died during the operation.

Darnell called and said he was withdrawing from his classes for the winter quarter. He needed to stay home to help his mother and sister plan his dad's funeral and wrap up his affairs. He and his mother and sister would have to decide whether it would be in his mother's best interest to remain in Macon or to sell the house and move to an apartment in Atlanta, where she could be closer to her daughter.

Darnell wasn't sure when, or even if, he would be able to return.

The guys sent flowers, and Hal traveled to Macon to attend the funeral.

# A Job Offer

Tuesday, January 31, 2012

When Ryan returned home after his jazz ensemble rehearsal, he checked his email. He received an email from Kendra Clifton, his manager from his internship at Technovations. He opened the email and almost crapped his pants. Kendra offered him a job in her department with a starting salary of $95,000.

Ryan leaped to his feet, pumped his fist into the air, and shouted, "YESSS!!!" He paced around the room, filled with triumphant excitement. He was accustomed to making that much money each year doing porn. But he was ready to leave that industry, along with its baggage and difficulties, to begin his professional career.

As the initial rush of excitement subsided, he realized he had a choice to make. Should he accept this job offer and move to Scottsdale, or apply for a job at Technovations' campus in Lehi, Utah, where an offer was less certain?

As he ate dinner and tried to study, he could think of nothing else. He enjoyed working at Technovations last summer and he liked living in Scottsdale. But then, there was Cody. He was the only guy who had shown promise as a boyfriend during the four-and-a-half years he had lived in LA. He was the only one who wasn't turned off by the fact that Ryan did porn. Ryan didn't know what living in Utah would be like, other than it would be cold and snowy in the winter and more politically and socially conservative. He'd still be working for Technovations, either way. He figured he might as well find out what opportunities were available and see what it was like.

He opened Kendra's email again and clicked on Reply.

Hi Kendra,

Thank you so much for the job offer! I am grateful and excited! I enjoyed my internship last summer and I would be thrilled to work for Technovations.

As you probably recall from our conversation last summer, I would also like to consider opportunities with Technovations at their Lehi, Utah site. Do you know who I could contact to learn more about the openings they may have for new college graduates?

I will give your offer serious consideration. By what date do you need to receive a reply from me?

Thanks again for your offer. I genuinely appreciate it.

Best Regards,

Ryan Robertson

On Wednesday afternoon, Kendra replied with the email address of Sherri Singleton, who coordinated their new college graduate interviews in Lehi. Ryan promptly sent her an email asking about opportunities there.

***

On Friday, he received a reply from Sherri Singleton. She informed him they would have five openings for new college graduates in June. The interview rush, as she called it, would take place on March 15th and 16th. She asked Ryan to send his resumé. She said she would reply within the next two weeks with an invitation to travel to Lehi for the rush if any hiring managers were interested.

# The Truth Will Set You Free

Tuesday, February 14, 2012

On Valentine's Day, Ryan hurried home after jazz ensemble rehearsal to clean up for dinner. He had invited Cody to dinner at Al Fresco's, the Italian restaurant in Santa Monica where he went with his high school friends for dinner on prom night.

After he took a shower, he changed into a nice shirt and dress slacks. He had a few minutes to spare, so he checked his email.

To his delight, he received an email from Sherri Singleton inviting him to travel to Lehi for the hiring rush. Their travel department would make airplane reservations for him to fly to Salt Lake City on Wednesday afternoon, March 14th, and return on Saturday morning, March 17th. They would reserve a rental car and three nights in a nice hotel nearby.

Ryan was ecstatic! This news made Valentine's Day even sweeter. He couldn't wait to share the news with Cody. He glanced at the time in the lower right corner of his computer screen. It was 5:15 – time to leave.

Ryan pulled up to the front entrance of Hedrick Hall at 5:26. He called Cody to let him know he had arrived, but the line was busy. He left a voicemail and sent Cody a text. About ten minutes later, Cody appeared at the front door and headed toward the car. Ryan was mildly disappointed that Cody wasn't dressed any nicer than he typically dressed for classes, but whatever. Ryan wasn't about to let that detract from his good mood and the romantic evening that awaited them.

Cody got in the car, and Ryan leaned toward him to kiss him. Cody pushed him back and said, "Uh… not right in front of my dorm, okay?"

Ryan was momentarily taken aback. But then he recalled the time in Kansas when Chris tried to kiss him when they were parked at Slush Fun. Ryan pushed him away because he didn't want other people to see him kissing a guy. He realized Cody probably wasn't out to people in his dorm, so he cut him a break.

As Ryan pulled away, he said, "So! How was your day?"

"It was okay, I guess. Just an average day."

Cody didn't seem very excited about going out for a nice dinner to celebrate Valentine's Day.

Ryan asked, "Did anything bad happen? Is anything wrong?"

"No, not really. I dunno… I guess I'm just having an off day."

"Well, hopefully, this evening will cheer you up. I just got some great news! I'll tell you about it over dinner."

"Okay. I can tell you're pretty excited about something." Cody figured that with Ryan in such a great mood, the sex later this evening would be fantastic. So there was that.

They arrived at Al Fresco's. Ryan said to the maître d', "Good evening. I'm Ryan Robertson. I believe I have a reservation for two at a table in the garden?"

She checked her list. "Yes, indeed. Right this way, please." She led them through the dining room to the rear door, then out to the garden. It was just as Ryan remembered it, with the beautiful roses and tall oleander hedges and overhead light strings. It was still light, but in half an hour the sun would go down and it would become even more romantic.

The maître d' showed them to a small round table for two at the far end of the garden, next to a few particularly attractive rose bushes. They sat down and she handed each of them a menu and placed a wine list on the table between them. "Your waiter, Giorgio, will be with you in a moment. Have a lovely dinner!"

As soon as she was out of earshot, Cody leaned over and said, "I had no idea it was going to be this nice." That was obvious from his choice of clothing, but Ryan didn't say anything. Cody glanced at the menu and said, "This place is awfully expensive."

"Relax! I'm paying for it. I want our first Valentine's Day to be special. Besides, as of tomorrow, it's been a year for us."

"What do you mean?"

"It was one year ago tomorrow that we met for lunch after I spoke at the Ethics class."

"Yeah, I guess so." Cody hadn't thought of that. He felt awkward.

Ryan glanced at the wine list. "How about a nice Sangiovese? That should go well with anything Italian."

"I don't even know what that is. I'll take your word for it."

"As they say, when in Rome…"

Giorgio arrived at their table and said, "Good evening, gentlemen. Would you like to start with something to drink?"

Ryan said, "Yes, please. I'd like a bottle of the Sangiovese."

"An excellent choice." He lowered his voice. "May I see your identification please?" Ryan and Cody retrieved their driver's licenses from their wallets and showed them to Giorgio. He smiled. "Thank you. I'll be right back with your wine and some fresh warm bread."

Cody scanned the menu, puzzled by most of what he saw. "Uh… what are you going to have?"

"I think I'll try the garlic roasted shrimp over penne pasta, with the pesto sauce."

Cody decided to play it safe and stick to spaghetti and meatballs. It was one of the cheapest things on the menu.

Giorgio returned with their wine. An assistant brought a basket containing a cloth-wrapped loaf of round bread and a sharp bread knife. The assistant placed a small plate between them and poured some olive oil and black vinegar onto it. Giorgio uncorked their wine and poured a small amount into Ryan's glass. Ryan swirled the wine for a moment, inhaled the bouquet, then took a small sip. He rolled it around inside his mouth before swallowing. He smiled and said, "Oh, yes! That's wonderful!"

Giorgio poured some wine into Cody's glass, then into Ryan's. "Have you decided what you would like to order, or do you need a few more minutes?"

Ryan glanced at Cody, who nodded. "I think we're ready. I'd like the garlic roasted shrimp over penne pasta, with the pesto sauce. And a Caesar salad."

"Very well, sir." Giorgio turned to Cody. "And for you, sir?"

"I'll have the spaghetti and meatballs."

"Would you also like a salad?"

"Yeah, I guess. Just a regular salad."

"Very well. Thank you." Giorgio hurried away.

Cody reached for his glass and was about to take a drink from it. Ryan said, "Wait! A toast! To one year together, and all that is to come!" Ryan reached over and clinked his glass against Cody's, then took a sip. Cody said nothing and took a drink from his glass.

Ryan could hold back no longer. "So! I got some great news today, right before I left to pick you up. Remember how I said I got a job offer from Technovations, the place I interned at last summer?"

"Yeah. In Scottsdale, right?"

"Yeah. But listen to this! They also have an office in Lehi, Utah. That's right next to American Fork, where you're from!"

"Well, yes, I know where Lehi is."

Ryan chuckled. "Yeah, I guess so. Duh, right? Well anyway, I checked, and they have some job openings for new college graduates there too! So I sent them my resumé, and I just found out today they're interested in me! I'm going there in March for interviews! They're going to fly me there and put me up in a nice hotel and everything! Isn't that great?"

Cody looked shocked. "Uh… why did you do that?"

"Well, you said you wanted to live in Utah after you graduate, and you're applying for jobs at the newspapers in Salt Lake City and Provo. So, if I get a job in Lehi we can stay together!"

Cody sighed. Then he took a deep breath and said, "Okay, look.

Uh… I don't know how to say this, but… You can't come to Utah."

"Why not?"

"Well, I guess you could. I can't stop you from going wherever you want to go. But if you come to Utah, we can't see each other."

"What…? Oh, wait a minute. You didn't tell your folks about me when you were home for Christmas, did you?"

"No."

"There's still time. Or we can go somewhere else. They have newspapers in Phoenix. You'd love Scottsdale. Have you ever been there?"

"No. I'm going back to Utah."

"Why? If you're afraid of your parents finding out you're gay, why not live someplace else? Why do you have to go back to Utah?"

"My whole family is there. So is Jennifer."

"Who's Jennifer?"

"My fiancée."

"Your *what*???"

"My fiancée. We've been dating off and on since high school. We got back together again last summer when I was home. I asked her to marry me over Christmas break, and she said yes."

"Wait… So, let me see if I have this straight. Bad choice of words, but whatever. You're gay, but you're going to go back home and marry a woman."

"Actually, that was a good choice of words. You keep talking about me telling my parents I'm gay. Well, I didn't tell them, because I'm not."

"What the fuck? What do you mean you're not gay?"

"Shhh… you're getting kind of loud."

Ryan made no effort to lower his voice. "I don't give a shit. You're telling me we've been seeing each other for a year, but you're not actually gay?"

"Yeah, we hang out a lot, and that's been cool. But I never told you I'm gay, 'cause I'm not. That's something you assumed."

"YOU LOOK PRETTY FUCKING GAY WHEN I'M POUNDING MY COCK IN YOUR ASS!"

All the other diners in the courtyard stopped their conversations and listened to what was going on. Some tried to be discrete and not look, while others couldn't stop themselves from staring.

Cody whispered, "Will you please keep your voice down?"

"If you knew I was assuming you're gay but you're not, when were you planning on telling me?"

"It didn't matter. I never wanted this to turn into some kind of relationship. Back when we first met, you said you weren't interested in having a boyfriend while you were still in college. I just thought we'd hang out and have fun together until we graduated, then we'd go our separate ways. You'll move to Scottsdale and I'll move back to Utah, and that will be that."

Ryan said, "Wow. Just wow. Un-fucking-believable. All this time, I thought we were boyfriends and there was something real happening between us. But no… to you, we're just… I don't know… fuck buddies. Is that it?"

"I'd rather think of it as friends with benefits. You know, bros helpin' each other out. And we can still do that for the rest of the year. We can keep things the way they are."

"No thanks. I'm not into expiration dating. Sorry, not sorry."

"Your loss. You know you like it."

"I liked thinking I was building a relationship with someone who cared about me. But I guess to you I'm nothing more than a life support system for a big dick."

Cody had no answer for that.

Ryan said, "So you're going to go back to Utah and marry a woman… just to keep your folks happy. Who's going to fuck you in the ass then? Or are you going to give Jennifer a strap-on on your wedding night?"

A couple at a nearby table chuckled. Giorgio, who was trying to take their order, snorted and abruptly hurried away.

Ryan continued, "Because let's get real. You're, like, a total bottom. You like sucking dick and you like getting fucked in the ass. You were never interested in topping me."

"I can do that with Jennifer. And I can honestly tell her I never fucked anyone else while I was away at college."

Ryan yelled, "Oh, don't fucking talk to me about honesty! You're the most dishonest person I've ever met! You've been dishonest with me, you're being dishonest with Jennifer, and you're being dishonest with yourself." Ryan rose to his feet, knocking his chair over behind him. He pointed his finger in Cody's face and shouted, "Because the truth is, YOU'RE A BIG FUCKING HOMO. YOU LOVE SUCKING COCK AND YOU LOVE GETTING FUCKED IN THE ASS. OWN IT! BECAUSE UNTIL YOU DO, YOU'RE A BIG FUCKING LIAR!"

Ryan grabbed his glass of Sangiovese and threw the wine in Cody's face. "GO FUCK YOURSELF!"

As Ryan stormed across the courtyard toward the door into the restaurant, the other diners broke into a round of applause.

As he entered the door, he ran into Giorgio, who was carrying a tray with their salads. "I'm sorry, Giorgio. We won't be having dinner this evening. Or at least I won't." He pulled out his wallet, counted out five twenty-dollar bills, and shoved them into Giorgio's free hand. "I think this will cover dinner, plus a tip. If it doesn't, call me. My name's Ryan Robertson. They have my number in the reservation book."

Giorgio replied, "Thank you, sir, that should be sufficient. I'm sorry about what happened."

"Thanks. And to think, I almost moved to Utah for that guy. Oh well, better to find out now than later."

"Yes indeed. Good night, Mr. Robertson."

Ryan left the restaurant and drove home.

***

The next day, he sent Sherri Singleton an email informing her that he was withdrawing from the hiring rush in Lehi.

He called Kendra Clifton and left a voicemail asking if there was still time to accept her job offer. Later in the day, she called to tell him yes.

# The Party's Over

Wednesday, March 14, 2012

When Ryan returned home after classes, he pulled his laptop out of his backpack and gently dropped the backpack to the floor next to his desk. He opened the laptop and pulled up his email. There was an email from Reed, the production assistant at the studio where Ryan did the majority of his porn shoots. The subject line read,

SHOOTS CANCELLED, PLEASE READ

Ryan clicked to open the email.

<table>
<tr><td>

Hey everyone,

    All shoots for the next two weeks are canceled, due to a few HIV cases reported at other studios. I'll be in touch soon to reschedule. Take care of yourselves, stay safe, and GET TESTED.

    Talk soon,

    Reed

</td></tr>
</table>

*Oh well*, thought Ryan. *It's not like I need the money. And now I can go to classes on those days.*

Ryan's next bi-weekly test was scheduled in two days, so that would be soon enough.

He checked his phone. A text with the same information arrived half an hour ago.

Ryan wondered whether Ricky had been notified yet. He usually worked for different studios, so their paths rarely crossed. But whenever a performer tested positive, it shut down production throughout the San Fernando Valley for two weeks.

Ryan walked over to Ricky's room and knocked on the door.

"Come in." Ricky's voice sounded softer and weaker than usual.

Ryan entered. Ricky was sitting at his desk with a dejected look on his face. An open beer bottle was sitting on the desk, and Ryan could see a couple of empties in the trash can.

Ryan said, "Hey, man. Did you get the message about the two-week shutdown?"

Ricky looked up at Ryan. His eyes were red and Ryan could see dried tears on his face.

Ryan asked, "What's wrong, man?"

Ricky replied, barely above a whisper. "I've got it."

"You've got what?"

"HIV." Ricky sniffled and a couple more tears dripped from his eyes. "It was me."

Ryan stared in disbelief, unsure what to say. He dropped to one knee and wrapped his left arm around Ricky's shoulder. "I'm really sorry."

"Yeah, me too." Ricky reached for his beer, took three big swallows to finish off the bottle, and tossed it into the trash can. "I found out this morning when I went in for my test."

Ryan asked, "Do you know how you got it?" He didn't know whether that was the right thing to say, but he couldn't think of anything else.

"I don't know for sure, but I was at this party a couple of weekends ago. It was pretty crazy, and I got really lit. I let a couple of guys fuck me, and I think one of them might not have used a condom. Or maybe both of them."

"Oh, man. I'm sorry."

"And I've done some scenes lately where they wanted creampies and… well, I don't know. It could have been any of them."

Ryan said, "I guess it doesn't matter. It happened."

"Yeah."

Sadly, Ryan wasn't surprised. Over the four and a half years he lived with Ricky, he was concerned that his reckless party-boy lifestyle would get out of hand. Ricky seemed to be 'getting lit' more often, and Ryan suspected his meth use had increased. He knew it wouldn't end well, sooner or later. Still, it was sad. He truly felt sorry for his housemate.

Ryan said, "Well, it's not the end of the world. With the meds they have now, most people can go on living full lives. Like Hal – he's been positive for over twenty years, and he's doing fine."

"Yeah, but now I won't be able to work in the business anymore."

"There are plenty of other things you can do."

"Yeah, but they don't pay worth a shit. And I don't know if I could handle a regular job. I have no idea what I'll do."

"Well, maybe you could start taking classes again and finish your degree."

"Maybe. I don't know. Anyway, I don't wanna think about that now."

"Yeah, it's probably better to wait a few days until things settle down and you can think a little more clearly. You don't have to rush into a decision."

"I guess. Well anyway… thanks, man."

Ryan interpreted that as his cue to leave. He stood up. "Well again… I'm really sorry. Let me know if you want to talk or anything. I'm always here."

"Thanks."

Ricky didn't look up. Ryan left.

***

Ricky's HIV diagnosis effectively ended his career as a porn star. Hal pointed out that a few studios hired HIV+ performers and matched them up with each other. But Ricky wasn't interested. "They're too skanky."

Ricky launched into a downward spiral. When he wasn't getting drunk on beer, he was getting high on meth. Everyone else in the house was concerned. Ryan and Mykel tried to express their concern to Ricky, but he would always say, "I can handle it."

# Paranoia

Thursday, March 22, 2012

When Ryan arrived home from the day's classes, he sensed something was amiss as he inserted his key into the front door. He glanced around and noticed the security camera mounted under the eaves above the front door had been destroyed. It looked like someone had smashed it with a baseball bat.

*Hmmm...* Ryan thought. *We live in a nice neighborhood. It's pretty safe here. The local kids aren't the type that would do something like this. Has our house been broken into?* There was no indication someone had tried to open the front door and no broken windows he could see. He unlocked the door and cautiously entered the house.

He could see no signs of disarray. He walked into the family room and saw that the large TV was still in its place.

He walked out onto the back patio. There was no sign anyone had broken into the house there, but the two security cameras in the eaves had been smashed too.

Ryan went back inside and locked the sliding glass door behind him. Hal had installed security cameras indoors in several inconspicuous places to monitor the doors and the main rooms. Ryan walked through the house to check on each of them. All had been smashed.

Just then, Ricky bolted out of his bedroom and charged into the family room. He was wielding a large butcher knife from the kitchen. "WHO IS IT???" he screamed. He had a crazed, maniacal look on his face. He was sweating, his pupils were dilated, and he seemed panicked.

Ryan shouted, "Whoa! Whoa, dude! Put that thing down!"

For a brief moment, Ryan and Ricky stood a few feet apart,

staring at each other. Ryan contemplated whether he should run to his room and lock the door, make a run for the front door and drive away, or attempt to wrestle the knife away from Ricky.

Ricky saw that Ryan was alone and decided he posed no threat, so he lowered the knife. He shifted out of attack mode, but he still looked like he was possessed.

Ryan tried his hardest to appear calm, and said, "What's wrong, Ricky? What's going on here?"

"They're after me! When I heard you come in, I thought it was them."

"Who?"

"You know, *them.*"

"What are you talking about?"

"They're spying on me. Didn't you see all the black cars parked on the street? They're all over the neighborhood."

"No, I didn't see anything unusual outside."

"Well, maybe they left. But I swear they were out there. And they'll come back. They always do."

"So… what happened to the security cameras?"

"You mean the surveillance cameras? I destroyed them. I don't want them spying on me anymore."

"What are you talking about? Who would be spying on you? And why?"

Ricky dropped his voice to a whisper. "There are secret government agencies nobody knows about. They're watching every move we make. They're listening, too."

"What? You think the house is bugged?"

"Shhh!!!" Ricky placed his finger to his lips, then nodded.

"Dude, this is crazy. And Hal's going to fucking kill you when he sees what you did."

Ricky whispered so softly Ryan could barely hear him. "I think he might be in on it."

Ryan's head was spinning. *What is going on inside Ricky's*

*head? Why is he behaving like this? Most importantly, what should I do right now?*

Ryan took a deep breath and reminded himself to remain calm and non-threatening. He said, "Okay, so why would people want to spy on us and listen in on us?"

Ricky put his finger to his lips and shook his head.

Ryan sighed. "Is there somewhere we can go that isn't bugged? Maybe out in the backyard?"

Ricky shook his head.

"Why not? You destroyed the cameras."

Ricky pointed upward, as if helicopters or drones could still spy on him. Then he asked, "Can we get in your car and go someplace?"

Ryan considered doing this, but he decided the more he played along with Ricky, the more he was lending credibility to what he was saying. "Let's sit down." Ryan led Ricky into the family room and sat down on one of the easy chairs. Ricky sat down on the sofa near Ryan. "Okay, so what is it you're afraid of?"

"They're going to bust me. 'Cause… you know."

Clearly, Ricky had been abusing drugs. Probably meth. "Ricky, I don't know what's going on here, but I promise you there is nobody spying on us. There is nobody listening to us. There are no black cars parked out on the street. Do you want to go look?"

Ricky shook his head. It began to dawn on Ricky that he had been hallucinating, and he was starting to come out of it. "You mean… I'm imagining all this?"

Ryan nodded. "None of it is real."

Ricky's demeanor shifted from panic to embarrassment. "There's nobody spying on me? Nobody trying to take me away?"

"Nope. I promise."

Ricky sat silently, as reality returned and he realized how foolishly he had acted. He buried his head in his hands. "Fu-u-u-uck."

Ryan asked, "Why did you think someone was going to take you away? Where would they take you?"

Ricky's voice dropped to a whisper again. "I was afraid if I got busted they were going to send me back."

"Back to where? El Paso?"

Ricky shook his head. "El Salvador."

"I don't understand. I thought you were from El Paso."

"That's where my family has lived for 15 years. But we came here from El Salvador."

"I still don't understand why anyone would send you back to El Salvador."

"We're undocumented."

It never occurred to Ryan that Ricky might be living in this country illegally. He decided to leave that unaddressed and deal with the present moment. "Okay. This has all been a false alarm. Everything's going to be okay."

"Promise?"

"I promise."

"Maybe I need to take a nap for a while."

"That sounds like a good idea."

They stood up. Ryan took a good look at Ricky. He looked like he had been losing weight and his face was drooping a little bit.

Ricky said, "I'm sorry. God, I'm so embarrassed. I feel like such an idiot."

Ryan could see a few brown spots developing on Ricky's teeth. He gave Ricky a hug, then Ricky went back to his room.

Ryan went to his room and opened his laptop. He searched for the side effects of crystal meth addiction. Weight loss, agitation, outbursts, mood swings, rotting teeth, paranoia, hallucination… All on the list.

Ryan called Hal to give him advance notice of what he would find when he arrived home.

***

Ryan was in the kitchen fixing his dinner when Hal walked in the door. Hal was visibly annoyed, and with good reason. "Where is he now?"

"He hasn't come out of his bedroom. He's taking a nap. I don't know whether he's sleeping now or not."

"Okay, well… would you talk to me in my office after you've eaten dinner?"

"Sure."

Ryan thought back over the past five years. His housemates frequently teased Ricky about his promiscuity and referred to him as a party boy. He thought about all the weekends Ricky spent partying and barhopping with very little sleep, only to crash for the next few days. He remembered the time Ricky took him out to the bar to celebrate his 21st birthday and those shady characters he hung around with. Ryan wondered, *Were they his dealers? One of them tried to offer me something to perk me up.*

*It's no surprise that Ricky has ended up in this condition. The signs were so clear. Everybody could see what was happening, but maybe they didn't realize how serious it had become. Yet, nobody said or did anything. Should someone have intervened sooner? Would Ricky have listened? Probably not. He would say, 'I can handle it.' Why does he need to indulge in such excess in the first place? What is he trying to escape from? What inner pain is he trying to suppress?*

Despite the fact that this conclusion was inevitable, Ryan still felt sorry for Ricky. He finished his dinner, cleaned up his dishes, then went to see Hal in his master suite.

Hal said, "So, before we dive into the matter at hand, how are you doing?"

"Okay. Part of me is really looking forward to this quarter being over and graduating. I mean, I've already got a job lined up. I've met all the requirements for graduation, so the next few weeks seem kind of pointless. On the other hand, I'm going to miss it. Someday, I'll look back at my college years and wish I could be here again. So I guess I should try to appreciate every day while I'm still here."

Hal smiled. "Yeah, I felt exactly the same way. That's why I bought this house that's so close to campus. In some ways, I relive college vicariously through you guys. I used to take walks through the campus and recall what it was like and think about my old friends. But then I realized it only made me depressed. Those were good times, but they're gone now. Life goes on, and you have to go with it."

"I don't know if I'll miss the campus itself. I don't have as much connection to it as I would if I lived in the dorms. But I'm going to miss living here. I'm going to miss you and the other guys. You guys have been so nice to me and so supportive. You've been my family. We had so many good times. Of course, Ted and Darnell are gone now, and I won't be here in a couple of months. And, well, who knows what's going to happen to Ricky."

"Yeah, people come and go – both in this house and in our lives. I've had some great guys living here at various times. But we need to talk about Ricky. What happened?"

Ryan told Hal everything from Ricky charging at him with a knife and saying he was being spied on, to Ryan calming him down and disabusing him of his fears. "After Ricky went back to his room, I did some research on the internet. The paranoia and hallucinations are all symptoms of crystal meth addiction. Plus, I can see he's been losing weight and he's getting some brown spots on his teeth."

Hal said, "I guess, with 20/20 hindsight, none of this should be a surprise. It all makes sense. I've been concerned about him for a long time, but I had no idea it had gone this far."

"I think when he found out he had HIV it pushed him over the edge."

"Yeah. But this situation has been developing for several years. And there's this. I rent rooms in this house to college students. He hasn't been attending college in any meaningful way for six years. He takes a class here and there and talks about going back full-time, but he never does it. I've been thinking about asking him to leave for over two years now, but I didn't have the heart. I always hoped he'd get his act together and go back to school."

"Still, it's not your fault he's gotten himself into this mess."

"No, not directly, but it was too easy for him to stay here for $500 a month and have no responsibilities. If he was out on his own and had to pay rent and bills, maybe he would have become more responsible."

Ryan asked, "Well, anyway, what are we going to do now?"

"We have to get him into rehab. There's no way around it."

"What if he won't go?"

"Then I'm afraid I'll have to kick him out. I can't have things go on this way and risk the health and safety of everyone else in this household. He came at you with a knife. The cameras can be replaced, but who knows what he'll do next time? No… he can't continue down this path. He needs help, badly."

"Yeah. Oh, and there's one more thing. Maybe I shouldn't tell you this, but I'm going to. He's undocumented. He and his family came to the US illegally when he was eleven. He was paranoid they would send him back to El Salvador."

"Okay, well… that's interesting to know, but it doesn't change the current situation. I guess I need to see if he's in good enough shape to talk to him."

Ryan asked, "You want me to check on him first?"

"Yeah, that might be a good idea."

Ryan walked over to Ricky's bedroom and knocked on the door. At first, there was no answer. He said, "Ricky, it's me – Ryan. Can I come in?"

He didn't hear anything, so he assumed Ricky was still asleep. He hoped it was nothing worse. As he was turning to go back to Hal's room, Ricky cracked the door open a few inches. When he saw that it was Ryan, he said, "Come on in."

He opened the door enough for Ryan to enter, then he closed it quickly behind him. The room was dark except for the light seeping in around the edge of the curtains. As Ryan's eyes adjusted, he could see that Ricky's room was messier than he had ever seen it.

Ryan asked, "Can we turn the light on?"

"No. I don't want them to know I'm in here."

"How are you right now?"

"Better. I slept for a couple of hours. I'm hungry now. I was thinkin' about gettin' something to eat. Then I'll probably sleep some more."

"That's a good idea."

"Yeah, but I don't have any food here. I can't go outside. I guess I could get something delivered, but I'm scared to answer the door."

Ryan decided not to try to rationalize with Ricky, at least not now. "I have a couple of frozen meals. You want one?"

"Thanks, man. Would you mind nuking one and bringing it to me?"

"Yeah, okay. Would you prefer turkey with mashed potatoes and stuffing, or chicken fettuccine?"

"Doesn't matter. Chicken, I guess."

"Okay, I'll be back in a few minutes."

Ryan got his chicken fettuccine entrée out of the freezer and started cooking it in the microwave. Then he went back to Hal's room.

"He's been asleep until now. I'm fixing one of my microwave dinners for him. He's scared to come out of his room."

Hal looked concerned. "I guess I should wait until tomorrow."

"Oh, and one more thing. There's a ziplock bag of white powder on his desk."

Hal suddenly became irate. "Oh, hell no! You know I don't allow drugs in this house." He slammed his fist on his desk. "Dammit! Why did I think he was only using it when he went to parties? Son of a bitch. How could I have been so stupid?"

"It's not your fault. Don't beat yourself up. He brought this all on himself."

Hal sighed. "Yeah, you're right, but… still, I'm kicking myself for letting it get this far."

They heard the microwave ding. Ryan said, "Well, I'd better go take him his dinner. Give him 15 minutes or so to eat it. And try to calm down. The way he is now, if you come at him forcefully it might trigger him."

Ryan retrieved the meal from the microwave, picked a knife and fork out of the drawer, and pulled a bottle of water from the fridge. He delivered the dinner to Ricky.

Fifteen minutes later, Hal came to Ryan's room. "So… are you ready to do this?"

"Do I have to be there? Maybe he would feel less threatened if it was one on one."

"Yeah, but what if he gets violent? And two people telling him he needs to go into rehab sends a stronger message."

"Okay." Ryan never imagined he would find himself in a situation like this. But he knew it had to be done. "Let's get this over with."

Ryan knocked on Ricky's door. "Ricky? It's Ryan."

"Come in."

"I've got Hal with me. We need to talk."

Ryan and Hal walked into Ricky's bedroom and closed the door. Hal flipped on the light switch. Ricky decided not to protest.

Hal said, "Ricky, I'm going to cut right to the chase. You have a problem. Wouldn't you agree?"

Ricky stared at the floor. "Yeah, I guess."

"We care about you, and we want to see you get the help you need. Will you let us help you?"

Ricky thought for a moment. "Yeah, I know I need to cut back. But I can handle it."

Hal said, "Let's look at where we are now. Today you busted all the security cameras, threatened Ryan with a knife, and you think secret government agents are spying on you. Let's be honest – it's out of control. It's gotten too big. You can't handle it anymore."

Ricky remained silent.

Hal asked, "Do you want to quit?"

Ricky hesitated. He was trying to assess his options and their potential outcomes, but his addled mind was preventing him from thinking clearly. "Yeah, I guess so."

"'I guess so' isn't good enough. Look where this has gotten you. There's only one way up, Ricky." Hal paused to let that sink in. "Do you want to quit?"

"Yeah."

"Are you willing to get help?"

"What kind of help?"

"You need to go into rehab."

"Rehab? Isn't that kind of extreme? I mean, isn't that for celebrities and stuff?"

"No, lots of everyday people go into rehab. There's no shame in it. It takes a strong person to admit that they need help and to go get it. It's what you need right now. You can do it."

"But isn't it expensive?"

"It depends on the place. But your health insurance should cover at least part of it."

"I don't have health insurance."

"WHAT??? You don't have health insurance? How can you not have health insurance?"

Ricky shrugged his shoulders.

Hal said, "You have HIV now. How do you think you're going to pay for your meds? Do you have any idea how expensive they are?" Hal had remained remarkably calm up to this point. Ryan knew if Hal lost his patience they might not be able to salvage this situation. He took a couple of steps toward Hal and put his hand on his shoulder to calm him down.

Ryan said, "We can find a way to work through that. But are you willing to come clean? Are you willing to stop using drugs?"

"I can reel it in. I can keep it to a party every now and then."

Ryan said, "No. You have a problem. Meth is ruining your life. You're addicted. You can't control it, it's controlling you. You need to give it up – completely."

Hal regained his composure. "Ricky, we love you, but it's come down to this. You have two choices. You either go into rehab or you move out. Those are your only two choices. If you commit to quitting, we'll get you into rehab. If you won't commit, you move out. Is that clear?"

Ricky nodded.

Hal said, "Think about it and let me know in the morning." He walked over to Ricky's desk and picked up the bag of meth. "You know I don't allow drugs in this house."

Ricky sprang to life. "What are you doing, man?"

"I'm flushing it down the toilet."

"No way, man. There's like $300 worth of chalk in there."

"Are you serious about quitting or not?"

Ricky realized the moment of truth was upon him. "You said I had until tomorrow."

"That's right. Okay, I won't flush it. I'll hang onto it until tomorrow. I don't want you using any more of this in the meantime. If you decide you're not willing to go into rehab, I'll return this to you when you move out."

Ricky said nothing. Hal and Ryan left the room.

***

The next morning at 10:00, Hal knocked on Ricky's door. He heard a weak, sleepy voice say, "Come in."

Hal entered. The curtains were still closed and the room was still dark. He flipped on the light. Ricky was still in bed.

"So, what have you decided? Rehab or move out?"

Ricky sat up and pivoted so he was now sitting on the edge of the bed with his feet on the floor. He stared at the floor, both to avoid the light and to avoid the decision he was being called upon to make.

"I guess I'll try rehab."

"Good. I was hoping that's what you would decide. It's for the best."

Ricky said nothing.

Hal said, "Now, would you come with me, please?"

Ricky wasn't sure what Hal had in mind, but he slowly got up and shuffled across the room. Hal led him into the bathroom, then handed Ricky his bag of meth. "Flush it."

Ricky hesitantly took the bag from Hal. He stood in front of the toilet, waffling back and forth. "Do I have to?"

"Yes. If you're serious about quitting, then you don't want this. You don't ever want to take an illegal drug again. This is your enemy. It's ruining your life. You should want to get rid of it. Flushing this will be a liberating experience. It's a physical expression of your commitment to your recovery and a better life."

Ricky pulled the ziplock seal apart. He looked back and forth between the bag of white powder and the toilet. He recalled the many all-night parties, the laughter, and the high-energy nights of dancing in the clubs. Good times. Good friends. Life in the fast lane. Flushing his drugs meant flushing away his social life – forever.

After half a minute that seemed to last half an hour, Ricky stepped back from the toilet. He pressed the ziplock bag closed again. "I can't do it. I just can't."

"Then you need to be out by Sunday."

"Where will I go?"

"That's your problem. Start calling your party friends. Surely one of them will be there for you." Hal turned and took a few steps into the hallway, then turned back. "And you owe me $800 for the security cameras."

# Everything's Going to Hell

Sunday, April 15, 2012

Hal informed Ryan and Mykel there would be no family night dinner this week. "I'm still working on my taxes. Besides, with only the three of us, what's the point?"

Ryan knew something wasn't right. Hal had become progressively more depressed and unhappy over the past several months, starting around the time he and Brent broke up.

After contemplating what he could do to help, Ryan went to Hal's bedroom and knocked on the door.

"What is it?" Hal sounded hopeless. It was a far cry from his usual cheerful 'Come in!'

Ryan opened the door and took a couple of steps inside. Hal was staring at his computer screen looking defeated. Paperwork was strewn all over his desk. Hal looked up at Ryan but didn't smile. Ryan could see a half-empty bourbon bottle and a glass with a few nearly-melted ice cubes.

Ryan said, "So… I know you're busy, but I was wondering… I'd be happy to cook dinner this week. Or I could get take-out."

"Thanks, but no. I'm not into it this week. Sorry."

"You've got to eat sometime. Can I bring you anything?"

Hal picked up his glass and extended his arm toward Ryan. "A few more ice cubes. Five is about right."

Ryan took the glass to the kitchen, dumped the remaining ice and water, and filled the glass with five fresh ice cubes. Then he headed back to Hal's room.

"Here you go."

Hal took the glass and muttered, "Thanks." He opened the

bourbon bottle and filled the glass.

"Hal… I know you're busy so I won't take up much of your time, but… what's bothering you?"

Hal was about to say, 'Nothing. Don't worry, I'll be fine.' But he realized Ryan would worry, he wasn't fine, and he wouldn't be fine any time soon. He heaved a huge sigh. "Sit down."

Ryan sat in Hal's reading chair. Hal swiveled around in his desk chair to face him. "Life sucks, Ryan. Everything's going to hell in a handbasket. I don't know what I'm going to do."

"Do you owe a lot on your taxes? I can loan you some money if you need it." Ryan would do that for Hal, but he thought it was highly unusual that Hal would be short on cash.

"No, it's not just the taxes. It's everything. Breaking up with Brent. The whole thing with Ricky. But the biggest thing is my production company. All my investors and business partners are pulling out. I've sunk everything I own into this business, and now poof! It's all turning to shit."

"How come they're pulling out?"

"Oh, geez… you name it. Brent invested a million dollars in it, but he wouldn't put in another half-million when we needed it. That's what led to us breaking up. So now I'm out both a romantic partner and a business partner. Others started getting cold feet about losing their money and what it might do to their professional reputations."

"Oh, wow. I didn't know that's why you broke up. I'm sorry."

"Yeah, that was part of it. I didn't say anything about that. But anyway, there's also this. I wanted this production company to be high-end like Eagle and Kinky Twinkies. You know, high class. Good production values. The best performers. The cream of the crop. But all that – the sets, the lighting, the cameras, the editing, the best people – it all takes money. And now, you have every Tom, Dick, and Harry making homemade porn with GoPros and cheap, consumer-level cameras. Hell, people are even making videos on their iPhones! Editing software is cheap now too. And now with all these cheap-ass porn sites on the internet, everyone thinks they can just record people fucking and upload it. Nobody gives a shit about quality, and they're not willing to pay for it. Why should they, when they can watch butt-ugly people fucking online for free? The whole market has gone to hell."

Hal took a huge gulp of his bourbon and emptied half of the glass.

"And then there's this. They're going to put a measure on the ballot this fall to require all actors in the adult film industry to wear condoms. And it looks like it might pass. And if it does, there goes every studio in San Fernando Valley – gay and straight."

"Why don't they go back to using condoms like they used to? It would be safer for the performers and it would send a better message to viewers."

"Because nobody wants to see condoms in porn. Porn is all about fantasy. You know that. Do you fantasize about wearing condoms? No. Of course not. Nobody else does either. Nobody's buying that shit. At first, there were only a few places that shot bareback porn. The rest of the industry howled about it, but those guys were making all the money. So one by one, all the other studios ditched the condoms. When Libertine Studios stopped using condoms, their sales shot up 50 percent."

"So what's going to happen if the ballot measure passes?"

"Everyone will go someplace else – probably Vegas. That, or stay here and lose money. And I'm just starting out. I don't have the resources to move everything to Vegas and I can't afford to add plane tickets and hotel rooms to the production costs. Especially since people are going to download it for free anyway."

"Yeah, that all sucks. I can't think of a good answer."

"I can't either. So anyway, now you know. I guess I should have left well enough alone. But nooo… I had to go chase this stupid-ass dream of being a big-shot production company owner. I thought I had friends all over the industry I could count on, but they scattered like roaches as soon as the going got tough."

"Well, even if you close up shop, can't you go back to what you were doing?"

"Maybe. But some of the other studios weren't exactly thrilled when they found out I was starting a competing business. They may not be real crazy about hiring me to be their attorney now."

Ryan had run out of things to say. He had no idea what he could suggest that might help. "I'm really sorry about everything. But thanks for sharing all that with me. You can always talk to me."

"Thanks. I appreciate it. I know you mean well, and that counts a lot. Now if you'll excuse me…"

"Yeah, I know – taxes. I won't take up any more of your time tonight."

"Thanks, Ryan." Hal got up to hug Ryan. He could barely stand up. As he approached, his breath reeked of bourbon. He wrapped his arms around Ryan and whispered, "Thanks for caring about me. Seems like nobody else does."

"Of course, I care about you! Hal, I owe everything to you. When I first arrived here, you offered me a place to stay. You've given me guidance and support and love. You've been more of a father to me than my own father."

After a few more seconds, Hal dropped his arms and stumbled back into his chair.

"Your father? Now you're saying I'm old?"

"You know I didn't mean it that way. And uh… I know it's none of my business, but I think maybe you've had enough for one night."

Hal resented that but didn't say anything.

Ryan needed something to lift his mood. He wanted to get out of the house for a while. After five years of family dinners on Sunday, that had become his favorite meal of the week. He decided to go to Burger Betty's. It wouldn't be as much fun to eat there alone, but he was okay with that.

***

When he returned home, the house was eerily quiet. Ryan spent a couple of hours trying to focus on his homework. At around 10:00, he decided to cap off the evening with a soak in the hot tub. It wouldn't be quite the same as those nights when he and Ted sipped wine and talked. Still, it would be relaxing.

When he reached the sliding glass door, he could see Hal was already in the hot tub. Under any other circumstances, Ryan would ask if he could join him. Tonight, he knew Hal wanted to be alone. And as much as Ryan was concerned about Hal, he knew joining him would only lead to more wallowing in misery. That wouldn't help Hal and it would bring Ryan down.

He returned to his room. He watched some YouTube videos, then went to bed.

# Tragedy Strikes

Monday, April 16, 2012

The next morning, Ryan entered the kitchen to make breakfast. He glanced out onto the patio. He spotted an empty bourbon bottle and a nearly-empty glass on the drink shelf on the side of the hot tub. He walked out onto the patio, figuring he would put the glass in the dishwasher and the empty bottle in the recycling bin.

When he reached the hot tub, he found Hal's motionless body. He had apparently blacked out from being so drunk. His unconscious body had slid down, submerging his head beneath the surface of the water. His face and torso were bloated and had started turning white.

For a few seconds, he stood motionless – shocked and terrified, with no idea what to do. Then he reached into the tub and tried to pull Hal up by his armpits. He jostled Hal – no response. He let go, and Hal's limp body slid back into the tub.

Ryan ran inside and pounded on Mykel's door. "Mykel! Mykel!"

Mykel cracked open the door. "What is it?"

"It's Hal! I just found his body in the hot tub! I think he's dead!"

Mykel and Ryan hurried outside. Mykel took one look and turned away, covering his face with his hands and fighting off the urge to vomit.

Ryan said, "Help me get him out. Let's try giving him CPR. Do you know how to do that?"

"Yeah, but I think it's way too late for that. He's probably been dead for hours."

Ryan's heart sank. He knew Mykel was right. But if there was even the slightest chance… No. It was hopeless.

"What do you think we should do?"

"Call 911, I guess."

Ryan ran back to get his phone. He wasn't sure why he was running. He dialed 911. Within ten minutes, two police officers arrived and took a report. They questioned Ryan extensively and took numerous photos. When they finished questioning Ryan, one of them asked, "Are there any other people living here?"

Ryan answered, "Yeah, one other guy named Mykel. Let me go get him." He went to Mykel's room and knocked on the door. No answer. "Mykel! Mykel!" Ryan shouted. Still no answer. Ryan jiggled the doorknob. It was locked.

Ryan returned to the police officers. "He's either not here or he's not answering. He was here half an hour ago."

"What's his name?"

"Mykel. That's spelled M-Y-K-E-L. He says he doesn't have a last name, or at least I don't know what it is. Do you want his number?"

"Yes, please."

Ryan gave the officers Mykel's number.

"Well, let us know when he returns." The officers gave Ryan their cards. An ambulance arrived, and medics lifted Hal's body onto a stretcher, covered it with a sheet, and loaded it into the back of the ambulance.

Ryan asked, "Where are you taking him?"

"To the county morgue. The coroner is going to want to do an autopsy."

"Then what will happen to his body?"

"It depends. Do you know if he had an end-of-life directive or if he designated a person to be responsible?"

"No, but I'll try to find out."

"Good. Let us know."

The medics climbed into the ambulance and drove away. Moments later, the police officers left.

Ryan had already missed his morning classes, and he knew there was no point in going to his afternoon classes. He paced around the house wondering what to do next.

He decided he should start notifying people that Hal had died. But who?

He started with Ted. He knew Ted would be at work, but he could at least leave a message. Ted answered after two rings. "Hey, Ry, what's up?"

"I'm sorry to bother you at work but I didn't know who else to call, and I figured you would want to know. Hal's dead."

"WHAT??? How? What happened?"

Ryan recounted the events of last evening and this morning.

"Oh my God… That's awful. How are you doing?"

"I don't know. I really don't. It's still sinking in. I'm just numb. I can't even think. I can't believe this is real. I know I should start calling people, but I don't even know where to start or what to do next. So I figured I'd start with you."

"Do you want me to come over?"

"That would be nice, but don't you have to work?"

"I can get away for this."

"Are you sure?"

"Yeah. See you in about an hour."

Ryan hung up. Then he tried knocking on Mykel's door again. There was still no answer. Ryan was trying to decide whether to try calling Mykel on his phone, but then Mykel entered through the front door with four of his friends. Ryan recognized some of them from the naked yoga sessions Mykel held on the back patio.

"Where did you go?" Ryan asked. "What's going on here?"

Mykel led his friends to his bedroom. He turned to Ryan and said, "I am *sooo* outta here!"

Ryan watched as Mykel gave instructions to his friends and they started carrying his possessions out of the house.

"What? You're moving out?"

"Well, duh… What's it look like?" Mykel stepped into his

closet. He pushed all of his hanging clothes together, wrapped his arms around them, and lifted the bundle to free the hanger hooks from the clothes rod.

He started carrying them outside with Ryan trailing him. "How can you just leave?"

"Like this." Mykel shook his head. "You ask the most obvious questions." One of his friends saw Mykel carrying his clothes and opened the rear passenger door for him. Mykel unloaded his armful of clothes onto the back seat.

Then he hurried back inside, trying to ignore Ryan. Ryan followed him back in. "I can't believe you left before the police got here. They're going to want to talk to you."

Mykel turned and glared at Ryan. "I have nothing to say to them. I have done nothing wrong. None of this was my fault. I didn't have anything to do with it."

"Well, neither did I, but…"

"I am *so* over this place. It has *sooo* much negative energy! First, there was the porn thing. Then Ricky and his meth addiction. And now Hal's dead body in the hot tub. My chakras are like totally blocked! I just can't deal with it. Like literally. I… Can't… Even! Now if you'll excuse me." He spun around and walked back into his room to gather the rest of his stuff. Two of his friends were carrying his yoga mats through the house and out to a pick-up truck.

Ryan pulled out his phone and dialed one of the officers. "Hello, Officer Cooper? It's Ryan Robertson, at the house with the dead body in the hot tub. The other guy who lives here, Mykel, came back. He has a few of his friends with him, and they're moving his stuff out now."

"Okay. I'm in the middle of another call, but I'll try to get there as soon as I can. It will probably be about half an hour."

"He'll be gone by then."

"Okay, I'll try to get there sooner. See if you can get his license plate number."

"I will. Thanks. Bye."

Mykel and his friends left before the police returned. Ryan called Officer Cooper to tell him that. He gave him Mykel's license plate number.

With Mykel gone and Hal's body removed, Ryan was now alone in the house. With nothing to distract him, the enormity of what happened crashed down on him. He ran to his room, plopped down on the bed, and cried his eyes out.

# Ted Arrives

Monday, April 16, 2012

An hour later, Ted arrived. They hugged, then Ryan led him into Hal's office. Ted said, "Geez, what a mess. I've never seen Hal's desk like this."

"Yeah. Last night he was working on his taxes. He was totally bummed out. He told me his new production company was failing and his investors were pulling out. He went on and on about how the industry is changing and things were going to get worse."

"That sucks. No wonder he was so depressed."

"Anyway, the police officer asked if he had an advance directive. Do you know what that is?"

"Yeah. It's where you specify whether you want to be kept alive on life support or they should not resuscitate you when it seems clear that you're going to die. Also, it states what you want to be done with your body after you die."

"Do you know if he had one of those?"

"I don't know. We can start looking around on his computer. Maybe there's paperwork in his file cabinet."

Thankfully, Hal left his computer on when he went out to the hot tub, and he didn't have a screen-saver password in place.

Ryan said, "Okay, I'll start looking in his files. You look on his computer."

"We also need to see if we can find a will or trust or anything else."

"And we need to figure out who we should notify."

Ted sat down at Hal's desk. He started looking through the directories on his computer to see if any folder names looked like they might contain Hal's estate planning documents.

After about ten minutes, Ryan said, "I haven't found anything in his file cabinet."

"I wonder where else he might keep important papers. Do you know if he has a safe?"

"Let me check." The first place Ryan thought to look was in Hal's closet, since his father had a safe in the closet in his home office. "Yep – there's a safe. But it's locked."

"Of course. But think about it. Why would you put documents that someone else will need after you die in a place where nobody can get to them?"

"Good question." Ryan walked back to Hal's desk and started picking up the various objects on the desk and looking under them.

"What are you doing?" Ted asked.

"Checking to see if he has the combination written down someplace. My dad had the combination to his safe on a little piece of paper taped under the canister where he kept his pens and pencils."

"Maybe there's a password file on his computer. I'll check." A moment later, Ted said, "Found it! Try 16-24-3."

Ryan tried that combination. It worked. After looking through the contents of the safe, he said, "I don't see anything that looks like an advance directive or a will. Of course, I don't know what those things look like."

"You know who might know? That guy he was dating. What was his name?"

"Brent. Yeah, he might know. Besides, we need to notify him anyway."

"Do you have his number?"

"No, but he's probably still in the contacts on Hal's phone. Same with a lot of the other people we'll need to notify. Do you see his phone laying around anywhere?"

It wasn't visible on Hal's desk, so Ted started looking under the rat's nest of paperwork. "Here it is." He handed it to Ryan.

Ryan said, "Shit. I don't know his PIN."

"Hmmm. Can you think of any four-digit numbers that would be significant to him? Try our house number."

Ryan typed 1-0-6-4. "Nope."

"What year was he born? 1965 or 1966?"

Ryan tried every year in that range. "Nope. Is it in his password file?"

Ted checked. "Nope. Hmmm… Try this. You know how they have letters corresponding to the numbers on the phone? Try UCLA."

Ryan typed 8-2-5-2. "Bingo! You're a genius!"

"I'm just a lucky guesser. Anyway, do you see Brent?"

"Yep." Ryan took a deep breath. "Here goes." He pressed the 'Call' icon. After 15 seconds, he said, "It's going to his voicemail."

"He probably doesn't want to talk to Hal."

The outgoing message finished, then Ryan heard the beep. "Uh, hi Brent. This is Ryan Robertson, you know, the tall guy who lives in Hal's house. Please call me back right away. It's important. My number is 817-555-7926. Or I guess you can call back on this phone. Thanks. Bye."

"I'm surprised you didn't tell him in the voicemail you left."

"I don't know – it seemed kinda wrong to tell someone that somebody died on a voicemail message. But I guess it's kind of weird that I called him on Hal's phone."

"Yeah, that might be a clue that something's wrong. Anyway, come over here and look at this." Ryan walked over to Ted's side. "I found this among all this paperwork. It's a foreclosure notice."

"What's that?"

"It says he has missed the last three payments on his loan. He has 30 days from the date on that letter to catch up on the payments, or the bank will take over ownership of the house. And the letter is dated April 10."

"That doesn't make sense. Hal told me he bought the house with the money he got when he won that discrimination lawsuit against the law firm he worked for. I didn't think he had a mortgage."

Ted read the notice again. "It looks like he took out a mortgage on this house for $800,000 back in September of 2011."

"Probably for his production company. But how can they just come and take his house?"

"That's how it works. The house is the collateral on the loan."

"So if he misses a few payments, they get the whole house?"

"That's right."

"Shit. How much does he owe?"

"His payment is almost $6,000 a month, and he's behind three months, plus this month. So, about $24,000."

Ryan asked, "So how will that change now that he's dead?"

"I'm no expert, but either we find $24,000 in other assets or the bank gets the house. Besides, when they find out he's dead, they're going to want to call the loan."

"I have close to $100,000 saved up. After I earned enough money to pay for the rest of my education, I started saving for a down payment on a house."

"Good for you. Most kids get out of college saddled with huge student debt. But I would hold off for now. Do you want to keep paying $6,000 a month on a loan that isn't yours?"

"I would do that for Hal. I wish he would have asked me for help when he was first getting in trouble."

Ted said, "Yeah, but there's no way he could have brought himself to do that. I'm sure he didn't want to burden you with it, especially since it was doubtful when or if he'd be able to repay you."

"So what are we going to do?"

"We're going to have to find his will and see who he willed the house to – assuming he did. Then that person will have to sell the house and pay back the loan."

Ryan's phone rang. "Hello?"

"Hey Ryan, it's Brent. What's up?"

"Hi, Brent. I'm afraid I have some terrible news. Hal's dead."

"OH MY GOD!!! What happened?"

"He got totally inebriated last night and got in the hot tub. He passed out, slid down into the water, and drowned. I found him this morning."

"Oh God, that must have been terrible. I'm so sorry. Thanks for letting me know."

"So, Ted and I are here trying to go through his things. Do you know if he had a will or an advanced directive or anything?"

"Yes. He has a trust. He and I both updated our estate documents when we were dating and it looked like it was getting serious."

"Do you know where it is?"

"I'm not sure where he kept his copy. But let me give you the name and number of the attorney that prepared it. She's the one who will get the ball rolling. And unless Hal changed it after we broke up, I'm the executor of the estate."

Brent gave him the name and number, and Ryan wrote it down.

Brent asked, "Would you prefer that I call her?"

"Yes, please."

"I'll call her as soon as I get off the phone with you. Now, all that aside, how are you doing?"

"I'm pretty shaken up, but I guess I'm doing okay. Ted and I are trying to figure out who we should notify and what we should do next."

"Well, don't pay any bills or move any money around in his bank accounts. From the moment he died, that responsibility falls on the executor. I have to be officially appointed by a judge, and the attorney will take care of getting that done. So really, there's not much you should do concerning his personal affairs."

"Okay."

Brent asked, "Would you like me to come over?"

"Yeah, that would be great."

"Okay, I'll stop by after work. I think I can get out early. Does 3:30 sound okay?"

"Yeah. We'll be here."

"Talk to you soon. Bye."

Ryan turned to Ted. "It's 1:00. I'm starving. Wanna go get something to eat."

"Sounds good. You pick the place."

"How about My Gyro?"

"Sounds good. Want me to drive?"

"Nah, I'd rather walk if that's okay. It will be impossible to find a parking place. Besides, it will be nice to get some fresh air."

They walked for five minutes without saying anything. Ryan couldn't get the image of Hal's body in the hot tub out of his mind. He wondered if he'd start having nightmares.

Finally, Ted spoke. "So, say something."

"Something."

"Very funny. What are you thinking about?"

"What else? I keep replaying everything that's happened today. And I wonder what's going to happen to the house. Now, I'll be the only person living there. It's not like I'm afraid of ghosts or anything, but it will feel creepy."

"Yeah, I can see how you might feel that way."

Ryan asked, "Would you spend the night with me?"

"I guess I could. Or maybe you can spend the night at my place. It would get you out of there."

"Yeah. That would probably be better. I'm not looking forward to spending the night alone in that house."

"That would work better for me since I have to be at work by 8:00."

"Okay, let's do that."

After a moment, Ted said, "Still, you're going to have to spend the night there on your own at some point."

"Yeah, I guess. But I'm never getting in that hot tub again."

"I get it. But are you never going to get in a hot tub again for the rest of your life?"

"I don't know. Lots of people live their entire lives without ever getting in a hot tub. Hell, I never thought of it when I was living in Kansas."

Ted said, "What I'm saying is that at some point you're going to have to move past this."

"At some point. Not now."

"Fair enough."

They arrived at My Gyro, ordered their lunches, and sat down.

Ryan said, "Let's talk about something else. Anything. Just not this."

Ted said, "Well, I have some news. I found out my transfer request was approved."

"I didn't know you had applied for one."

"Yeah, I wasn't going to say anything until it was approved. Anyway, I'll be moving to London around the end of June. I start there on July 2nd."

"Oh. Well, congratulations, I guess."

"I guess??? Is that the best you can do?"

"Sorry. I'm happy for you – really. I know this is something you've talked about doing for years. I guess I just… well, it kind of took me by surprise. Now, on top of everything else happening, you're going to move away."

"Well, you're moving to Scottsdale. It's not like we'd be in the same city either way."

"Yeah, but LA is a lot closer to Scottsdale than London."

"True, but they have these really cool inventions – you know, like the telephone, Skype, email, and Facebook. And there are these magical flying machines called airplanes that will transport you from one place to another in less than a day."

Ryan forced a smile. "Yeah, I know. But it won't be the same."

"Life moves on, Ryan. Things change. People move."

"Yeah, tell me about it."

"Look. I want you to promise me right now that you'll come to London for a visit next year. By then, I'll know my way around and I can show you all kinds of stuff."

"Okay."

"Promise?"

"I promise."

"I'm going to hold you to that."

They finished their lunches and started walking back to the house.

Ryan asked, "So are you going to have all your stuff shipped there?"

"Only a few things. I'll be renting a furnished apartment. Even if I wasn't, shipping all my stuff there would cost an arm and a leg. It would be cheaper to buy what I need once I get there."

"So what about all the stuff you bought for your apartment here?"

"Actually, I was going to offer it to you."

"Really?"

Ted said, "Sure, why not? You'll be getting an apartment in Scottsdale. You'll need furniture for it."

"Seriously? You've got some nice stuff! At least let me pay you something for it."

"Tell you what. You can take care of renting the moving van. I'll drive over with you and help you move it in."

"Oh, man. That is so nice of you. Thanks! What are you going to do with your Beemer?"

"Sell it. It would cost a fortune to ship it over there, and I won't need a car in London anyway. Besides, they drive on the left, so their cars have the steering wheel on the right."

Ryan thought for a moment. His old Toyota had over 250,000 miles on it and it was due for some major repairs. "Can I buy it from you?"

"Yeah, sure. I'll look up the blue book value on it and sell it to you for that. How's that sound?"

"Great! Thanks."

They arrived at the house, climbed the front steps, and let themselves in through the front door.

Ted said, "Just think – whenever you're riding in your car, or sitting on your furniture, or sleeping in your bed, you'll think of me."

Ryan laughed for the first time today. "You're probably right. But I'll be thinking of you anyway. I'm going to miss you." He turned toward Ted.

"I'm going to miss you too." He paused. "Aside from Alex, you're the best friend I've ever had."

They hugged and held each other for a good 15 seconds.

Ryan said, "So don't move away."

"It's what I need to do."

Ryan knew Ted was right.

Ted said, "Don't worry, you'll make friends in Scottsdale."

They walked around the eerily quiet house. Ryan said, "So many memories."

"Yeah, good times for sure."

"I can still hear Darnell being fabulous and everyone teasing Ricky about being a slut."

"Speaking of Ricky, remember that time not long after you moved in when you came home from school and they were filming an orgy out at the pool?"

Ryan laughed. "Oh my God… And there was Ricky right in the middle of it. Man, what an eye-opener that was. Oh, and I don't think I told you this. After I got back from Europe a couple of summers ago, after you moved out and Mykel moved in, I came home one day and there were a bunch of naked guys out there doing yoga – including Hal and Brent."

Ted laughed, "No, you didn't tell me about that."

"But of course, compared to coming home and seeing an orgy, that was nothing."

"I remember Hal's parties. Sometimes things got pretty wild."

"I'll say." Ryan thought of people getting frisky with each other in the hot tub. Then he thought of Hal's lifeless body in the hot tub. *Move on, move on...* "I remember the times you and I went running together. Especially the first couple of times right after I moved here."

Ted smiled. "Yeah. I remember all the nights we spent together in the hot tub."

Ryan's mind flashed onto the image of Hal's body. "Uh… can we not mention the hot tub?"

"Oh, yeah. Sorry."

"And his family night dinners. That was such a great tradition."

"Yeah. He was so generous. And such a good cook."

Ryan said, "It's like we were his kids. Last night when I was talking to him, I said he was more like a father to me than my own father. And he got all upset about that, like I was saying he was old." Ryan felt like he could start to cry at any moment. "He gave me a place to stay. He was always there with encouragement and advice. He was always willing to talk whenever I needed someone to talk to. I told him I owed him everything. And it's true, I do."

Ryan's tears started to flow. Ted stepped up and hugged him. Ryan said, "And that was the last time I saw him. He was already really drunk. I told him he shouldn't have any more, but obviously, he did. I saw him out there at 10:00. I should have gone out and checked on him, but I didn't. Maybe if I had, he'd be alive today."

Ted pulled back from their hug and looked Ryan in the eyes. He wiped a stream of tears away with his finger. "Now don't start thinking like that. This isn't your fault in any way, shape, or form."

"I know, but…" Ryan's crying intensified.

"Go ahead, let it out."

Ryan sat down on the couch in the family room and cried. After a few seconds, he laid down on his left side and let it flow.

Ted decided to give him some privacy, so he went back into Hal's office and started straightening up his desk. He did his best to separate all the paperwork into relevant piles. He pulled up the calendar on Hal's computer and started looking for upcoming appointments he or Ryan would need to cancel.

Fifteen minutes later, Ted glanced at his watch. 3:15. Brent would be there soon. He walked back into the family room. Ryan had stopped crying but was still laying on his side on the couch. "Brent's going to be here soon. Why don't you step into the bathroom and wash your face?"

# Brent Arrives

Monday, April 16, 2012

At 3:30, Brent arrived and they got down to business.

Brent said, "I think I know where his estate documents are." He walked into the master closet and open the bottom drawer of the dresser. He pulled out a couple of loose-leaf binders and a thick manila envelope. "Yep. Here it is." Brent glanced through the paperwork.

"Okay, here's his advance directive. Hal wanted to be cremated. He didn't want a big funeral with people viewing his body in a casket or anything like that. He said just a small memorial service with some of his friends was all he wanted."

Ryan said, "They took his body to the morgue to do an autopsy."

"Okay, I'll contact them and advise them about what to do with his body after they're finished."

Ted said, "Who else should we notify?"

Brent said, "I'd start with his gay Jewish group. I met some of them. I'll be able to recognize their names in his email and phone contacts. We should probably let the LGBT Youth Project know."

Ted said, "Before you got here I was looking ahead in his calendar to see if he had any appointments. We should probably contact those people."

Brent said, "Yeah, that's good. You probably don't need to contact everybody. If you only tell one or two people in a group, they'll tell everyone else."

Ryan said, "What about his family? I know he wasn't speaking to them, but they should probably know."

Brent lit up. "NO! NO! Do NOT tell anyone in his family. I don't even know if we could find out who they are or how to get a hold of them. Hal would not want his family to know. They would probably swoop in like hawks and try to take everything he had."

Ryan said, "Really? You think they would actually do that?"

"Absolutely. It happens all the time, especially with the families of gay people. They think just because they're the biological next of kin, they should be entitled to everything."

Ted said, "Even when there's a will or trust?"

"Yep. They'll challenge it. Then all the money gets eaten up by attorney's fees. Even in happy families, when someone dies and there's money and possessions to be had, people suddenly get really nasty."

Brent skimmed the contents of one of the binders. "Okay, this looks like it's the document we created last year. I wasn't sure whether he would change it again after we broke up, but he didn't. So yeah, I'm still the executor of the estate. Now, this was drawn up before his business started failing, but at the time, he wanted all of his monetary assets donated to the Los Angeles LGBT Youth Project. That was fine with me. I know how passionate he was about that organization, and I support them too. I don't need his money."

Brent turned to Ryan. "He left the house to you."

"What? Really? Why would he do that?"

"He hoped you would continue to live in it. You'd move into the master suite and rent the rooms out to gay college guys like he did."

"But I've accepted a job in Scottsdale."

"He didn't know that at the time."

"So now I have to stay and live in this house? Honestly, given what has happened, I don't think I could do that."

"That was his hope. It's not stipulated in the will. The house will be yours, and you can do what you want with it."

Ted said, "Unfortunately, now there's an $800,000 home equity loan he took out back in September to fund his business. As soon as they find out Hal's dead, they're going to call the loan. They're going to want to have the loan paid off."

Ryan said, "And he was behind on the payments. They're going to foreclose on it in less than a month."

Brent said, "But if they receive the outstanding payments, the loan will be in good standing again. That will end the foreclosure process."

Ryan said, "I have $24,000. I could pay it."

"Would you be willing to do that?"

"Yes, of course."

Brent thought for a moment. "Yeah, that would work. Because even if we sold the house within a month, they would receive that money at the settlement. They're going to get that $24,000 either way."

Ted said, "But if the money comes from Ryan rather than Hal, wouldn't that tip them off that Hal has died?"

"It could, but probably not. They just want to get their money. They don't care where it comes from."

Ryan said, "Ted, does it show where to send the payment on that foreclosure notice?"

Ted retrieved the notice from the piles of paperwork and looked it over. "Yeah. There's also a place to pay it online. That would be a lot faster." He pulled up Hal's password file on his computer. "Here's the login information."

Within ten minutes, Ryan had paid the outstanding balance on the home equity loan.

Brent asked, "Can you tell what other outstanding bills he has?"

Ted replied, "I don't know. Let me start looking for that stuff."

"Also check the balances on his credit card statements. We can't pay any of them from his account until I am appointed his executor, but if you would make a list for me, that would be a big help."

Ryan said, "Before you get too engrossed in that, can I get a few names and numbers of people I should notify?"

Brent said, "I know some of his friends in his Jewish group. I'll call them. But if you could call the LGBT Youth Project and his business colleagues, that would be great."

Ted scanned through Hal's emails and the contacts on his phone, created a list, and handed it to Ryan. "Why don't you use Hal's phone, so they'll recognize the caller ID?"

"Good idea. Hey, you want anything to drink?"

Ted replied, "If there are any beers in the fridge, that would be great. Otherwise, water."

"I'll go look." He turned to Brent. "How about you?"

"I'll come with you and see what's in there."

Ted started creating a list of Hal's outstanding debts, while Ryan and Brent walked into the kitchen. Ryan looked in the fridge, and there were several bottles of beer. He pulled one out for Ted. Brent said, "I'll have one too, please."

Ryan said, "I still can't believe Hal left the house to me."

Brent clasped his hand on Ryan's shoulder and said softly, "Between you and me… you were his favorite of all the guys who ever lived here. I think he saw a lot of similarities between him and you – being rejected by your parents, being out on your own, and doing porn to earn money for college. There were a lot of parallels. He told me on several occasions how he thought you were a very fine young man. He thought the world of you. You were like a son to him."

Ryan felt like he could start crying again at any moment. "It's funny… last night I told him he was more of a father to me than my own father, and he said, 'Don't say that, you're making me sound old.'"

Brent smiled. "Yep. That sounds like Hal. I think he wished he could be a college student for the rest of his life. That may be why he rented rooms out to you guys, so he could at least be around college students."

"Yeah, you're right."

Brent smiled. "And he was correct. You're a fine young man."

Ryan stopped in his room long enough to retrieve a Dr Pepper from his fridge, then he returned to Hal's bedroom and handed Ted the beer. Brent stayed in the kitchen and started making calls. Ryan picked up Hal's phone and started making his calls.

After about 20 minutes, Brent returned to Hal's bedroom. Ted said, "Well, this isn't good. It looks like Hal maxed out all his credit cards. He was keeping the utility bills paid, but he was making only the minimum payments each month on his credit cards. He's about $40,000 in debt, in addition to the home equity loan."

Ryan said, "Jesus. What are we going to do about that?"

Brent said, "I don't know. I'll have to ask the attorney. The creditors may have to write it off. Or else it will be taken out of the proceeds of the house. But don't pay anything from his account."

Ted said, "Here's something else I noticed. In going back through his bank statements over the past year or so, I don't see any indication that Mykel was paying rent."

Ryan said, "Are you shittin' me?"

"Doesn't look like it. I see checks deposited from you, Ricky, and Darnell, until they moved out, but nothing from Mykel."

Brent said, "Maybe he paid in cash."

Ryan said, "Maybe. But Darnell and I were talking one time not too long after Mykel moved in. Darnell was suspicious of him. He wondered how Mykel made enough money teaching yoga classes and doing medium readings to be able to afford to live here and pay for college. I wondered about that too."

Brent said, "Maybe Hal was letting him slide until the lawsuit about his inheritance money got settled."

Ryan looked puzzled. "What lawsuit?"

Brent said, "Oh, you didn't know? Hal was serving as his attorney. There's probably some stuff on his computer and in his filing cabinet about it. Here, let me sit down."

Ted got up and Brent sat down at Hal's desk. Brent navigated through Hal's directories for a few seconds, then said, "Here it is. Michael Boyce vs. the Estate of Frederick Boyce."

Ryan said, "Boyce was his last name? He always told us he didn't go by a last name. And besides, Mykel spells his name M-Y-K-E-L."

"Well, I don't know what's up with that, but his legal name is

Michael Boyce. Anyway, I remember Hal telling me about this. Frederick Boyce was Michael's grandfather. He was a billionaire, several times over. He was a big commercial real estate developer in the LA area. Had some properties in the Bay Area too, if I recall. Anyway, he died a couple of years ago. He transferred his share of the business to his sons when he retired. But when he died, he left around five million dollars to each of his grandkids. Michael's father was trying to stop Michael from getting his share of the inheritance because he didn't approve of him being gay."

"But how can he do that?"

"I don't know, but he was trying. According to Hal, Frederick Boyce was a real right-winger. He gave a lot of money to Family-Focused Ministries, the National Association to Prevent Homosexuality, a bunch of anti-abortion groups, and stuff like that. Hal said they were trying to make the case that since Grandpa was so vehemently opposed to homosexuality, he wouldn't have wanted any of his money to go to a homosexual."

Ryan said, "So I guess Hal figured that once Mykel had the money, he'd be able to pay him the rent."

Brent said, "Yeah. And he promised Hal he would invest in his production business too. But the lawsuit dragged on and on, and he never saw that money."

Ryan said, "I wonder if it's still going on."

Ted said, "I saw some appointments for court dates coming up on his calendar."

Ryan said, "I wonder if that has anything to do with why he moved out of here so quickly this morning."

Brent said, "Maybe. Who knows what else is going on and what else he knows? If nothing else, he won't have a free place to live any longer."

Ted added, "Not to mention a free attorney."

Ryan said, "I guess Darnell was right to be suspicious of him."

Brent looked at his watch. "It's 4:45. I'm getting hungry and we need a break. Can I take you guys out to eat?"

Ryan and Ted glanced at each other with looks that said, 'Why not?' Ryan said, "Sure."

Brent said, "Where would you like to go?"

Ryan shrugged his shoulders. *Brent's paying. He should get to decide.*

Ted smiled and said, "I know where Ryan would like to go. There's this place in WeHo called Burger Betty's."

Brent said, "Oh, I love that place! I don't go very often because it's not exactly diet food. But we could use some fun."

Ryan was about to say, 'No, I was just there last night,' but he stopped himself. *What, are you crazy? Go to Burger Betty's!* "Yeah, okay. Let's go!"

They left through the front door, and Ryan turned around to lock it.

Brent said, "Does anyone else have a key?"

Ryan said, "Shit. I didn't get the key back from Mykel."

They stood and looked at each other for a moment. Then Brent said, "Well then, on the way back, we'll stop at a hardware store and pick up a set of doorknobs and deadbolts. We can install them when we get back."

***

After they arrived, ordered, and had fancy cocktails in front of them, they tried to engage in small talk about any subject other than Hal's untimely death. Finally, Brent said, "I know we would all rather talk about anything other than Hal, but let's face it. It's what's on our minds. It's what we have to deal with today. So let's talk about what we'd like to do for a memorial service."

Ryan said, "I've never been to one. What happens at a memorial service?"

Ted said, "And what's the difference between a memorial

service and a funeral? You said Hal didn't want a funeral."

Brent said, "I've been to plenty of memorial services, unfortunately. Twenty years ago, guys were dropping like flies because of AIDS. I lost so many friends. You guys are lucky they have good drugs now. But enough about that. To me, a funeral is a sad, somber occasion. Most of the time, religion is involved unless the deceased's family is not religious. It's usually held at a funeral home or church a few days after the person died, so everyone is still mourning their loss. If it's at a funeral home, the person's body will be lying there in a casket. A memorial service is more like a celebration of the person's life. It's usually held in a meeting place or at someone's home if it's large enough. The body isn't there, but there are usually pictures or other memorabilia from the person's life. People will stand up one at a time and share stories and memories of the person. There's usually food. After the structured part of the ceremony, people stand around and share more stories."

Ryan said, "So instead of 'We're here to mourn the death of Hal Morris,' it's more like, 'We're here to celebrate the life of Hal Morris.'"

Brent said, "Yeah. That's a good way to put it."

Ted said, "So where would we have it? And how many people do you think would show up? He knew a lot of people."

Brent said, "I don't know. He probably wouldn't want it to be held at the synagogue. Hal was Jewish, but he wasn't particularly observant. I wonder if they have a meeting room at the LGBT Youth Project office that would be large enough?"

Ryan said, "I went there the day I arrived in town. That was almost five years ago, but I don't recall seeing a large room. We could ask, though."

Brent said, "Yeah. Or they might have connections with another place we could use."

Ted said, "My apartment complex has a clubhouse I could reserve. We could probably fit 30 or 40."

Brent said, "That might not be large enough. We might get 50 or more people."

Ryan said, "Why don't we have it at the house? The backyard is probably big enough for 50 or 60 people."

Brent said, "We'd have to rent some folding chairs, but that's no big deal. And the kitchen island is large enough to hold a lot of food."

Ted said, "If the point of this event is to remember Hal, I think it would feel a lot better to do it at Hal's house instead of some neutral place. He loved to throw parties. Everyone who would come has probably been there."

Ryan said, "Yeah, that house has 'Hal' written all over it. It might get a little crowded, but so what?"

Brent said, "Okay, then all we need to do is pick a date. Maybe a Saturday or Sunday afternoon in May. Since I've been to so many other memorial services, I'll organize it if that's okay."

Ted said, "Fine by me."

Ryan said, "Yeah, that would be great. But do you think you'll have time for that on top of everything else you have to do, like putting the house on the market?"

Brent said, "I'll make the time. This is important."

Ted said, "You could have it on Memorial Day, or at least Memorial Day weekend. That would be appropriate."

Their entrees were delivered to the table. The conversation paused while everyone dug into their food. After a few minutes, Ryan said to Brent, "This is an awful lot of work for you to take on, especially since you and Hal weren't a couple anymore."

Brent paused, then said, "I still love Hal. I never stopped loving him. I didn't really want to break up. But last fall, when it became obvious Hal's business wasn't working out, he tried to get me to invest another half a million dollars. I just couldn't do it. I could see the handwriting on the wall. The business wasn't going to make it. I tried to get him to see that and either change course or cut his losses, but he wouldn't hear of it. And I refused to sink more of my money into it because I knew I'd never see it again. It was just prolonging the inevitable." Brent took a bite of his oversized bacon bleu cheese hamburger while Ted and Ryan processed everything they had just heard. Then Brent continued. "One day Hal said, 'If you really believe in me – if you really believe in *us* – you'd invest your money. But it looks like you don't. I guess your money is more important than me.' I didn't think it was right to tie being in a relationship to being in business together. And I wouldn't tolerate being guilt-tripped or given an ultimatum. So we ended it. I hated to do it, but I felt like I didn't have a choice."

Ryan said, "Wow. I'm really sorry. I didn't know it got that intense."

"Thanks. Yeah, it was."

Ted said, "It looks like he took out that home equity loan to get the money instead."

"Yeah. He was going to do that anyway, for half a million. I guess he upped it to $800,000 when I wouldn't give him any money. But anyway… I hoped one day we would get back together. Maybe after his business failed and he finally had all that behind him, I would give him a call and we could work things out." Brent sighed. "Oh, well. But as I said, I still love Hal. I want to do this for him. It's the least I can do."

Their server came and cleared their plates and left the check, which Brent paid. They picked up new doorknobs and deadbolts for all the doors, then went back to the house and installed them. There was no indication Mykel had returned while they were gone.

They decided to call it an evening. Ryan went to his bedroom to pack a few things to take to Ted's apartment since he was going to spend the night there.

While Ryan was in his bedroom, Brent asked Ted, "So, uh… when all this is over, would it be okay if I gave you a call?"

That took Ted by surprise. He briefly considered it. Brent seemed like a nice guy. He said, "I guess so. But you should know that I'm only going to be living here for a couple more months. At the end of June, I'm moving to London."

Brent's smile faded. "Oh well."

"But thanks."

# Wrapping Things Up

Saturday, April 21, 2012

On Saturday morning at 9:00, Brent arrived at the house. He let himself in since, as the executor of Hal's estate, he kept one of the keys from the new set of locks they had installed. He called out, "Hey, Ryan!"

Ryan emerged from the kitchen, where he had just finished cleaning up after breakfast. "Hey, Brent." They gave each other a quick hug.

Brent asked, "How have you been?"

"A little better each day. I spent Monday night with Ted. But from Tuesday on, I've stayed here. I've been going to all my classes since Tuesday and doing a lot of catching up on my studying."

"I'll bet it's hard to keep your mind on school."

"Yeah. Trying to stay in my normal routine helps. But it's weird being in this house all by myself. I don't think I've ever slept alone in a house in my entire life. It's not like I'm scared, but it feels so … empty. So different."

"Yeah, I'll bet. Anyway, I got in touch with the morgue. Hal had a Blood Alcohol Concentration of 0.41, which is lethal in many cases. That's five times as much as you would need to get arrested for DUI."

Ryan shook his head. "He drank that whole bottle in less than four hours."

"To get that drunk he probably had more than that. Anyway, they didn't find any evidence of drugs or poisonous substances, so they concluded that he died by drowning. They're sending the body to a crematorium. I picked up the death certificates. In other news, the attorney has an appointment with the probate judge on Monday to have me appointed as the executor. And a realtor I know is going to be here at 3:00 to see the house."

"Wow. Things are moving quickly."

"There's no sense in letting this drag out. Even so, it will take several months before everything is settled. I went through this a few years ago when my dad died."

"So, I know I'm getting the house. Does that mean all the furniture too, or is that separate?"

"Legally, it just means the house. But as far as I'm concerned, if you want any of the furniture or any of the stuff in the kitchen, you can have it."

"Well, it's not like I have any place to put it. I'm moving to Scottsdale after I graduate." *Besides, Ted's already giving me the furniture in his apartment.*

"Well, you'll have an apartment to furnish there. And we'll know more after we talk with the realtor, but after we sell the house and pay off the loan, you'll still walk away with several hundred thousand dollars. You could probably buy a house for yourself in Scottsdale or Phoenix. Prices are a lot lower there."

"Yeah, but what would I do with it in the meantime?"

"Rent a storage unit. They're only like a hundred bucks a month. And there's no contract. You can rent for as long or short as you need it."

"What about the stuff I don't want?"

"We have several options. We can donate it. There's a consignment shop downtown run by the Lambda Foundation that donates the proceeds to local organizations, including the LGBT Youth Project. Or we could have an auction or a garage sale and donate the proceeds."

"It's up to you, but I'd say donate it – especially if the Youth Project would benefit. Hal would have wanted that."

"Yeah, that's what I was thinking. Anyway, let's start going through his stuff."

# Final Arrangements

Saturday, May 19, 2012

A month later, Ryan and Ted got together for dinner on Saturday night. Ryan suggested Al Fresco's, the Italian restaurant in Santa Monica. Despite the fiasco with Cody on Valentine's Day, Ryan still liked this restaurant. Ted arrived at the house at 5:30, and they made it to the restaurant in plenty of time for their 6:00 reservation. The maître d' escorted them to a table in the outdoor courtyard. The warm spring evening was perfect for dining outdoors.

As they were looking over their menus, the maître d' led six high school kids dressed in tuxes and gowns into the courtyard and seated them at a table nearby. Ryan leaned toward Ted and whispered, "See those kids over there? They're probably going to their high school prom. That would have been me and my friends four years ago."

"Yeah, I remember that night. Wasn't that the night someone scratched 'FAG' on the side of your car with a key?"

"Yeah. I forgot about that. That was an interesting night in a lot of ways."

Ted said, "Do you suppose any of them are gay?"

Ryan looked at the group again. There were four boys and two girls. "Well, at least two of them are. Maybe all six. Or some of them could be going solo. But whatever… I hope they have a good time."

Ryan thought back to his senior year of high school and his prom night. It seemed so long ago. "I went with Mike Nguyen. That was a week after Payton found out I did porn and dumped me. We went with LaTanya and her girlfriend Angelica and a couple of our straight friends. We were all scared to dance, but at one point during a slow dance, LaTanya and Angelica started dancing. Then Mike and I joined them.

Everyone else stopped dancing and stared. But ten minutes later, it was no big deal." Ryan looked over at the kids again. They were laughing and having a good time. "I hope they can dance with each other tonight."

Ted said, "You know what else? I think tonight's the night they're having the annual gala to raise money for the Los Angeles LGBT Youth Project."

"I think you're right. Come to think of it, Hal didn't buy tickets this year like he always did before. Now I know why. He didn't have the money." Ryan paused. "If I had known, I would have bought a table of tickets."

"Man, those were some fabulous evenings, weren't they?"

Ryan said, "Yeah, I remember the first time I went. The limo ride, all the fabulous outfits… I was totally overwhelmed. I had never seen anything like that before. I had never been around so many gay people in my life, either. And they were so affluent and successful. It really changed how I thought about myself and how my life as a gay man could turn out."

"And remember Darnell performing as Whitney Austin, and that speech he gave? That was something else." Ted paused. "I wonder how Darnell's doing. Did you tell him about Hal?"

"Yeah, and I told him about the memorial service next weekend. He can't come, but he's going to send a video as Whitney. I think she's going to sing something."

"I know she'll come up with something fabulous."

Their food arrived, and Ted poured each of them another glass of wine. After they had eaten a few bites, he said, "So, how are you holding up?"

"Pretty good, I guess. There's been so much going on the past four weeks, it's like I don't have time to stop and think about how I'm doing. The first weekend, Brent came over and we went through a lot of Hal's stuff. A realtor came by to look at the house. For the next couple of weeks, we had to clean the house and get rid of a bunch of stuff. You should have seen Ricky's room. He left behind a whole bunch of junk and it was filthy. Anyway, they put the house on the market a couple of weeks ago, and it sold in like ten days."

Ted said, "Wow, that was fast. Did they get what they were asking?"

"Yeah, we got two offers, so we didn't have to drop the price. Anyway, between all that and school, I haven't had time for anything. It's been crazy."

"Sounds like those first few months after you moved here. You were going to school, playing in the marching band, and working as many hours as you could at Pure Foods."

"Yeah. But in a few weeks, it will all be over."

"When's your graduation?"

"Saturday, June 16th. Four weeks from today."

"Can I come?"

"Of course. Thanks. It will be nice to have someone there for me."

Ryan thought about Hal, and how much he wished Hal could be there. He tried to chase that thought from his head. "Wow. Hard to believe it will all be over soon. As of now, closing is set for Thursday, June 14, a couple of days before I graduate. But it could change. That means I need to have all my stuff out by then. I'll probably stay in a hotel or something."

"Don't do that. You can stay with me."

"Are you sure? I don't want to inconvenience you. You're going to have plenty of stuff to do to get ready for your move to London."

"No problem. Seriously. Come stay with me."

"Okay, thanks. When do you leave?"

"I fly out on Friday, the 22nd."

"Hmmm… I was going to drive over to Scottsdale on Sunday, the 17th. But if I take your stuff, that means you'll have an empty apartment for a week. Maybe I can push back a week."

"I guess I can sleep on the floor. Maybe I'll buy an air mattress and a sleeping bag. Are you going to hire movers?"

Ryan said, "I was thinking I'd just rent a truck. I don't have an apartment there yet, so I figured I'd find an apartment within the first couple of days, then move in. If I use movers, I won't have a place for them to move my stuff into."

"You're going to move all that furniture by yourself? You don't know anyone there, do you?"

"Hmmm… Well, there's Eddie, the guy I stayed with last summer. He'd probably help. But if I drive the truck, how am I going to get your car there? I guess I could fly back and get it."

"Or you could rent one of those car trailers and hitch it to the truck."

"I guess I haven't thought this out very well."

Ted thought for a moment. "Okay, I have an idea. How about this? On Sunday, the day after you graduate, we'll move my stuff into the truck. One of us can drive the truck and the other can drive the car. I'll help you look for an apartment and move in. Then I can stay with you for the rest of the week. I'll book a one-way flight from Phoenix to LA on the 22$^{nd}$. You can drive me to the airport. Then I'll fly from LA to London on the flight I already have."

Ryan thought about it. "That makes sense, but are you sure that's okay?"

"Yeah. It solves all the problems. Besides, then I'll have a few more days to spend with you and I can see what Scottsdale's like."

They finished their dinner and went back to the house.

Ted walked around. The bedrooms where he, Darnell, and Ricky had slept were now empty except for a bed, desk, and dresser in each. Hal's bed, desk, and other bedroom furniture were still there, but all his clothes and personal belongings had been donated or disposed of. About half of the things in the kitchen had been cleared out. "Wow. It looks so empty."

"Yeah. We cleaned a lot of the stuff out before they put the house up for sale. Now that it's sold, most of the furniture is going to be taken to a consignment shop run by the Lambda Foundation. Some of the proceeds will go to the LGBT Youth Project.”

“Hal would have appreciated that.”

“Yeah. Brent said I could take whatever I wanted, so I’m going to take Hal’s bed and desk, some of the videos and games, and some of the cooking stuff from the kitchen. Between that and everything you’re giving me, I should be pretty well set.”

“You’ll be able to furnish a house.”

“Yeah. I’m hoping to buy one before too long. I may have to get a storage unit in Scottsdale for some of it.”

They walked into the family room. Ryan said, “It’s been strange living here by myself. It was kind of creepy the first few nights. I’ve never lived alone before.”

“Well, you’re going to be living alone when you move to Scottsdale.”

Ryan thought for a moment. “Yeah, you’re right. But that’s kind of different. There were always five people living here and now there’s only me. My apartment is supposed to be for only me. After you moved out, how did you deal with living alone?”

“It was fine. But then, I’m more of a loner than you are, so I’m okay with it. After living in barracks, then the dorm, then the house, it was a nice change. I missed the family night dinners, though.”

Ted and Ryan walked onto the back patio. It was dark and the sky was clear. Ted said, “You know what would be nice? I’d like to spend one last evening with you in the hot tub. Just for old time’s sake.”

Ryan shuddered. “I don’t know… that hot tub still creeps me out every time I see it. It’s like I can still see Hal’s body in there.”

“I get it. But you’ll have to face your fears sooner or later. Either that or never get in a hot tub again.”

“It’s not so much *a* hot tub, it’s *that* hot tub.”

Ted tried to mask his disappointment. “Yeah, okay. How warm is the pool water?” He walked over to the edge of the pool and stuck his hand into the water. “It’s pretty cold. We might have a shrinkage issue. Even you!”

Ryan chuckled. "Yeah. I think Hal stopped running the heater a few months ago."

"Given his financial situation, that makes sense."

They walked back inside. Ryan realized this was the first time in a month he was able to relax. It might be his last, given all the things that needed to be done in the next four weeks. After nearly five years, his days of living in this house, with all its fond memories, would come to an end. He was excited about moving to Scottsdale and starting his first career job, but he knew he would miss Ted. He glanced at Ted. He could tell he was having similar nostalgic feelings.

Ryan said, "Hey, I still have two bottles of wine. Shall I open one?"

"Sure. What do you have?"

"I have a nice buttery, oaky Chardonnay with a smooth subtle palate of apple, pear, and apricot; and a bright, intense, yet silky-smooth Merlot with flavors of plum, blackberry, and cherry."

"Listen to *you*! I remember that night, not long after you moved here. We were out in the pool and I had to show you how to swirl the wine in your glass and sip it."

"Yeah, I was so clueless about everything. But I've learned from the best! So what'll it be?"

"I think I'm more in the mood for the Chardonnay."

Ryan pulled the bottle from the fridge, then expertly wielded the corkscrew to cut through the seal and open the bottle. The wine glasses in the cupboard were among the items that Ryan chose to take with him. He took two glasses down and filled them to the shoulder, twisting the bottle at the end to prevent any drops from running down the side of the bottle.

He and Ted sat down on stools at the kitchen island. Ryan raised his glass and said, "To good friends, good times, and many fond memories!"

They clinked their glasses and sipped.

It seemed weird to be sitting at the kitchen island sipping wine.

Ryan could tell Ted was disappointed they weren't enjoying this wine in the hot tub. He thought, *Come on, don't be such a buzzkill. Get over yourself. This is a special evening. Man up and get in the hot tub with him. Besides, it's your chance to do what you've dreamed about doing in there for five years.*

Ryan smiled and placed his hand on Ted's knee. "All right, tell ya what. I will get in the hot tub with you on one condition."

"What's that?"

Ryan paused for dramatic effect. Ted eagerly waited to hear what Ryan would say next. After Ryan had milked the moment long enough, he said, "We fuck each other's brains out."

Ted threw his head back and burst out laughing. "Hmmm… I think I might be able to *accommodate* your request."

"That, and you spend the night."

Ted said, "That's two conditions."

Ryan raised an eyebrow and threw Ted some good-natured shade.

Ted added, "…but who's counting?"

# Afterword

Thank you for purchasing and reading this book. I hope you enjoyed it.

This is the third in a series of six books that follow Ryan as he finishes high school, goes to college, launches his career, forms relationships, and comes to terms with his past.

I invite you to subscribe to my newsletter. I'll keep you informed about my upcoming books and offer them to you at a discount. I'll share background information about the stories and the writing process. From time to time, I may solicit your input which will help make the books even better! To join, visit my website: AuthorDaveHughes.com.

To thank you for joining, I will send my short story, *Cruise Virgins.* In it, Ryan (as a young adult) and Ted experience their first gay cruise – and confront their feelings for one another.

Now, I have a small favor to ask.

As a new, self-published author, it's incredibly difficult to get my books noticed in a world in which hundreds, if not thousands, of new books are released every day. It's challenging to build an audience for my work. If you enjoyed this book, please consider posting something about it on your social media platform of choice. All it takes is something simple, like 'I thoroughly enjoyed reading *Open Books, Closed Sets,* by Dave Hughes. Check it out!' Also, please consider leaving an honest review on the website where you purchased this book.

Thanks! I truly appreciate it.

I would like to thank my beta readers who provided valuable feedback that helped me improve this book: Tom Bogardus, Aaron Chavez, Jeff McKeehan, and Russ Smith. Also, I would like to thank my launch team: Gary Brenkman, Aaron Chavez, Jeff McKeehan, and Mike Triggs. And thanks to Chad Anderson for sharing his subject

354

matter expertise.

Thanks to my author friends for their invaluable support and advice (in no particular order): Mark McNease, David S. Pederson, Andrew Michael Flynn, Martin Wilsey, Debra Gaskill, Mike Triggs, Sandor M. Lubisch, Russ Smith, and Kevin Allen McKeehan. (Sorry if I missed anyone!)

Thanks to my email subscribers for their loyalty and support. I've made numerous decisions based on your feedback. And thanks to the Chandler Public Library Downtown Writers Group, led by Andrew Flynn, for their support and useful, constructive feedback.

Very special thanks to Gregg Edelman of Exposed Studio & Gallery. His charming art gallery is the perfect location for my book signing events. Thanks for all you do for the community!

Most important, I would like to thank my husband, Jeff McKeehan, who has supported and encouraged me every step of the way, provided great ideas and valuable feedback, and tolerated all those times when my mind was immersed in the world of my characters. Every spouse of an author knows exactly what I'm talking about.

# Other Books by Dave Hughes

## Fiction

Maybe Next Year

Instant Adult

If I Seem Quiet...

## Retirement Lifestyle

Design Your Dream Retirement

Smooth Sailing into Retirement

The Quest for Retirement Utopia


AuthorDaveHughes.com

# About the Author

This is author Dave Hughes' third novel. It is the third of four published novels in the series "Gay Tales for the New Millennium," with two more scheduled for release in 2024.

Before writing fiction, Dave wrote three retirement lifestyle planning books, *Design Your Dream Retirement, Smooth Sailing Into Retirement,* and *The Quest for Retirement Utopia.* Dave created the website RetireFabulously.com, which enables readers to envision, plan for, and enjoy the best retirement possible. In addition to writing hundreds of articles for RetireFabulously.com, Dave's writing has appeared on US News & World Report, lgbtSr.com, Medium, Yahoo! Finance, CNN/Money, Next Avenue, Tiny Buddha, and others.

Aside from his writing, Dave is also a jazz musician. He plays trombone and steelpan in various bands in the Phoenix area. He owns an embarrassingly large collection of jazz, Brazilian, exotica, steel band, jazz/rock, and vocal ensemble CDs and videos.

Before retiring early at age 56, Dave was a software engineer for 34 years, working for companies such as Intel Corporation, Computer Sciences Corporation, McDonnell Douglas Space Systems, and NCR Corporation. Throughout his career, his assignments included software development, customer support, training, course development, and management.

Dave resides in Chandler, Arizona with his husband Jeff and their dog Maynard.

Dave is available for interviews, book readings/signings, speaking engagements, and panel discussions. You may contact Dave at Dave@AuthorDaveHughes.com.

Visit AuthorDaveHughes.com to learn more and subscribe to his newsletter.